Praise for E. J. Mellow

"Lyrical, vibrant, imaginative. E. J. Mellow's striking, original voice will draw you into a mesmerizing world."

—Emma Raveling, author of the Ondine Quartet

"E. J. is one of those authors who deserve to be immortal just to continue writing mind-blowing novels for their readers."

—Book Vogue

"It's so easy to lose yourself in Mellow's evocative and engaging prose."

—Charlie Holmberg, author of *The Paper Magician*

SCORCHED SKIES

OTHER TITLES BY E. J. MELLOW

The Mousai Series
Song of the Forever Rains
Dance of a Burning Sea
Symphony for a Deadly Throne

SCORCHED SKIES

WAY OF WINGS

BOOK ONE

E·J·MELLOW

Montlake

This is a work of fiction. Names, characters, organizations, places, events, and incidents are either products of the author's imagination or are used fictitiously. Otherwise, any resemblance to actual persons, living or dead, is purely coincidental.

Text copyright © 2025 by E. J. Mellow
All rights reserved.

No part of this book may be reproduced, or stored in a retrieval system, or transmitted in any form or by any means, electronic, mechanical, photocopying, recording, or otherwise, without express written permission of the publisher.

Published by Montlake, Seattle

www.apub.com

Amazon, the Amazon logo, and Montlake are trademarks of Amazon.com, Inc., or its affiliates.

ISBN-13: 9781662526848 (hardcover)
ISBN-13: 9781662515439 (paperback)
ISBN-13: 9781662515446 (digital)

Cover design by Faceout Studio, Tim Green
Cover images: © GoonDu, © Mike Taylor, © queso, © setia69, © therealtakeone / Shutterstock
Map design by Emil Mellow

Printed in the United States of America
First edition

For Christopher,
who forever encourages me to soar to new heights.

NOTE FROM THE AUTHOR

As with all art, there is subject matter I have explored that may be of a sensitive nature to some. I have worked to handle it with great care, but you, the reader, know best what may be triggering. This book contains the following explicit content and dark elements. It includes mature language, violence, sexual assault, substance use, death, animal cruelty, racism, classism, explicit romance scenes, and grief. It is intended for readers eighteen-plus years of age.

MAP OF CĀDRA

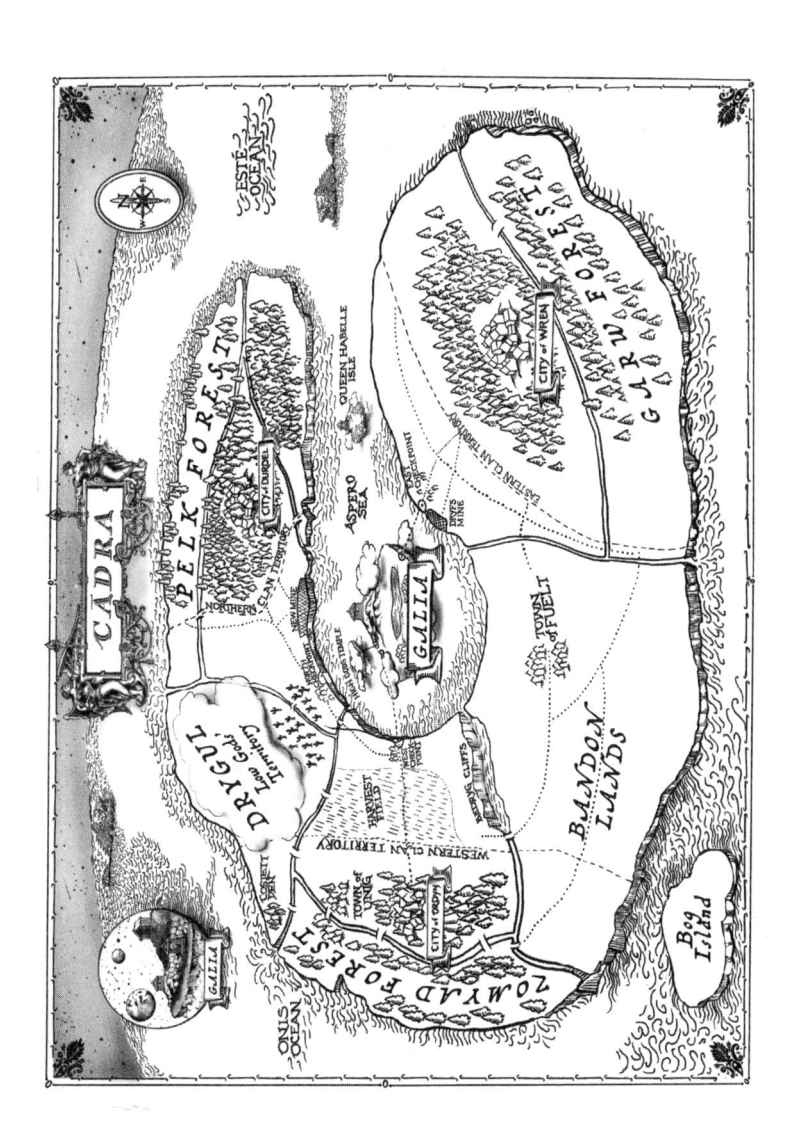

Tanwen Coslett

GLOSSARY

Süra Horns by Clan

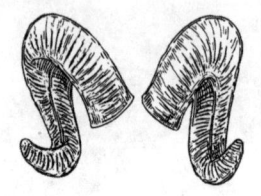

Northern Clan

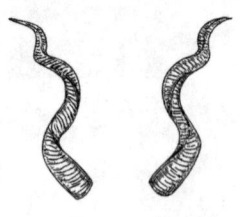

Western Clan

Eastern Clan

Volari Sky Magic Symbols

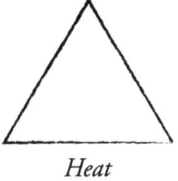

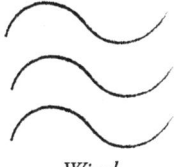

△

Heat

≈

Wind

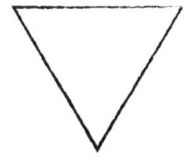

▽

Freeze

/ / /

Rain

PANTHEON OF GODS

The Twelve High Gods

- **Ré**—God of the heavens, sun, and sky. Father of the High Gods. Brother of Maryth.
- **Nocémi**—Goddess of night. Wife of Ré.
- **Maja & Parvi**—Twin moon goddesses.
- **Orzel**—God of the sea.
- **Hyfel**—God of war and justice.
- **Leza**—Goddess of beauty.
- **Ilustra**—God of love and lust.
- **Udasha**—Goddess of fortune and luck.
- **Naru**—Goddess of artistry.
- **Izato**—God of revelry.
- **Zenca**—Goddess of destiny.

The Twelve Low Gods

- **Maryth**—Goddess of death and time. Mother of the Low Gods. Sister to Ré.
- **Ridi**—God of mischief and chaos.
- **Bosyg**—Goddess of the forest.

- **Nen**—Goddess of river and water.
- **Eya**—Goddess of fertility.
- **Tyrith**—God of land, soil, and mountains.
- **Poti**—God of cleverness and wit.
- **Thryn**—Goddess of nurture and healing.
- **Hylio**—God of summer.
- **Mog**—Goddess of winter.
- **Fohl**—God of autumn.
- **Wynya**—Goddess of spring.

PART I

Hunted

1

Only fools with a death wish left the forest at night.

So it was no surprise that the trees loomed disapprovingly as Tanwen Coslett traded their safety for the open field. Though she had hoped they wouldn't chastise her so loudly.

A sharp warning cry from an owl mixed with a fox's high-pitched scolding. *Turn back,* they all demanded. *Too risky.*

Thankfully, Tanwen was well practiced in ignoring the prodding advice from those with whom she did not agree. She had not traveled this distance during the full moons to return home empty handed.

Yet still, as Tanwen eyed the glowing jadüri bloom in the center of the tall grass, her pulse quickened when her current vulnerability became clear. Without the woven tangle of trees, she was an easy mark. Foolish prey.

She scanned the night sky once more, pointed ears on alert, as her legs continued to carry her toward the sacred flower.

High above, the twin moon goddesses, Maja and Parvi, tracked her movement, unblinking orbs of white and gold amid their dusting of stars. There was not even a cloud disturbing their brilliance as their moonlight cascaded across the stalks that rustled with Tanwen's steps.

She remained alone.

See, she silently rebutted to the wildlife who waited, reluctant sentries at the forest's edge. They had kept her company on her trek here, but their companionship always ended at the tree line. *All is fine,* she reassured.

For now, their dubious collective thoughts replied.

Despite disagreeing, Tanwen hurried her pace.

Her ability to communicate with animals was an irritant at times. They tended to offer unwanted opinions more readily than eldoth Yffant, the oldest member of her clan.

As she neared the flower, a gentle summer breeze ran encouraging fingers across her back.

Tanwen pulled free her small blade from her thigh holster.

With blood pumping quickly through her veins, she parted the tall grass, coming to kneel before the cerulean bloom. Its warm glow touched her cheeks, caressed her lips.

You found me, she imagined it sighing.

Tanwen carefully dug the plant out by the roots before laying it upon a clean strip of cloth. The petals were like gossamer, more fragile than glass, and within the center of the bud danced nectar of the gods.

Magic.

And it grew right here, on the soil of Cādra, for any Süra to take.

It never ceased to amaze Tanwen, this small gift from Maja and Parvi, the only High Gods who seemed to care for her kind. For it was under their full moonlight that jadüri bloomed.

"Thank you, Goddesses," Tanwen whispered skyward before she wrapped up the flower, dousing its radiance, and slipped it into the pouch at her hip. It was a bag she had constructed herself, padded and sturdy, made specifically to hold such a fragile find.

As if Tanwen's ears were stuffed with wax, her surroundings went deadly quiet. No longer did the noise of insects or nightfowl fill the air. And this, more than their earlier shouts, caused Tanwen's hairs on her neck to rise.

Danger, their stillness announced.

With heartbeat in her throat, Tanwen gave no hesitation as she stood and sprinted back toward the forest.

How? she wondered in her panic, arms swinging, booted feet kicking up soil. *I was alone! I swear I was alone!*

Foolish. Foolish. Foolish, scolded the animals within the tight cluster of trees, the dark entrance still stretching much too far away.

A whooshing shadow passed overhead.

A heavy whip of wind.

Tanwen refused to look up.

Instead, her lungs burned as she forced herself to pick up speed. Her foraging satchel bounced at her back, her pouches slapping along her hips. Suddenly, obtaining the jadüri felt more than foolish. It appeared suicidal.

Not if I make it to the trees! she pleaded to any High God who might be listening.

But she should have known they turned ears only to their children, for her path became blocked by a great expansion of wings. An eclipsing silhouette fell over her, snuffing out the observing eyes of moonlight.

Tanwen jerked to a halt as her pulse tumbled forward.

His wingspan was as terrifying as it was magnificent. He gave one last push of his feathers, forcing the tall grass to bow with its gale as he planted booted feet on the ground.

Recklessly, Tanwen entertained turning and running the other way. But there lay only more endless field. Her safety was in the past, before she had stepped foot from the forest.

The blood drained from her as she curled her hands into fists to keep them from shaking. She lowered her eyes and dropped to one knee.

As she had been taught.

As she was meant to before a child of the High Gods.

She loathed prostrating, but she was not ready to die this night.

"I mean you no harm." His voice startled her, so deep, a storm thundering over the quiet grassland.

Tanwen kept her gaze down, knowing better than to reply, but internally her galloping heartbeats thumped *Lies, lies, lies.*

Volari and Süra were not comrades. Celestial beings did not befriend vermin, or so their winged kind liked to say. Any Süra found alone by a Volari rarely returned to their clan to tell the tale, or so her kind liked to say. And if this man knew what Tanwen *really* was, what mixed blood her Süra appearance masked, well, his knife would not have remained sheathed at his hip.

"I am searching for a man," he continued as he towered over her. "Rumored to be living with the western clan of the Zomyad Forest. Three ambrü will be given to any who can share sound information about his whereabouts."

A small fortune, thought Tanwen, her mind racing. Who would be worth so much to find?

"His name is Gabreel Heiro," the Volari went on. "Though we expect he has not used that name in a very long while. He may appear as one of your own, but his lack of horns and the scars on his back will prove otherwise. For he was once a Volari, but no longer does he have his wings."

Dread. A cold, unforgiving grip to Tanwen's spine caused her to look up. A misstep, for she found the piercing blue gaze of the Volari regarding her much too intently.

He was tall. Broad. Light-brown skin flawless over his sharply cut features. The light of the twin moons outlined the crest of his white wings, now tucked in, the color matching his long tied-back hair. His beauty was eclipsing, a consuming spot in her vision that sent shivers through her before a cascading of heat. He was every bit a creature born in the clouds, meant to take up the sky.

Tanwen's attention was pulled to the four gold stripes and sun insignia decorating his high-collared coat.

A renewed twist of fear filled her gut.

She knelt before a kidar of the royal palace, though perhaps she should be prostrating, for she could not be further from his equal.

"Do you know of such a man?" he inquired again.

Tanwen swallowed past the tightness squeezing her throat as she quickly bowed her head.

"I do not, sir," she lied, praying now to the Low Gods that he'd believe her.

Because Tanwen *did* know of such a man.

But unfortunately, that man was her father.

2

The Süra was lying.

Zolya knew this, for he had been born into a den of deceivers. To be a child of the High Gods meant one also had to live with them. Or, more aptly, survive their influence. As a youth he had learned the subtle mannerisms of falsehoods. The tightness in shoulders. The heightened octave of a voice. The way distorted confidence tended to sour a gaze or how nerves could cause it to shift.

This Süra had fallen victim to the latter.

Though, in her defense, most of her kind were skittish around his.

But it wasn't merely nerves that had lifted her attention. He saw her truth from what flickered through her green eyes: fear.

There was only one reason his inquiry would spark such terror, and that was to know the answer but be unwilling to share it.

Was she a friend? A neighbor? Did she work for him? What loyalty would hold her tongue?

Zolya's heartbeat thrummed harder.

Despite the answer, he was now convinced he was back on Gabreel's trail.

A wash of relief touched his tired shoulders, slightly eased the ever-pressing ache in his wings from endless flying. Especially since the rumors he had chased west had dried up a fortnight ago.

"Are you certain?" Zolya pushed, studying the Süra more closely as she knelt before him. She held the blessings of Leza, to be sure, her beauty woven through her high cheekbones and delicate brows. But she seemed young. Though, to him, most Süra appeared as such when decades made up their lives rather than centuries. Her white skin was smooth under the twins' moonlight, her hair spilling a midnight river around her shoulders. Her one peculiarity was that her horns—tall and slightly curved—claimed her eastern-clan heritage despite her clearly living within the western clan. She also wore the common brown-and-green-dyed threads of those from Zomyad, with dozens of pouches strapped to her person. Zolya recalled eyeing her harvesting jadüri before he had descended. *A meddyg,* he thought. A reckless one to be foraging out in the open, alone at night. Or perhaps desperate.

"May I remind you there are ambrü waiting to be given for what you may know of this man," he repeated. "Surely that is a sum that can gain you priceless wares for your practice."

Zolya watched her already clenched fists tighten further. "Indeed, you are correct, sir," she replied with forced calm. "It is also a sum that could gain priceless food for many Süra families. Which is why it pains me not to have heard of such a person this far west."

"Yes, how unfortunate," he mused. "Especially since there have been others before you who have said otherwise."

"If that is true, sir," she countered, continuing to speak to the grass between them, "then my ignorance should not stop your search. I merely apologize that I cannot be more useful in your endeavors."

Zolya almost smiled, noting the slightest pinch of derision buried beneath her even tone.

She was bold, this one.

And lucky.

Another Volari would not have found her words amusing or allowed her to leave unscathed if they sensed she was lying.

Exactly the reason Zolya had insisted he lead this search over the other willing kidars—or, rather, one of the reasons he had insisted.

With great effort, he kept his thoughts from shifting to King Réol, unease creeping through his veins. Instead, he refocused on the girl.

Despite her claims, Zolya had gathered what he needed for his next task.

With the moons cresting well past midnight, he held no desire to further this line of questioning. That way only ever led to a Süra in pain. And as determined as Zolya was to end this search, he was equally exhausted from hurting, from watching his men hurt. He merely wished for a hasty flight back to camp, where he could indulge in a hearty meal and uninterrupted sleep before the next inevitable long day ahead.

Another mark toward this woman's luck, which he decided on a whim to enhance.

An atonement for the unlucky before her.

"You have been more useful than you perhaps realize," he said. "Here." Zolya fingered out a payment from the purse clipped to his belt. "For your troubles." He bent down, holding it out for her to take.

The woman drew away as she registered his nearness, no doubt finding it unsettling that a Volari would lower themselves to her level. Her frown twisted further into a scowl as she saw what was in his gloved hand.

He held an ambrü between them. Its glowing scarlet center pulsed as though knowing its worth to her kind and whispering, *Take me, take me, take me.*

Her eyes rose to his, and this time it was not fear that Zolya registered in their depths. No, it was the seed of their races' shared history: hatred.

The look would have startled Zolya if he had not seen it many times prior from Süra.

He may also have been mistaken regarding her age. This close, he now saw her years woven through her eyes, the speckling of scars across her skin. A worn-down stone, a collection of hardships.

An imprisoned part of Zolya's heart thumped, saddened.

Though none of it dimmed her beauty. In fact, it merely enhanced it and stirred awake questions from Zolya.

What life have you already lived?

"I cannot take that, sir," she said, though her declaration was weak. Which, of course, was exactly the reason for her disdain. She was no doubt reminded of the truth of their world: the ones who held valuables hardly valued them.

She needed this more than he did.

"Then don't take it," Zolya replied. "I shall leave it here for someone else to find."

He dropped the ambrü into the tall grass before standing, stretching out his wings.

The effect was as he desired. The woman shrank within the shadow of his feathered expanse, but her eyes still held what was in her heart.

Careful, he wanted to warn. Such a strongly held gaze toward a Volari for too long had led many of her kind to Maryth's Eternal River.

To curb her future behavior for when she inevitably met a Volari less lenient than him, Zolya sent a quick reminder of his threat.

He took a deep inhale, gathering the power of the High Gods that lived within his blood. It was a racing of fiery cords through his veins as he balled it together in his chest. *Be my storm,* he ordered before he released his sky magic with a burst.

A rumble shook their surroundings. Dark clouds formed above, curling droplets of ink, and then it began to rain.

The woman fell to both her knees as she shielded herself from the abrupt wet onslaught. Her dark hair was quickly plastered to her pale face, her horns standing more prominently.

"I'd find cover within your forest," Zolya suggested from where he remained bone dry, the rain curving around him. Created magic did not affect the creator. "Before your jadüri gets drenched."

With a large push of his wings, he shot into the air, leaving the girl behind, but not before he saw her ignore his advice. Instead, she was bent forward, frantically searching the grass for the discarded ambrü.

◆ ◆ ◆

"I was about to wake the camp to come find you." Osko stood by the dark cliff's ledge as Zolya ascended onto it.

"Then it is good I have returned before you did." Zolya tucked in his wings, walking past his joint-in-command to find the nearest fire. One still flickered with life between a cluster of tents by the south-facing wall. He turned, warming his frosted plumage. The heat seeped into him, healing, a mother's embrace. Zolya let out a soft sigh of contentment.

Though it was summer in Cādra, when this high up in the Bedryg Cliffs, the night air held tight to a chill. An effect the winds coming from the rough Aspero Sea to the east only amplified. His men would be wrapped in their thickest hides tonight.

As he took in the stillness of the camp, the last curls of smoke from doused fires, and the weak aroma of stew long since enjoyed, Zolya surmised they had been tucked in for some time. Despite him still having been out flying.

But he could not fault his men.

Zolya knew they were as beaten down as he was from their endless monthlong search. Cādra was vast, with many places to hide. And while it had been twenty-odd years since Gabreel's banishment from Galia, Zolya had not expected their hunt to recover the infamous inventor to go on for quite this long.

But it shall end soon, he reminded himself. *Tomorrow we will know for certain where you disappeared to, Gabreel Heiro. We will know where a dead man might find sanctuary to live again.* And then history would repeat itself.

Zolya frowned, that disquieting whisper in his heart awakening again. But it wasn't his place to question the desires of his king—and especially not his orders. King Réol acted from the voice of the High Gods in his ear. Whatever his intentions, they were from divine reasoning.

"Well?" Osko came to stand before Zolya, arms crossed, black wings twitching behind him with telling agitation. "Was searching the northern perimeter of the forest as uneventful as the last three times?"

"You really must have more faith in my instincts," replied Zolya as he worked off his leather gloves, then slipped them into his coat pocket.

"It is not your instincts I question," countered Osko, his dark brows furrowed. "It's the risk you pose to yourself by doing these searches alone. What is the point of us keeping this unit if you do not use them?"

"May I remind you," began Zolya, his tone skirting an edge. "It was not my desire to have a unit at all for this mission. Süra do not exactly grow conversational when a horde of armed Volari approach. Or shall I recount the past failed fortnight of interactions? We have made the progress that we have *because* of my solo flights."

Osko's chest puffed up, his features a twist of ire. He was an ox poised to charge but knowing the result would yield little reward. It was the exact expression he had worn since he was a boy, whenever he found himself in an argument with Zolya.

"I take your silence as you coming to the conclusion that I am right." Zolya turned, warming his hands next.

"You're a cramp in my wing is what you are."

Zolya flashed Osko a grin as the large man drew up beside him. "Spoken like a true friend."

Osko merely grunted, his attention settling on the fire. The dancing glow brushed across his pale cheek, casting a shadow against the black-inked triangle exposed on the side of his neck.

At the sight of Osko's tattoo, Zolya's mood sobered, and he looked away.

Not every Volari marked themselves with their craft of sky magic. Those who could wield heat were a particularly proud lot, however. They believed they were the closest in blessings to King Réol. He who upon descending to the throne inherited not only the god of the sky's namesake but his magic as well. The all-powerful Ré, the father of the High Gods who ruled the heavens, sun, and sky.

King Réol certainly thought this, too, for he favored the heat wielders, having originally been one himself.

Zolya was born with rain in his blood.

Like his mother.

His first indiscretion.

Zolya curled his outstretched hands into fists, lowering them to his side as he fought a twist of agitation. For a star fall he was back as a boy still sorting out his wrongdoings. But with a calming exhale, he forced his mind to return to the present, to their mission—the one he was going to succeed in.

"Tomorrow we shall seek an audience with Nyddoth Marwth," Zolya announced, his resolve as hard as the rock beneath his feet.

"We will?" Osko's shock was clear in his voice. "On what grounds? None of our brothers assigned to the western harvest have said they've heard of Gabreel or the likes of a wingless Volari in this area. We will need more than your instincts for us to be allowed entry into a Süra forest, let alone to seek an audience with one of their clan leaders. The intel gathered in Garw was either old or a blatant misdirect. We should search Both Island as we had decided this morning."

"I met someone tonight who knows Gabreel," Zolya explained, his gaze meeting his friend's widening one. "Or I highly suspect knows of him."

"Suspect?" Osko's brows drew in. "Did you not get the truth from them?"

Red splashed across Zolya's vision. Blood and screams and tears. A Volari soldier's way to truth.

But did it always have to be *the* way?

A question Zolya knew was safest left a thought.

"I did not need to hear the words to know it was their truth."

"Zol," Osko huffed as he shook his head. "This is why I should have accompanied you. Or a kidet. Süra are clever. They've prospered as long as they have because the Low God of mischief has blessed them with the art of evasion. How do you know this Süra did not merely tell you what you wanted to know to secure his profit and leave? There certainly have been others on our search who have tried."

"I know the ways of Süra," Zolya rebutted, his tone a pinprick of a blade. "And I am not a greenhorn kidet. I am a kidar of the royal palace, same as you, and do not need to defend my findings."

"You are *not* the same as I," grunted Osko.

Zolya cut his friend a glance, their gazes a clashing of tides, but he knew the only way to address such a comment was to ignore it. "We have already searched the Pelk Forest and the Garw," he reasoned. "All that is left is Zomyad, and despite what you may think, Gabreel *is* there. Or has been recently. If I am wrong, we will go to Both."

"And what are we to say to Nyddoth Marwth, hmm?" Osko challenged. "We need proof to search the Süra's sanctuary forests. You should have snagged this Süra to present to their nyddoth and make him share what he had with you. If you indeed caught him outside the forest, then he had left his territory on his own."

Zolya ground his teeth together, knowing Osko was right. Why hadn't he grabbed her?

For the same reason you do not correct your friend that he *is in fact* she, a voice whispered through him.

Zolya's skin prickled with awareness as his attention danced over the collection of nearby tents. To the tired men inside. The hungry men. The men who assuredly missed their comforts found back in Galia.

No woman would be safe here, especially not a Süra.

And this concerns you why? asked a cutting internal voice, one that brought shame to fill Zolya's chest, a scolding scalding. *Weakness is a decision made from the heart.* Words from his king. *Do you wish to be a weakness, Zolya?*

Zolya was poised rigidly as the echo of the question burned through him.

Do you wish to be a weakness?

The answer always a tapestry: layered and complicated.

"Without such proof we'll need to be prepared to offer a generous sum," Osko continued. "Süra clan leaders are proud. The nyddoth will not be bribed easily. Do you think King Réol will approve of such a bounty?"

Zolya dropped his gaze to the fire, quick to bury the provoking voice in the back of his mind. As he churned over his friend's question, a vision of the woman from tonight manifested in the jumping flames. Her strength had shone through her eyes, reflecting her will to survive. Yet he couldn't help but notice her slender frame, the collarbone protruding too prominently from beneath her shirt.

A plan slithered into place.

"Leave it to me for what we will offer," he said. "To King Réol, the inventor is worth any price to be returned. If Nyddoth Marwth knows of Gabreel's whereabouts, we will come to an arrangement for him to give him up. And by week's end we *will* have him."

Osko poised to respond but then held off. He studied Zolya, and Zolya let him, a matching of silent calculation and histories shared. In the end, Osko gave a terse nod because there was not much else he could do with such a command.

Zolya's stance relaxed. *Thank you, blessed High Gods,* he thought, eager to be done with the conversation, to finally end this painfully long day.

"Is there any supper left?" he asked after another beat, wanting to rid the air of tension.

Scorched Skies

Osko walked the short distance to a discarded covered pot beside the fire. As he picked it up, the base of the metal glowed red for a spell, Osko warming it with his hands.

"Here," he said, ladling a bowl and extending it to Zolya. "I made sure the kidets left you some."

The two men sat together on nearby stools, each of their wings brushing the ground at their backs. The pop and sizzle of the fire became their music, the pulsing of stars overhead their entertainment as Zolya nearly drank the stew in one go. It lacked salt, and taste, but it was warm and filled the empty yawn in his stomach. Once he was finished, his exhaustion fell upon him, unyielding. His recent use of magic had not helped. When already fatigued, to expel such energy merely heightened every soreness and discomfort in his body. But it had felt necessary at the time, and by morning he would be restored to his old self. They *all* would be once they were set to return home.

"I want you to know," said Osko, breaking their stretch of quiet, "it was not I who insisted so many of our men joined this mission."

Zolya set his bowl aside, a new weariness slipping into his bones. "Yes, I know."

"You're his son," Osko continued, reasoning. "It's natural he'd want to keep you safe."

Zolya remained silent, though his rebuttal rang loud through his mind, a clawing of truth against his heart.

I'm his heir, he wanted to correct. *He wants his legacy safe.*

For what other reason would a king need a son?

3

Tanwen stood bottling salves in her family's kitchen, but her nerves were a waterfall of disruption. Her attention kept drifting to her bedroom door, which lay down the hall to her right, to the scuffed floorboard under her mattress where a leather pouch hid the ambrü.

Tanwen swore she could hear its pulsing red glow as though an unwanted guest were knocking on their den. Particularly the kidar who had offered it to her last night.

There are ambrü waiting to be given for what you may know of this man.

His rumbling words had chased Tanwen the entire distance back to her home. Had rung out with each creaking step she had climbed to her family's tree den and whispered in the thick forest air filtering through her window as she slipped into her bed, unseen by her dozing twin brother across the room. As Tanwen gripped her covers close, her swirling confusion and fear-tangled thoughts had made sleep futile.

Despite the kidar's threat, he had surprised Tanwen.

He was intimidating, to be sure, but hadn't acted like any other Volari she had yet encountered.

Where had been his forceful demands? Or his condescending tone and rough handling when he hadn't gotten what he sought?

Instead, he had stood assessing, poised, calm.

He had even sunk to her level to offer up the ambrü.

It had sent Tanwen reeling with uncertainty, not enjoying how her blood thrummed from his nearness, how his restraint had teased the promise of her safety.

A dangerous mirage.

And Tanwen had already been born into danger. *Was* a danger.

She was an abomination to hide.

Her grip tightened around the jar she held, frustration scratching up her throat.

Why? she wanted to scream to the High Gods. *After so many years, why* now *are the Volari looking for my father?*

And what would happen if they found him? Found them?

Tanwen's anger tumbled to worry, a cold clasp to her spine.

She did not wish to be forced further into the shadows. A phantom at the fringes of life, back on the run.

Reasons enough for why she had refrained from going to her parents last night, waking them to warn of the kidar who was out searching for a wingless Volari. A kidar who had used a name for her father that had long been buried. A name Tanwen was forbidden to even mutter in her thoughts.

Her father was Flyn Coslett now. They were all Cosletts.

Heiro was a surname her parents had abandoned after the birth of her and her brother, a history best left severed along with her father's wings.

While there were many pockets of mysteries within her parents' pasts, Flyn and Aisling Coslett had made sure their children knew of their deepest-buried secret: their love. Or, more aptly, their love that broke crucial Cādra law—that a Süra and Volari were never to reproduce—for Tanwen and her brother, Aberthol, were the repercussions of such sin.

They were Mütra.

Mixed blood.

A plague on Cādra.

Unnatural creatures born to possess unnatural abilities. Thieves of celestial magic, which swam through their blood, never destined for any but the Volari to have and to wield.

Tanwen frowned as she set aside another filled jar, then absently reached for the next.

Not that her parents would ever call them by such names. Their mother often said they were her wyrthia, her miracles. But Tanwen didn't know of any miracles that were meant to be so thoroughly hidden. Or destroyed.

She only understood they were blessed to appear as Süra, with their horns that matched their mother's. No differences marked their backs, no partial wings or misshapen physical traits, like many other Mütra they had happened upon had.

As for Tanwen's father, without his wings he had been passing as a Süra for as long as she could remember.

Only at home, in the privacy of shuttered windows and locked doors, did he dare remove the band of horns from his head.

A gift from a Süra long swimming in the Eternal River, he had explained to Tanwen and her brother when, as children, they had asked how he could come to own horns. Meaning, he had cut them from the head of the dead. Tanwen remembered how her own horns had throbbed as she was tucked into bed that night, imagining a shadow slipping into her room to carve them out.

Tanwen shivered at the memory, stopping in her work.

The extremes to which her family had gone to hide were exactly why she hesitated in confiding in them now. Despite the potential danger the kidar's sudden appearance brought, she understood what outcome would follow her confession: Her family disappearing, *again*, and with it Tanwen vanishing from another home. Forced to become invisible. Or, rather, further invisible.

No. She couldn't allow it. She wouldn't survive it! Tanwen clenched her teeth as her resolve settled. *Why should I continually suffer from an act I had no part of?* A life she had never asked for.

"Wen," breathed her mother as she swept into their workroom, drawing Tanwen's attention away from her rising ire.

Her mother fluttered like a hummingbird as she pulled down dried roots over the sleeping hearth and flowers hanging by the window. She paused only to gently spread them out on a table along the far wall.

"Are you almost done?" asked her mother as she eyed the stack of bottled salves beside Tanwen. She answered her own question with a satisfied nod. "We must make it to the fields by midbreak," she explained, continuing her spin about the room. "And we must stop in Unig on our way. I told elda Anora I'd deliver her ointment for her foot. Here." Her mother offered up a small filled glass vial, which she had swiped from an organized row. "Put this along your belt. I'll help pack these salves up between us."

Tanwen did as she was told, and soon they were loaded up to leave.

As she adjusted the weight of the pack across her back, Tanwen studied her mother doing the same.

Aisling was tall for a Süra, with delicate features that softened her stronger personality. Her father often joked that it was Aisling who was Tanwen's twin over Aberthol. While it made her mother blush, Tanwen was always hit with a pang of guilt.

They might share visual traits and duties—Tanwen training to follow in her mother's footsteps as a skilled meddyg—but her heart's true desire lay outside their kitchen. In a workshop along the forest floor.

But in there, women were not suited to roam.

"What is this?" asked her mother, unfolding a cloth near Tanwen.

The room was flooded in blue light as the jadüri was revealed. Aisling snapped her gaze up to meet Tanwen's. A race of emotions flooded her mother's features—suspicion, no doubt, for how she had acquired it; worry with her realization; relief in finding her safe—and then settled on an expression that left Tanwen swallowing an ache in her throat: pride.

"Maja and Parvi were generous during my foraging," explained Tanwen, having nearly forgotten about the sacred bud that she had set out to show her mother.

Instead, all morning her thoughts had been weighed down by the kidar. The threat of which she was now hoping would merely fly away as quickly as he had from her last night. After all, she hadn't revealed anything to him. There was no use in causing her parents alarm from someone who could very well already be headed back to Galia.

"Well done," said her mother, re-covering the plant with the cloth. The blue glow was snuffed out. "We will make docüra from it tonight, while the nectar is still rich. Your father has some business in the capital at end of week. We'll go with him and sell our mixture to meddyg Lyral. The gods know we can use the gem." Within her palm, Aisling cradled the linen like a newborn as she bent below one of their cupboards. "We will also give an offering of gratitude to Thryn so she may bless our endeavors."

Tanwen watched as her mother hid the jadüri. It was from her that Tanwen had learned how to bury treasure in floorboards.

"Ready?" asked her mother as she stood.

Tanwen nodded, and together they left the workshop, then exited their home.

As Tanwen stepped across the threshold, the full sweetness of the forest filled her lungs.

An endless sea of brown-and-green foliage spilled out on the other side of the balcony. High above the sky was a canopy of leaves, stretched open like interlocked hands grasping for the sun. Only speckled slashes of light dived into the bowels of the woods, poked holes in cloth to grace the forest floor.

It was a leafy tangled net, the Low Gods' gift that kept the Süra safe. For only the smallest of winged creatures could fly in here. If any Volari did dare enter the Zomyad Forest, it would be on equalizing terrain—their feet.

As Tanwen followed her mother, descended the curling steps that hugged their tree den, she held tight to this reminder of their security. *In the forest we are safe. My family is safe.*

A large reason, Tanwen knew, they had made the long voyage to live here those ten years ago.

Her and her brother's childhood had not been made up of consistencies. Because of what their family hid—past and present—they had moved often, living in tight abandoned quarters dug throughout the wild open Bandon Lands of southeast Cādra. It wasn't until they had reached Zomyad, a place farthest from where they were born, that Tanwen experienced what it was like to put down roots. Decorate a home. *Have* a home. One she was desperate to hold on to as long as she could.

With determined strides that matched her thoughts, Tanwen kept pace with her mother as they turned from the staircase to cut their way to another tree by way of a large extended branch outfitted as a bridge.

Most of the woods was connected similarly, their city and towns most of all. A twisting of stacked buildings along tree trunks and roads along grand branches, hanging bridges that swayed from one great sapling to the next. And like all Süra dwellings in Zomyad, the Cosletts' den was built high within an anfith tree: the largest and oldest of its kind found in Cādra.

But unlike other homes, theirs, of course, was in the most inconvenient section of the forest: in a pie slice of land on the northwest edge.

As one would guess, it was not a quick trek to Unig, the closest town, but it was a familiar journey, and soon Tanwen and her mother had reached the cluster of buildings that made up its border.

"Wait here," instructed her mother as she took the vial Tanwen handed to her from her belt. "I should only be a moment with elda Anora. Do not talk to anyone."

Tanwen pursed her lips at the repeated instruction she had endured since birth.

Do not draw attention to yourself.
Do not speak to others.
You do not need friends. You have your brother.
You must stay close. It's the only way to stay safe.
Safe. Hidden. Forgotten.

But what her parents hadn't taken into consideration was that to stand alone was to stand apart, and often that drew worse attention than better. The Cosletts had built a reputation for themselves.

"Tanwen, did you hear what I said?" asked her mother, who had remained awaiting her reply.

"Yes," Tanwen assured. "I will be as though the moss on this tree," she added, unable to keep the dryness from her tone as she leaned against the trunk. At two and twenty, she was more than tired of her leash.

Her mother seemed to pick up on her discontent, for her gaze narrowed, but in the end, she left to make her delivery.

Tanwen let out a bored sigh, pulling at the weight of her sack across her chest as she eyed the surrounding web of town. Children ran across a bridge high above, while citizens moved about to buy or sell wares from stalls built into the massive protruding tree roots below.

And here Tanwen stood, meant to be as though the foliage she hid beside—a backdrop. An unremarkable detail to their world. She crossed her arms over her chest, her annoyance prickling.

To blend in was a seemingly impossible request when, since birth, Tanwen had felt more like the sun, a beacon reaching far and wide.

I cannot believe you left our den without me, came a familiar, though out of breath, voice within her mind.

As if on cue, Tanwen glanced down to find a mouse scurrying up her pant leg. *Eli,* she thought with a smile, drawing her small friend into her hand. His whiskers tickled her palm. *I'm sorry,* she replied silently. *Mother was in a hurry, and I thought you were napping.*

I was, rebuked Eli, *until your stomping out of the workshop woke me up. You really must be more courteous of those around you. Especially if they are sleeping.*

Tanwen rolled her eyes.

She had found Eli a month ago after he had made himself at home in their bread box. When he had squeaked his apology and Tanwen had replied with her forgiveness, he had frozen, clearly in shock to have understood her and she him. Ever since, he was never far from her side.

Eli was an example of what her magic attracted. Wherever she traveled, the creatures followed.

And within the forest of Zomyad, creatures were aplenty. Animals squeezed out of cracks and shadowed knolls to be near her. Millepedes skittered along her boots to curl within her laces as if seeking her warmth. When she walked at night, glow beetles gathered to light her way; lynxes and foxes followed as her guards. Owls soared forward to scout her destination. Since her earliest memories, Tanwen could feel the nature around her and hear the nearby creatures, and in exchange they could hear her.

Friend, they would coo. *Ally, cousin, familiar.*

This was her one reprieve in being a Mütra, in their family moving from place to place to eventually be sequestered to the farthest reaches of this forest. The animals here had become her confidants, her companions to chase away the spells of loneliness. Her protectors and the only reason her parents ever let her forage alone. The very magic that put her in danger gave her the smallest taste of freedom.

We are blessed to have these abilities, she would often argue with her brother. *Instead of another Mütra trait to call us out. We can hide our magic.*

I'd rather not have to hide anything at all, Aberthol had huffed, flicking his finger to cause a puddle out of arm's reach to splash. While he could not communicate with animals like Tanwen, her parents had come to decide Aberthol could affect sky elements. While the Volari could manifest them, Aberthol could move them. Push away raindrops, redirect a breeze, shield himself from heat or freeze.

Their father thought their magic was fascinating.

Their mother found it terrifying.

What if they draw attention to it without thinking? As a reaction or a form of defense? Aisling's fearful rebuttal had traveled down through floorboards to where Tanwen and her brother had sat together as children on their bed, listening to their parents' whispered debate.

Then we will teach them to hide it even under the worst pain.

And their father had.

Tanwen could still recall the searing agony of those lessons with her father. The nausea of hearing the screams of her brother and then, after, each of them sitting together—silent and tearstained—as their mother cared for their burns.

Her father might pass as a Süra, but they would never forget he was born a Volari, and while he no longer had his wings, he still held his powers. And that was to wield heat.

"I was wondering when Bedryg's critter would be back in town." The deep voice returned Tanwen's attention to where she leaned against a tree trunk, two men having approached. She realized with dismay Eli was still in her palm, her fingers having been absently stroking his fur.

Tanwen bit back a curse.

Begone, friend, she thought to Eli, stirring the mouse to run up her arm and leap into the foliage at her back.

Osian snorted his disgust, turning to his companion. "See, Luwyg, I told you she's always covered in rodents."

Luwyg replied with a bored assessment of Tanwen, his gaze snagging on her horns before his lips pursed in clear disdain.

Tanwen stiffened, wishing to draw deeper into the shadows.

If her parents had wanted them to blend in, it would have helped if her horns weren't of the eastern clan. Being so obviously a foreigner was only met with distrust in these smaller towns of Zomyad.

"Tell me, critter," began Osian, smile pointed. "Have you been sleeping on the forest floor again? Or have you finally dug your bed underground like all straight horns?"

Tanwen gritted her teeth, fighting a reply. She might hold no loyalty to the eastern Süra, but the slurs still stung, if only because those were her mother's people.

If I don't say anything, they will get bored and leave, she reminded herself. *They always get bored and leave.*

Do not draw attention to yourself.

Do not speak to others.

You are Mütra. You are Mütra. You are Mütra.

It was the mantra Tanwen had clung to since she was a young girl, when those in town had begun to have an appetite for heckling her, the shy foreigner who lived on the fringes of their forest.

"Where else is she meant to find her worms to eat?" countered Luwyg, idly picking at his nails.

Tanwen's ire prickled.

If I don't say anything, they will get bored and leave. If I don't say anything, they will get bored and leave.

"Speaking of worms," continued Osian. "How's your brother these days? Still cowering behind your father?"

Hate was a slithering sensation, one that filled Tanwen's veins as she curled her hands into fists at her side. *If only I could give you something to cower from,* Tanwen silently shot back, her rage frothing.

As soon as she had the biting thought, Tanwen was too late in sensing the danger.

A snake lunged toward Osian from behind her shoulder. An uncoiling yellow rope from the tangle of leaves. Fangs bared; venom poised.

There was a collection of gasps as the men jumped apart.

The snake was knocked from the air by a thrown stick. It hissed as it slithered quickly back into the bushes.

"We are all done here, Wen." Her mother's tense voice cut into the moment as she strode toward her. "Osian, have you not left blessings for Bedryg lately?" Aisling glanced worriedly to the wide-eyed man. "It seems you have upset our goddess of our home if her children are acting out like that. I'd return to your den immediately and offer up your best spirits to atone."

Osian merely nodded, still regaining his bearings as Tanwen's elbow was gripped by her mother, who practically dragged her away.

Only when they were a good distance from town did she stop, spinning to confront Tanwen. "That was foolish, girl! What were you thinking?"

"I didn't do anything!"

"So that snake decided to attack Osian all on its own?"

Tanwen folded her arms over her chest. "It's entirely possible. If I were a snake, he certainly seems like someone I'd want to bite."

"That"—her mother poked her arm—"right there is why the snake tried. Your thoughts can become theirs. You *must* refrain from drawing suspicion onto our family. Onto you."

Annoyance flared hot through Tanwen, dry leaves catching flame. "And living reclusively from the rest of our clan isn't suspicious?" she countered. "Keeping Thol and me from having friends isn't odd? Making sure we don't utter more than a handful of words when in town is completely normal behavior? Parading around with horns that are clearly foreign makes it so easy to blend in? *I* have not drawn suspicion onto our family; you and father have. Or are you truly unaware of our name, the Curious Cosletts, which is whispered throughout Zomyad?"

"Wen." Her mother sighed, the fight seeping from her like she was an overwrung wet cloth: exhausted. "It is better they remain curious than wise to what we hide. I am sorry for it, but you *know* why we live as we do, so far from where you were born. Why your father and I demand all that we have from you and Thol. We wish our world was different, but it is not. It never will be, which makes these constant arguments tiresome. All your father and I want is to give you and your brother a home, for us to live together safely. You cannot fault us in that."

No, but what if that is not all I want in life? Tanwen wanted to scream.

Instead, she remained close lipped.

Despite how it curdled her blood with frustration, she knew her mother was right. She was always right. And these arguments were indeed growing tiresome because they always ended the same: Tanwen boiling with the same conclusion.

The gods had cursed her life.

And no amount of kicking and screaming would change that.

"I do not blame you for wanting to retaliate against Osian," her mother went on, clearly trying to soothe the tension swirling. "His father is just as troublesome, but no good will come from engaging with those sorts. Only more trouble."

"But I *didn't* engage," Tanwen huffed. "*I* remained silent when he called me critter and a straight horn and called Thol a coward. I cannot help it if my friends wish to engage for me. And despite how you might disapprove," she said hurriedly before her mother could reply, "I am glad they did. Someone needs to knock Osian down a branch or two."

Her mother let out a long exhale, looking to the High Gods as though they could instill in her more patience. "All right," she said. "I see this is currently as far as we will get on the matter. But please, for now, just . . . try not to have your *friends* help any more today. Especially not while we are at the harvest."

Aisling turned, officially ending the debate as she strode away.

Tanwen followed, fighting the urge to pout. And not merely because of their argument but because of what her mother had said regarding her friends.

Aisling had nothing to worry about there.

After last night, Tanwen knew even if she were to beg, no animal within the forest would save her from a Volari.

Unfortunate, indeed, given the destination they now sought would be swarming with them.

4

It was never pleasant stepping into the full light of day.

Tanwen squinted, shielding her eyes from the accosting sun as she and her mother left the tranquil shadows of the forest to enter the harvest fields. Though it was a short distance to the northern outbuildings, the summer's heat did quick work in plastering Tanwen's shirt to her back, her exposed skin growing slick with sweat.

Tanwen hurried her pace, her steps kicking up dust along the dirt road, to find a shadowed reprieve under the nearest covered pavilion.

She never understood how any creature could live so unprotected under the searing gaze of Ré. The father of the High Gods was a demanding master, greedy to cover every strip of Cādra with his bright and blistering fingers.

But it was not merely the midday blaze that gripped Tanwen with discomfort or set her longing to retreat into the forest; it was what else filled the sky.

In the distance, dozens of Volari peppered the blue expanse, massive wings pumping as they hovered over various plots of farmland. *Vultures*, her people often called the Volari stationed here. A necessity to their clan's process of life as well as a warning of its vulnerability.

Here flew the children of the High Gods assigned to oversee and aid in the western land's agriculture. For these fields were what fed most of Cādra, including the floating isles of Galia and the king and queen themselves.

While this forced a symbiotic relationship between the two races—both needing what the seasonal harvests yielded—it was not without a lack of injustices. The Volari might extend their magic to bring rain to thirsty crops, heat to frosted ones, and a breeze to spread pollination, but the Sūra did the backbreaking work on the ground. The labor that left hands bleeding, skin puckering from sunburns, muscles overworked, and bodies parched. But such was the price for food grown on their own soil—and the reason Tanwen and her mother were here.

By midday, any meddyg was a welcome sight to the workers.

Her mother greeted the other women stationed within the outbuilding, cooks and seamstresses, while Tanwen unpacked supplies in their assigned section. The open pavilion was outfitted simply: a few cots, chairs, and rows of benches for the workers to sit and eat.

"I'll finish setting up," said her mother, handing Tanwen one of their water sacks. "Go find your father and brother. They will need a refill after working all morning in this heat."

"Use one of the horses," advised Venya, the female warden of their post. "There was a handful of equipment the crop master needed your pa to check. They are most likely further south by now, near the squash."

Tanwen gave Venya a thankful smile, but before she could take leave, her mother grasped her forearm, stilling her.

"Remember what we spoke of," Aisling whispered, eyes earnest, features stern.

Do not draw attention to yourself.
Do not speak to others.
Stay safe. Blend in.

Tanwen clenched her teeth together, her frustration with the unceasing reminder never far. But she managed a nod, which released her mother's grip.

She hurried to the stables, her mood lifting when she spotted the white-and-brown mare in one of the stalls.

"I had hoped you'd still be here, Rind," whispered Tanwen as she stroked the horse's nose, the scent of hay lying thick in the space between them.

Friend. Rind nuzzled her neck. *Sister.*

Tanwen's chest heated with the honor of such a greeting.

"I need to find my father and brother," she explained, continuing to keep her voice low so no nearby stable hands could hear. Curious Cosletts, indeed, if they found her conversing with a horse. "Do you mind giving me a ride?"

Rind huffed, prancing as she gave her consent.

"Thank you." Tanwen smiled before she saddled the horse and led her outside.

Despite being back beneath the expansive sky, the pumping wings of the Volari in her periphery, her pulse jumped with excitement as she mounted Rind.

Women were not extended many of the same activities as the men, but riding was blessedly one she could partake in.

The summer heat turned to an exhilarating wind as she urged Rind into a gallop, traveling down the harvest road. The breeze fingered through her hair and across her cheeks, and for a moment, she dared to close her eyes, wondering if this was what the Volari felt when they flew: free.

As she neared the beginning rows of squash, Tanwen pulled on Rind's reins, slowing the mare to a trot. Workers were busy, bent over the infinite strips of vegetation. Their only respite from the heat was the shade made by their large straw hats, their horns poking through holes at the top. None paid Tanwen mind as she passed. Distractions were never well met here.

As she neared the middle of the plot, Tanwen easily spotted her father and brother hunched together by a wagon. Two other Süra stood to the side. The crop master, no doubt, and a farmhand there to help.

Her gaze hooked on to her father's western horns protruding from his wide-brimmed hat. Beneath would be the headband that secured them in place, hidden beneath a fashionable wrapping that many Süra wore to push back their hair. Her father tied his so tight that he often suffered headaches. *A necessary pain for my freedom,* he had once remarked. *And a penance.*

Tanwen wasn't sure what he had meant by the latter, but she had noted the tender gaze from her mother as she handed him a tonic to ease his discomfort. It was a look that spoke of their past, but Tanwen and her brother knew better than to pry into that domain. Unless they wanted a father who brooded for days and a mother who handed out unnecessary chores.

At the sight of her father, a sense of relief loosened Tanwen's tense muscles. If he felt comfortable working in the fields under the watchful eyes of the Volari here, then he must feel safe. Confident in his and his family's disguises.

More reason not to tell him about the kidar, thought Tanwen. Her father had passed as Süra this long, unrecognized by those flying above; he would certainly continue to.

At the sound of her and Rind's approach, their group turned, regarding her. Well, all except her father, who remained thoroughly absorbed in tinkering with a hinge on the wagon's front axle.

"Wen." Her brother smiled up at her from beneath the brim of his hat. He helped to steady her mare as she dismounted. "I was praying to Udasha that she might lend a sliver of her fortune to bring you here."

"You really must be suffering dehydration to extend such a kind greeting, brother," said Tanwen sardonically.

"Let us find out, shall we?" Aberthol stretched out his hand. "Pass over that water sack, and we'll see if I remain glad of your presence once my thirst is quenched."

"No need for tests," said Tanwen as she gave him the pouch. "Dehydration or not, it's already been proven neither of us can tolerate the other for long. The Low Gods only know how we were able to live in such tight quarters all those months in Mother's womb."

"We did come early," he reasoned.

"Exactly my point." Tanwen huffed a laugh.

Aberthol shot her a wry grin before taking hardy sips.

While she and Aberthol were born with their mother's dark hair, her brother was the one who inherited their father's tight curls. The edges of which were currently plastered with sweat against his temples and neck.

"Oy." Tanwen poked his arm, causing a bit of water to slip from his lips and trickle down his cheek. "Save some for Father."

"You should have brought two," Aberthol grumbled, lowering the sack.

"We *did*. The other is back in the pavilion for when you all break for midday meal."

"Thol," called her father, drawing them both to look to where he now lay halfway under the wagon. "Get the pliers and the larger of our springs."

Aberthol did as he was ordered, Tanwen coming to stand beside her brother as they watched their father twist and knock loose a rusted spring housed between the axle and the wagon's floor. He grunted and groaned as he worked. Tanwen often wondered how annoyed he must feel being forced to use tools instead of his heat magic to shape metals like clay.

"Are these the wheel shocks you installed last season?" asked Tanwen, her mind hungry to remember every move and twist and fix her father orchestrated from the ground. Neither he nor Aberthol was a farmhand, but they were often hired to repair and better the equipment the Süra used for the harvest.

While her father never spoke about his time in Galia, she knew his occupation had been of the engineering sort. His mind was quick to invent, to create, to better the best.

Tanwen remained a riveted audience as she grasped her hands tightly behind her back, resisting her urge to reach down and assist her father.

That was Thol's role.

"Yes, these are them," answered her father, pushing out from under the wagon. As he took care to readjust his hat, he did nothing about the dirt covering his pants, shirt, and beard. "We'll need to grease them more often than I had calculated so they don't grow so brittle as quickly."

"I can experiment with creating different oils," suggested Tanwen. "Find a mixture that would last longer so greasing more often isn't necessary."

Her father met her gaze, a flash of curious delight that filled Tanwen with a rush of warmth.

See, Father, she wanted to say. *Like Thol, I also am worthy of your time.*

A painful howl turned Tanwen's attention to where a Volari descended from the sky like a hawk onto a mouse, clamping down on a worker two rows away.

A dust cloud awoke as Bastian, the head Volari of the harvest unit, pumped his massive gray wings to steady his hold on a squirming Süra. "Be still!" he demanded. "Running is never a match for our flight."

At his words, three more male Volari landed nearby.

The captive man grew slack, but his terror-stricken features remained. "Please," he begged of Bastian. "I have done nothing wrong!" His basket of squash lay tipped over and forgotten at his feet.

Tanwen did not recognize the man in Bastian's grip, but with how little she interacted with her clan, there were always unfamiliar faces.

"Are you sure this is him?" asked Bastian to an approaching Süra. "You will be punished in his stead if what you say is untrue."

"I *know* he is Mütra, sir," assured the accuser. He appeared about the same age as Tanwen, but there was a sick pallor to his complexion, with chipped horns and signs of malnourishment hinting that he might be nearing his final swim in the Eternal River. He reeked of desperation.

"The truth of their abomination is on their backs," he said, pointing to the captive man.

Tanwen's blood drained from her, Aberthol's hand now a vise grip on her arm.

"What?" cried the man. "No! He lies! He's a liar. I am a Süra of the Zomyad Forest!" He attempted to turn so he could speak directly to Bastian, but he was forced to his knees, his hands slapping against the dirt to catch his fall.

"If you are," said Bastian. "Then you will have no issue removing your shirt."

Tanwen's stomach clenched with dread as she forced herself not to glance to her father, to what he hid beneath his tunic.

"You cannot order such a thing," the man pleaded desperately. "Süra of the Zomyad are under the protection of—"

"Take off your shirt," ordered Bastian once more, this time each word a swinging hammer to steel. "If you do not, then one of us shall."

The wings of his nearby brethren shifted, as though they were awaiting his command.

The man at his feet began to tremble in clear terror, a sob escaping him.

Tanwen no longer held her breath as panic curled its fingers around her neck, squeezing, squeezing as she was helpless to do anything but watch.

I know they are Mütra. The hateful words sliced along her skin.

The memory of her previous night hurtled down on her from the heavens. When she had been forced into a similar prostrating position before the kidar.

Nausea gripped Tanwen.

Terror drowning.

How different last night could have turned out.

How all her future days could still transpire.

Despite how Tanwen loathed it, her mother's warnings were clearly justified.

A collection of gasps brought Tanwen back to the scene within the field.

The man on the ground had slipped off his shirt.

And there, in the clear blaze of day, was his guilt.

Two tiny wings, useless and flesh covered, twitched on either side of his shoulder blades. But it wasn't the crooked appendages that nearly made Tanwen buckle in anguish. It was the raw markings made by the band the man had used to confine them and the angry, vicious scars covering them like a tapestry. Knife wounds sliced across the base of his wings. Red and puckering. A history of the man's desperate attempts to rid himself of the sin of his existence.

Tanwen swallowed past the burning ache in her throat. How similar these scars were to her father's. But where this man's work had failed him, whoever had seen to her father's dismemberment had succeeded.

Bastian glared down at the Mütra, distaste a pinch to his dark features, before he turned to one of his nearby men, giving a nod.

The small blade hardly made a sound as it was drawn from his belt.

"No!" cried the Mütra, scurrying back, but he tripped over his own hands in his hysteria. "*No!*" he shouted louder, his desperation echoing across the field as he was grabbed by his executioner. "I am not bad," he cried. "I am not bad. I have no magic. I am worthless. I am worthless!"

"Then nothing shall be lost here this day," replied Bastian.

Death was but a flash. A reflection of sun against a blade as it was raised to slit a throat. Somewhere behind Tanwen, Rind whined her distress. Birds stirred into flight as the Mütra's body collapsed in the dirt.

Stillness.

Silence.

And then there was an exchange of money into hands. The accusing Süra's sharp smile as he gazed into the bag of gem passed on by one of the Volari. Not even ambrü worthy, the ending of a Mütra's life, and yet still enough to hunt them.

There was a shouting of orders for the crowd to get back to work, but Tanwen stood rooted, unflinching as the gale made by the children of the High Gods taking flight pressed into her.

The Mütra took up her vision as he was dragged away, the scraping of his bent wings along the dirt. A red trail of death followed him, a path that marked the last spot he had lived.

Later, he would be burned alone. Even if he had those who loved him, they would not come to stand by his flames. They could not.

To be Mütra was a plague.

To be Mütra was a mistake.

One to be corrected.

Eradicated.

Tanwen hadn't realized she was shivering until a hand to her shoulder caused her to flinch.

Her father had come to stand between her and her brother. Beneath his hat, his gaze was lowered, but she saw the tenseness in his jaw, the rough swallow in his throat.

She wondered if he was reliving a flash of his own tortured past, when his brethren had stripped him of his wings. If so, it was not a long haunting, for he eventually let out a sigh, squeezing her shoulder before nudging Aberthol's.

Back to work, the gesture said.

As their father turned, she momentarily met her brother's gaze. Aberthol's green eyes held a storybook of fear, of worry, but then—just like her father—he blinked, and it was gone and so was he, returning his attention to the wagon.

Tanwen was left alone, her only companion the mare who stepped forward to nuzzle her neck.

I am here, the horse's warm huff said. *But we should go. It isn't safe.*

No, agreed Tanwen. *It isn't safe.*

But neither was their forest when Süra were out hunting Mütra.

If their neighbors were ready to betray neighbors for a bag of gem, what wouldn't they do for an ambrü?

A curl of icy dread spilled into Tanwen's veins at the thought, a heavy sinking of understanding.

The ambush of the kidar last night and the killing of the Mütra today were more than a coincidence, more than a reminder of their vulnerability. They were a Low God forewarning.

Tanwen and her family's time in Zomyad was up.

And she would have to be the one to tell them.

5

Walking often felt foolish when one could fly, but Zolya supposed that was rather the point in being forced to traverse their current tight, dark tunnel. *Your wings are useless here,* the thick tangle of vines seemed to taunt as he and Osko followed a wall of Süra guards.

They were being led through a maze of sorts, a private corridor that fed from the forest's edge into the center of Ordyn, the capital city of Zomyad. Though Zolya could see no great buildings or dwellings or hear the bustle of citizens from within their covered passageway. There was only the scent of damp dirt and the surrounding thick woven branches and vines that made up the tunnel, lit every few paces by hanging jarred glow beetles.

Their visit was evidently meant to be kept a secret.

Understandably so.

It would not make for a calm clan, the witnessing of two kidars of the royal palace striding through town, let alone if he was recognized as the prince.

Still, Zolya wished there had been another way to meet with the nyddoth than walking endlessly through such a constraining space. His wings bumped and brushed and grazed his surroundings, an ever-growing irritant that forced him to tuck his plumage in tight despite his heightening desire to stretch it wide.

The claws of claustrophobia were threatening to pierce through Zolya's composure by the time they finally made it out of their covered lane to enter a large reception room.

It was empty save for four new guards who stood beneath blazing torches on either side of tall, ornately carved wooden doors. They were the last barrier to an audience with the western clan leader. And though their group was expected, it did not keep hands from grasping swords' hilts as they approached.

Distrust was thick in the Süra soldiers' gazes as they raked over Zolya, narrowed as they caught the taunting grin from Osko, and sharpened further on the tucked-in wings at both their backs. But after showing that no weapons graced his or Osko's person, despite their held sky magic, they were waved through.

The air was warm and perfumed within the domed hall, a pleasant wafting of cedar that lifted from blazing bowls. More displays of Süra artistry spiraled along the wide columns that drew them forward. Intricate depictions of the Low Gods and their myths, the most prominent that of Ré's betrayal of his sister, Maryth, when he severed her wings and banished her from the heavens to live on the soil of Cādra. Her tears of rage and mourning had become the Eternal River, where she collected souls to fill her lonely existence. Zolya had always despised that story, not understanding how the Volari could praise the father of the High Gods for such deception. Though it did illuminate the temperament of the two races, each dedicating their lives to a different pantheon of gods, both opposing.

With unease settling in his chest, Zolya tore his gaze from the carving toward the throne they approached.

At the back of the room rose a manicured canopy tree, its leaves feathering out to become one with the ceiling's decor. At its base sat Nyddoth Marwth; his wife, Nydda Clyfra; and three of his elder councilmen, who flanked his sides.

Upon their approach, the clan leader rose, along with his entourage of advisers.

Once they reached the base of the platform, their Süra guides dropped to their knees, heads bent in reverence before their leader.

Zolya and Osko remained standing.

"Your Royal Highness," said the steady voice of Nyddoth Marwth as he stepped forward, his dark complexion warmed by the nearby torchlight. He gave a slight bow, one that was not as low as customary before a Volari royal but respectful nonetheless. A reminder to Zolya that, yes, he might be a child of the High Gods and the prince of Cādra, but he currently stood in another's domain. "It has been many seasons since this forest has been honored by the presence of those of the Diusé bloodline," exclaimed the nyddoth. "In fact, if our history books are written true, the last your family visited here was during the signing of the peace agreement of our two races."

Words that meant more than what was spoken.

Remember what has been sworn by centuries of blood.

"Yes," replied Zolya. "It was a day that has benefited both Süra and Volari since."

We are not here to undo progress.

"Indeed," mused the clan leader, eyeing Osko at his side before returning his gaze to Zolya's. "I hope today can also be such a day. Please, let us sit so we may talk easier."

With a wave of the clan leader's hand, the guides in front of Zolya rose, then shuffled out of the way for new attendants to arrive. They settled plush benches behind Zolya and Osko, room for their wings to skim the floor as they sat.

"Now," began Nyddoth Marwth, sinking into his throne. "Let us hear what has brought His Royal Highness and his company of soldiers so far west."

Zolya held the clan leader's steady gaze. He was not a large man. In fact, Zolya found him to be quite small. Minuscule, even, with how his thick wrapped green tunic and decorative beading seemed to weigh on his thin frame. How heavy his tall curling horns appeared to sit atop his gaunt features. But while his outward appearance might lack gravitas, what spun within his eyes held his strength. Here was his cleverness, his power, his lived wisdom, and it was all hooked on to Zolya, waiting.

"We come seeking a man," Zolya began. "Said to be living within your forest. A Volari that is of great importance to King Réol. One who I am charged to return to Galia."

"A Volari, you say?" Nyddoth Marwth steepled his fingers, brows raised. "Living in our woods?"

"That seems highly unlikely," chimed in one of the eldoths, who sat like a slice of old bark to the nyddoth's right, a face full of grooves. "I do not wish to offend, sire, but all Volari stationed here live in their allotted territory outside the forest. If one had made home within our trees, it would not go without notice or debate amongst our people."

"This is not a Volari who is tending to the harvest," explained Zolya. "This is one who no longer has his wings. He will appear middle aged by your standards, dark curly hair, and I suspect has been passing as a Süra."

"Passing as a Süra?" questioned the eldoth, incredulous. "Our horns are not accessories or a disguise easily worn."

"He is very clever. He would have found a way."

"And what of his name?" asked Nydda Clyfra. While the clan leader was made up of night and shadow, his wife glowed like one of the twin moons. Her pale skin seeped effortlessly into her graying hair and white-painted horns. Yet despite her contrast with her husband, her gaze was just as direct.

"The man we seek is Gabreel Heiro," answered Zolya. "But I suspect he has not used that name for a long while."

"The king's inventor?" Nydda Clyfra's brows rose.

"You have heard of him?" inquired Zolya.

"Who has not heard of the man who fathered the Dryfs Mine? Remind me again, husband"—she turned toward Nyddoth

Marwth—"how many Süra die each year working within that labyrinth? Has it accumulated to the number of the Great Collapse yet?"

"You forget who is in your presence," warned Osko, a tense boulder at Zolya's side.

"On the contrary, Kidar," countered the nydda, her eyes narrowing on the two of them. "It is near impossible for us to forget when wings are present."

Zolya sensed Osko's desire to stand, but the shifting forward of the Süra guards who flanked them and his own hand to his friend's shoulder kept him seated. *Stand down,* Zolya's tight grip said. Osko sucked in the side of his cheek, his agitation palpable, but he settled back into his bench.

"You will allow your woman to address His Royal Highness in such a way?" Osko challenged Nyddoth Marwth, to which he received a laugh.

"She may be my wife," said the clan leader, mirth still a glimmer in his brown gaze. "But you must remember she is also the nydda to this clan. Is Queen Habelle so easy to command?"

Zolya was now the one to grow tense at the mention of his mother, though not as rigid as Nydda Clyfra. He noted how her folded hands curled tightly within her lap, her shoulders drawing back. Evidently, she did not enjoy mention of her demeanor needing taming. A trait she indeed shared with his mother.

"We have not come here to discuss the queen or the mines," Zolya explained, attempting to loosen the tension in the room while regaining control of the conversation. "We have come because information has been gathered that Gabreel lives within this forest. Enough to warrant us seeking an audience with you and your council."

Nyddoth Marwth studied Zolya for a beat. "And if this . . . information was to be true, what exactly is it you wish of me, Your Royal Highness? As I recall, your inventor was banished from Galia by the very king who desires him now returned. Süra forests are sanctuaries. If this man has been living here, it is not my place to force him out."

"Süra forests are sanctuaries to Süra," Zolya corrected as his pulse skipped with renewed assurance. *Gabreel is here. Gabreel is here. Gabreel is here.*

"Even so," said Nyddoth Marwth, "in accordance with our peace agreement, Volari are prohibited from hunting within our forest."

"It would not be a hunt if we were to know exactly where to find him," clarified Zolya. "King Réol is prepared to offer a handsome trade for any leniency shown by the western clan to aid us in returning his inventor."

One of the eldoths harrumphed. "It would not be considered lenient—"

"A trade?" interrupted the nyddoth, hand raised to silence his council. "That King Réol has allowed you to bless in his name?"

Zolya nodded. "A generous one if it leads us to directly obtaining the inventor."

"And this will be upheld with a contract?"

"If one is desired, of course," said Zolya, heartbeat racing with anticipation. "We will have it drawn and signed before any party leaves here tonight."

The silence that followed was a physical apparition. A stretching assessment of what little trust might lie between a Volari prince and a Süra clan leader. Meeting the scrutinizing gaze of Nyddoth Marwth, Zolya dared breathe as his heartbeat kicked into a sprint. He sent a silent prayer to Udasha, a plea for her fortune in this moment.

"I dismiss my council and my guards," announced the nyddoth.

Zolya barely held back his grin, a burst of gratitude soaring toward the High Goddess for answering his prayer.

"But, my nyddoth," began the same overopinionated eldoth, "I do not advise you to be alone, unprotected with—"

"You are quite right, eldoth Yffant," agreed Nyddoth Marwth, cutting him off. "My wife shall stay. As we've seen, she is quite equipped at diverting danger from myself."

As Nydda Clyfra remained seated, her expression pinched, there was a great show of disapproval from the elder council as they groaned and griped with their shuffling from the great hall. The guards were the last to leave. With the shutting of the door, the room now vibrated with promise.

What is spoken, none but us shall hear.

"You have known that Gabreel Heiro lives in your forest," stated Zolya. As the words left his lips, they were heavy and light all at once, a reweaving of his desperation with certainty.

He is here. He is here. The inventor is here.

"A clan leader always knows who enters his territory," answered the nyddoth. "Just as we know when others go sniffing around our brethren's."

"Our search for the inventor has never been a secret," explained Osko defensively.

"Then your search has been successful in that regard," replied the nyddoth.

"What do you want to grant us access to the inventor?" inquired Zolya. He no longer held patience for argumentative diversions. Gabreel was here, and his nerves danced with hunger to grasp him.

"Want?" repeated Nyddoth Marwth, his shrewd gaze unyielding. "Or need?"

Zolya remained silent. He would not be the first to show what he had to barter.

"There are needs my clan certainly has," the nyddoth continued. "But will they truly be met by King Réol?"

"Voice them to find out," offered Zolya.

The clan leader drummed his fingers on his armrest, pensive silence spreading thick within the domed hall. "The Volari's take from each season's harvest has always been disproportionate compared to the Süra's," he began. "A detail we were able to abide until recent years. My clan has grown since our last harvest contract. What was sustainable three decades ago to feed families is no longer."

Zolya almost laughed. How neatly this was all going according to plan. "You wish for a larger percentage of what the western harvest yields." He quickly got to the point.

"Fifteen percent more," clarified the nyddoth.

Osko scoffed beside him.

"Ten," countered Zolya.

"*Sire*," hissed Osko, snapping his attention to Zolya. "Are you sure King Réol—"

"Ten," repeated Zolya, his gaze never wavering from the clan leader's. He and Osko had agreed for him to play the part of a startled and offended companion, causing their offer to shine with advantage. Zolya had to admit, his friend had missed his calling for the stage.

Nyddoth Marwth appeared to chew on the number. "I will agree to ten if we can also agree to a pause in the hunting of Mütra."

"By the High Gods." Osko nearly snorted his incredulity, his acting breaking into true emotion. "If we are living in dreams, then forget contracts. Let us leave here now, my prince, and tear through this forest ourselves to find Gabreel."

"Such words threaten war, Kidar," said Nydda Clyfra, her tone the steel unsheathing of a blade.

"A war that Süra would lose," countered Osko. "As your kind have lost before. Or do we need to call an orator to recount the decade-long drought the last Süra uprising brought to Cādra?"

The nydda's gaze caught fire, untampered animosity flashing in her blue depths.

Zolya fought back a frustrated sigh. "There will be *no* war," he appeased. "My companion merely speaks of our surprise with such a request regarding Mütra. What causes this?" he pressed the nyddoth.

"A Mütra was killed today in our harvest fields," he explained.

"Not a rare occurrence, surely?"

"No, but one that always creates a greater disturbance in my clan than if a Mütra remained living within it. The bounty hunters are growing in number, their tactics more brutal and conniving. There are

Mütra sympathizers who have begun to retaliate. By killing one Mütra today, five of my clan are now dead."

"We cannot be held responsible for Süra who hunt Mütra," reasoned Zolya. "Or for how those react to the ones who do."

"No, but it was not Süra who put a bounty on Mütra's heads."

"They are abominations," spit Osko. "Creations neither High nor Low God intended to exist."

"Perhaps," mused the nyddoth. "And yet *both* our kind are responsible for making them."

"Careful, Nyddoth," warned Osko. "It sounds as though you might be counted amongst the Mütra sympathizers you speak of."

"The only ones I sympathize with are my clan people," he corrected. "I merely point out facts."

"It is impossible to eradicate this law," explained Zolya, wanting to return the conversation back to the original request. His father had deemed Mütra treasonous to the crown, and there was very little one could do to reverse the king's decisions once made.

"I do not ask for its removal, Your Royal Highness," said Nyddoth Marwth. "Merely a lifting of their bounty and hunting within Zomyad for a time. It does not need apply to the rest of Cādra, but to my forest alone. As I said, this latest killing was done in front of our harvest workers. We need them compliant, not defiant and on edge. I would like tensions to ease so nothing escalates further to disrupt production. May I remind you, it is not only our clan's food at stake, but all of Cādra's."

"You are their nyddoth," Zolya reminded him. "Do not allow it to escalate within your clan."

"What do you think I'm attempting to do here tonight?"

Zolya eyed the clan leader. "You ask much."

"Perhaps," countered Nyddoth Marwth. "But how much do you need your inventor?"

Zolya narrowed his gaze, a swirl of frustration filling his gut.

He needed Gabreel desperately, and he hated that the nyddoth understood this.

Zolya could not return to Galia, to his father, empty handed.

"One year," offered Zolya. "That is the most I can offer without our king present. But this will reduce your ten percent to five percent more harvest yield."

Nyddoth Marwth rubbed his lips together in thought. "I will settle for six months to regain ten percent."

Zolya let the counter settle within the room, ignoring the waves of tension coming from Osko. He knew his friend was annoyed that they had to barter for what they wanted. But here, in this forest, different rules applied. No longer were they in their skies, free to do as they wished.

"Do we have an agreement?" the nyddoth pressed.

Zolya took a deep breath in. "We do," he said.

Despite his answer, the nyddoth did not smile. He merely appeared more weighted, as though the burden of sacrifices to keep sanctuaries was growing tiresome. "Very good." He nodded. "Let us discuss how you are to collect your inventor."

6

Tanwen would tell her family everything.

She would.

But not tonight.

Tomorrow.

After breakfast.

Tomorrow after breakfast, Tanwen would tell her family about the kidar and the ambrü.

Until then she would do her best to enjoy her last precious moments in this forest, in this home, in the only place she had friends—despite them being animals.

She would have to tell them too.

She would have to do a lot soon.

Like pack.

Tanwen's stomach turned over as her thoughts slid to her room, to what items she might be able to take with her, to which were worthy of their weight on her back.

Do not cry, she silently chastised herself as an aching sorrow tightened around her throat. *Do not cry.*

"*Tanwen.*" Her mother's curt voice snapped her back to where she stood at her side within their dark workroom. Though it was night, their windows still had been covered, the only light made by a cluster of candles and the jadüri partially dissected on the table in front of them. "Your mouse is about to eat a very precious petal," pointed out her mother.

"*Eli.*" Tanwen shooed her friend from the glowing bud. He scampered down the table to hide behind a bottle. "You won't be allowed in here if you act like that."

"He shouldn't be allowed in here at all," huffed her mother. "Rodents aren't the most hygienic for a meddyg's workroom."

"He assured me he cleaned himself thoroughly," said Tanwen. "He won't be a problem again. Right?" She glared pointedly at Eli, who squeaked his compliance.

"Wonderful," said her mother. "Now, if you don't remove the anthers soon, the gods' nectar will grow less potent."

Tanwen blinked back to her task. "Yes, sorry, Mother."

They were making docüra; a coveted hallucinogen whose key ingredient was the very flower Tanwen had regrettably dashed from the forest to acquire.

"Those tweezers are too big." Her mother plucked the instrument from Tanwen's hand. "You know we use the thinner forceps for this."

"Yes, of course," said Tanwen, her cheeks growing flushed with her chagrin.

She sensed Aisling's scrutinization as she bent to gather the small glowing buds within the jadüri bloom. The warmth of their illumination touched Tanwen's cheeks, the subtle fragrance of vanilla and honey lifting as she carefully scraped the thick pollen off and into an awaiting bowl of tonic. As soon as the pollen hit the liquid, the room erupted with blue light. Tanwen squinted against the brightness, waiting as the nectar of the gods fully dissipated within the mixture. The liquid changed from clear to what appeared like a pulsing night sky, the shimmering stars pinpricks of magic.

Despite Tanwen's mournful mood, making docüra always gave her a rush, a sense of strength to be one of the few who knew the art. For docüra was sought by both Süra and Volari, though used very differently. Süra applied it ceremoniously, in trauma healing or to converse with the Low Gods. The Volari preferred it recreationally.

A single drop to a shallow cut was enough to send the user into a prolonged haze. And the price of such a drop was more than a handful of gem. Normally a worthwhile reward for the risk of obtaining the jadüri bloom. Though now, Tanwen would have gladly paid that amount tenfold to erase the last two days. To not have to do what she would in the morning.

Her chest was gripped with that ever-present mixture of anxiety and dread.

"Good," said her mother as she reached for the bowl. "And now for a dash of the Coslett secret spice." She added in the last ingredient.

"Will you ever tell me what that is?" asked Tanwen, watching as her mother stirred in a fine brown powder before recapping the bottle and setting it aside.

"Eventually," said Aisling. "When it's necessary."

"Why even teach me how to make docüra if you won't teach me all of it?"

"Because you can make docüra without the Coslett secret spice."

"Yes, I am aware, but it's evidently not as good."

"Of course it's still good," corrected her mother. "But this makes it more potent."

"Perhaps I will make up my own secret spice, then," challenged Tanwen. "To rival yours."

Her mother smiled as she stirred the mixture. "I certainly welcome you to try. Experimenting is what sets apart a good meddyg from the best, but remember, with any of your experiments—"

"You must be the willing first subject to test them." Tanwen finished her mother's usual rhetoric. "Yes, I know."

Her mother shot her a wry glance. "And why do I always say this?"

"Because empathy is the key ingredient to all healing."

Aisling nodded, pleased, before refocusing her attention on the docüra.

"So you've really tried all your altered docüra mixtures before discovering the secret ingredient?" wondered Tanwen.

"Your father helped on occasion."

Tanwen thought on this answer. "Does that mean Thol can help me with my experiments?" she asked.

"If he agrees, I don't see why not," said her mother as she wiped clean her spoon before setting it aside.

Tanwen couldn't help but smile at the thought of putting her brother through all sorts of tests under the guise of perfecting her craft. *I'd paint his face with dung first,* she thought, *and tell him it was an ointment to help bring in his facial hair faster.*

"I see the mischief of Ridi spinning through your mind, girl." Her mother tut-tutted. "What torture are you concocting for your loving brother this time?"

"Loving?" Tanwen raised her brows. "Loving does not rub poison moss all over my mattress."

"If I recall correctly," countered her mother, "you had put pepper ants in his first."

"Only because he had cut off a chunk of my hair while I slept so he could have a tail for his silly toy horse."

Her mother huffed a laugh, shaking her head. "And here your father and I thought we had to protect you both from the outside world, not from each other within our own home."

Home.

The word snagged sharp.

Home.

Despite Tanwen's desperation to enjoy one last night pretending all was good and happy and safe, the inevitable danger that hovered over her shoulder suddenly pressed down, unyielding.

Tell her, the small voice of Eli urged within Tanwen's mind. She glanced to her friend regarding her on hind legs. *Tell your mother,* he prompted again. *She needs to know.*

Tanwen's resolve wavered. She didn't disagree, but . . . *I need tonight,* she silently rebuked, quietly begged. *I need one final night of peace. Something to keep my heart beating when all in Cādra want it still.*

The sudden heavy stomping of feet a floor below turned Tanwen's attention to their workroom's door.

"Your father and brother must have finished early in their workshop," said her mother. "We need to set out dinner. Come, Tanwen," she instructed as she began to clean up. "We'll let the docüra settle overnight before preparing to sell it in Ordyn."

Another weighted pull of guilt to Tanwen's shoulders at the mention of their capital city. They would not be making it to Ordyn.

But we can sell the docüra on the road, she silently reasoned. *Between that and my ambrü, we'll have plenty to ensure our survival away from Zomyad.*

It was a small but welcome reprieve to Tanwen's burden. A similar press of comfort as when Eli jumped from the table to scamper up her sleeve before situating himself on her shoulder.

I'm here, he said. *I will go wherever you go.*

Tanwen held back the threat of tears.

Thank you, she thought, running a gentle finger over Eli's soft fur before she followed her mother downstairs, hoping her smile didn't appear as forced as it felt.

◆ ◆ ◆

Supper was uneventful.

Almost boring.

Tanwen couldn't stand it.

Not with her secret rattling inside her chest.

Despite barely touching her food, she quickly excused herself, fearful that if she sat for another moment, her confession would burst free.

Thankfully, her family hardly paid her leave mind. Thol was too content to finish her meal, while her mother sat on her father's lap, the pair consumed with one another, ogling and sharing sappy grins.

It would have disgusted Tanwen if she was not already used to their displayed affection.

With Eli on her shoulder, Tanwen had stepped from their den, never more thankful for the cool night air racing into her lungs.

The woods were a pulsing glow over their balcony. After the sun set, the forest awoke with new light. A diverse tangle of blue- and green-bioluminescent organisms. Glow beetles, moon moss, starlight spiders, and a thousand other plants and animals lit the thick weave of ancient trunks and leaves.

Tanwen never could decide which she enjoyed more: the richness of the forest during the day or the effervescent illumination of it at night. She remembered only her awe when they had first arrived.

If ever proof was needed of the Low Gods' existence, one merely needed to visit the Zomyad Forest. Their magic vibrated within the soil. Bosyg's beauty.

Tanwen wanted to bottle this moment, this view. Trap it beneath glass so she may take some of this home to wherever they ended up next.

Her melancholy stirred, but she quickly turned from it as she ignored the long winding stairs that led to the forest floor and instead set loose the rope ladder near their door, a faster exit to the ground, then climbed her way down.

The air grew damper the farther she descended, the sweet fragrance of plumeria richer as her booted feet hit soil. Tanwen set off on a path that wove from their tree den to where her father and brother's workshop lay hidden.

Eli sat quietly on her shoulder, nibbling on a piece of bread. As Tanwen twisted along the lane, glow beetles gathered to better light her way, dancing and twirling at her side, a happy greeting. An owl screeched overhead, causing Eli to momentarily hide within Tanwen's collar.

Hello, Willia, thought Tanwen before the owl rushed forward and into the dark.

Her usual companions were coming to see her toward her destination.

Despite her somber mood, she smiled, welcoming the company.

It didn't take long for Tanwen to reach the workshop, which was tucked beside a small waterfall. The rushing waters fed into a small river that snaked through an open glen before dropping into the western cliffs. The fast current was a key component in powering many of her father's tools, which was why he had risked situating his workshop so close to the forest's clearing.

Still, he left nothing to chance.

If one didn't know where to look for the door, it was easily missed.

Tanwen stood before a massive boulder covered in moss and hanging vines. But there, disguised as a crooked piece of wood, was a door handle and a simple metal keyhole.

Tanwen located the spare key tucked beneath a nearby rock. After making fast work of the lock, she slipped inside.

The workshop smelled of papers and ink, wood shavings, and the tang of greased metals. It was also utterly consumed in black. No bioluminescence reached the bowels of this windowless domain, but soon the darkness was overtaken by light as Tanwen lit a nearby lamp.

As she carried the lantern, the room awoke, with long stretches of tables covered in schematics and numerous miniature models of innovations. An automated water lift, a zip line for transporting heavy supplies long distances, a resetting sundial. Tanwen skimmed over the inventions that her father had shared with the western clan over the years. These she had seen before. Many times. Tonight, she was on the hunt for new.

While she might not be allowed within the workshop when her father and brother were here, she still knew its floor plan as if she were an apprentice herself. Tanwen had made a habit of entering at night, alone, to take in what women were thought too feebleminded to understand. Though her father might not publicly contradict such beliefs, his behavior certainly did behind closed doors. Within their den, Tanwen had been taught the art of arithmetic and physics alongside her brother. *If you are learning to read,* he had said, *you might as well learn how to read everything.* It had made much of her childhood filled exclusively with lessons, fitting in teachings from both parents, but it was a blessed distraction from the daily danger that loomed.

As Tanwen walked the room, she drank in the sharp scribblings from her father and brother. New ideas and calculations.

She stopped at a particularly interesting project regarding the funneling of water from their well up to their tree den. She studied the rough sketch done by her father's hand, trying to make sense of the pressure system. Though none in her family spoke of it, there was an understanding regarding Tanwen's occasional evening trips. Over the years papers had gone from being stacked and filed each night to left out, spread out. An invitation.

Come look, and see what you might understand.

No doubt an experiment of sorts for her father.

But Tanwen did not mind.

She would take any scrap given to learn all she could about the power of invention, for it stirred an elated frenzy in her veins.

Being an inventor was not so unlike being a meddyg.

Both practices used trial and error, both sought to fix, better, innovate.

Which was why Tanwen found it confusing that women couldn't learn the trade, a thought her mother didn't disagree with but advised her to remain quiet about.

Aisling believed a woman's power held more value by remaining unassuming. *A heavy blow might make a dent,* her mother had once shared, *but think of the noise. A well-sharpened blade is much quieter and can easily cut straight through. You must remember, my wyrthia, more can be accomplished when no one is looking.*

Tanwen let out a tired sigh. Her mood for learning had faded. In its stead rose her inevitable fate that would come with dawn's approach.

After taking one last glance around the workshop, Tanwen doused her lantern and slipped out.

Her family's tree den lay quiet when she returned, sleep filling the dark halls as she softly padded toward her room. The weak glow of candlelight creeping from beneath her bedroom door alerted her to Aberthol, still awake. As she pushed in, he glanced up from where he sat in bed, book in hand.

"Learn anything of interest on your nightly stroll?" he asked, a knowing grin present.

"Nothing of exceptional interest, no," she countered, coming to sit on the edge of his bed.

Aberthol shifted his legs to give her more room as she helped Eli down from her shoulder. The mouse scurried across the floor and into the small home she had built him out of slats of wood and straw.

She made a mental note to figure out how to fit his bed into her pack tomorrow.

The true weariness of her tasks ahead collapsed around her. She stared out the window, which sat across the room. The croaking and buzzing of night spilled in through the open shutters, filling the silence.

"Are you thinking about the Mütra?" asked Aberthol.

Tanwen turned to her brother. He wore a pinch between his dark brows, the low-burning candle on his bedside painting half his face and horns in warm light, the other in shadow.

"I'm thinking about a lot," she admitted.

"Me too," he said, putting down his book.

He moved to sit beside her, both their feet now pressing into their floor. His bare, hers booted.

Tanwen never knew if it was because they were siblings or twins, but she and Aberthol always seemed to understand when the other had something heavy on their mind. Something they would not press to learn unless the other wished to share.

Tanwen wished to share what was on her mind very much. The words had been fighting their way up her throat for the better part of today. And now it was time. Telling her brother first felt a bit less intimidating than telling her parents. That way they could go to them together. It was always easier when they were together. But how to start? Where to begin?

With the weight of her admission causing her chest to grow tight, the sick dread of knowing she could not come back after speaking what she would next, Tanwen stood and went to her side of the room.

She pushed aside her bed and bent to remove a slat from the floorboards.

"I *knew* you had a hiding spot," said Aberthol, his triumph clear in his voice as she returned holding a small pouch.

"Yes, well, it won't be my hiding spot any longer."

Her brother frowned before his features changed to shock as she revealed the ambrü.

The red glow was a glint in his green eyes as she held it up between them.

"Thol," she began. "There's something I need to tell you."

7

Tanwen had assumed they'd be leaving, but she hadn't expected them to be forced to pack so quickly.

"Fill as many water sacks as you can carry," ordered her father from where he was digging through the back of a cupboard. "We can find food easier than clean water." He pulled free two small go bags and dropped them on the kitchen table. "Thol, go through these, and add anything else of value. I know we have better knives."

Tanwen stood motionless, numb, as she watched her brother do as he was told, listened to the fast footsteps of her mother two floors above in their workroom. Aisling had run up there as soon as it was decided they'd be leaving that morning, hurrying to gather as many important meddyg supplies as she could fit within their sacks.

It seemed only a moment ago that Aberthol had insisted they wake their parents to tell them everything Tanwen had confided to him within their room. And yet the sun had somehow risen; a new day's light was creeping into their kitchen's windows.

Tanwen's confession about the kidar searching for their father along with the bounty of ambrü had been met with thick silence before her parents had overwhelmed her with questions.

What did he ask you?

What answers did you give?
Did he say what he wanted?
You need to remember your exact *words spoken!*

There was a thankful breath after Tanwen's answers, but then she mentioned that the kidar was of the royal palace, repeated his physical description: White hair, matching wings, golden brown skin, blue eyes. Big, very big. He had made it rain.

And that's when everything had burst into chaos.

They were to leave immediately.

Tanwen and her brother had plenty more questions, but her parents had cut them off. There would be time for explanations later; for now they needed to get somewhere far—and fast.

"Tanwen," called her father, bringing her back to their kitchen, to the swirl of movement. "Go help your mother," he instructed. "Thol and I will finish here and gather what we can from the workshop." When she didn't move, he snapped, "Tanwen, now!"

She jumped, a rush of shame rising to her cheeks.

He was mad.

At her.

She dashed from the kitchen, climbing the steps two at a time as her guilt burned hot in her chest.

This was her fault.

This was all her fault.

She never should have gone foraging for the jadüri.

Why did she always have to test the rules, push the boundaries of what her parents said was safe?

This was the repercussions of such defiance.

Tanwen's tears were warm on her cheeks as she entered their workroom. Her mother was busy sorting through their different ointments in the far corner.

"I need you to bottle the docüra," said her mother over her shoulder. "And pack it within one of those sturdier pouches you've made."

Tanwen did as she was asked, fighting the urge to sob as her vision blurred. More tears overflowing. The starlit bowl of docüra shook in her grasp.

Be stronger! she silently chastised herself, attempting to force away her anguish. *You knew this was to come.*

But knowing never eased pains.

"Wen." Her mother's soft voice had her looking up. Worry creased Aisling's brow as she no doubt noted her daughter crying.

In quick strides Tanwen was within her mother's embrace. Nothing could stop her sobs now.

"My wyrthia," hushed her mother, rubbing her back. "I know this is a lot, but we have done this before. We will be fine."

"I'm so sorry," said Tanwen, burying her face in her mother's shoulder. Her familiar scent of gardenia was a slight poultice to Tanwen's aches.

"For what?" asked her mother. "Tanwen." She gripped her shoulders, pushing her back so she could look at her. "None of this is your fault. You do understand that? Don't you?"

"But if I had not gone foraging—"

"No." Her mother cut her off with a shake of her head. "This kidar had obviously been searching for your father long before he stumbled upon you," she reasoned. "You did well. You didn't tell him anything. He does not know who you are. *What* you are. It was fortuitous that you were in his path."

"It was?"

"Yes, otherwise we would never have known the danger we currently are in."

"But we have always been in danger."

"Well, yes," agreed her mother, managing a small smile. "But this is of a different kind."

"Who is this kidar?" asked Tanwen. "Why is he looking for Father now?"

Her mother appeared ready to answer until their attention was drawn to the rustling and hurried pecking against one of their windows.

"Willia?" Tanwen frowned, walking to open the pane, allowing the owl inside. "I never see you during the day."

Danger. Volari. Your father and brother. Volari are in our forest!

Willia hooted and pumped her wings with her panic, causing various dried flowers and lists of ingredients to fly about the room.

"Can you calm her down?" asked her mother, shielding herself.

But Tanwen was seized in a grip of paralysis as she took in Willia's message. "No," she whispered and then repeated louder: "No!"

Hurry, urged Willia. *Waterfall,* she hooted before hopping back to the window's ledge and flying out.

"What's going on?" asked her mother, brows drawn in with confusion. "Tanwen, what did she say?"

"Volari," Tanwen managed to sputter as she ran from the room.

Her mother was quick on her heels. "What about them? Tanwen!" She snagged her arm, forcing her to a stop on the stairs.

"She said there are Volari in our forest," Tanwen rushed out. "She mentioned Father and Thol. They had gone to the workshop. We must help them!"

They were wind as they blew from their home, down the rope ladder to run toward the glen.

Even in her panic Tanwen noted how the forest lay quiet, animals hiding from prey.

Tanwen's pace quickened with her consuming fear, her lungs burning as they reached the final slope that would bring them to the waterfall's clearing.

She was ready to dash over, but her mother nearly knocked her to the ground, stopping her.

"Hush." She covered Tanwen's mouth as she forced them to crouch, voices reaching them. "We must see what's happening first," she whispered, breath labored from their sprint.

With heartbeat in her throat, Tanwen edged forward with her mother, peeking through the wide-leafed bush they hid behind.

The sight beyond froze Tanwen's heart.

Her father and brother stood on the final path that led to their workshop, bridging the shadow of the forest's edge and the sunlight of the open glen, surrounded by Volari guards. The door to their hidden workroom was flung open. Exposed. Discovered. Winged soldiers stomped in and out, adding to a pile of scrolls and miniature models nearby. Burn marks led from the door along the dry grass, smoke lifting from a recent fire being snuffed out. A quick fight had taken place. One her father had lost. His band of horns had been removed from his head, now a useless heap by his feet. Blood trickled from his nose, and Aberthol was held by a soldier, a knife at his throat, his eyes wide with panic.

A wave of nausea crested over Tanwen as she took in the tallest of the group, the one whom the rest seemed to bend toward. His white wings were blinding from where he stood beneath the sun, his plumage soaking in the daylight. His matching hair was a stark contrast to his brown skin. His gray high-collared coat strained over his broad shoulders.

"That's the kidar," Tanwen hissed. "The one who questioned me."

"That's Zolya Diusé," replied her mother.

Tanwen whipped her gaze to Aisling, an ocean of shock crashing through her. "The crown prince?"

Her mother nodded, attention not wavering from the scene taking place mere paces away.

Holy gods, thought Tanwen, her mind tipping in every direction.

She had stood before the crown prince.

The one soul in Cādra who would slit her throat without hesitation if he knew she was Mütra.

The son of the king who had banished her father from Galia and ordered his wings to be ripped from his back, all for falling in love with a Süra.

The crown prince of the children of the High Gods was *here*, trapping her father and brother with his small army.

But why?

"What should we do?" Tanwen asked, her heartbeats yelling at her to rush forward. Her instincts were weighted shackles to her ankles, keeping her still.

"We wait," said Aisling.

Tanwen hated that answer, but she noted how her mother must have as well, for her fingers were digging into the dirt by her knees, her back a tense coil.

"There is no use fighting, Gabreel." Prince Zolya's deep voice reached them, his sharp features made harsher by his look of indifference. "The king wishes you returned to Galia, and what the king desires will always come to pass."

"But what value do I have to King Réol?" asked her father. "The last words he spoke to me carried the name of traitor. His last orders were the tearing of my wings so I may become like the Süra I loved so much."

"Whatever lies in the past, your mind will always be of value," said the prince. "King Réol requests another mine."

Tanwen could not see whatever expression her father might have made to such a comment, his back toward them, but she sensed the air mount with new tension, heard the quick, shocked gasp from her mother.

"Then I would suggest," began her father coolly, "that His Eminence implores the services of André Bardrex. For isn't that who replaced my services to the crown?"

"Bardrex unfortunately proved . . . unfit for the position," explained the prince. "You are who King Réol has requested be reinstated as his royal engineer."

"I respectfully decline," said her father.

There was an impatient sigh from Prince Zolya. "You know well enough, Gabreel, requests from His Majesty are orders."

There were fast heartbeats of quiet. The harrowing silence of a soul cornered.

"I will *never* create another of those catacombs," seethed her father, his tone the slamming of a door. "I would send myself to Maryth's Eternal River before I repeated such a mistake."

The prince cocked his head, studying her father. "And what of your son's life?" He nodded to where Aberthol was held captive by a brown-winged kidar. "Would you send him there with you?"

"That is my apprentice," her father quickly explained.

The kidar holding Aberthol huffed his disbelief. "Do not lie to us, Heiro. Even with your beard and his horns, it is easy to see he is your kin. You and your Süra lover sure do know how to make trouble."

There was a pause before her father replied, "*Did* know."

The kidar's gaze narrowed. "She left you?"

"She was taken by Maryth with my son's birth."

"Penance for her sins bearing this abomination." He spit on the ground. "*Mütra.*"

"Enough, Osko," ordered Prince Zolya as his eyes scanned the forest's edge, suspicion clear in his furrowed brow.

Tanwen and her mother lay flat, panicked breaths stirring the dirt.

Please, do not let the Volari enter the forest. Tanwen sent a desperate plea to Bosyg. *Please keep us safe beneath your branches. Please, please, please.*

The goddess of the forest must have listened, for the prince's attention returned to her father. "While this is the king's orders, you still have a choice, Gabreel," he explained. "Stay and see your son's throat cut before your own, or come with us and see him live."

"How do I know you will not kill him as soon as I am gone?"

"Because if you come, so will he," explained the prince. "And so long as you stay alive, so shall your son."

Despite his promise, Tanwen's mind screamed *Trap, trap, trap* from where she remained tucked behind the bushes. At some point, she and her mother had gripped each other's hands, a small tether to the anguish ripping apart Tanwen's heart.

I need to do something!

I need to act!
I need to save them!

She felt the presence of her animals at her back, sensed their own heartache. But they remained at a distance, this scene a too-familiar part of their world. There were those who hunted and those who were hunted. Tanwen's family was the latter.

She wanted to scream! Or cry. Or both.

Her father shifted his head just so, as if he wished to turn and steal one last glance at whoever might be watching from within the woods. To find her and her mother. But then his attention turned to his pilfered workshop before Aberthol, who was held pinned by his throat. Her father's shoulders lifted and fell with a heavy breath. "I will come."

No! Tanwen made to rush forward, but her mother held her down. "It will not help." Her mother's hiss was hot and harsh in her ear as she kept them pressed to the ground, a quiet tremble in her voice, a breaking of a soul. "It will not help, my wyrthia."

Her father and brother were shoved together as they were swallowed within a net and lifted into the air. Her father's inventions and research were gathered into another.

Tanwen and her mother remained motionless, in shock, as the children of the High Gods grew to mere silhouettes within the blue sky before disappearing entirely.

Gone.

Empty.

Vanished.

Tanwen barely registered her mother crying, her shaking body lying beside her in the dirt.

She was too deeply consumed in her own grief, in her own remorse of inaction.

Her family had been ripped apart, and all Tanwen had done was hide.

PART II

PASSAGE

8

Gabreel Heiro had planned never to see Galia again.

A banishment he had not once mourned.

It had taken months for the wounds of his dismemberment to heal, weeks to learn to walk properly without his wings, and years for the phantom sensation of their weight on his back and his desire to stretch them to leave.

No, Gabreel Heiro did not yearn for his place of birth.

He despised it.

As the celestial islands that lived high within the clouds came into view, a sun-glistening white expanse of ornate architecture sprawling between greenery and the great pumping of hundreds of winged citizens, he forced his eyes closed.

He had failed.

Failed in his promise to Aisling that they would have a different life, a better life, so long as they were far from here together.

Now, Gabreel was back in the clutches of a vicious king, and this time so was his son.

He gripped the finely woven net he was trapped in, the icy wind funneling through doing little to cool the fury thrumming within his veins. *Burn,* his anger whispered to his magic, gathered beneath his skin. Every part of him wished to incinerate the threads of his cage so he could fall to the rough sea below.

But even if the taking of his own life hadn't meant the taking of Aberthol's, Gabreel could not cut away the net he was tangled in.

The material was infused with a mixture of blood from every type of sky magic, making it impenetrable. A science he had created.

Perfected.

For his king.

"Father," a voice called through the wind.

He opened his eyes to see Aberthol being carried by another group of kidets.

Gabreel put a finger to his lips. *Hush,* he instructed his son. *Strength.* He placed a hand to his heart before making a fist. *Courage.*

Aberthol mimicked the gesture, though his furrowed brows remained marked with worry. He looked so much like a boy in that moment, a child pretending bravery to please his father.

Gabreel swallowed past the anguish that threatened to choke him, refocusing on the approaching kingdom in the sky.

It had taken two sleepless nights and endless flying to reach Galia, which floated above the center of Cādra. The rough journey was made rougher by the promise of hurt Gabreel saw simmering within the soldiers' eyes whenever they looked upon Aberthol. And despite Prince Zolya's strict orders for none of his men to touch the inventor or the Mütra, Gabreel had dared not sleep, curled beside his son—his watchdog. Though he knew it wouldn't stop the pain his son would inevitably endure.

Galia was pain. A place where suffering was used to erect beauty, carve perfection.

And Mütra were the worst sort of flaw.

Gabreel dared to imagine what horror awaited them.

He also regretted his decision to come. It would have been a mercy to have had his whole family's throats cut beneath the shadows of the

Zomyad Forest. At least then they would have known peace, have found their final resting ground in the Eternal River together.

Instead, Gabreel had been weak.

And once again he was paying the price.

He merely hoped Aisling and Wen remained safe. If they were smart, they'd be a long way from Zomyad by now, searching for a new home where they could live out their days.

Grief, sharp and unforgiving, clawed at his chest once more. After the Great Collapse, Gabreel hadn't thought he deserved a second chance at life. He now realized this was to be his payment for such a gift. Zenca, the High Goddess of destiny, had finally come to collect, and her price was to be all that Gabreel loved.

As their group banked left, pushing Gabreel into the net, they rapidly descended toward the palace. The gargantuan pillared expanse, tiered with domed citadels, was situated at the highest point of Galia. Its white was so pristine it rivaled the clouds, a bleaching that concealed the bloodstains of the workmen who built it.

Long landing platforms, lined in plush manicured grass, greeted them as they touched down. Barely was Gabreel deposited when the familiar wash of jasmine and honeysuckle invaded his senses. The melody of macaws and cockatoos. Crisp air and the light press of heat. His body was seized in an all-consuming panic.

Back.

He was back.

The full weighted reality of this—where he was being dragged to, his feet and hands covered and then shackled, before being corralled forward with his son—nearly buckled his knees.

But the audience that gathered to watch their procession kept him standing, kept his chin lifted along with his strength.

He would never cower before this court.

Word had evidently spread quickly of the prince's return, along with whom he had in his company. Sun and Isle Court members filled the towering bright hall they traveled, the scene a collection of billowing peplos and immaculately woven chitons, delicate epaulets all garnished with elegant gold detailing and ornamentation. Pointed ears covered in jewels.

It was a wash of riches, fashion that dripped listlessness, flaunted idle occupations.

Despite himself, Gabreel's interest snagged, finding Galia's extravagance had now extended to wings. Intricate mosaics of color were dyed into feathers, visions of beauty when spread wide. Peacocks, all of them.

A low gasp brought Gabreel's attention to his son shuffling forward at his side.

Aberthol was trapped in utter wonderment as he took in the surrounding splendor.

Even with the danger that loomed, his son remained spellbound, curious, delighted.

It was a thousand daggers to Gabreel's heart, witnessing such innocence in his child. How soon would that light be snuffed out by the cruelty this utopia hid?

Gabreel fought back tears as he squeezed his trembling hands in anger. He forced his gaze to the white polished stone beneath his feet.

He could no longer stomach the view.

As their procession continued, he sensed the rustling wave of bows to the prince ahead, heard the growing whispers before shouts of "Traitor!" that were aimed his way as he passed. Each echoed with heightened viciousness against the surrounding columns.

Gabreel clenched his teeth, his ire for the crowd of hypocrites rising. *Traitor, indeed,* he thought with a sneer. The very traitor who had helped create many of their comforts of the past century, enabled everyone in this palace, on this island, to grow richer. A traitor who had been hunted down and then returned because of the value their ruler believed he still held in his mind.

Gabreel had feared this day might come.

It was why he had taken such precautions to hide, not only because of his wife and children.

It had not been an act of benevolence that King Réol had spared his life after his transgressions.

No, it had been insurance.

The king wished for another mine, and evidently only Gabreel could provide him with one.

Though he didn't yet know how, Gabreel would repeat no such act.

With a slow, steadying breath, he worked to erect his internal armor, prepared himself for what would come next as best he could, the only way he knew how.

Gabreel became the man he had been when still he had his wings, the man who had once been like the watching crowd.

Heartless.

◆ ◆ ◆

"Do not look him in the eyes or utter a single word," Gabreel ordered Aberthol from where they were being adorned in simpler Galia garb: white tunics with gold edges and loose-fitting tan pants that hugged their ankles.

Two Süra servants were readying them for an audience with King Réol, their gazes dutifully averted from meeting his or his son's.

Earlier they had been fed and washed, and Gabreel's beard had been shaved clean. A pretense to appease any court members they might happen upon. It was much easier to ignore that the palace held prisoners when they blended in as guests.

"Even if the king commands you to speak," Gabreel continued, "do not. Press further into the floor, prostrate more dramatically, but do *not* speak."

"Won't I then be disobeying His Majesty's order?" asked Aberthol, frowning as one of the attendants urged him to lift his feet so he could step into slippers.

"Your existence is disobeying his orders," Gabreel explained. "To hear a Mütra's voice he will consider tainting his divine ears. It will only be interpreted as disrespect. If requested, I shall do the talking. You must trust me. The execution of Mütra began under King Réol's rule. He is not like a nyddoth, nor are the Volari of Galia like those stationed in Zomyad. This place . . ." He cut himself off, eyeing the nearby kidets who loomed outside their dressing room's open door. "Beauty is never soft," Gabreel went on in a whisper. "You must remember this, my son. Beauty is hard, sharp, vicious. It carves away anything and everything that it believes threatens to make it grotesque. It does not care if what it eradicates is in fact helping it thrive or grow or remain nourished or protected. All beauty cares about is being beautiful, even as its innards grow rotten. *That* is Galia and especially our king."

At his words their attendants paused their work, a shifting as their eyes met, but they knew better than to linger long in their silent exchange.

The servants here were all Süra and paid better than other forms of labor found on Cādra. This, mixed with the promise of living closer to the High Gods, spurred many to apply for the Recruitment—a lifetime of work in Galia. Though once they arrived, quickly did they realize these isles were in fact a prison. The only true way out was with wings or the large gondolas that connected to various parts of Cādra.

And those borders were heavily monitored.

"I'm to understand that I'm the grotesque," remarked Aberthol, brows furrowed.

"Here, yes," said Gabreel. He had never shielded his children from the harshness of this world. It was better they knew what may await them, prepare for it.

"And what about this new mine?" Aberthol questioned. "Did you really help make the Dryfs?"

Gabreel looked away from his son, shame a hot wash to his cheeks. How many souls within the Eternal River was he now responsible for?

Too many Süra had been lost within that underground maze, were still lost weekly.

"I engineered it," he admitted. "A regret I have carried for many decades. The only solace to my atrocity was in meeting your mother. She had been one of the assigned meddygs to the mine. Though I know I should not have been so blessed after surviving the Great Collapse when so many did not, it was because of her I did and why I came to understand the horror of my invention. Of all the ways of Galia rule."

The silence that engulfed the room was excruciatingly loud. Even the attendants had stopped in their work.

"Why . . . ?" Aberthol's voice trailed off. "Why did you never tell us?"

Because I could not bear my own children's disdain, thought Gabreel.

"Because your mother and I did not want to taint your lives any further," he explained instead.

"Further because I am already Mütra?" Aberthol's voice wavered, anger and ache. "Already a misdeed?"

"You are extraordinary," Gabreel corrected, his tone the sharp decisiveness of a falling blade. "Which makes you a threat. Especially to those who believe they are the only ones meant to hold such a title."

Gabreel noted the hard swallow to his son's throat, the conflicting emotions in his green gaze, fury and fear.

"What is going to happen to us, Father?" Thol asked.

The question nauseated Gabreel.

Visions of his past flashed, fast and red and angry.

The scars along his back screamed their agony as though the fire that had been held to cauterize his wounds was still present.

Gabreel shook uncontrollably from where he crouched on all fours. The stone was hard beneath his hands and knees, wet and putrid from his own vomit mixing with his blood. He could not see past the pain, could not breathe for fear of smelling his own burning flesh. He toppled to the ground, imbalanced, out of body.

That's when he saw them.

A mass of gray in the corner of his blurred vision.

Feathers.
His feathers.
His wings.
His life.
Cut away.

Gabreel screamed but ended up retching again instead, a trickle of bile all that was left inside before the darkness took him. A blessed reprieve from the scorching brightness of his torture.

Gabreel took in a shaky inhale, snapping himself back to the room where he and Thol stood. Though the image of his nightmare remained reflected in the mirror in front of them, where wings should have replaced the empty air at his back.

What is going to happen to us, Father? his son had asked.

"Whatever does happen," Gabreel said, voice hoarse as he grasped Thol's shoulder. More to steady himself than an act of reassurance. "I can promise you, it will happen with us together."

◆ ◆ ◆

Once dressed, they were escorted to where Prince Zolya and a few of his entourage waited in a large pavilion. Doors, let alone walls, were not details found in many Volari buildings. Wings liked wide-open halls, large skylights. Easy exits and entrances.

Only clouds and sky could be seen beyond the surrounding massive columns from where they walked, leaking sunlight to send dramatic shadows across the marble floor.

Though high up, the air here always held a warm, gentle breeze.

All an illusion, of course.

Wind, freeze, and heat wielders were stationed around the palace day and night, ensuring the perfect atmosphere.

As they approached, the prince stopped his conversation with one of his companions. It was the same kidar who had held a knife to Thol's throat.

Osko Terz, ambitious adolescent and companion to the prince. For over fifty years Gabreel had watched the two grow up and grow inseparable.

A pity, for he always found Terz too hotheaded to be a proper adviser to anyone.

"Follow us until the throne room's threshold," instructed the prince to their kidet escorts. "Kidar Terz and I will take the inventor and his son from there."

Prince Zolya had changed since their flight, adorned in the proper royal garb of his station. His gold-and-white chest plate bled seamlessly into the design of his silk tunic and decorative cape. His laurel crown was a delicate weaving through his alabaster hair, pearls and diamonds winking from each leafy tip. He was a vision of power and excess.

As Prince Zolya turned, guiding them forward, Gabreel noted how he seemed to make a point of avoiding eye contact. An interesting tell of guilt.

While they had never been close, the prince had often visited Gabreel's workroom within the palace as a child and well into adulthood. He had always shown interest in Gabreel's inventions, the idea of improving something or creating new things. But whenever he visited, there was always a guard, keeping their relationship formal. A purposeful move by the king, no doubt.

Gabreel surmised the prince did not have many trusted companions. More reason why Terz was dangerous.

As they neared towering doors made from a mosaic of ambrü, Gabreel's feet stuttered. A cold sweat erupted along his skin as he stared at the entrance to King Réol's throne room.

It had been twenty-three years since he had been on the other side, the day of his sentencing, and yet it was as if he was the same man as then: terrified and desperate.

Gabreel glanced to his son, to his wide gaze fixed to the entrance.

A renewed consuming panic surged through him.

Grab him now!

Grab him and fly!

Gabreel's heart screamed for him to do whatever he could to help them escape. Help his son be free of the awaiting nightmares. Even if that meant throwing them both over the pavilion's ledge.

But then the doors were opening, their group pushed into the white pantheon, and Gabreel's vision was swallowed by light.

It was said King Réol's throne room was crafted by Naru, the High Goddess of artistry, herself. A claim that could not be denied once inside.

As if her brush had been dipped in the rays of the sun, the towering domed expanse shone like a womb of a star, a celestial paradise. One instantly felt their inadequacy beside such pristine beauty, their insignificance as they walked forward between the laboriously carved columns. So wide and tall they rivaled the ancient trees of Zomyad.

And there, at the center of it all, wings spread wide as he sat at the very top of hundreds of rising alabaster steps, beneath a beam of sunlight, was their almighty king.

A pulsing of power.

Eternal brilliance.

Vicious, unnatural beauty.

Gabreel did not understand how he was moving when everything inside him had stopped. While King Réol was not a High God, he emanated as though one, so much of Ré's divine powers bestowed in his blood.

King Réol was shirtless, besides a woven cage of a chest plate, and his golden brown skin glowed as though light was trapped beneath. The gold of his epaulets reached over his strong chest and covered his shoulders, where feathered hammered adornments blended into his massive white wingspan. Plumage that was sharp and soft at once, like the gold laurel crown atop his head.

There was no mistaking Prince Zolya's parentage.

The similarities were uncanny.

But where the prince's eyes still held shards of humanity, of warmth, King Réol's were hallowed from centuries of brutality.

Gabreel quickly lowered his gaze as their group fell to prostrating bows at the base of the stairs. The stone floor was ice to Gabreel's forehead, his heartbeat loud in his ears, but between the galloping echoes, he could still hear the quick breaths of Aberthol crouched at his side.

Terror.

His son was terrified.

As he should be.

Still, Gabreel's heart was shattering at the reality of witnessing his child's fear and not being able to reach out to console him. Protect him.

Gabreel gritted his teeth just as the thunderous voice of King Réol washed over him.

"My son has returned home," he began, "and he has brought me gifts."

"I exist to serve, Your Eminence," said Prince Zolya from where he remained bowed in front of Gabreel.

"You may rise."

There was a shuffling as the prince and Kidar Terz stood. Gabreel and his son remained cowered.

"Given your reports over the past month," said the king, "I was preparing to be disappointed. However, you have proven your worth today, my son. Present to me that which you have found scurrying on the soil of Cādra."

Rough hands gripped Gabreel as Kidar Terz pulled him to his feet. With his gaze cast downward, he was brought beside Prince Zolya. A gift presented.

"As wished by our divine king," said the prince, "I have returned the inventor, Gabreel Heiro."

There was a stretching of silence, and though Gabreel was not looking at His Eminence, he could sense his sharp smile. It was a cut of acid energy through the air.

Gabreel's magic stirred in his blood, a rising of heat to protect as the scars along his back prickled with awareness. Wariness. As if the remaining wing shards beneath his skin knew they were back where they had been broken.

"Were you always this small, Heiro?" asked the king. "Or has living so long in the dirt of Cādra tugged you down like a root?"

Gabreel dared not speak; instead he further clenched his bound hands, which rested in front of him.

"No, I suppose it was always your wings that gave you such height," mused the king. "A true tragedy, that. Especially when they were such a tasteful plumage. Do you remember their coloring, Heiro?"

Slow, steady breaths. That's all Gabreel could manage.

"Luckily, you do not have to strain too hard to recall." There was a shuffling a distance away, footsteps as servants dragged in something heavy. "Think of this as a welcome-home present."

Gabreel's surroundings warped, blood draining as his gaze collided with gray outstretched wings at the base of the King's podium.

My wings.
My life.
My freedom.

Gabreel barely swallowed down his sob, his feet stuttering forward before he was wrenched back by Kidar Terz.

"Not so fast, old man," he hissed.

But Gabreel hardly heard him, his mind splitting and tipping in every direction.

King Réol kept them.
Kept my wings.

But of course he had.

He was a hunter who prized that which he killed.

Rage—blinding, consuming—swallowed Gabreel.

His magic erupted along his skin, causing Kidar Terz to hiss as he released him, his hands scalded.

A cracking slap whipped Gabreel's head back.

"Stand down, inventor," Kidar Terz growled. "It is a lashing crime for any sky magic to be used while in attendance with His Eminence." Gabreel's jaw throbbed, but he was thankful for the hit. His mind had been cleared. Or as cleared as it could be under such circumstances.

"I must admit"—the king's deep voice punctured the room—"our reunion has far exceeded expectations. Despite your continued efforts to disobey the laws of this land, I'm pleased you are here, Heiro."

Gabreel knew better. Knew the risk. So it was with apparent madness that he turned his gaze up and met that of King Réol.

It was a mouse staring at the teeth that had already punctured his heart.

The king seemed to enjoy the defiance. His lips twisted into a deeper grin. "Yes," he continued. "I am happy of your company, Heiro, despite how you dishonor this throne with the presence of your Mütra spawn."

Gabreel swallowed the terror working up his throat, did his best not to flinch at King Réol mentioning his son.

His child who was still prostrating on the ground behind him.

"But the spawn only makes this all the more entertaining, does it not?" observed the king. "As does the news of your Süra succubus finally entering the Eternal River. Despite her eluding our soldiers all those years ago, it appears Zenca still had her pay for her insolence against me. Isn't this correct, Zolya?"

"Yes, Your Eminence," the prince replied, expression neutral. "His Süra mate died in childbirth."

Gabreel did not need to fabricate his heartache from such a statement.

To him, Aisling was dead, as he knew he would never see her again. Low Gods willing.

Pain erupted like a thorned vine in his chest, a desperate ache accompanied by regret. He should have kissed her more that morning, held her longer, told her he loved her.

He should have done a lot differently—like not keeping them so long in Zomyad. Aisling had been growing nervous, voicing her wish for them to leave, but he hadn't listened. He was too determined to give her the home, his family the home, that they deserved.

"More proof of the gods not condoning such creatures," scoffed the king, redrawing Gabreel's attention. "To kill off the mothers who bore them."

Gabreel clenched his teeth, watching with growing trepidation as King Réol's gaze slid to Aberthol on the floor.

"Do we know what powers it might possess?" he asked.

It, not *they*, not *he*.

It.

"If the Mütra has any," answered Prince Zolya, "we will find out, Your Eminence."

"I shall enjoy the reports on your progress," the king declared. "In the meantime, let us get our inventor settled into his workroom. There is much to accomplish to get my new mine operational. You'll find, Heiro, that Bardrex has left you quite a mess to clean."

With the king's dismissal, Gabreel was pulled to the side, different guards coming to collect his son. His heart leaped from his chest, terror consuming as they were torn apart.

"Your Eminence," Gabreel called out, fighting against Kidar Terz's unforgiving grip. "Prince Zolya promised my son would remain alive so long as I did. To ensure this agreement is met, I require my son beside me as I work."

"Your *son*?" the king sneered, as though testing the name for such a creature as a Mütra, finding it most foul. "Your son," he repeated, eyes narrowing on Prince Zolya before shrewdly on where Aberthol crouched. "Yes," he mused slowly. "Very well, inventor. You have my word as the conduit for our almighty Ré that your spawn shall live, as well as remain with you, so long as your work proves progress. After all"—the king's smile was sharp—"we need something to keep you motivated, Heiro."

As Gabreel and Aberthol were herded from the throne room, he was submerged in a cold drowning of dread.

The king's declaration was less of an assurance than a threat.

One that was carried out that very night when Aberthol was dragged from their guarded room for his first night of torture. A taste of what would happen if Gabreel didn't make progress.

But his child was returned.

Alive.

As the king had promised.

9

As soon as Zolya touched down on his mother's private isle, he regretted his choice to visit.

The air was sweeter than usual. The lush gardens oversaturated with creeping blooms.

And the gentle breeze carried a vibration of celestial power. Cool and hot at once.

A High God was present.

Zolya curled his hands into fists, in no mood to be tested by the divine.

Every waking moment of his life was already riddled with tests.

But it was too late to depart, for a servant had caught sight of him and was already bowing and offering him a refreshment before ushering him through to a shaded veranda.

His mother's home was a physical manifestation of herself. An island full of vibrancy and art, flowing paths that led to an array of meditation pools, each dedicated to one of the twelve High Gods. It was a space of expression and reflection. A sanctuary.

Or usually was, when Zolya wasn't being announced before the presence of Naru, the High Goddess of artistry.

Despite standing before his queen, Zolya strode directly to where Naru lounged against a silk settee. Her divine power rippled in hot currents, and it took extra strength to hide his flutter of fear as he came to kneel.

"My benevolent creator," Zolya addressed the goddess as he bent over her outstretched hand. He took special care not to touch any part of her. "I am eternally humbled and honored to be in your presence."

"And yet," said a lyrical voice tinged with birdsong and the echo of time, "you held the desire to leave as soon as you had arrived."

Zolya's muscles tensed.

He was not surprised Naru had sensed his earlier emotions from such a distance away, but it was unpleasant nonetheless. "It was a desire merely born from not wishing to intrude on my queen's precious moments with you, my almighty goddess," he appeased.

Naru's amused laughter was a tinkling of bells. "You may look upon me, Prince Zolya."

He did as he was told, finding a face too radiant to hold within his mind. Though Naru sat beneath the shade of a wisteria tree, her skin shimmered from light to dark, vibrant to muted, a changing of every color in existence and those yet to be born. Her painter's palette.

As for her clothes, the details were lost in the bright glow of the fabric and the great draping of her fiery wings at her side. The gods were not physical beings by nature, but incorporeal. To present themselves as flesh and bone was an attempt to gather in their immensity. A small gesture of kindness to avoid overwhelming their subjects when they visited from the heavens.

Though overwhelm they certainly still did.

"One of our more accomplished children, your son is, Habelle," said Naru to the queen while still fixated on Zolya. Her words might have been complimentary, but the goddess regarded him with indifference. A common expression of the gods, all their gazes the cold expansive universe. "He grows handsomer with every passing decade. Perhaps by too much," she mused. "We know how our almighty father enjoys being the only one to shine."

A flippant threat that still froze Zolya's next words.

The gods were as fickle as they were vengeful.

A menial offense could spark great despair, while a larger atrocity could be wholly ignored.

His response had to be perfect, for it, no doubt, would be heard by Ré.

"I am but a dull reflection," replied Zolya, "beneath the glorious sun of our creator."

Naru tilted her head, and though she did not smile, he could sense her pleasure at his words. Her entertainment in a prince prostrating. "Indeed," she agreed. "Now, what say you of your mother's creation? She and her ladies have been engaging me with their talents during my visit."

Zolya stood, taking in the glistening ice sculpture in the center of the veranda, his mother and her ladies-in-waiting nearby.

He had arrived during one of the queen's sculpting sessions. An art where she summoned a small rain cloud and controlled the droplets precisely as she wanted.

A few of her ladies—daughters of the highest born of the Sun Court—who held the power of freeze were there to capture her water in place. The finished result was an immaculate depiction of the surrounding wisteria trees. The icy blooms so detailed he could reach out and pluck one off without compromising the piece.

"An accomplishment, to be sure," he replied. "I am forever in awe of the blessings you've bestowed upon our women. The delicate crafting they can accomplish with their magic is always stunning."

"You make their abilities sound minuscule," observed Naru. "To carve something delicate takes great strength. It is far easier to push a boulder off a cliff than to chisel it into pebbles where it lies."

"Yes, of course." Zolya bowed his apologies. "That was not my intended meaning."

"You must forgive my son's attempt at appreciating my art, Naru," interjected his mother. "I fear I may have favored my time sculpting over my time with him when he was a boy. More than one shattered piece did I find whenever he was near."

"Is that so?" questioned the goddess.

Zolya could feel Naru's hard gaze on him.

Mother, he wanted to chastise, though he sensed that his discomfort was her current joy.

"Merely a repercussion of my own inadequacy in trying to be as my queen," he quickly explained. "My rain may be mighty, but never could I direct it as precise."

"Then I advise you to allow your mother to teach you her art, child."

Zolya laughed but soon realized the goddess had been serious.

He had a multitude of replies on his lips, though none were complimentary.

A man be taught delicate magic? A prince sit for art lessons?

If he wasn't challenged enough by his father, that would surely give the king fodder for the next century.

"Is artistry so amusing?" questioned Naru, the very goddess who mothered it.

Zolya's wings stiffened. He was flying in dangerous skies.

"You must remember *all* that I command, child." Naru's voice grew heavy with her reprimand, power gathering. "One can have artistry with a blade, with ideas, with lies." She fluttered her fingers, awakening tiny depictions of her words within her palm, one piece folding into the next. "It does not merely belong to the brush or the chisel. I am talent. I am skill. I am mastery. Do you laugh at that?"

"Never, my almighty goddess." Zolya came to one knee. To grovel to a god was the quickest way to be forgiven.

"Good," said Naru, snuffing out her creations with a clamped fist. "As for finding artistry within your magic, I ask you to meditate on this for when we meet again, young prince. Perhaps then you will learn how dangerous *delicate* can be."

In the next breath, Naru became nothing but light, a star gathering inward as she winked out of existence, leaving them.

Zolya's muscles instantly relaxed, a long exhale. "Thank you for that, Mother," he said as he came to his feet, tugging his coat straight.

"I had no part in you flying yourself into such a storm," explained Queen Habelle from where she remained beside her tree of ice. "It was not I who laughed at a god's advice. Really, Zolya, I may be a favorite of Naru, but you know better than that."

Zolya sucked his teeth in annoyance, knowing she was right. His mother may have protection under Naru, certain informalities agreed upon when she visited, but that did not mean it extended to himself.

"Yes, well," he began, chin lifting. "Let us excuse my lapse in behavior from not eating a proper meal before my flight here."

"Ah," exclaimed his mother. "Now we learn of the real purpose of your visit. You've come for my chef's food."

"And to be amongst the best company while eating it," added Zolya, shooting her a wry grin, which stirred from her a laugh.

Not to have been outdone by her divine visitor, Queen Habelle was resplendent. Styled in a flowing peplos of white and orange that wrapped her lithe frame. Her black skin shone with youth—despite her being well over two centuries in age—while her amber wings matched the color of her braided hair that was gathered into an intricate updo.

"Let us get you fed, then," she ordered, waving to a nearby servant. "But before you begin your feast, your queen requires a proper greeting."

Zolya strode to his mother's outstretched arms, then laid a kiss to each of her cheeks. Her familiar lilac fragrance was a calming inhale, her hazel gaze a tender hug.

Though his father held the power to harness the sun, it was his mother who had always showed him warmth. Beyond any of Zolya's scholars, she nourished his mind, challenged his ideas, and allowed space for him to voice them.

Which was why he had the habit of visiting her after an audience with the king.

Her tranquil presence washed the bitter tang from his mouth, eased the tightness in his spine. Her private isle was not merely her place of respite but his.

"I am glad you are home," she said. "My favorite child."

Zolya huffed a laugh. "I am your only child."

"Lucky for you, then." She smiled, stepping back. "You might not have remained my favorite otherwise."

"Despite such a threat," countered Zolya, "I am confident I would have. My abilities to charm *are* rather notorious. Wouldn't you agree, ladies?"

A tittering of giggles and blushed cheeks greeted his wink from the trio of women peering at him from behind his mother's wings.

"Yes, sire." They curtsied in unison.

Zolya caught the tail end of the queen's eye roll.

"You may leave me, girls," she announced. "So I may talk with my son without damaging your delicate eyelashes from all that fluttering."

Two of the ladies looked offended, the other embarrassed, but all obeyed. With a quick leap into the air, they retreated to the queen's palace.

As servants laid out a spread fit for royals, Zolya and his mother settled into the plush benches beneath the blooming lavender trees. Zolya wasted little time before filling his plate with wrapped dates and warm glazed lamb, the flavors euphoric as they settled onto his tongue.

By the High Gods, he was eternally relieved to be eating this and not another tasteless soup.

"Thank you, Mariel," said the queen to one of her attendants as she poured them tea.

Zolya eyed how the Süra barely contained her pleasure at the queen's spoken gratitude.

"You spoil them," pointed out Zolya once all the servants had slipped back to the fringes of the balcony, awaiting when they'd next be needed.

"For what?" questioned his mother as she raised her teacup.

"For whenever they are sent back to Galia."

"I have no intentions of sending anyone back anywhere," she countered. "Unless they desire to return to their lives in Cādra with their families, of course. All who work on my isle know they can leave if requested."

Zolya paused midchew, blinking at his mother.

"Oh, don't look so shocked, my son. These Süra *do* have lives and families apart from their roles here, you know. Many of whom they support with their Galia compensations."

"Of course I know this," he said after a hard swallow, annoyance stirring.

"Then what has you frowning?"

"I merely wish you were more careful with your behavior. Thanking servants, addressing them by their given names, granting them pardons from their positions if they so wish."

"What a snob you are, my son."

"I am a prince," replied Zolya, tone indignant. "One *you* have raised to understand his place and role in Cādra and those of others."

"Mmm, yes." She sipped her drink. "Perhaps I am to blame for some of your snobbery."

"I am not above showing kindness to our staff," he explained in a hush. "Of course I am not. But I understand how certain . . . observed relaxed behavior could lead to whispers of being a . . ."

"A what?" pushed the queen.

"A Süra sympathizer," he answered curtly.

And we all know what our king and courtiers think about such positions, he finished to himself, wings tense at his back.

"And what if I was?"

"*Mother*," he chastised, cutting her off as he glanced about their surroundings. "Please, keep your voice down. Your ladies are not so far off. This may be your island, but rumors spread fast on wings."

She swatted away his concern with a wave of her hand. "Clouds fill each of their minds."

"Then why have you chosen them for your ladies?" Zolya frowned, discarding his plate on the low table between them.

"It is called *politics*, my child. To be a lady-in-waiting to the queen helps each of them in their matchmaking. I pet the wings of their families so they can pet mine. A tactic I know you are familiar with."

"Yes," Zolya replied dryly. "Another lesson you are responsible for. Which begs the question, How do you not see the politics regarding my earlier point with your servants?"

His mother merely smiled at his barb, her amber hair glistening from the sunlight coming through the tree canopy as she leaned forward to pluck a grape. "What I see is this conversation leaving one of us ill at ease with the other," she countered. "Now, tell me of your recent exploration, my son. I hear it was a success."

Success, not sentencing.

Exploration, not manhunt.

Zolya swallowed down the acid taste that quickly rose at his mother's request, unwelcome memories from yesterday's audience with his father awakening like a dreaded dream.

Gabreel's preserved wings, spiked and spread wide.

The inventor's silent rage and palpable desperation to protect his son.

The Mütra trembling beneath his feet.

So new to this world.

And Zolya made responsible for showing him the horrors of it.

Do we know what powers it might possess? his king had asked.

We will find out, Your Eminence, he had complied.

Zolya had felt crazed afterward. Did still. He loathed himself as he ordered the arrangements for the Mütra to be studied that night. As if the boy were a soul with no feeling, no conscience.

Despite the decades Zolya had witnessed and carried out similar orders for his father, despite having been present during Gabreel's original banishment, he had never grown the stomach for their form of discipline. Only better armor for his mask of indifference toward it.

Zolya often wished he could be as pure of purpose and conviction as Osko or even his father regarding their laws and beliefs. As many of their court members.

It seemed a much simpler existence.

But he had always been more like his mother.

Full of thoughts, questions.

Disobedience stalked the corners of his heart.

Traits wholly unbecoming of the only son of the king, one specifically created to be the next in line for the throne. Which was perhaps why he found himself so provoked by his mother's informalities with her staff.

Such small freedoms he was hardly allowed.

"Tiring, was it?" The queen's voice brought him back to the shaded veranda, to where she regarded him carefully. Her gaze dipped to his clenched hand along his thigh, as though that was where he could trap his spinning emotions.

"It was a long voyage," answered Zolya, loosening his grip. "One I'm glad is over."

"Yes," appeased his mother. "As am I. I never enjoy when my child is long gone."

Her words stirred up more disquiet in Zolya's chest.

"Speaking of children," said Zolya after a moment. "Gabreel had a son . . . with his Süra lover."

The queen's brows rose. "Did he?"

"We brought him with us to Galia."

"The child?"

"Yes."

"Alive?" His mother's concern was clear in her tone, in her pinched expression.

Zolya looked away, unable to stomach her disapproval, to allow further guilt and uncertainty to twist into his heart.

Instead, he concentrated on the slowly melting ice sculpture that sat beneath the heat of Ré. Despite the king's promise, Zolya knew what would become of Gabreel's son eventually.

"Yes, alive," he replied.

A stretching of silence.

"And the mother? Gabreel's Süra lover?" asked Queen Habelle.

"Apparently dead."

"You are not sure?"

Zolya rubbed his lips together, unease a cold slither through his veins.

It had been subtle, but he had noticed how Gabreel wanted to look into the forest behind him when they were in Zomyad. Zolya had wondered who might have been watching from within.

Who might the inventor have wanted to catch one last glimpse of before they took flight?

Zolya's aptitude for knowing when someone was lying was not always a blessing. Especially when the terms of their arrangement to acquire Gabreel had specifically stated they were to stay within the clearing.

They could not penetrate the forest but must remain waiting on the fringes to catch the inventor when he emerged, as he was rumored to do whenever traveling to his hidden workshop.

Though, for Zolya, that was preferred.

He wanted to fly as far and as fast from that forest as possible.

Gabreel's son was a surprise enough.

The nyddoth had deliberately left out the detail of the inventor having a family. Which made his request to lift the hunting of Mütra all the clearer.

Even if they had wanted to kill Gabreel's son that day, they couldn't. Not while still in Zomyad, at least.

Blood the nyddoth did not want on his hands.

Blood Zolya did not want on his either.

But that was the way of their world. Of the crown prince's position.

Which was exactly what had Zolya remaining quiet now, fearful that if he voiced his uncertainties regarding the death of Gabreel's lover, someone else might hear besides his mother. If not a servant or one of the queen's ladies, then a High God.

Zolya had no wish to reengage his hunt. He already had his hands full with the inventor and his Mütra offspring. He did not want to produce any more pets for his father to play with.

"All that I'm sure about is this new mine," Zolya eventually reasoned. "The Aspero Sea erodes the Dryfs year by year. The ambrü- and gem-output reports have become minuscule. The treasury will soon grow unstable, and despite the hard labor this build will require, an unsteady government would be a far worse fate for all in Cādra."

His mother's gaze was a narrowing of calculations. He could tell she had many thoughts regarding his proclamations, but in the end, she settled on "Then it is good you have returned our inventor."

For some reason this was more maddening than if she had challenged him.

Then it is good.

Good.

Zolya clamped his teeth together as the word settled like hot embers on his skin, a flutter of frustration down his spine. He glanced to the wide-open sky beyond the veranda. The endless blue expanse. A promise of freedom. Of escape. And yet forever the domain of their almighty creators. A reminder of the duty his bloodline carried. To rule over it.

"Yes, it is good," he repeated, shoulders tense.

"Zolya, look at me." There was a light clink as his mother placed down her teacup.

Hesitantly, he met her hard stare.

"You did not have a choice, my son." She reached out, placing a gentle hand on his knee. "Do you understand? With the inventor, you did not have a choice."

Remorse was a sharp clawing up Zolya's throat. One he swallowed down with unknown force. His mother, for better or worse, always saw him. "Didn't I?" he asked.

"No." Queen Habelle shook her head as she sat back. "You had moves. They are very different," she explained. "You are the son of the king, Zolya. A royal child of gods and heir to the throne. You were born into a dangerous game. You must, *must*, move through it carefully. You have done that. Triumphantly. Do not berate yourself. Not for actions that were inevitable. As I said, with this you did not have a choice."

The truth of his mother's words was a vise grip to Zolya's lungs. Shackles to his wings. He could not breathe; he could not escape.

He didn't have a choice.

Never did.

But would he ever?

Something hot and dangerous awoke in his blood, sparking the magic that swam there. The ever-present gnawing of independence he had been taught to smother since birth. But not kill. No, the queen made sure he kept this internal fire alive, merely in secret, in her private company.

And this was the danger of his mother, of visiting this island.

Here he believed he had space to set himself free. Lower his masks of duty and responsibilities to the Diusé bloodline. Merely be her son. A man. A person.

But the difficulty lay in how to be recaptured.

An animal did not easily return to their cage.

It was this fight, this frustration of the queen's dual expectations of Zolya that had him lashing out now.

"But what of your choices, then, Mother?" he questioned coolly. "You speak of moving through life carefully yet so flippantly mention sympathizing with Süra for everyone to hear. I fear that is hypocrisy at its best."

Queen Habelle sat back, not at all offended by his cutting remark. This was the very freedom she allowed him, after all. "I have lived more than two centuries, Zolya," she said. "My flippancy is allowed due to the protections I have carefully—and *artfully*, I might add—put into place around me."

"Protections," he scoffed. "Just as Aunt Callia had protections? Sister to the queen yet still susceptible to the king's impulses."

Zolya regretted the words as soon as they left his lips.

The veranda fell quiet. Even the breeze seemed to die as his declaration echoed around them. Queen Habelle's eyes flashed, her wings stiffening.

"Mother, I apologize. I did not—"

"My sister," the queen interjected, voice the frost of winter, "did not move through her life carefully, now did she?"

Zolya dared not reply.

With a pinch to her brow, his mother regarded her softening sculpture. Its magnificence was now reduced to an unidentifiable melting mass of ice, soon to be nothing but a puddle at its base.

"One's title or blood is hardly ever sturdy armor," she said after another moment. "In fact, they are likely the weakest form of protection, for they are often desired by others. A title can be easily taken. Blood easily shed. Callia may have been a queen's sister, but that also meant she was near power. And power, as you know, Zolya, is dangerous." She looked back at him, expression hard. "Power clouds judgment, cloaks consequences. Why do you think I live on this isle at the western edge of Cādra? So far from Galia, from you, my son. I can tell you now, it is not for the views. Absence does not always make the heart grow fonder. Sometimes, one is blessed with being forgotten."

Forgotten by her king.

Forgotten by her husband.

Shielded from occupying the thoughts of a dangerous man.

Zolya swallowed past the ache wrapping his throat. Pain brought on by the idea of his mother experiencing any of her own.

He did not remember exactly when his mother had moved to this isle, only that there was a distinct *before* and *after*.

Before, Queen Habelle was reserved, mute, obedient.
After, she had interests, hobbies, opinions.
After, she smiled.
She laughed.
She held him.

"My sister was a fool to not follow me here," continued Queen Habelle. "Instead, she decided to move closer to power, and look at what that got her. A bastard and then killed."

"Mother," whispered Zolya, her words a blow to his chest.

"Is it not true?" she challenged.

"I'm sorry" was all he could manage.

"The only remorse I have is that you cannot also live here permanently," she countered. "You and Azla."

Zolya frowned at the mention of his half sister and cousin. The very bastard child his mother had just accused his aunt of having.

While Zolya had a relationship with Azla, Queen Habelle hardly spoke of her.

Despite the sixty-five years since Azla's birth, Zolya still wasn't sure of the queen's feelings regarding her niece. He knew only that what had transpired with his aunt was a wound that had never quite healed for his mother. Either because of her betrayal or because of her execution, he could not say.

"I hope you are watching over her," the queen went on, shocking him further.

"You astound me." Zolya shook his head.

"Why?"

"To care for the bastard child of your husband."

Her brows drew in. "You *are* kind to her, aren't you, Zolya?"

"Of course. I have no issues with Azla."

In fact, Zolya felt more kinship with her than he cared to admit. Both were blood of the king. Both were utilized at court for others' gains. Both were judged by what they represented over who they were as people.

"Good." His mother nodded, settling into her bench. "While I may not support what my sister did, a child shouldn't be judged for who their parents are or what they did before their birth."

Zolya huffed his disbelief. "If only all felt as you, Mother."

"I *am* one of a kind," she managed with a smile.

"Yes," he agreed. "But I certainly would not judge if some animosity filled your heart toward Azla."

The queen tilted her head, assessing him. "Does some fill yours?"

Zolya let the question swirl in his chest, testing his true feelings, but too easily he knew his answer. "Azla is headstrong, too much at times," he began, "but I have grown fond of her. She . . ." He clamped his lips together, keeping his next words from flying free.

"What?" urged his mother. "You can say it, my son."

"She reminds me of you," he said hesitantly.

His mother merely nodded, a faraway look entering her features before she shook it off. "I am not upset that you have a relationship with her," she explained. "I am glad of it, in fact. I can only imagine how lonely her life would have been without your favor."

This was true, of course. Princess Azla had been a pariah at court for many decades following her birth. Not until Zolya accompanied her as her chaperone during her debut year did she fall into favor. With the king hardly acknowledging her existence—a burden of many daughters of the court with their fathers—all had waited to see how his bastard would be entered into society. To be on the arm of the prince, well, that was one advantage of Zolya's title: his power to influence others' thoughts. At the very least, their behaviors in public.

"She would be glad to know her queen thinks kindly of her," explained Zolya.

"You may share that I do," stated Queen Habelle. "And perhaps, one day, she can visit me here."

Zolya nodded despite how the offer rippled unpleasantly down his spine. He might care for Azla, but this isle was for him. This time alone with his mother was his. Dare he admit he would be jealous to share it?

"I have been meditating on this for a while now," continued his mother, smoothing out her skirts. "It is not often Volari bear children. If the High Gods blessed Callia with a child, it was for a purpose. Perhaps part of that purpose was to teach me compassion."

As his mother regarded him expectantly, Zolya kept his expression neutral.

Compassion was not a trait he believed the High Gods cared for. Devotion, beauty, talent, ambition, along with humility in the face of their greatness—these were attributes they seemed to crave.

"If that is the case, Mother, you have succeeded in your learnings," he appeased. "A more compassionate person I have yet to meet. Just ask your staff. I'm sure they would all agree."

Queen Habelle raised a brow at his barb. "Yes, I'm sure they would," she replied. "As I'm sure they would also agree it is time we visit my meditation pond."

Zolya was unable to hold in his groan.

"You cannot fly here and eat my food, Zolya, without a prayer session of gratitude," she scolded. "Naru also gave you clear orders to meditate on her earlier words. Now is a perfect time to do so. We will pick something beautiful from my gardens for her altar, as well as the rest of the gods."

"The rest?" Zolya exclaimed, eyes wide. "If we are to visit all twelve, it will be dark by the time we are finished."

"Good thing you have a room within my palace, then, hmm?" countered his mother. "You will stay the night. I'm sure you did not find much time for prayer when you were out searching for our inventor. Luckily, you have that time now."

Yes, how fortunate for me, Zolya silently grumbled as he followed his mother.

Yet when he found himself prostrating, forehead kissing the cool marble floor of Naru's altar room, his mind did not tumble to the goddess's teachings. His thoughts, instead, were consumed by his mother's earlier words regarding purpose.

If the High Gods blessed Callia with a child, it was for a purpose.

Zolya wondered if his only purpose was to follow in his father's footsteps. Or, perhaps, could the High Gods have created him for more than wearing a crown?

His mother had spoken of compassion.

A trait he had difficulty only hiding, not feeling.

Why give the son of a stern king compassion when his daily duties were riddled with inflicting pain? With upholding rigid laws and decorum and beliefs he didn't completely believe himself?

Why sculpt him in the image of his father but fill him so completely with his mother?

It all reeked of amusement for bored eternal beings.

Anger was a crescendo building in Zolya's veins, stroking along the magic that swam there, rain clouds brewing.

Here he bowed, meant to be thanking the High Gods.

Instead, all Zolya wished to do was curse them.

10

Tanwen was a storm as she threw together a travel bag. Her thoughts were the rumblings of thunder, harsh and loud, visions of her father and brother abducted playing over and over in her mind. Her heartbeats were cracks of lightning in her chest, painful shouts, remorseful screams against her rib cage.

She had done nothing to stop them.

Nothing to keep her family from being torn in two.

I am a coward!

Selfish. A fool.

If I had only told my family sooner.

Tanwen's guilt nearly buckled her knees as she clutched a sack of rice, shoving it into her pack. She was hardly aware of what she was pulling together. She only knew she had to pull *something* together.

Because Low Gods as her witness, she was falling apart.

"We can't follow them," reasoned her mother as she stood in the corner of their kitchen, eyes still swollen from tears, shirt and trousers plastered with dirt. Her gaze tracked Tanwen as she ran from cupboard to closet to bedroom. Eli was also there, perched on a chair's back. His whiskers twitched in telling agitation. He was quiet, however.

Eli knew better than to interrupt Tanwen when she was on a mission.

"We can certainly try," Tanwen ground out, dunking her canteen into one of their water troughs by the kitchen door. The cold seized her hand, momentarily clearing her frenzied mind.

Tanwen blinked back to her surroundings, noting the half-drunk tea of her father's still on the counter, now cold. The bags he and her brother had been packing, now tipped over, abandoned.

After the soldiers had left, Tanwen and her mother had sat clutching one another for what felt like an eternity, the morning somehow shifting to afternoon. It wasn't until a fox had poked its nose into Tanwen's back, questioning if she was all right, that she stirred from her drowning grief.

But barely.

Tanwen was certainly not all right, but that would not stop her from correcting this wrong.

How was she to do that?

She wasn't yet certain.

She knew only that it would include Prince Zolya suffering the same pain he was causing her now. Tanwen would be just as cold and uncaring when she unleashed her anger as he had been when he threatened her brother's life and forced her father's hand so heartlessly.

Humiliation burned along her skin.

How could she have thought he was any different from any other Volari?

When, in fact, he was the worst of his kind.

In a haze, Tanwen had helped her mother to her feet, then returned them to their den.

But once there, she realized her mistake. Their home now felt like a mausoleum.

She and her mother the reluctant mourners.

They needed to leave.

"No one can get onto Galia without the proper paperwork," reasoned Aisling, her hoarse voice returning Tanwen to their kitchen, to where her mother regarded her. "And even if we could," her mother went on, "how do you plan to infiltrate the palace? Or find where they might be keeping your father and brother? If they are even together? You have no plan, Wen. If we are packing, it should be to head north. It is no longer safe in Zomyad. We'll go to the Low Gods' territory, in Drygul, until we can figure out our next steps. There are places on its fringes where mortals can roam. That was always the plan your father and I—"

"Well, Father isn't here anymore, is he?" Tanwen regretted her words instantly. Especially when her mother flinched as if Tanwen had thrown daggers rather than voiced her anger.

But by the twin moons, Tanwen *was* angry.

She was furious.

Scared.

Lost.

"I'm sorry," said Tanwen, pulling up her now-filled canteen and placing it on the table. Water sloshed from the top, staining the wood grain below dark. She stared at the wet spot, watching as it was absorbed and vanished. Tanwen swallowed down the sob she felt reaching for freedom. She had cried enough. Could cry again later. Currently, she desperately needed to act. Do. But perhaps more importantly, she needed to understand.

"Mother . . ." She hesitated. "Why did this happen? Why would the king need Father to make a new mine?"

As if the answer pained her, Aisling drew in her brows, glancing out the window to her right. The energetic buzz of insects and languid birdsong filtering through was a taunt to their tense moment.

"Do you remember how your father and I met?" she asked.

"You were a meddyg at the Dryfs Mine, where Father also worked," said Tanwen, repeating the story she had been told many times since she was a child, one that always warmed their colder nights on the road. "He had helped carry in some workers who had been hurt, which had startled you, because you never see a Volari so openly offer their aid to Süra."

"Nor do you see them freely enter such tight quarters like that of our meddyg hut," added her mother, a fond faraway look in her gaze. "He knocked over half my supplies that day with his wings, making more of a mess for me to mend in the end."

"But you found him charming," added Tanwen with a smile, always liking that part of the story—imagining her father clumsy in the presence of her mother.

"I did," she replied, small grin awakening. "Despite myself, I did."

"That's when he started to visit you more often, always with an injured worker, however."

"Yes, and though he wasn't meant to, he'd stay long after they had gone. He was fascinated with my work," she added, features growing sober. "But most of all he wished to understand my hatred of the mine, to change my opinion. But I could not be swayed. Despite how the Dryfs gave me and my people work, it suppressed us more, *killed* us. It is the worst invention in the history of Cādra."

Tanwen swallowed her discomfort, never liking when her parents disagreed, even if it was in a past life. "And he didn't like that you thought that," said Tanwen, knowing what came next. It was a part of the story she hated even though it was what ultimately brought her parents together. "You fought. Told him you never wanted to see him again. And then . . ."

"The Great Collapse," finished her mother, tone hollow. "I can still taste the dirt coating my throat from that day. The screams of men buried alive, dying."

"And Father . . ."

"Was among the Süra digging for survivors, right there in the chaos, on the ground. Until he fell into an air pocket, rocks half covering him."

"That's how you came to tend to him and for him to confess his love for you, laid out on your meddyg table."

Her mother nodded, meeting Tanwen's gaze. "It is, but there is more to the story we never shared."

Tanwen remained quiet, her unease awakening.

"There was a reason your father was so offended at my hatred for the Dryfs," explained her mother. "And that is because he was not stationed there to oversee the workers like the other Volari. He invented the mine."

Tanwen blinked, heartbeat stuttering. "Invented? As in . . ."

"It was from his mind that the Dryfs came to exist." Aisling's features were hard. "He was King Réol's engineer. His trusted inventor for over a century."

Her mother's words seeped into her skin, ice piercing veins. Disbelief rendered her frozen. Tanwen knew her father was old, but . . . more than a century? And his mind was certainly great, but . . . adviser to the king?

New words prickled awake in Tanwen's mind, ones spoken by Prince Zolya to her father.

You are who King Réol has requested be reinstated as his royal engineer.

Understanding flickered awake.

"We have remained hidden for more than just Thol and I, haven't we?" asked Tanwen, disquiet churning in her gut. "For more than a Volari falling in love with a Süra."

"We have stayed *cautious*," clarified Aisling, "for many reasons."

"Mother," Tanwen pleaded. "There could not be a better time to tell me everything than now."

Her mother let out a long exhale, as though she had been holding it in for years. "Yes," she breathed. "You are right." Her gaze seemed to grow unfocused as her mind tipped back to the past. "After the Great Collapse," she began, "your father was ordered to rebuild the Dryfs, but he had finally seen the damage his invention could do to those who worked the mine. There were many areas his schematics had not accounted for. Conditions weren't entirely safe, the hours of labor beneath ground unhealthy, the food provided unfit for the energy expended by the laborers. And pay, well, there is a reason the most desperate along with criminals work the mine. But the king would not agree to his proposed changes to make the Dryfs more suitable. It would have been too costly, he had told him. Too time consuming. The king wanted his mine rebuilt and rebuilt fast. Your father refused."

Tanwen stared wide eyed at her mother. "Refused the king?"

Aisling nodded. "I have never been prouder of him than in that moment. It was shortly after that he and I were discovered. The king had Flyn—*Gabreel*," her mother corrected with a frown, "followed, suspicious for his insolence after decades of faithfully obeying orders. There had to be another reason, after all, than a man merely growing a conscience on his own. I was the reason the king eventually found for Gabreel's transgression. I was the Süra harlot who poisoned his precious inventor's mind. It was treason of the highest degree."

Tanwen desperately grasped every word her mother set free, empty corners of her parents' past filling in. "But why didn't the king have Father killed?" asked Tanwen. "Why merely take his wings and banish him?"

"To take a Volari's wings is like having them killed," explained her mother. "In fact, some would argue it is worse than dying, being robbed of the air they were born to fly in. After all, it was what Ré had done to his sister, Maryth. But you are right to wonder why King Réol ended his vengeance there. It was a question your father also wondered about for a time. The king does not easily forgive, if at all, nor is he known for his benevolence. Treason or not, he must have seen the worth of your father's mind. He has created many innovations for the king and Galia over the centuries. Despite your father leaving with his life, he feared a day would come when the king would seek him out again for his services. And as we've seen today"—her mother grew paler—"your father was right."

"And you?" wondered Tanwen. "Why would the king spare you?"

A blunt question. One that was met head on by her mother.

"He didn't," said Aisling, chin lifting. "But you must remember, I am a soul born from the soil of Cādra, a Süra from Garw, and know better how to hide in dirt than winged creatures. Their hunt for me faded after a year. Thankfully, since during that time, I discovered I was carrying you and your brother."

Despite her mother's softening expression, Tanwen felt only a growing churn of fury. Perhaps because she was still grieving the events of this morning, still sifting through her disdain for Prince Zolya and guilt for potentially being a reason he had found them.

She hated how helpless she felt.

"Why did you never tell us this full story?" asked Tanwen. "Why only share parts?"

"It was your father's wish," said her mother. "He . . . is deeply ashamed for the Dryfs. For what it has done to the Süra. The further divide it has instilled between the classes. He and I both wanted a fresh start with our family."

"A fresh start?" scoffed Tanwen. "But all we have ever done since our earliest memories was run. Run from a past we had no part in!"

"Wen," breathed her mother. "I understand why you are upset, but—"

"You understand nothing!" Tanwen snapped, her ever-pressing frustrations regarding her life again uncapping. "You know nothing about being scorned by the two races that make up your blood. The guilt of believing your life is what causes your family to be forced into seclusion."

"Tanwen, *stop*." Her mother grasped her shoulders, tugging her to her chest. Tanwen tried to push her away, but Aisling's grip was iron strong. "You must stop," she ordered again. "Please, it breaks me to hear you say such things."

"But it is the *truth*," seethed Tanwen, ignoring the hot tears streaming down her cheeks.

"It is not mine." Her mother met her gaze, features sharp. "You say I do not understand what it is like to be scorned? I am still a woman, Wen. One who fell in love with a Volari. I know what it is to disappoint, to be ostracized from a community, disowned by my own parents simply for following my heart. It wasn't until we had you and Aberthol that your father and I realized the rest of the world could hang. So yes, we hid, we ran, we have stayed tucked away in this corner of the forest for safety, but we have also done so because we no longer agree with the structures of Galia. Why live close to neighbors who would so quickly turn on us for a bag of gem?" Her mother's words echoed Tanwen's earlier thoughts. "You and Thol may not be like me or your father," she continued, determined. "But that's because you are better. Your first breath as you left my womb was a gift from the gods. You are proof that something new and different can exist in this world. You are our future, Tanwen. You are—"

Their den shook, the sound of wood splintering as Tanwen tumbled back into her mother's arms.

The Volari! They are back, thought Tanwen in terror as the walls of their kitchen bowed. She barely registered Eli jumping from his chair to scurry up and into her shirt's pocket, burrowing deep.

"Mother!" shouted Tanwen, steadying them both as foliage burst through the floorboards, snaking across their kitchen. The air became sweeter, headier, glistening. Flowers bloomed, radiant; a multitude of bugs, large, colorful, and winged, invaded. They no longer stood inside their den but in a woodland cave of wonder. One that continued to bend and build from the center until a form made of vines and moss and mud shifted forward.

An unfurling face of leaves stared down at them, eyes so black they might as well not have been there.

"*Bosyg,*" whispered her mother as she pulled Tanwen to kneel. "Revered goddess of our home," she said, head bowed. "Creator of all we honor and nourish, we are humbled to be before you."

"I have interrupted a moment between you and your child," stated the goddess, her voice the turning over of soil, rough and smooth at once.

"Nothing is of greater importance than the purpose of your visit," said her mother.

Tanwen's gaze was also on the floor, or what was once their floor. Now it was an ever-moving landscape of plants and bugs cycling through their birth and death.

Tanwen held in a shiver; the endless power she felt pressing against her was terrifying. She had never been in the presence of a god, and so far, she was not sure it was something she enjoyed.

"I have been dishonored this day," said Bosyg, her roots shifting. "Those who are not meant to roam in my woods have stolen from it."

"Yes," answered her mother, voice breathless. "My mate and one of my children were taken from your sanctuary by Prince Zolya and his soldiers this morning."

Their kitchen thickened with vines, a pressure of displeasure wafting from the goddess. "It is audacious of the children of the High Gods to believe themselves above the laws of my forest," exclaimed Bosyg. "They may live in the clouds, closest to my cousins, but their rule ends at my tree line."

Aisling remained quiet, no doubt unsure how to appease the Low Goddess without angering any of the High.

"I have spoken with your nyddoth and nydda, however," continued Bosyg. "And I have heard their plight regarding the trade. While I have accepted it along with their repentance, I am not fully satisfied."

"The trade?" questioned Tanwen. The words slipped out, unchecked and regrettable, as she glanced up.

To be in the presence of a god was one thing, but to stare into one was wholly another.

And it was indeed to stare *into*. For whatever magic made up Bosyg was consuming. A pulling of the mind to fall forward, as if leaping from a cliff's edge to grasp the unobtainable. A bottomless descent of yearning.

Tanwen looked away, trying to calm her fast-beating heart as she focused on a sturdier branch.

"Offering up the king's inventor has helped your clan gain more provisions from the yearly harvests," explained Bosyg.

The room tilted farther. "Our nyddoth traded my father and brother for . . . *food*?"

"*Tanwen*," admonished her mother before bowing lower before the goddess. "I apologize for my child's outburst—"

"But this is insanity!" exclaimed Tanwen. "How are you not upset?"

"Of *course* I am upset," Aisling hissed, cutting her a look. "But now is not the time to share such emotion."

"Do not worry, Mother," stated Bosyg, hand lazily stroking a python, which wove in and out of her viny abdomen. "I am not above understanding that your child's anger is directed elsewhere. I may be eternal, but I know the nuances that make up the beings that live in my forest. Even the kind that are most rare."

As the goddess's gaze bore down on Tanwen, her skin dusted with goose bumps, terror seizing.

Even the kind that are most rare.

Mütra.

Bosyg knew what she was.

But of course she did.

She was a god.

Still, Tanwen didn't know if she was meant to run or beg for forgiveness.

"You are safe here, little one," said Bosyg, as if sensing her fright, her inner turmoil. "You are no threat to me or this forest."

You are no threat. You are safe.

It was as if the air was knocked from Tanwen. Words she had not known she needed to hear grasped her heart, held it beating. A touch of acceptance. And from Bosyg, mother of their home. A Low Goddess.

Still, a flicker of anger ignited in Tanwen's chest as she sensed the contradiction in the sentiment. "Then why allow us to be hunted in your forest?" challenged Tanwen.

"Why allow a deer to be felled by your blade?" returned Bosyg, head tilting. "Or flowers to be plucked by your hand? I do not dictate how life behaves in my woods. I merely nourish the soil it grows from."

Tanwen wanted to sneer at the response, at the excuse, but instead she reluctantly understood. She was a small piece in the circle of life, and Bosyg was not responsible for where she fell in the pecking order. Still, Tanwen's cheeks burned in frustration. By the gods, she wished to change that. For once be in power, in control. To no longer hide or cower but soar free.

"However, I have always been curious why your kind became banned by King Réol," Bosyg mused. "Life is not given unless for a reason. To fight nature is futile. It is ever changing, adapting, surviving, conquering."

Around the room the foliage morphed and grew and receded with Bosyg's words; time sped up, showing every stage of life in her forest. The effect was dizzying.

"Yes, how curious," repeated Bosyg. "Why would King Réol want to prune what wishes to grow? Why would our almighty Ré grant him the power to do so?" The questions hung in the air. "Such actions are usually a sign of fear. But I wonder, little one"—the goddess's endless black gaze bore down on her—"what about you would scare a god?"

The assessing silence shifted to scheming.

Unease filled Tanwen's rapid heartbeats.

"I . . . I do not know," answered Tanwen.

She might have held unique abilities but nothing as spectacular as the children of gods had. Of the gods themselves, high or low.

"Hmm," mused Bosyg thoughtfully. "No, I don't suppose you do, which begs the question, Are you willing to find out?"

The hairs on Tanwen's neck rose, the goddess's inquiry a dangerous temptation.

What about you would scare a god? Are you willing to find out?

"Goddess," interjected her mother, voice wary. "We thank you for your concern and are humbled for your time, but we understand an immortal power such as yourself has other, more important, matters to attend to."

"I would not be here if I did not find this worthy of my attention," said Bosyg. "Are you implying my judgment is flawed?"

"No," her mother quickly replied. "Of course not, Goddess."

"We have both been wronged this day," said Bosyg. "I demand retribution. Let us see how my cousins' children like to be stolen from. It appears they are in need of a reminder that without land, there is no sky. High or low, we are all gods. I am offering you the opportunity to return home your mate and child."

Tanwen jolted in shock as her pulse kicked to racing.

I am offering you the opportunity to return home your mate and child.

Miraculous words.

"How?" breathed Tanwen, leaning forward.

Despite her better instincts not to bargain with a god, she knew this kind of opportunity would not be repeated.

And Tanwen and her mother were not currently in a position to be selective in where they found help.

"There are other ways to Galia than with wings," explained Bosyg as she captured a dancing butterfly from the air, closing her palm around it. "Ways that will allow you to enter unnoticed but remain invited." She opened her hand, letting free now dozens of butterflies, the original one lost in the crowd.

Tanwen's mind churned.

There are other ways to Galia.

"The Recruitment," whispered Tanwen, her heart a pounding drum beneath her rib cage.

Bosyg grinned.

"No." Aisling shook her head, tone the slamming of a door. "No, Wen. Absolutely not. I won't allow it. We will not become servants on Galia."

"No, *we* won't." Tanwen met her mother's hard gaze with her own. "Because you won't be coming with me. I will sign up for the Recruitment, not you. We can't risk you being recognized. Plus, they only ever want younger servants, anyway. And I am a meddyg, trained under the most gifted of meddygs. They will not pass up my skills, especially when they learn I can make docüra."

"This is madness," her mother seethed. "I will not allow you to sign your life away, Tanwen! There is no way out once enlisted. Please"—Aisling turned back to the goddess, eyes wide in her panic—"we truly thank you for your aid, but we will find another way. We will—"

"If my mother stays behind"—Tanwen cut off her mother's desperate plea, this new plan quickly hardening her resolve—"where will she go? It is no longer safe for us in Zomyad."

"Your clan does not know of what has transpired here this morning," stated Bosyg. "Your nyddoth has ensured it. There is no harm in your mother staying, but even so, I will extend my influence for additional protection. For as long as your father and brother are gone, so will their memory be from your neighbors. Your mother and your home shall remain safe in your absence."

Home.

Safe.

All Tanwen had ever wanted in life.

But with her whole family, together.

This was her opportunity to grasp that dream.

Still, Tanwen understood her mother's wariness. There would be no way out of the Recruitment once in. Her life would be owned by Volari. She'd be at the mercy of the position she was enlisted into and in debt to a Low God.

But what other solution was there? What other plan would get her access to Galia and ensure her mother was protected?

Tanwen chewed her bottom lip. This was the only way.

"And for your offered safety?" Tanwen tentatively asked. "What is it you will require in return?"

"I will grant you this favor," said Bosyg, "but a time will come when I will need a favor of my own."

And there it was, the terms of their deal.

A favor for a favor.

But why a god might seek the aid of a mortal, and a half-bred one at that, Tanwen did not know.

She only understood she could not remain still this time. She would not hide.

Her parents had been her protectors her whole life; now it was time she repay their efforts by protecting them.

"So, little one," asked Bosyg. "Do you accept this offer?" The goddess extended a single pale-pink dahlia that grew from the tip of her finger. "Shall we learn the might of a Mütra?"

"Tanwen." Her mother grasped her shoulder, desperation in her tone. "Let us think on this."

But Tanwen was already reaching out.

"Yes," she answered the goddess as she plucked free the flower.

Bosyg's smile was the stretching of moss growing over stones.

And then their surroundings blew apart, every vine and branch and plant and animal erupting before their kitchen snapped back to its original state.

Her father's cold tea and discarded bags had returned.

Bosyg had left.

Yet her flower remained, pinched between Tanwen's fingers.

A deal with a god sealed.

11

"Mother, please stop fidgeting," demanded Tanwen from where they stood in line outside the Recruitment Office. "You're making me nervous."

"Good," said Aisling as she continued to play with the buttons on her shirt, her gaze incessantly darting to every passing citizen. "You should be nervous," she went on. "This is a mistake."

"Yes," huffed Tanwen. "You've been saying that since we left our den."

It had taken them a full day to travel to Ordyn, and despite the early hours, the Recruitment Office was busy. It appeared Tanwen wasn't the only one looking for passage to Galia. A group of people, some older and others barely past puberty, waited for their interviews.

"Because it remains true," said her mother. "We should be heading north."

"It is too late for that," reasoned Tanwen, more than tired of their cyclical argument. "We agreed that heading north held no plan except hiding, *again*. Besides, it's not as though I can back out of what's been agreed upon with a god."

"*Hush*," admonished her mother, gaze bouncing to those beside them in line.

None paid them mind, too absorbed in their own whispered conversations with loved ones or standing alone wearing hollow stares. Their thoughts were clearly preoccupied with their own reasons for being here.

Still, Tanwen lowered her voice. "Well?" she questioned. "Do you think we can back out?"

Her mother exhaled her frustration. "We could have changed course if you did not accept the offer."

And here they were again.

It wasn't as if Tanwen *wanted* to be indebted to a Low God or to be signing up to be a lifelong servant to the Volari, but with each day's fading light, she knew whatever fate her father and brother faced only grew closer. With every moment they waited, mourned, questioned, Tanwen feared the possibility of their family ever being reunited grew slimmer, more impossible. The vision of Thol and her father receding into the sky haunted her.

She could not let them fade further from her memory.

She could not wait.

She could not hide.

Not this time.

If only because she knew Thol wouldn't hide either. He'd do whatever it took to get her back.

As for her parents, how could either of them remain motionless when their mate and child were taken?

The thought sent a rush of fire to Tanwen's lungs.

"As I see it," began Tanwen, tone sharp, "you should be thanking me. I'm stepping up to save our family. Or do you not want to get Father and Thol back?"

Aisling's gaze swung to meet hers, wide and furious. "You are being unfair and cruel," she snapped. "I want more *than my own life* for my husband and son to be safely returned, but nothing done right is done in haste."

Tanwen's cheeks flushed with her shame. "I apologize," she said, not enjoying how erratic her emotions were becoming. How quickly she wanted to scream before pulling her mother into a hug. It was as if she was reliving her adolescent years. "Of course I know you want to save them," she reassured. "It's just—we can't afford to wait. Bosyg came to us. She suggested this route. Promised her protection for you while I'm gone, and as it appears"—Tanwen nodded to the passing citizens, none of whom glanced their way—"she spoke true about no one knowing what transpired yesterday."

"For now," countered Aisling.

"Mother." Tanwen placed a gentle hand on her shoulder, wanting to erase the worried crease in her mother's brow. "You have the promise of safety from a Low God. The relief of not needing to explain Father's and Thol's absence to anyone. What more reassurance do you need?"

"That *you* will be safe," said Aisling, covering Tanwen's hand with her own, her grip tightening. "I . . . have already lost a husband and son. I cannot also lose you."

Anguish pooled inside Tanwen's chest.

"Father and Thol are *not* lost," Tanwen reasoned, though as she spoke, she felt the uncertainty of her words. But she could not go down that road of thought. They *had* to be capable of being saved. "And I will send you letters as often as I can," she reassured.

Her mother shook her head. "All notes from Süra are read before they are sent from Galia. It won't be safe."

"I do not intend to send my letters by way of regular post." She eyed her mother meaningfully.

Volari weren't the only ones with wings in Cādra. Tanwen had requested favors from birds before. Nothing a bit of sweet bread couldn't bribe.

"No, Tanwen," urged her mother. "You can't risk—"

"Next six in line," interrupted a gruff voice.

Tanwen looked up, realizing they had moved to the front of the office. The burly guard at the entrance waved the next group forward.

"I'll be right back," Tanwen said to her mother, trying to ignore the panic in her gaze, which only worsened her own rising anxiety.

What am I about to do?

As Tanwen was funneled in with the next group, she eyed the two painted posters that hung on either side of the entryway. Each depicted a Süra smiling as sunrays warmed their cheeks, standing in front of parted clouds and a blue sky.

SERVE THEIR CHILDREN, AND YOU WILL SERVE THE HIGH GODS, one of them read.

LIVE HIGHER. SOAR WITH PURPOSE. PROSPER AS IF YOU HAD WINGS, read another.

Neither helped ease Tanwen's disquiet as she was guided through a brightly lit hall and into a circular room filled with desks and chairs arranged along a curved wall.

Despite its clean appearance, the air still hung stale: the breath of too many people mixed. Tanwen wrinkled her nose as she was directed to a stall.

As she sat, she was met by an older man sitting across from her, desk between them. The tip of one of his horns was chipped, and his mess of dark hair alluded to his lack of a hairbrush. The only orderly part of him was the shiny silver wings pinned to his shirt, a symbol of a high-ranked employee for Galia.

He didn't care to look up at Tanwen as he readied new papers and refilled his ink holder.

"Name?" he asked, tone revealing he cared little for what her name might be.

"Tanwen Cos—ters," she corrected quickly, realizing in a panic it would likely be best not to use a surname associated with her family.

"Tanwen Costers," the Recruitment officer repeated, scribbling her answer onto a form.

"Age?"

"Two and twenty."

"Your trade?"

"Meddyg."

"Mmm, Volari don't use Süra healers," he grunted. "And we have enough meddygs for the staff on Galia."

Tanwen's hands tightened on her thighs, nerves spiking, though she had been prepared for this.

"I can make docüra," she explained.

The recruitment officer finally looked up at her, eyes narrowing. "Can you now?"

"Yes, and I have brought some as proof." Tanwen unclasped her side purse to pull out a small vial. The docüra churned a midnight galaxy as she handed it to him.

The man gave it a swirl, brows pinched before he uncorked it and sniffed. His eyes shot wide as he looked back at her with new interest.

"If you did make this," he began while pocketing her sample, "you'll do well in Galia. They prefer those who already know how to make docüra over needing to teach the craft. I'll recommend that you be stationed at Sumora. They only take the pretty ones, anyway."

Tanwen frowned. "What is Sumora?"

"A docüra den," he explained. "One of the best in Galia, actually. You are lucky I am feeling so generous this morning to suggest you be stationed there. The clientele are usually all court members."

When Tanwen didn't react to such intel, the man huffed at her ignorance.

"This means you'll be making a higher compensation than most, muffin," he clarified. "Eight gem a week is what I hear it starts for green recruits."

"Eight gem . . . a *week*?" Tanwen breathed out her shock.

"Mmm," grunted the man, finally satisfied with her reaction. "And if you prove worthy, your tips could outmatch that. So you're welcome," he added gruffly while feeling over where he had pocketed her docüra.

By the twin moons, thought Tanwen, *no wonder people seek work on Galia*. She had never made such a weekly sum.

This Sumora must really be one of the best dens to offer such compensation, which had Tanwen wondering . . .

"Is Sumora near the palace?" she asked.

The recruiter's gaze lifted, a pinch between his brows. "It is in Fioré, the town below. Why?"

"I . . . just have friends who work in the palace," Tanwen quickly explained, heartbeat tumbling, to remove his suspicion. "I didn't know if I'd be able to see them."

"I would not waste prayers to the High Gods about it," he huffed, returning to completing her form. "Do you have anyone in Zomyad you'd like to send a percentage of your monthly earnings?"

Tanwen shifted, not prepared for such a question. Wariness filled her gut. Her mother could certainly benefit from the money she would make now that she'd be alone, but Tanwen was unsure of the risk of mentioning the exact location of their den or Aisling by name.

"No," she said. "There is no one."

The recruiter recorded her answer before continuing with a litany of other questions. The interview felt simultaneously excessive and too short before a stack of papers was swiveled her way. "Sign here, here, here, and here." He indicated.

After Tanwen scratched her name onto the various parchments, the rest of the process went by with a blur. Soon the recruiter was handing her a copy of her file along with a leather bifold wallet. Inside was a small card with her details: her name, new surname, worker number, and place of employment all stamped with a winged seal.

She was officially recruited into serving the Volari in Galia.

Indefinitely.

Oh gods, what have I done?

Tanwen swallowed down the bile rising in her throat as she gripped her papers, her hands beginning to shake.

This is a mistake. The voice of her mother rose, worried and regretful, in her mind.

No, thought Tanwen. *No.* It wasn't a mistake. At least not yet.

"Do *not* lose that card," the recruiter advised, snapping Tanwen's attention back to where he pointed to her bifold. "That is your entrance paper to Galia. You will not be able to get in or out without it."

Tanwen nodded, hugging the document closer.

"Even with your mark, you'll need your papers."

"My mark?" questioned Tanwen.

"Yes, let me see your wrist."

"Why?" She held her arm rigidly against her chest, brows furrowing.

"Give it here, girl," huffed the recruiter impatiently, holding out his hand. As he did, Tanwen noticed a faded scar on his wrist peeking out from his shirtsleeve. "It is the smallest discomfort, and then you will be an official recruit. Unless you want to revoke your application and stay here?"

Tanwen rubbed her lips together, uncertainty swirling as she glanced around. No one seemed to be screaming, and a few Süra who had entered with her were already taking their leave, approved papers in hand.

Another had been denied and was pleading for the officer to reconsider as he was dragged out of the room.

Tanwen hesitantly offered up her wrist.

With quick work, the recruiter cleaned her skin with a blot of alcohol, picked up a stamp that rested in a shallow bowl of clear liquid, and emphatically pressed it to her wrist.

Tanwen hissed, the burning instant, but then it was but a tingle as the man lifted the stamp to reveal a red marking of a pair of wings now on the inside of her right wrist. The same symbol that was pinned to the man's shirt and peeking out from his sleeve.

"You stamped me with acid," said Tanwen, already noting her skin blistering. She hadn't noticed this mark before on others who worked on Galia. But then again, she wasn't usually around many other people.

"A mild mixture," the recruiter explained. "By tomorrow it will be a light scar. It is a symbol to be proud of," he reasoned.

More like a branding to regret, thought Tanwen morosely.

"Congratulations," said the recruiter. "You are welcomed onto Galia. Go through that door." He pointed to an exit on the other side of the room. "You'll wait for the next convoy there. One should be leaving before midmeal. May the gods bless your journey." He placed a hand over his silver pin. "And the children of the High thank you for your service."

Tanwen stood on shaky legs, mind in a fog before she realized exactly what was about to happen. What already *had* happened. "Wait," she said, pulse hurrying as she turned back to the recruiter. "I need to say goodbye to someone outside. She also has another of my satchels."

"Make it quick." He waved her off. "A guard will accompany you back to where you need to be."

With a whooshing filling her head, Tanwen felt unsteady as she met her mother outside.

Aisling instantly pulled her into a hug.

Tanwen fought the tears wrestling to be free as she soaked in her mother's warmth. If she cried, it would only make this parting worse. Would only put more fear into her mother's heart and mind. Aisling had been a rock most of Tanwen's life, her stoic guide. Tanwen needed to be that now for her mother.

"I've been accepted to work in one of the docüra dens, called Sumora," explained Tanwen, stepping from her mother's embrace. "They said it is one of the best in Fioré."

Aisling's attention was momentarily pulled to the winged red mark on Tanwen's inner wrist. A shadow passed across her features, but then it was gone as she met Tanwen's gaze.

"Yes," said her mother. "Sumora is one of the best." A swallow in her throat. "Wen," she began, brows furrowing. "Now that we know where you'll be stationed, there's something else I need to tell you." There was a pause, as if her mother was gathering the words but loathed to speak them. It did not instill confidence in Tanwen. "While you have administered docüra during Süra ceremonies," said her mother, "and have seen its effects and learned the purpose for its use here on Cādra, you must know that what has been said about the Volari is true. They use docüra very differently. It's their blood," she explained. "The magic it holds, I suppose. It makes them react differently to the drug than Süra. Because of this, they use docüra for pleasure and parties. It is but a form to help with their entertainment, like wine."

"That is a very expensive glass of wine," said Tanwen.

"Yes," agreed her mother. "One they can afford. But there is something else you must understand about this. The docüra dens in Galia are not like the dens in Zomyad."

"What do you mean?"

"They are more like . . . taverns."

"Taverns?" questioned Tanwen, confused by such a comparison. Where in a tavern were the meditation rooms and altars to the gods one wished to commune with? Where were the alcoves where a meddyg could help a patient heal from a hardship?

To administer docüra in a tavern felt sacrilegious.

"Yes," assured her mother. "Like I said, Volari react differently. While I'm sure they could still use it as Süra do, they do not seek that experience. After all, why fall into a trance to speak with a god when they are often visited by them in Galia?"

Tanwen took in this information with unease, as well as its implications.

"I tell you this so you can prepare yourself for what you will find at Sumora," reasoned her mother. "You are skilled in your craft, yes, but at Sumora you will be seen as if a barmaid. A pretty and entertaining companion to their patrons."

Tanwen shot up her brows, a creeping of disquiet icing through her veins. "I fear that is not all you wish to tell me."

"It is not." Aisling shook her head. "While it is forbidden for Süra and Volari to marry and reproduce," she continued, her voice lowering to a mere whisper, "that does not keep many from . . . taking liberties. *Especially* with servants. Do you understand? You *must* be careful, Wen, and not for the usual reasons."

Tanwen blinked, that whooshing filling her head once more, the numbness returning to her legs.

They only take the pretty ones, anyway.

Regret was a chill working up Tanwen's spine, one she quickly forced away. She could *not* regret this.

She could not!

Her mother was warning her of the possibilities, not the predictions.

Besides, Tanwen had learned how to extricate herself from many undesirable situations. Had taught herself how to be invisible in a crowded room. She could do this. She *would* do this.

Because she had no other choice.

"I understand," said Tanwen, the words coming out heavy on her tongue.

Aisling nodded but appeared no less appeased. "Just remember to administer the docüra fast. Once under the drug, they will not be a threat. They will be sluggish, and you should easily be able to remove yourself."

"I'll remember," she said, forcing a tone of confidence, but her mother must have seen through it, must have still caught the waver of fear in her gaze, for she placed steadying hands onto Tanwen's shoulders, her stoic self returned.

"You are not merely my wyrthia, Tanwen," said her mother, expression earnest. "You are also Thol's and your father's. I am *so* proud of you. For who you are right now, in this moment. You are strong and intelligent and brave. You are special. Which is why you *must* come home to me—do you understand?" Her mother's grip tightened, her eyes glossing with unshed tears. "If ever there was a time to listen to me, it's now. You *must* come home."

Tanwen only nodded, scared to speak lest she sob.

"Oy, girl," called a gruff voice, turning their attention to the guard who had guided her out. He stood waiting by the Recruitment Office's door. "You said you'd be quick."

"She's coming," answered her mother before pulling Tanwen back to face her. "The last thing I need to tell you is this." She reached into her pocket to draw out a small glass jar filled with fine gray dust. She pushed it into Tanwen's hands. "It's Volari feathers," she whispered.

"What?" Tanwen frowned, glancing at the small bottle.

"That is the secret spice," explained her mother. "What it is that I add. What makes my docüra a more potent mixture."

"Volari feathers?" breathed Tanwen in awe, pulse skipping quickly as she studied the small dark grains more intently. "But . . . how did you get—"

"Your father," interrupted her mother, furtively glancing behind Tanwen to the waiting guard. She urged Tanwen to put the vial into her pack. "Before they were taken from him."

"Why are you telling me this now?" asked Tanwen, clipping her bag back in place.

"Because now it's necessary," she explained. "I did not know where you'd be stationed, but I suspected it could be in a den if you shared your abilities with the recruiter. You will be tested there, Tanwen, made to prove that you are an asset. One that can bring in money. This can help with that"—she nodded at what was now hidden in Tanwen's bag—"but you must remember, *only* use it when you must. When it will mean something. And *only* a pinch. You mustn't let anyone know what makes your mixture different. Let them think it is special because *you* made it. Because *you* administered it. If you want to get into the palace, you'll want to rise above the others, but not by too much," she added quickly. "The beautiful roses are the ones who get cut and brought inside. The ones who grow too tall get pruned."

"How do you know all this?" asked Tanwen. "About the dens in Galia."

"You forget who I am married to." Aisling's smile was soft, pained. "And that I worked the Dryfs Mine. Much of what transpired in Galia flowed through those tunnels. Gossip was more filling than the served stale bread. But you must go now. That guard looks as though he's ready to stomp over here and drag you back inside."

Tanwen glanced behind her, noting that her mother was right. The man eyed her impatiently as he waved rather dramatically for her to return.

This was it.

She was about to leave, alone.

"I love you." Tanwen fell back into her mother's arms. She breathed deep her scent of gardenia, attempting to hold it forever in her heart's memory.

"I love you," replied Aisling, grip squeezing before she let her go and handed Tanwen her other pack.

As Tanwen shouldered both of them, the heaviness of her task and the need for her to succeed suddenly pressed down on her like the weight of the surrounding trees. Crushing.

"I'll see you soon," said her mother.

Tanwen nodded, her voice held hostage by the pain slicing across her heart.

She then turned and walked away from the only family she might have left.

PART III

ASCEND

12

In a windowless room, on the outskirts of the palace, a father and son together were trapped.

But despite their tight proximity, they could not be farther apart.

No longer would Gabreel's son look at him.

Nor would he talk.

They were now estranged, divided by invisible insurmountable suffering.

And the inventor wished to set everything aflame.

Gabreel's sky magic pulsed at his fingertips, cascaded like a wash of lava across his palms as he leaned on the worktable. The papers beneath his hands hissed as they burned, but Gabreel cared little for the damage. He was too busy eyeing Aberthol, who sat chained on the far side of the room, nearest the locked door.

Gabreel worked to find any cut or bruise or break peeking from his son's washed and pressed clothes. But besides his hollow eyes, wilted posture, and disheveled hair, Aberthol appeared whole.

As he was the first time he had been returned.

Which only spurred worse imaginings from Gabreel.

What internal monstrosities has my son faced?

The question sent Gabreel reeling in anguish, knowing the answers were unending.

He had tried to approach Aberthol multiple times, but his son always shrank away, shielding himself as if Gabreel was there to continue his torment.

And perhaps he was.

Everything they now faced was because of him.

What he had done and yet now could not do.

Gabreel leaned more heavily on the table, bile rising up his throat as he returned his gaze to the papers in front of him. He forced a deep breath, drinking in the thick scent of ink and parchment and fresh balsa wood that filled the room. Once a fragrance that had calmed his nerves, it now only sent them buzzing in disquiet.

Gabreel was not here to better. He was not locked up in the hopes that when he reemerged, he would birth wonder or ingenuity.

No, Gabreel was here to dig another catacomb.

And his son was allowed with him not for comfort but as a threat.

See who will suffer if you disobey. This was the king's everlasting vow of encouragement.

A vow he upheld.

If Gabreel worked, proved progress in his engineering, Aberthol would remain by his side. If he showed that he was stalling or had stagnated, his son would be pulled away, not to be returned until the morning.

As had happened last night.

When Gabreel had dared to once again choose his conscience, his wife's people over his king's wishes.

Over his child.

At the thought, a roar surged up his throat, the suffocation of his position caving in, but he clenched his teeth to keep his scream at bay. Making noise would only attract the guards outside his workroom.

Gabreel could not afford for them to see how little he had done today.

More importantly, his son could not afford that.

With a frustrated exhale, Gabreel pushed aside the burned papers to study the old ones he had been supplied.

Each held failed attempts from his predecessor to build a strong enough infrastructure for the new mining site. Most held similar issues Gabreel had endured at the Dryfs, but this time, despite this new location proving wealth, it was situated dangerously close to the exposed cliffside. Closer even than the Dryfs. The unceasing pounding waves of the Aspero Sea were forever an obstacle and an unfortunate by-product of their gems and ambrü forming only in such rough conditions.

But that was the way of precious commodities.

Currency held value only in its scarcity and the effort required to obtain it.

Though Gabreel knew the treasury didn't wish for their currency to be *this* scarce.

Gabreel shuffled through the drawings, drinking in the different crosscut proposals, shaft designs, and ways André Bardrex had wished to access the various veins of precious rock. But every calculation kept collapsing at the same point. So far Bardrex had only been able to tap the shallowest ore body, and that would not long sustain what the treasury needed.

The soil was too wet at this new location. Too easy to crumble, fall, fail.

This was what Gabreel needed to solve.

Solve so more Süra could be sent into its bowels.

Ire bubbled through Gabreel's veins before a rattling cough snapped his attention to Aberthol.

His son was bent over, hacking for breath.

Gabreel sprang to his side, cup of water in hand.

"No," wheezed Aberthol, recoiling from his touch, but his cough had him barreling over again.

Gabreel caught him, whispered gentle comforts while urging him to drink.

A wash of relief filled him as his son finally accepted the cup, the shackles on his wrists clanking as he drank.

But Gabreel's reprieve was short lived when he spotted the blood marking his son's hand, splattered from his lips.

Fury was an explosion that left Gabreel hotter than the sun.

What have they done to my child?

Aberthol cried out, snapping Gabreel back to where he held his son, grip burning.

In a panic, Gabreel sprang away, his eyes wide in horror as he caught the tears tracking down Aberthol's cheeks.

But it was not anguish that filled his son's gaze; it was hatred.

Hatred that pierced Gabreel.

A thousand blades puncturing Gabreel's heart as he took in a stuttering breath. Never had Aberthol looked at him thus. Never had Gabreel thought it possible.

Despite all he and Aisling had sacrificed to raise their family, it was his children's love that kept him going. Kept him determined in their chosen life, their hidden life.

But how quickly the king had stolen everything he had worked so hard to acquire. First his freedom, then his family, and now his son, turned against him.

A crippling pain flooded through Gabreel, a desperate apology poised at his lips for hurting his Aberthol, when the door swung open.

"What is going on?" asked the stern voice of a guard. His brown wings twitched at his back, no doubt feeling the discomfort of the tight-walled and windowless space.

"What have you done to my son?" Gabreel seethed in return, his remorse redirecting to ire. "He is coughing blood."

The guard looked to Aberthol, and Gabreel instinctually positioned himself in front of him.

"Well," said Gabreel. "Don't just stand there. I require warm water and crushed barlimant. And I need them quickly, or you'll be blamed for my delay in today's work."

The guard appeared unsure what to do with such a command, but evidently Gabreel still held a bit of his Volari demeanor, for the man eventually left to do as he was bid. The lock on the door clunked into place.

"Aberthol," said Gabreel gently as he turned back to his son. "I am so sorry."

Sorry for burning you. Sorry for bringing you here. Sorry for everything.

But his son had slipped back into whatever fog he had swum in earlier, where the pain of his present and past must not have existed. Where even the voice of his father—once capable of gleaning the reverent wonderment of his child—could not awaken him.

Blood still stained the corners of Aberthol's lips, but Gabreel left it there, fearing another rebuke. He did not want to be the cause of any more of his son's pain.

Gabreel realized then grief was like drowning. It burned, sparked panic until there was no fight left. Until you gave in to the cold darkness of your fate.

With a chill enveloping his heart, Gabreel returned to his worktable.

But this time his mind was clear as he gathered the papers and readied his pen.

He was not a hero of a story.

Not someone built to carry the weight of the world's problems.

He was merely a father desperate to protect his child.

And if that caused him to fail others, fail another of his vows to himself, so be it.

Forgive me, he thought silently to Aisling, his chest splintering. *It's what must be done, my love.*

So long as he was the key to keep Aberthol from suffering more nightmares, Gabreel would build the king's new mine and any other monstrosity he commanded.

13

Tanwen was flying.

Her stomach was permanently lodged in her throat as the gondola raced upward through the clouds. She gripped the railing as the cage swayed in the wind. She didn't want to think about the single thick rope their contraption clung to, the only support keeping them from plummeting into the angry Aspero Sea below.

By the Low Gods, I'm going to be sick, she thought.

As am I, squeaked Eli within the pack on her back.

Tanwen could sense him burrowing beneath her clothes, fighting the chill. She had found the cheeky bugger hiding inside quickly after departing Ordyn, and, despite reprimanding him because of the dangers in coming, she was glad he had stolen away. His presence kept her from being overwhelmed by her uncertain future.

At least we made it past the checkpoint, reasoned Tanwen silently, attempting to shift her thoughts from where they precariously dangled.

I might have preferred being back beneath all those vultures, Eli griped.

I certainly do not, Tanwen argued. *I will take freezing-cold cloud coverage over suffering those whooshing shadows any day.*

They had reached the western Galia checkpoint at dawn, and despite the early hours, the skies had been filled with dozens of Volari soaring home. It had been difficult for Tanwen not to constantly flinch as she shuffled forward in line.

Tanwen yipped—a sudden whip of wind smashed into the gondola.

The cage groaned its protest as her stomach bounced into her throat, her grip white knuckled on the banister.

Still prefer the clouds? Eli taunted.

Tanwen's rebuttal was stolen as they finally pierced through the last bit of cloud and into the raw, uncovered light of day.

The brightness was a slap to her senses. Intrusive and harsh.

Tanwen squinted, shielding her eyes as the massive island of Galia rose from the clouds like the barnacled back of a turtle breaching waves. A jutting expanse of carved perfection that could have been made possible only by the luxury of endless time.

Tanwen gasped, the beauty nearly overwhelming.

Everything was green, lush, alive. And it sparkled. All of it.

Ré's wash of sunlight bounced off every manicured surface, saturated each piece of foliage, and brushed open the petals of every flower. It was a deluge of colors and blooms.

Of life.

Fioré, the town they rushed toward, sprawled like dollops of rich icing, white roofs with massive skylights, pantheons and open-air markets reaching and hugging the edge of a glistening lake. The water was so blue it might as well have been the sky that filled it.

The only thing breaking the peace was the flapping of hundreds of wings.

Volari were everywhere.

Tanwen instinctively shrank back, her senses on high alert as her attention was drawn, up and up and up, to the top of a jungle mountainside.

The palace glowed as if a piece of Ré himself had been carved out and placed meticulously at the tip. The white marble of the domed citadel radiated with power; the massive, reaching pillars shimmered, a beating heart.

And her father and brother were somewhere within. Trapped. Possibly in pain. Suffering.

But not for long.

Daydreams of vengeance blossomed in Tanwen's mind, thawing her chilled skin.

The prince had swooped into her home, stealing away her family. Now here Tanwen soared, promising to do the same.

◆ ◆ ◆

"Line up against this wall," commanded their Süra guide after Tanwen and the new recruits had been divided into their respective services. "The den madams will be here soon for your inspections."

Tanwen was pushed and jostled into a row with ten other young women, her nerves anxious like plucked strings.

The energy around her was chaotic, a bustling Fioré spilling out on all sides.

Their gondola had docked next to an outdoor market, where the air was filled with the lively chatter of vendors hawking their goods and citizens negotiating prices. Ré's morning light glistened over the endless displays of ornate pottery and drapes of fine silks hanging in stalls, while the tantalizing scent of spices mixed with caramelized fruits.

If it wasn't for the surrounding ostentatious architecture, bright sun, and endless swooping shadows of Volari overhead, Fioré could have been mistaken for Ordyn. The diversity of citizens was vast. Horns of every shape and curve filled the crowd. Even the shop attendants were Süra.

Tanwen felt the energy in her line change, drawing her attention to a group of elegantly dressed older women approaching. The girls beside her stood straighter.

Of the newcomers, a curvaceous woman in flowing lilac silk approached their line first. Her horns were tall and twisted like those of Süra from Garw. Her dark skin shone smooth in the morning light as she glanced down her nose at the first girl in their row. By her side was an assistant, reading aloud the information provided on the recruit's papers.

"Who's that?" asked Tanwen in a whisper to the recruit to her left.

"That's Madam Kyva," said the girl, a waver of fear in her voice. "She runs Sumora."

The hairs rose on the back of Tanwen's neck.

That's where we're meant to go, said Eli from where he remained hidden in her pack. *I want to see.*

No, Tanwen hissed silently. *You must stay put,* she instructed, watching as two of the recruits whom Madam Kyva inspected were pushed to form another line, their expressions grave.

"What's happening?" Tanwen asked of the girl beside her again.

"They weren't chosen," she explained with a swallow.

"What does that mean?"

"They will be left for the other madams to review. If they are passed up again, they will most likely go to the dens in the Shadow District."

Tanwen frowned. "What's the Shadow District?"

Fearful blue eyes fervently caught hers. "Nowhere either of us wants to be."

Tanwen's blood ran cold, the wait for her inspection torturously long, but eventually Madam Kyva stopped before Tanwen. Her floral perfume pressed into Tanwen as their gazes collided.

Tanwen dutifully lowered her eyes, but she could feel Madam Kyva's scrutinization sliding over her body, calculating, measuring.

At Sumora you will be seen as if a barmaid. A pretty and entertaining companion to their patrons.

The sobering words of Tanwen's mother rose up in her mind.

You must be careful, Wen, and not for the usual reasons.

Tanwen held out her papers for the awaiting attendant.

"This is Tanwen Costers from Zomyad," he read. "She is recommended to serve in Sumora. Her trade was meddyg in her clan, and it says she knows how to make docüra."

The following silence was thick, a slow assessment.

"How many clients have you served docüra?" asked Madam Kyva.

Tanwen was momentarily caught off guard by the question, but she recovered quickly.

"No fewer than two dozen, ma'am," she answered.

"Hmm," replied Madam Kyva. "Show me your hands."

Tanwen did as she was commanded.

"You will need a good scrubbing," observed Madam Kyva before she walked to the next girl in line.

Tanwen blinked, her fear spiking.

What does that mean?

But then her papers were shoved back into her grip, a new red mark stamped on the top: **APPROVED**.

Tanwen's hands shook as she read the word over and over.

Her future was decided.

She was in.

Despite her nerves, Tanwen looked up, finding the shining palace atop the distant mountain, and smiled.

14

Zolya decided he needed to stop attending these dinners.

Despite the stretch of steaming and teeming savory dishes laid before him, the accompanying conversation succeeded only in souring his appetite.

Which was a quick path to souring his mood.

As Zolya leaned against his armrest, he idly sipped his wine, the rich flavor inspiring little enjoyment as he listened to the exchanges taking place within the banquet hall.

There was the hostess of the evening, Princess Azla, and her lady-in-waiting, Lady Esme, hands grazing where they sat beside one another at the far end of the table. Osko was in attendance along with Zander Aetos, another of their senior kidars. The final guest was Lady Lorelei, of the Sun Court, a past lover of Zolya's and someone whose company he usually enjoyed but whom he currently was in no mood to entertain.

From the echoing of voices rising toward the skylight, one would think he sat before his entire court rather than the intimate gathering of six.

Zolya took another swig of his drink, wings shifting at his back with his annoyance.

Or perhaps he was bored.

Whichever he was, he was assuredly tired.

Tired of the same discourse.

Tired of his presence needed at every affair.

Tired of—

"My prince," said Lady Lorelei, drawing his attention to where she sat to his left. She was a vision of lavish expense, muted silks, and drapes of jewels. The distant night sky was her backdrop, framing her sand-colored wings, the plumage matching the massive billowing curtains hung around the room. "You have been awfully quiet on the topic," she observed. "What say you of the uprising of Mütra sympathizers Kidar Terz tells us of in Zomyad?"

The table fell silent as every eye turned his way. Even the towering columns appeared to bow forward, the stars in the heavens glowing brighter in anticipation of his answer.

The High Gods were listening.

"I waste little thought on them," replied Zolya. "They are for Nyddoth Marwth to handle, as they are in his domain."

"Surely such sympathizers are not only in Zomyad," said Princess Azla, her brown complexion made warm by the light of the nearby candelabras, her white wings and hair a matching pair to Zolya's. When together, there could be no denying their shared blood or shared father. It was also only because of her that Zolya suffered through these affairs. There was little he wouldn't do to help Azla have an easier time at court. If becoming the gatekeeper to a private dinner with himself helped, then so be it.

"The law against Mütra stretches the whole of Cādra," explained Zolya. "So your assumption is likely correct."

"And still you do not waste time thinking of them?" countered Lady Lorelei, her pale cheek catching the light bouncing from her ambrü earrings. "When there could very well be sympathizers in Galia?"

"If there are, they keep their thoughts to themselves," reasoned Zolya. "An effect of them knowing their fate if they voiced their beliefs here, let alone attempted to stir an uprising. As it is now, there is little we can do about one's quiet musings." *And thank the stars for that,* finished Zolya to himself. He would certainly never admit to it, but he understood why there were those who were displeased with the treatment of Mütra. He himself found the discrimination against them barbaric. After all, they held souls like the rest of them, were given the gift of life despite the rarity of the two races procreating. If anything, their existence was more of a miracle.

But there, of course, lay the problem. Only the king was meant to be a marvel.

"The issue, I see," began Zander as he swirled his glass, his twiglike form poised on the edge of his bench, "are these stories the Süra sympathizers are spreading."

"What stories?" inquired Princess Azla.

"Tales that we are scared of the Mütra."

Osko snorted his disbelief. "Is a hawk scared of the fish he hunts? What is there to fear of these mongrels?"

"Mütra do hold magic," said Lady Lorelei. "And an unpredictable kind."

"*Some* hold magic," corrected Osko. "And even then, it is a watered-down, useless trick. Nothing compared to what the High Gods have bestowed to us, their children. The Mütra are thieves of blood not destined for them."

"Then why are they created?"

The dinner table fell quiet, heads turning toward Lady Esme.

"My love?" inquired Princess Azla, a nervous flutter to her voice.

"It is not a shocking question," reasoned Lady Esme, a single amber brow raised. "And I certainly am not the first to have asked it. I'm merely offering a counterpoint to your argument, Kidar Terz. If life is not meant to be, why would the gods, high or low, bestow it on the coupling of a Süra and Volari?" she challenged. "And, besides, isn't proclaiming that Mütra are thieves of High Gods' blood insinuating that our benevolent creators are capable of being stolen from?"

Zolya fought back a grin, observing Lady Esme more closely as her words echoed his thoughts. Born into one of the oldest families of the Sun Court, Lady Esme had been beside his sister for over three decades, her fiery wings and hair always an accompanying accessory to the princess, stirring from her a laugh or warm smile. But despite the proximity, Zolya had not paid much mind to what beliefs she might harbor.

Or perhaps that was Lady Esme's intention.

As she held Osko's gaze, Zolya noted the keen spark in her eyes. Quickly did he then ascertain that he had sorely underestimated the intelligence of his sister's lady-in-waiting.

"I am insinuating no such thing," huffed Osko, offense clear in the slamming down of his brows.

"Of course you are not," appeased Lady Lorelei from across the table. "The High Gods rule over the entire universe. They cannot pay attention to every weed that sprouts."

"Precisely." Osko nodded.

"That is why they have created us, is it not, Kidar Terz?" continued Lady Lorelei, dazzling smile aimed at Osko. "To watch over that which they have made. Or, more specifically, why we have the strength and powerful sky magic of our men and the wisdom of our king: to retain order in our otherwise wild lands."

"Well, aren't you charming." Zander tutted beside Lady Lorelei. "I can now see how you have risen in ranks to charm our prince. Tell us, sire," he engaged Zolya. "Does she spin similar beautiful bedtime stories for you after you've lain with her?"

Osko laughed at Zander's coarse remark.

The women at the table, however, appeared less than amused, much like Zolya.

He watched in annoyance as Lady Lorelei forced herself to control her expression, settling on a placating grin as she nodded her acknowledgment of his jest.

Displeasure was a sour bite across Zolya's tongue.

"Lady Lorelei *is* the beautiful bedtime story," he replied curtly, pinning Zander with a hard stare. "The likes of which I fear you will never experience, Kidar Aetos. From what I hear, you seem only capable of nightmarish bed partners."

This had Osko guffawing even harder as Zander's features flattened.

Zolya met Lorelei's gaze. Something flashed too quickly through her features to note, but she gave him a small grateful smile, a blush filling her cheeks.

He had an urge to reach out and touch her hand in reassurance, but he thought better of it. They may have shared relations for a time, but it had ebbed naturally. Zolya did not want to send her the wrong message. Too often his acts of kindness were interpreted as debts, ones that the women of court felt they needed to repay with their bodies.

Such behavior never sat well with Zolya.

He wanted his bed partners to be with him out of desire, not duty to a crown. Moreover, the additional pressure from courtiers offering their daughters at every function, wishing to tie themselves to a future king, made Zolya even more cautious and deliberate with how and whom he pursued.

"While we are on the topic of late-night trysts," interjected Princess Azla, sitting straighter on her bench. "I wanted to discuss an idea those at court have been wondering about, sire, and something I would very much like to grant."

Unease danced up Zolya's spine as he met his sister-cousin's stare. He knew that look, and it never brought him joy. "I fear you will tell me whether I wish to discuss it or not," he replied.

"Your fears are sound." Azla's grin widened. "I would like to host a welcome-home celebration in honor of your return, sire, along with the success of your and your men's mission."

"No."

"Oh, Zolya," she huffed, wings drooping along with her polite decorum. "It has been too long since the palace has had anything worthy to celebrate."

"She is not wrong," agreed Osko as he carved up a slice of meat, then talked through his chew. "Our kidets would certainly appreciate the gesture after such a lengthy time away."

"Not that I enjoy treating those fools," added Zander, "but I agree. This would also be well timed for more than inspiring our soldiers. An extravagant soiree could distract from the nervous chatter at court."

"What chatter?" questioned Zolya, brows pinching.

"Well, as you know, sire," said Zander, "the reappearance of Gabreel Heiro and his Mütra spawn has caused quite the stir."

Zolya waited for the point of such an apparent observation.

"And many are saying," Zander continued, though less assured, "that Galia must be in a dire state to return the traitorous inventor to his former role for our king. They wonder"—he paused, sending regretful furtive glances to the dinner guests—"well, if more than filling an already hearty treasury hinges on the success of this new mine."

Annoyance was a pouring of heat in Zolya's chest. Not only to hear that the courts appeared wise to the palace's current affairs—never a pleasant situation to assuage—but to have mention of Gabreel. Zolya's thoughts had finally had a few blessed days of silence regarding the inventor and his son, from the guilt in bringing them here. To suffer.

"Is this true?" Zolya asked Azla. Like her lady-in-waiting, the princess might play the innocent, but he knew it only disguised her cunning. If something was happening at court, she would know.

"No offense to the princess," interrupted Zander with a frown, "but these political nuances are surely too complicated for a lady's mind to grasp."

Zolya made a mental note for Zander to be forbidden from attending any future dinners with him. "Azla?" questioned Zolya pointedly, not wasting breath on addressing Zander's ridiculous comment.

The princess appeared unsure for a heartbeat, as if revealing she had a crumb of intelligence might put her at risk.

It made Zolya only more infuriated. Not at her, of course, but at their ridiculous society for forcing women to be so thoroughly reduced in nature.

But after Lady Esme placed an encouraging hand atop Azla's, she finally spoke. "It is true, sire. What is spoken between Sun and Isle Courts is most unpleasant regarding the status of the palace, let alone Galia. They jest about burying their valuables in the soil of Cādra in case we all fall to such low ranks."

Zolya inhaled his frustration. "By the High Gods," he said. "The courts might as well take to the stage for their desire to spin such melodrama."

"We agree, of course, sire," added Zander, appearing desperate to get back within his good graces.

Zolya drummed his fingers on the table, the tiredness that seemed to forever haunt him tugging at his wings.

He met the expectant gazes of each of his guests.

But is it true? their expressions still wondered, begged for him to answer.

This will not do, thought Zolya.

Especially if his father learned that his courts doubted their stability, *his* stability as their king to rule so they may remain satiated, comfortable. The king's anger would only come down on Zolya.

"Have your celebration, Princess," he announced. "And spare no expense. If the courts question the abundance of the Diusé household, we must be thorough in our answer. I want everyone who attends to be reminded of the centuries of comforts our king has provided them—and that it will continue."

Azla's smile was radiant as the table awoke in excited chatter.

But Zolya could rejoice in none of it.

His mind was once again plagued by thoughts of the inventor.

If Gabreel Heiro had been under pressure before to find a solution to the new mine, his timeline had just become shorter.

15

Despite the silk of her dress and the soft leather of her sandals, Tanwen was severely uncomfortable.

But she supposed her clothes were less to blame than the Volari who was slowly running a finger down her exposed arm.

"If you keep that up, my lord," she said with a teasing grin—because she now had teasing grins—"I will miss where I drop your docüra."

"Why are you all so soft?" mused Lord Caseer, ignoring her words. Her client sat in repose along one of the many lounge beds within the main courtyard of Sumora. A great heap of wings and muscle illuminated by torchlight and the squinting eyes of Maja and Parvi. "Does Madam Kyva make you scrub each other nightly?" he asked.

Though Tanwen's gaze was lowered—as she had been trained—she could feel his hooded stare, taste his lurid thoughts.

She desperately pushed away the shiver that accompanied her flash of fear, doing her best to disregard the forced laughter echoing through the courtyard, emanating from the other atentés—the servants hired to administer docüra—and the occasional moans from their patrons.

A wash of unease slipped down Tanwen's spine. Cold, foreboding. This session needed to move faster.

"My madam does not," replied Tanwen, honey sweet despite her nerves. "But it is a suggestion I will gladly pass along. In the meantime," she continued, "I am honored to aid you in what you have come here for this evening." Tanwen raised the delicate glass of docüra. The dark, star-filled liquid churned with anticipation. "The jadüri in tonight's mixture was harvested when the royal wisteria trees were in full bloom." She repeated her script as she filled her dropper. "And the docüra made that very night beneath Maja's and Parvi's gaze, ensuring your experience will be extra sweet."

"I am with the most beautiful new atenté," replied Lord Caseer, finger haphazardly grazing the side of Tanwen's breast. "My night is already sweet."

Tanwen remained rigid, though her pulse kicked into a sprint. Despite her long peplos, she might as well have been naked, given its sheer material. Her mind tumbled through her next moves as she eyed Lord Caseer's other hand.

Frustration mixed with her disquiet.

His meaty paw rested in his lap—a small sanitized knife forgotten in his grip. *Cut yourself,* she silently begged. *Make the nick so I can end this.*

Tanwen had been at Sumora two weeks, but already in that time she had been a quick study to an atenté's role: their required mannerisms and rote replies. It was not so different from following the orders of her mother when accompanying her on meddyg visits. *Be helpful but not intrusive. Speak only when spoken to. Make our clients feel comfortable.*

Of course, her clients in Zomyad could not have been more different compared to those at Sumora.

The only reason she was able to suffer through the lewd stares and inappropriate gropes was because of the promise her highborn patrons held: that they might let slip *something* useful regarding events in the palace. Specifically, around the return of the king's traitorous inventor.

Tonight, however, was proving disobliging. Lord Caseer might be part of the Sun Court, but his interest appeared focused more on her bosom than on gossip.

Tanwen's only goal now was to finish this session, and quick.

"You are too kind, Lord Caseer," said Tanwen, doing her best to ignore his ever-roaming touch. "Which is why I know you will help me impress my madam with successfully assisting you with your docüra this evening."

His grip on her wrist was sudden. Hard as he tugged her closer. "Make the cut with me." His whisper was hot on her cheek, soured wine.

Panic shot through Tanwen, and for a moment she forgot herself. "No—I mean . . . I cannot, my lord. It is against house rules."

Though so was *never deny our patrons*.

But Lord Caseer's request broke a more important Galia law: no Süra was to take a blade to a Volari.

"I am *not* asking." He pulled her hand to cover the hilt of the knife. The leather was smooth, warm, tempting.

Think, Tanwen! she silently demanded of herself, heartbeat pounding. *Think.*

But she could recall no training that extricated an atenté from a wanting client. They were told only to obey. Accept.

Tanwen had done both those actions enough in her life. She had not come to Galia to continue similar behavior. She had come here to save her family and, Low Gods willing, never be touched again by another winged man.

"First show me how you prefer your cut, my lord," she reasoned gently, attempting as much composure as she could muster. "Then the next time you visit, I will know precisely how best to assist you."

She could see the displeasure in his furrowing brows, the twitching of his wings, and the tightening of his grip. Renewed fear leaped across Tanwen's skin. Was her madam watching? Was the entire courtyard?

"I only wish to please you, my lord," she went on quickly, another grin flashing. "To make sure I do it properly, I must first observe. I *am* new, after all. And what better teacher to what you enjoy than yourself?"

This logic seemed to placate him, for he relaxed into his settee, loosening his hold.

Tanwen's entire body wanted to collapse with her relief.

"You are lucky Leza has been so kind to you," he said, "that I would wish to look upon you again. Now"—he took up his blade—"watch what I do carefully, my little goat."

Tanwen ignored his use of a Süra slur, merely grateful to find his knife poised on the underside of his forearm. A storybook of knicks and pricks peppered his skin. Openings from past nights of pleasure. "I don't like it long but deep," he explained, eyes darkening as he broke through flesh. It was a small cut but indeed deep, as blood pooled quickly.

Tanwen was quicker.

With practiced efficiency born from her decade of meddyg experience, she blotted the opening with a clean cloth before releasing four drops of docüra into the fresh cut.

The effect was instantaneous.

Her client sucked in a breath in stunned pleasure before exhaling ecstasy. His eyes dilated and rolled back, and he slumped into his settee.

Tanwen snatched up his loosened knife before it could clatter to the floor. She held the blade as she gazed down at Lord Caseer, his arms and wings limp at his sides.

She studied the flutter of his pulse along his neck, his closed eyes, his mind and body elsewhere.

Dangerous fantasies filled Tanwen as the haunting of his unwanted grazes still burned cold along her skin. His condescending remarks and demanding grip.

It would only take a simple slice, she thought. Fast. Fatal. Right where his lifeblood jumped against his throat.

Her fingers tightened around the blade.

Don't. Don't. They watch. They watch.

Tanwen blinked out of her dark musings, finding a midnight dove perched within a blossoming cherry tree nearby. The bird repeated its warning with a rustle of its black feathers.

Don't. Don't. They watch. They watch.

Tanwen shook herself lucid, furtively glancing at the guards hidden in shadowed alcoves of the courtyard. Their wings were pressed tight at their backs, hands idle on sword hilts at their hips, expressions bored but alert.

Süra may have been trusted to administer docüra to Volari, but they certainly were not trusted after.

Rightfully so.

Not that Tanwen had it in her to kill anyone.

She had been trained to save lives, not end them.

Still, she silently thanked the dove before making quick work of wrapping Lord Caseer's forearm in a thin bandage. After she collected her supplies, she made to exit the courtyard.

At home, in Zomyad, she would have remained by her client's side, ensuring their journey to the spirit realm of the gods transpired safely. She would have offered whatever comforting words were needed to guide them back to their realm.

But her mother had spoken true: the only voyage the Volari seemed to experience was a euphoric high for one lazy dip of the moon.

There was no need for Tanwen to linger.

Thank the Low Gods.

As she made her way to slip behind a curtained door, she did her best not to stare at the other atentés and their clients within the garden.

Never had Tanwen imagined she would be a part of such a scene.

Süra were draped over the laps of Volari. A peppering of exposed breasts before exploring fingers covered them. Other atentés stroked wings, singing a soft lullaby as they released docüra into shallow cuts. It was a collection of depraved sweetness and completely contradictory of the two races' history.

Something that had thoroughly befuddled Tanwen when she had first arrived. But now, as she leaned against the cool stone wall within a tight corridor, their moving shapes in her periphery blessedly blocked out by a thick drape, she didn't think much else could surprise her anytime soon.

The theme for her time at Sumora had been set her first night by Madam Kyva herself. Before they were sent to bed, she had called Tanwen and the other two new atentés into her office. Madam Kyva's expression had held its usual austere mask as she regarded them.

"Do you know the tale of Nocémi?" she asked.

None of them replied, clearly too terrified.

"It's a love story many enjoy hearing," she explained. "How when Ré first saw the goddess, he was transfixed by her beauty. Each passing year he only became more obsessed and relentless in his desire for her, eventually demanding she marry him. Being sought after by the father of the High Gods was considered an honor, especially given he had never before sought a wife or shown interest in another sharing his throne. He offered Nocémi rule of the night, a grand gesture of his adoration. But what many do not know about this story," explained Madam Kyva, with a pinch to her brows, "is that it was not Ré's idea to gift the night, but Nocémi's. The goddess saw what happened to those Ré desired, how quickly his flames, when held too long, burned away their existence. The goddess was clever, and she agreed to marry Ré so long as he gifted her rule of the night. Upon doing so, she freed herself from the dangers of her husband. Only during the brief moments of dusk and dawn did the two ever meet. Ré's light would forever be a gentle graze of yearning as Nocémi slid away."

Silence had filled Madam Kyva's office, a prickling of unease working up Tanwen's spine.

"So you see, girls," said Madam Kyva, hard gaze piercing. "Nocémi's story is not one of love, after all. It's a story of survival. And at Sumora you are each Nocémi. If you are clever, you will survive."

A rattling stirred Tanwen from her memory of standing before her madam. That terrible tale echoed in her mind as she found her hands were shaking. The items on her tray quivered across the smooth metal surface.

Tanwen tightened her grip, steadying the tray.

I survived, she thought. *I survived another night. I am Nocémi.*

"Others could learn from you," said a husky voice within the dimly lit stone hallway. "Caseer is usually not so cooperative."

"Huw." Tanwen nearly jumped. "I did not see you."

"Most don't," he replied.

Huw leaned on the opposite wall, beyond the light of the sconces, which was why she had initially missed him upon entering. From the shadows, Huw dug a fingernail into the skin of an orange. A tangy sweetness filled the corridor, a welcome reprieve to the overincensed den.

"Have you had Caseer as a client before?" asked Tanwen, forcing her thoughts away from Madam Kyva's lesson.

Huw was one of the few male atentés at Sumora. Another oddity Tanwen had encountered in Galia. Men were traditionally not taught meddyg skills on Cādra, but it appeared the dens here would teach anyone pretty enough the art of making docüra. It was all about pleasing their clients, after all.

"I'm not his type," explained Huw, biceps shifting as he popped a slice of orange into his mouth. He wore nothing but low-slung tan trousers that billowed before collecting at his ankles. "He likes them, well, like you."

"A girl?"

"Innocent." His gaze slid to her grip on her tray. "Scared."

Tanwen tensed, chin lifting. "I am not scared."

"Then that's your first mistake." Huw stepped into the sconce's light, his blond hair glowing as shadows played over his thick, curling northern horns. His pale skin gleamed with scented oil. He reminded Tanwen of the wheat fields outside Zomyad at sunset, reedy but stubbornly strong against the breeze. "We all are scared here, little fawn," he said. "Some of us have just learned to hide it better."

He placed his perfectly spiraled peel on her tray.

"Smell it," he advised. "It will help clear your head. At the very least settle your nerves."

Huw smiled, though it appeared heavy, as if his cheeks were exhausted from the constant effort to be lifted.

He's surviving, thought Tanwen, a press of melancholy to her chest.

Huw walked past her, picking up an awaiting tray of docüra on a side table before slipping out and into the courtyard.

Tanwen stared as the drape swung closed, Huw's words playing over in her mind.

We all are scared here.

Well, it certainly didn't seem that way. So many of the seasoned atentés appeared to glow under the attention of their Volari patrons. Many of them fighting over who could attend whom.

Even Tanwen's arrival had been met with suspicious glares, as if she had come to rob the place. Distrust simmered in the gaze of each atenté. Bullish acceptance when Tanwen was meant to shadow them.

"Girl." Madam Kyva stood at the far end of the corridor, fists plunked disapprovingly on ample hips. "Just because your floor time is over," she said, "doesn't mean your shift is. There is plenty to fold and clean and prepare for tomorrow before the night is up."

"Yes, Madam Kyva," said Tanwen, hurrying forward, but before she discarded her tray, she plucked up Huw's orange peel.

That night, when she lay exhausted but awake in the dormitory, the erratic snores of her nearby bunkmates filling the high-ceilinged hall, Tanwen slipped out the peel. It had grown limp in her pocket, the skin dry, but the fresh fragrance still lingered.

She lifted it to her nose, inhaling deeply.

Tanwen waited for her thoughts to clear, for the buzz of her anxiousness to ebb.

The only change she experienced was her feeling foolish.

She meant to laugh at her absurdity, but it came out as a sob.

Tears rolled unchecked down Tanwen's cheeks as she curled into a ball on her floor mat, orange peel forgotten somewhere by her side.

She wasn't sure why she was crying, what exactly about her current mess of a life had pushed her over the edge, but she wasn't exactly in the state to figure it out.

As she silently wept, the first time since leaving her mother, she felt a gentle touch on her hand. Tiny paws tickled along her forearm as Eli arrived from wherever he hid all day, to burrow into her chest.

Here was the only friend she could count on.

It'll be all right, Eli told her. *I'm here.*

His words only made Tanwen cry harder.

The emotions she had buried deep since leaving Zomyad leaked unchecked.

She wept out of fear—fear of never finding her father or brother, of being too late when she did. She cried from the uncertainty of ever returning to Zomyad or seeing her mother again. And from the growing dread that one day she might not be quick or clever enough with a client, their demands pushing her to a place she could not come back from.

I am not scared, she had told Huw.

Which had been true.

Tanwen wasn't scared.

She was terrified.

16

Sumora was in chaos.

"What's going on?" Tanwen asked a kitchen maid hurrying down a hall within the servants' quarters.

Her eyes were frantic as she gave Tanwen a once-over, recognition sparking. "You better get a move on," she urged. "The warden is coming!"

"The warden?" Tanwen repeated.

But the girl had already rushed forward, leaving behind a stunned Tanwen. She had barely risen for the morning meal when the den shook with a panicked commotion.

Despite her hunger, Tanwen rushed from the kitchens to sprint forward with the rest of the flock.

The atentés were corralled back into their dormitory, where Madam Kyva yelled for them to make themselves presentable and to gather in the larger garden immediately.

Tanwen was all puffs of breath and wiping sweat from her brow when she finally came to stand within the courtyard along with the other twenty-three atentés. The white wrap dress she had changed into felt clingy against the perspiration made by her haste, and she hadn't had the time to fix her hair. It currently rested in a haphazard mass around her shoulders.

She would certainly be reprimanded by Madam Kyva, but that worry was for later.

Presently, her—and everyone's—attention was held by the form descending into their courtyard like a High God come to bestow mortals with his magnificent presence. The warden's wings were painted an array of colors, more complicated than any tapestry Tanwen had ever seen. And they glistened as the sun touched them, light passing through stained glass. He gracefully landed in the center of the garden, wings tucking in as he peered down his nose at them. His black skin was youthful, despite him no doubt being well over a century in age, and his hair rested in tight braids on the nape of his neck.

Tanwen had met Lord Bacton, their warden, only once when she had first arrived, and his visit then had been terse. A swift assessment of Tanwen, the property he had inherited, before he had left as quickly as he had arrived. No words shared, only judgment.

"My lord," said Madam Kyva, coming to a deep bow before him.

Tanwen and the rest of the atentés followed.

"We are most honored by your visit," she continued. "We would—"

"I haven't the time for pleasantries," interrupted Lord Bacton with a dismissive wave of a manicured hand. "Show me those on your list."

Madam Kyva appeared uncharacteristically flustered for a moment, but she quickly recovered, calling out various atentés and instructing them to step forward.

"Tanwen Coster."

Tanwen snapped her head up, her pulse stopping before racing forward.

Me? she wondered in a panic.

"Go." Someone nudged hard at her back.

Tanwen's feet were boulders, impossible to lift, but she somehow managed to stand in the new line of atentés presented to the warden.

Why am I here? Why am I here? Why am I here?

Tanwen's mind spun for what she might have done wrong, for certainly this was not promising. *I take too long in the washroom,* she thought with dread.

Instincts to flee raced down her spine, her gaze shifting to every break in the columns, past the guards to the doors that lay beyond.

Her thoughts went blank, however, when Lord Bacton stopped in front of her.

The warden's cologne was thick, floral mixed with cinnamon. Tanwen's breath held as she sensed his gaze raking down her body. He even lifted a lock of her hair, feeling it between his fingers.

"Turn," he demanded.

A burst of ire awoke in Tanwen's gut, but she did as she was told. She turned.

When she faced Lord Bacton again, he was already walking away. Tanwen let out a slow breath, her heart restarting.

Similar assessments of the other atentés went on for far too long, a few being told to step back while new ones were pulled forward.

Tanwen remained where she stood, her worry compounding.

Finally, Lord Bacton spoke. "There is to be a celebration at the palace," he said, "to welcome home his crown prince and his brave kidets on their recent voyage across Cādra."

Tanwen was stone, frozen in shock.

The palace.

The prince.

"Like with most palace celebrations," continued Lord Bacton, "the size of the affair as well as the prestige of those invited requires favors from those at court. As done in the past, Sumora has been called upon to offer up some of my atentés for the event. Those standing in this line"—he waved to where Tanwen and nine others stood—"are due at the palace by end of the week to prepare for the festivities. You will be representing this den, but more importantly, you will represent *me.*" His tone dipped low, a warning. "I expect perfection from each of you." He allowed the severity of his order to stretch for an uncomfortably long beat before adding, "This is a time to show off why Sumora has the most prestigious clientele. Do *not* disappoint."

With that, Lord Bacton spread his wings, an angry peacock, and shot up into the air.

Tanwen shielded herself against the storm of dust his flight awoke, dirt coating her lips, but she could have been facing a sandstorm and she would not have cared.

She was going to the palace.

The palace!

Where her family was being held.

Where she would be another step closer in finding her father and Thol and freeing them all from this floating prison.

Udasha, she thought, glancing up to the sky at the High Goddess of luck, *thank you.*

"Well, well, little fawn," Huw remarked at her side, causing Tanwen to start. She hadn't noticed that she had been standing beside him this entire time. "Seems the warden likes them scared too." He winked at her before sauntering away.

Tanwen stared at his retreating form with indignation, shoulders stiffening.

Once again Huw had misread her.

Tanwen wasn't scared.

This time she was ready.

◆ ◆ ◆

Under the cloak of night, when the last patrons had left and the atentés were finally granted respite in their beds, Tanwen slid from her mat and into the bathhouse.

The vacant marble expanse echoed her hushed footsteps, the tiles still slick from their earlier washing. Her path was lit by nearby torches and an additional spill of moonlight through a skylight, but despite the illumination, Tanwen knew how to move through shadows better than most.

Unseen, she slipped into a corner toilet, concealed by a partition, and raised a loose stone from the wall.

It might not have been a floorboard, but it still did the trick.

Eli sat on her shoulder, watching as she pulled out the small glass jar that held the dust of her father's wings.

Tanwen had not trusted the others enough to keep it with her belongings in the dormitory. Too nosy were her bunkmates; plenty of her items had already gone missing as part of the hazing of being a greeny.

But all that was forgotten as Tanwen turned over the jar, the dark grains rustling as they fell over one another.

Her pulse kicked a quick rhythm through her veins.

It's not the best plan, said Eli.

No, agreed Tanwen, *but it's all I've got.*

As she held the delicate container, her mother's words floated forward in her mind.

Use it when you must. When it will mean something.

This certainly was such a time.

Tanwen was going to the palace.

Finally.

And when she got there, she would use her family's secret spice in her docüra mixture.

She didn't know if it would work—if her docüra would turn out as good as her mother's or, if it did, that it would even matter—but this was her one chance to try.

The atentés had been in a fluster after Lord Bacton's arrival, whispered debates filling the dining hall about who among them might end up staying at the palace.

Tanwen's ears had burned at the discovery, her heartbeat a stampede of desperation.

Evidently, the palace used these gatherings as unconventional auditions for new recruits working in Fioré, aiming to refresh their staff. The court tended to tire quickly of familiar faces among their entertainers.

Tanwen had been unable to finish her meal, her stomach a ball of nerves as the reality of her situation had pressed heavily upon her shoulders.

The gods only knew when another opportunity like this would come again.

Tanwen *needed* to bloom at this event so she might be the flower that got picked and brought inside.

Her family was depending on her.

She would do her very best to search the palace while she was there, but she understood her success in locating her father and brother and getting them out relied greatly on her length of stay.

It was an insane gamble, but much like the risk she had taken in striking a deal with Bosyg, Tanwen found herself with limited options.

This must *work,* she thought, gripping the glass.

Maybe if you got the prince as your client, it could, said Eli from her shoulder.

Tanwen wasn't sure if he was jesting, but suddenly her thoughts turned in a new direction, her veins pulsing with ire at the mention of Prince Zolya.

The man who had allowed a blade to be pressed to her brother's throat, who had taken away her father and best friend. Who had upended her entire life.

As Tanwen caressed the glass bottle, revenge was a dangerous poultice to her pain.

"Yes," mused Tanwen, "how fortunate would it be to serve the prince."

A dark imagining flooded her mind then: Tanwen beside His Royal Highness, so close to the sharp knife in his hand, to a precarious vein.

While Tanwen had learned much since coming to Galia, perhaps her most profound lesson had been imparted the first time she had watched a Volari cut into their skin.

Blood had trickled out, as red as her own.

In that moment, Tanwen had learned an invaluable truth.

The children of gods could bleed.

And if they could bleed, then they could die.

17

Full of regret, Zolya flew toward the royal gardens.

I should never have agreed to this, he thought, eyeing the horde of guests roaming the expansive grounds. The manicured shrubs had been soaked in droplets of blue and purple phosphorus light, the marble paths had been scrubbed until they shone like reflective ice under the twins' moonlight, and the torches had been laid in a pattern that mimicked the constellations. Lounge beds, draped gazebos, and salt baths were tucked away into secluded shadows. All hugged by the sweet scent of jasmine and a light tepid breeze manifested by circling wind and heat makers.

Azla had outdone herself.

Unsurprisingly.

A repercussion Zolya would suffer through tomorrow.

Tonight, he was meant to appease his court, be a symbol of merriment to assuage any worry that their current comforts may be in trouble.

Certainly, an ironic salve for a looming unstable economy.

As Zolya banked left, his entourage of guards following, he landed within an open-air temple at the top of the garden, the moons nearly fully formed at his back.

A wave of bows greeted his arrival, rippling out to the farthest corners of the garden.

And there they remained, bent low, waiting for his command.

"Let us give thanks to our creators," he said, voice traveling over the crowd, "for they have blessed us with the success of our mission across Cādra and the healthy return of myself and our kidets. Now, please, let us enjoy this beautiful gathering Princess Azla has manifested. Make Izato proud with your revelry."

Cheers and light clapping answered him, the music returning louder as servants entered the grounds with steaming dishes and overflowing glasses. Atentés in their revealing attire slunk between guests, smiling and offering any who desired drops of docüra.

Expense, expense, expense, thought Zolya.

"You look stunning, sire," said Azla as she came to curtsy before him, Lady Esme at her side.

His sister-cousin was the resplendent one in her bronze-plated bodice, the details rippling away like leafy vines toward her shoulders and over her hips, her brown skin dusted with gold. She appeared as if the daughter of Leza stepping from a bramble.

"Where would you like me?" he asked.

"Oh, Zolya." She nearly rolled her eyes at him. "This is *your* party. You can roam wherever you'd like."

He gave her a dry look. "Where would you like me, Azla."

She smiled, a child who got not only a toy but sweets. "I have made up the perfect cropping of benches and pillows for you and your friends over there." She pointed to a stone gazebo that had been brought into the temple. It had been done up intimately but was still very much on display within the center of the party. He would be sitting like a pampered parrot at the top of a cage.

"Very well," he replied.

"Sire." She touched his arm, momentarily stopping his retreat.

He glanced down at her, waiting.

"Thank you," she said.

And there it was, the desperate gratitude sparking in her eyes. His whole reason for being here, agreeing to this: to make her happy.

Or as happy as an illegitimate, motherless offspring of a stern king could be.

"Of course," said Zolya, managing a small grin.

She and Lady Esme gave him another curtsy before he walked away.

As he settled into a low lounge bed, draping his wings on either side of him, he accepted the plate of cheese and meats brought by servants. At least here Zolya would be saved from conversing with too many of the guests. He knew how he appeared: intimidating, unapproachable in his display case.

Here sat a reminder of the king who ruled them, a token of royal blood for guests to feel important to be so nearby.

As a few brave souls came to wish him well, Sun and Isle Court members presenting their daughters and sons, Zolya politely entertained them before the next in line stepped forward.

Osko visited briefly to drink half his spirits, offering Zolya a slight respite from unwanted conversation, but soon left to chase an Isle courtier into one of the flower mazes.

Zolya let out a bored sigh, swirling his wine. He would have gladly been doing many other activities than this, like lying along the tallest roof in the palace, gazing up at the Kaiwi River, the celestial home of the High Gods. He often went there alone so he could relax, unwatched and unjudged.

Zolya understood why his father rarely attended these social gatherings.

It was the purpose of the prince: to fulfill the undesired obligations of the king.

Though Zolya tried not to think too long regarding King Réol's absence from an event celebrating his son.

It certainly wasn't the first disappointment from his father, nor would it be the last.

Desiring a change in temperament, Zolya was about to chance a walk through the gardens when he spotted her.

A feat that was not hard, given she was gazing full force at him.

Not an act many practiced—specifically not servants.

At the edge of the temple, a woman stood half-hidden behind a column, her other half lit by a nearby torch. Her dark hair was thick and flowing around her shoulders, her tall horns capped with gold that matched the thin piping along her white chiton, the neckline temptingly low to display ample cleavage.

She held a tray of docüra, sparking a flood of questions in Zolya's mind.

The foremost question was, How?

How was the meddyg from the fields outside of Zomyad standing here, on palace ground, as an atenté?

Despite her change in costume, there was no denying this was the same woman. It was hard to forget a face like hers or the fiery gaze that swam within such a fragile-appearing creature, not to mention the woman who had unintentionally helped him find Gabreel.

After three long breaths, she quickly averted her attention, as if remembering herself.

Something uncomfortable twisted through Zolya, a desire for her to look at him again.

Before he knew what he was doing, Zolya turned to one of his guards, giving them a command.

In an instant, his man was beside her, talking low.

A wave of emotions fell across her features, each tinged with fear—an animal in hiding that had been found out—but then her expression went blank, professionally masked as she was ushered forward.

She came to prostrate on her knees before him, a reenactment of their first meeting, yet this time Zolya held an uneasy certainty it would not end the same.

18

Tanwen was out of her depths.

If this was how the children of gods celebrated, she could not begin to fathom how the High Gods themselves entertained.

The palace party was less of a party and more like a bloated enchanted spectacle.

Yes, it had drinks and music and food, but the overabundance was sickening.

How could such wealth exist when half the citizens of Cādra went hungry? Surely *some* of the funds to erect a multitiered glowing floral arrangement could be redirected to put food on Süra children's plates.

This was how much of Tanwen's initial days had transpired once she had been brought to the palace. She had stumbled into the compound in a mix of devastated awe and appalled outrage. The palace was certainly an imposing sight atop its mountain, but once within its walls, never had Tanwen felt so infinitesimal, so inconsequential among the soaring columns and exhaustively painted ceilings.

The lush lawns and gardens and orchards wove like colorful brushstrokes around the towering temples and domed citadels. And the sky—it was everywhere, as if the mountain's tip floated alone in the clouds and no town or lake lay beneath them.

It left Tanwen constantly on edge, a lingering unease that she might slip at any moment from a precipice and fall to her death.

Her discomfort had been intensified by the cold greeting from palace staff. Tanwen now understood the hierarchy among recruits in Galia. There were those privileged enough to serve within the palace—and then everyone else.

"Snobs," Huw had declared beside her when they had been paraded through the servants' quarters, receiving judgmental glares and upturned noses. "As if we don't all indulge the same commands at the end of the day."

Tanwen had paid the rudeness little mind, too used to such coldness. Instead, she had forced her attention on every door or hall or alcove they passed. *Could Thol and Father be down there?* she'd wondered. *Behind those doors? Or those?*

She had been desperate to find out, but her hope to explore the grounds had been quickly robbed by thoroughly packed days of preparation.

It had begun with an exhaustive tour of every atenté domain: their dormitory, bathhouse, dressing chamber, docüra workroom. Each space opulent and meticulously neat. But what had truly taken Tanwen's breath away was the jadüri greenhouse. At the western tip of the palace sat a marvel of engineering with its soaring glass-paneled walls and domed ceiling. Rows of garden boxes holding the sacred flower stretched endlessly, mocking the lengths to which Tanwen had gone to pluck her single bloom in Cādra. Here, in carefully controlled conditions, the plant flourished abundantly. The palace held exclusive rights to cultivate the flower, the Fioré dens purchasing what they needed to make their docüra.

They had then been introduced to the infamous Madam Arini, a lithe middle-aged woman hailing from Garw. Her beauty matched Galia in its cold perfection, her sculpted blond hair catching the sunlight as she walked the rows of borrowed atentés. She had surveyed them as one would when purchasing a horse, demanding they show her their teeth, turn, walk, and bow. She had given nothing away as she clicked her long nails against her gold armbands, hands crossed over her chest, assessing.

The only proof of her satisfaction had been when they were dismissed to wash and dress in the palace atenté uniform before enduring endless training for the celebration. Madam Arini had been relentless in her desired perfection for how they were to approach courtiers and administer the docüra.

"You walked forward too quickly," she had scolded Tanwen. "You mustn't seem desperate to please but pleased to obey. And you must offer the dropper with your wrist up. Gaze on the floor! Your bandage needs to be folded in thirds, not halves."

Tanwen's nerves had been a fluster under the constant scrutiny, but she had tried her best to remain poised, calm. An achievement made possible by her upbringing, in which she had learned not to be provoked by those in her village.

Do not draw attention to yourself.

You are Mütra. You are Mütra. You are Mütra.

Soon, Madam Arini had moved on to harass another.

But Tanwen's anxiousness had not ebbed.

It had only intensified when they were meant to make their docüra for the event, all under Madam Arini's watchful eye. Tanwen had stood frozen, at a loss for how she was to add the dust of her father's wings without being noticed.

It was Eli who had come to her rescue.

He made quite a scene of scurrying over a row of atentés' sandaled feet, eliciting shrieks and turning everyone's attention to the rodent who had gotten into the palace.

Tanwen had only a moment, but she seized it. With her pulse pounding through her veins, she removed the small vial from where she had wrapped it to her inner thigh and released a pinch of ash into her mixture.

By the time the room was righted, Eli sprinting to safety, her docüra spun innocuously in front of her, the vial once again hidden.

Tanwen clenched her hands together to keep them from shaking, her breaths uneven as her adrenaline rushed through her veins. Especially when Madam Arini came to inspect her bowl.

"Yours is darker," she accused, gaze narrowing.

"It is how I stir it, ma'am," Tanwen explained, forcing her tone even despite her stampeding heart. "My mother is a meddyg with two decades of experience making docüra. She says to stir with purpose and prayer—"

"I don't care for your past, girl," interrupted Madam Arini with a raised hand. "I care that this mixture is usable and up to palace standard—otherwise the cost of the jadüri will come out of your weekly pay."

"Oh, yes, ma'am," breathed Tanwen. "My docüra is quite sound."

She desperately hoped.

"Taste it."

Tanwen blinked, confused. "Excuse me, ma'am?"

"I am not of a kind to repeat myself," Madam Arini stated, eyeing her expectantly.

Tanwen's skin grew hot as she sensed the attention of those around her.

Do not draw attention to yourself.

You are Mütra. You are Mütra. You are Mütra.

Tanwen tasted her docüra, a pinkie dipped and licked.

It was syrupy sweet, headache inducing, but she kept herself from wincing.

Madam Arini stood waiting—for what, Tanwen did not know—but after a moment she took it upon herself to taste the docüra as well.

Her eyes went wide for a breath before slamming down to calculating slits as she regarded Tanwen.

"Your mother is a meddyg, you say?" she asked.

"Yes, ma'am."

"*Mmm*" was all she had replied, a thoughtful glimmer in her gaze before she had sauntered to the next atenté.

Now roaming within the palace gardens, Tanwen tightly gripped her tray of docüra. Courtiers were clustered in various parts of the expansive grounds, wings painted in a tapestry of colors, gowns and jackets sparkling with jeweled adornments and metallic thread.

She wove unnoticed through the flock as a contradiction of emotions swirled within her chest, anticipation as well as dread to test her mixture.

She hoped, prayed, that it would be as good as her mother's, but she was also terrified to discover if it wasn't.

What if she hadn't added enough dust or had added too much? What if she had unintentionally ruined her docüra completely? She had been in a panic, after all, hardly in a state to ensure precision when throwing in the grains of her father's wings.

Oh gods, thought Tanwen, heart seizing in terror. *What have I done?*

"You there," called someone nearby.

Tanwen turned, finding a group of guests sitting in repose within a twinkling pergola. A man in the middle beckoned her over.

Tanwen swallowed down her rising regret as she approached. There was no turning back now. "How may I assist you this evening, my lord?" she asked as she came to a low bow.

"You are a welcome new face to our usual atentés," stated the man, eyes raking over her body. His painted wings shimmered like snake scales in the dim light, his pale features pointed. "Tell us, which den have you been borrowed from?"

"Sumora, my lord," said Tanwen.

"I say." He tutted to his companions. "Lord Bacton might have a prettier collection of atentés than the palace."

"Indeed," agreed another courtier. "But let us see if her skills in attending to us are as well met."

"A sound solution." The first man smiled, gaze turning predatory as it remained locked to Tanwen. "Come closer, pet," he demanded. "And show us how well you can offer pleasure."

Tanwen's throat tightened, her indignation spiking at being treated like an object, but she approached nonetheless.

Though her steps faltered when a cluster of glow beetles swarmed into the pergola.

They must have sensed her agitation, for they buzzed in front of her, a fluttering of concern keeping her from walking any farther.

"*Eww.*" A lady swatted one that had dipped too close. "Get these wretched things away!"

Tanwen's panic soared.

Please, she silently begged the bugs. *I am fine. You must go!*

They didn't listen, her quickening heart rate saying otherwise.

The guests' alarm within the pergola began to draw notice, and Tanwen silently cursed.

Please, she urged again. *Please go.* This time she forced a deep breath of calm, her white-knuckle grip on her tray loosening.

I am safe, she said to the beetles, working to believe it. *I am safe.*

As her heart rate settled, so did the bugs. Soon they were gone.

Relief washed over Tanwen.

"How horrifying," said one of the ladies, settling back onto her bench.

"And odd," added another.

"It was probably your perfumes," stated one of the men. "You ladies do spray it on rather thick."

Offended mouths popped open; glares were thrown.

"All right," chided the original man who had called for Tanwen. "We are here to have fun, not bicker. Let us save the latter for dinner parties, not palace ones. Come, pet." He waved Tanwen forward. "I now find myself in even more need to escape this lot."

Tanwen obeyed, coming to kneel at his side and resting her tray on the bench beside him.

She felt his perusing gaze along her exposed skin, lingering on her breasts, which were uncomfortably on display.

"My lord." She offered him the small blade.

He didn't look away from her as he made his nick, but Tanwen's attention remained dutifully on administering her docüra as quickly as possible.

Her breath held as the dark droplets hit the cut.

A groan, and then another. The man grew limp upon his bench, wings drooping as his moans turned sensual, the sound of unrivaled euphoric pleasure.

The guests within the pergola sat silently as shocked observers.

Before they were all calling to her at once.

By the Eternal River, she thought, a strange giddiness jumping inside her chest, *it worked.*

Tanwen became thoroughly occupied the rest of the evening.

And would have remained such if it had not been for the arrival of one man.

One man who awoke a potent hatred within Tanwen's heart.

The crown prince of Galia.

19

Tanwen scowled as he soared into view like a shooting star, his winged entourage of guards trailing behind.

The entire celebration stilled to watch the prince's approach, his large white wings soaking in the moons' light before he settled within the temple. He was dressed in an intricate high-collared white coat, decorative gold feathers fanning over his broad shoulders and a gilded laurel crown woven into his alabaster hair.

Something hot and uncomfortable unfurled in Tanwen's chest, cascading through her entire body as she drank him in.

No one that beautiful should exist.

Certainly, no one as coldhearted or, at the very least, not someone she despised so thoroughly.

His deep voice rolled across the lawn, evoking memories of the night she had first knelt before him—terrified, regretful—and then of later, when he had commanded her father and brother into a net to be taken away.

Tanwen's grip on her tray stiffened, her fury mixing dangerously with her grief.

After attending to her recent clients, she hadn't exactly planned on slowly making her way toward the prince's secluded gazebo. Tanwen felt only an innate desperation to be closer to the man who had upended her life and undoubtedly knew the location where her father and brother were being held.

Could she discern any emotion from him that might provide a clue of their whereabouts? Had he kept his word that Thol would live so long as her father did?

The jar of docüra on her tray swashed back and forth as she slunk forward, a spinning galaxy as she came to hide behind one of the temple's columns. She was now close enough that she could catch the torchlight reflecting off the prince's jeweled rings as he lazily held a glass of wine. His brown skin was smooth, taut along his angular jaw.

She watched as the kidar who had gruffly held her brother's neck joined the prince.

Tanwen clenched her teeth, ire as hot as the sun filling her chest as she observed the men together, laughing and jesting. How unconcerned they were with the life-altering pain they had manifested within Tanwen and her family. No doubt within many citizens on Cādra.

And why would they be concerned?

Here they sat wrapped in their comforts, the ugliness of life's hardships nowhere in sight.

As Tanwen remained hidden, she had no idea why she remained torturing herself by standing there. But she did.

It wasn't until the prince once again sat alone that she made her mistake.

As she angled for a better view, Tanwen slipped a step too far into the light.

Like an animal knowing when he was being hunted, the prince turned his gaze on her.

Everything in Tanwen stopped, numbed, as their eyes collided.

But as their connection held, a surge of fire burned across her skin.

It was a heat that only intensified as a dangerous spark of recognition flashed in the prince's blue depths.

Tanwen sucked in a panicked breath.

You fool! she scolded, about to dart back into the shadows when a whip of wind had her attention snagging on a royal guard approaching.

The kidet's words jumbled in Tanwen's head as he stood towering over her. Surely, he had not said the prince wished for her services. Surely, she was not abiding the command by following.

Tanwen was out of her body, floating overhead as she watched herself crouch before the crown prince.

Again.

But this time she knew exactly who he was. Not a kidar, not even a prince, but her enemy.

"We have met before." His voice was a velvet touch, smooth, calm, not a question.

Tanwen's pulse fluttered like hummingbird wings; thoughts of lying spun quickly, but something told her it would be futile. "We have, sire," she said, attention remaining on his shining leather boots.

"You are the meddyg from the fields outside Zomyad."

How? Tanwen thought, roiling in shocked dismay. *Why?*

Why would the prince remember a dirt-covered meddyg from so many weeks ago?

"I am, sire," she managed to reply.

"Why are you here?"

Tanwen almost laughed, her answer so obvious in her mind. *To hurt you,* she quietly seethed. *And hopefully save my father and brother in the process,* she silently swore.

"You are amused by my question," said the prince. Another statement. Here sat a man who was confident in his assessments.

For who would dare contradict him?

"Of course not, sire." Tanwen quickly schooled her features, bending lower.

Do I have a death wish? she wondered in a panic. *Pull yourself together, Tanwen.*

"You may look at me," instructed the prince.

Tanwen hesitated but then did as she was ordered. Slowly, she sat back on her heels, tray of docüra remaining on the stone floor by her knees.

Prince Zolya's blue gaze pored over her, a liquid sky. He was luminous in his gold-and-white adornments, his flawless brown skin, and the delicate jewels woven into his laurel crown. The view of him was almost painful as he sat leaning one elbow against a padded armrest. He stared down at her like a predator eyeing a potential meal, wondering if it might taste good or merely cause him indigestion.

As he sat assessing, Tanwen remained very, very still. She could not look long at him. Her skin grew flushed when she did, the fabric of her dress becoming too suffocating.

She loathed how exposed she felt in her low-necked dress, wished instead to be wearing her sturdier clan pants and tunic with the comforting weight of her medicinal pouches at her hips.

"Shall we try this again?" asked Prince Zolya. "Why are you here, meddyg?"

Tanwen must have been mad, or tired, or desperate. Assuredly annoyed by his placating tone, for she found herself replying, "The same reason every servant is in Galia, sire: because I must be."

Her regret was instant.

Tanwen waited, breath held for the prince to order her dragged to whatever dungeon was hidden within the palace or beheaded on the spot for such insolence.

Instead, he shocked her by appearing concerned before bewildered, as though this might be the first moment in his decades of life that someone had spoken their mind to him. From her class, it certainly must be.

"I apologize, Your Royal Highness," Tanwen began. "I do not know what—"

"You answered my question," he interrupted with a wave of his hand. His white wings shifted at his back as he sat straighter. "Which is what I had requested."

Tanwen swallowed, nodding her gratitude for his lenience. She had not been around many royals—Prince Zolya was the first, in fact—but she surmised a subject should *never* act as she had.

She blamed it on being so near the man she had grown to hate, blamed it on her desperation to find her father and brother, on her losing conviction in succeeding, on being so torturously close to the prince who could give her all her answers but being unable to ask. Tanwen was growing rash with her actions, and she needed to snap out of it.

Be Nocémi, she reminded herself, taking a slow inhale. *Survive.*

"You wished for my services, sire?" Tanwen offered up her tray of docüra. Under the torchlight, the knife beside the bowl winked with dark temptation. Tanwen's fingers flexed along her tray.

But then what? she silently admonished herself.

Guards were an impenetrable circle around them, His Royal Highness's clear strength his own shield. Tanwen would no doubt be tackled before she could grasp the blade.

Besides, she now realized, causing harm to the prince would in no way help in her efforts to retrieve her father and brother.

"While my subjects may enjoy the euphoria made by the nectar of the gods," said the prince, redirecting Tanwen's attention, "I do not indulge in the stuff." He must have noted her surprise, for he leaned forward, almost conspiratorially, adding, "You see, it is not advantageous for the sole heir of this kingdom to be laid out publicly. One never knows if an angry subject might use such a moment to strike."

Disquiet was a rushing of water filling Tanwen's veins from how similar his musings had been to her own.

"Surely that is why you have your guards, sire?" Tanwen inclined her head to the surrounding kidets. "To keep threats at bay."

Prince Zolya's lips twitched, as if resisting a smile. "Yes, they do serve their function in protecting me," he said while holding her stare. "Still, I suppose I prefer to indulge in my pleasures privately."

Tanwen dared not breathe.

Heat was melting her from the inside out; visions of what sort of pleasures he might be referring to sparked in her mind. Beautiful slick skin, featherlight caresses, and ruffled sheets.

Tanwen swallowed, blinking away the imagining.

What was that? she silently chastised.

She was abuzz with confusion, her atenté training scattered within her mind. What was she meant to say again? How was she supposed to react? Divert?

Tanwen knew only that the man in front of her was not behaving like the man whom she had met in Zomyad. The coldness in his features had been replaced by a curious spark; his hard gaze now held only warm interest.

Tanwen glanced at his forgotten wine on a nearby table, noticing the almost empty decanter.

Is he in his cups? she wondered.

Hoped.

This would certainly clarify the tone of their exchange.

"Then how may I be of service to His Royal Highness?" It almost pained Tanwen to ask, to put such power into his already powerful hands, but this was her role. An atenté never left a client wanting, certainly not the prince.

He must have noted her discomfort, for a small displeased pinch appeared between his brows before he sat back, breaking whatever rope had been coiling around them.

Tanwen let seep a relieving exhale.

"Are you part of the royal atentés?" he asked.

"I . . . have been hired for this evening's events from Sumora," she explained.

Thoughtfully, Prince Zolya drummed his fingers on his thigh before nodding. "And how are you finding Galia compared to Zomyad?"

Tanwen frowned. *Why do you care?* she wanted to argue. *Why does a prince desire to know how a servant is getting on?*

"My question confuses you."

My gods, she thought with further annoyance, *more of his assured assessments.*

Not that he was wrong.

"I am merely wondering," Tanwen began slowly, carefully, "why His Royal Highness would concern himself with a servant's thoughts on their time in Galia."

Her directness hit, for his brows rose ever so slightly. *Why indeed?* his expression seemed to say.

"It is part of my duty to understand the lives of those my family rules over," he explained. "You do not need to worry of upsetting me with your answer."

Tanwen almost snorted. "You are the crown prince," she pointed out. "Everyone must worry about upsetting you, sire."

This time, Prince Zolya allowed his grin to grow. Something Tanwen could tell he rarely indulged. If possible, it left him more dazzling, more disarming. "Well, for the moment you do not," he assured. "For me to reconnect with those I meet along my travels through Cādra is rare. I wish to hear of your voyage here and—" He paused, a puzzled expression overtaking him. "I apologize; what is your name?"

"My name?" she repeated, confused.

"I assume you have one."

"Yes, of course, sire."

He waited for her to give it, but she was stuck in her indecision as her thudding pulse sent a warning to her brain.

Lie, lie, lie.

But her name was already known in Fioré, and if she was ever to be found out in her lie . . .

"Tanwen Coster, sire,"

"Tanwen Coster," he repeated.

Never had her name, fake or real, sounded so . . . alluring when spoken out loud.

"So tell me, Ms. Coster," he began. "Are you enjoying Galia?"

"It is very beautiful, sire."

"It is," he agreed, allowing the following silence to stretch, as if knowing she had much more to say.

"It is also . . . different," she added.

"In what ways?" he pushed.

"Well . . ." She refocused on him. "I am not used to being so often under Ré's light," she explained. "I did not realize there would be so few trees in Fioré."

Prince Zolya's brows furrowed, as if he had not considered such a detail nor realized what a difference it could make to those who lived most of their lives exclusively within forests.

"But my opinions hardly matter," she added. "What of you, sire? Are you glad to be home?"

Tanwen knew it was a precarious branch to tread, but if the prince was willing to converse, she would use it to her benefit.

"I am certainly glad to no longer be sleeping near the snoring of a dozen men," he replied easily.

"That does sound unpleasant," Tanwen agreed. "But at least it wasn't all for naught? You eventually found the man you were looking for, this Gabreel Heiro."

At her words, Prince Zolya appeared to wake from a dream. He blinked, features hardening. "That is what this celebration is about, is it not? My and my men's successful mission and return."

"Of course, sire," said Tanwen, understanding she was mad to keep prying, but she would not get a better chance than this. "I asked around about him," she added boldly. "After our meeting."

Stars of blue held to her, Prince Zolya regarding her with a curious glint. "And what did you learn?"

"I learned he was the father of the Dryfs Mine and was the inventor for the king."

"Is," corrected the prince, tone chilling. "He *is* the inventor for the king. He has been reinstated."

Tanwen's hands tightened on her thighs. "What an honor for Mr. Heiro," she said tensely. "Is he here, then? At the celebration?"

Tanwen's pulse rushed, her breaths shallow. "If so, I would very much like to meet this legendary Gabreel Heiro. Perhaps he would like to indulge in my docüra."

"He is much too busy to attend such affairs," Prince Zolya replied, tone despondent. She could sense his attention drifting, his displeasure in discussing the inventor evident.

If he is so burdensome, let him go! she wanted to scream.

Or, at the very least, tell me where he is!

Tanwen was poised to pry further when their bubble of seclusion was disturbed.

"I believe I have found her, Lord Bacton," said a lilting voice from behind. "Yes, over here! She fits the description my ladies gave exactly."

Tanwen turned from where she knelt to find her den warden approaching along with a stunning woman adorned in gilded leaves and a small group of courtiers.

Tanwen's throat closed in a panic, taking in Lord Bacton's hard glare.

"Is this her, Lady Beatrice?" inquired the woman of a nearby companion.

"It is, Princess," answered Lady Beatrice.

Princess?

Tanwen's pulse kicked into a sprint.

She furtively glanced back at Prince Zolya. He was watching the exchange with furrowed brows.

So this is the infamous Princess Azla, thought Tanwen.

Bastard half sister and cousin to the prince.

Tanwen had heard many tales about the affair between the queen's sister and the king, but the only details she cared to hold on to were the repercussions of a king's desire: the queen who now lived in solitude and a mistress who was dead.

"Azla, what is this about?" asked Prince Zolya.

"Oh, sire, I apologize," said the princess, appearing as if she had just realized he was there. "We have been on the hunt for this atenté for a solid dip of the moons."

"And why is that?" he inquired.

"Because she is said to be spectacular!" she explained, giving an emphatic wave of her hand. "Or her docüra is," she added. "Is your docüra spectacular?" asked the princess as she bent toward Tanwen.

Tanwen could just make out the sweet scent of wine on Princess Azla's breath.

She realized then that it was the princess who was in her cups.

"I . . ." Tanwen faltered for a moment as she caught the pointed stare of her den warden.

I expect perfection. Lord Bacton's earlier command was a digging grip to her shoulders.

"Yes, ma'am," said Tanwen as she bowed her head demurely. "My docüra is, so long as I administer it."

Bloom, she thought, heartbeat pounding. *Now is my chance to bloom.*

The princess smiled, a spirit-glazed beam of pleasure. "I must have you," she said, returning to her full height. "Sire, if you are done with her services, I must procure this atenté for my party."

A spark of irritation flashed in the prince's features before it was covered up with cool indifference. "Who am I to keep you from what you desire, Princess?"

"Oh!" She clapped, a contented child. "You really do spoil me, my prince."

"I know," he muttered.

Before Tanwen collected her tray, she dared to meet the prince's blue gaze.

It grabbed her, an invisible hand cupping her chin, forcing her to hold his stare.

I see you, he seemed to be saying.

A sense of forewarning thickened the air, of looming dangers with each breath their connection remained.

This was not proper.

This was not right.

He was Volari, the man she was meant to hate, and the crown prince of Galia, for god's sake.

And yet . . . Tanwen could feel it. With her subsiding fear, an odd tethering was forming between them.

Quickly, Tanwen lowered her gaze, her mind reeling along with her pulse.

What was that?

She dared not look at him again as she gave a departing bow before she was shuffled to the far end of the garden.

There she would remain for the rest of the night.

Only once, when her wits had returned, did she indulge herself, glancing back to the far-off temple.

But the gazebo within now stood empty.

Prince Zolya had left.

20

The servants' dining hall was an accosting of laughter and gossip, the energy fit for a tavern at midnight rather than such a cruel early hour.

Tanwen groaned, rubbing at her temples as she sat, staring at her barely touched plate of food. She had piled it high with fresh fruits, soft steaming rolls, and cheeses, but despite its allure, she held the stomach for none of it.

Her entire body was broken.

Or felt that way after the strenuous evening of serving practically every member at court. Her feet and knees were throbbing, her arms sore, fingers stiff, throat hoarse.

Tanwen had nearly sobbed in relief when she finally collapsed into her bed, but dawn was already encroaching Nocémi's night, and too soon the servants' bell had rung out.

Tanwen had whimpered, a kicked dog, as she forced herself back on her feet.

"You can sleep on the gondola ride back to Fioré," said Huw sympathetically from where he sat beside her. "And we'll likely have a slow night at Sumora, given most of our patrons will be busy recovering from yesterday's celebrations."

Huw sipped his tea before stealing one of her rolls.

"How can you be so chipper so early?" groaned Tanwen.

"I wasn't nearly as busy as you were, little fawn. Princess Azla certainly has stamina."

Huw was too right.

Princess Azla and her entourage had been wild in their indulgences. The more inebriated they had become, the more unabashed they had grown in their manners and magic. Tanwen learned quickly that the princess was a wind wielder, as she had been too pleased to blow off straps of gowns and lift skirts of passing guests, chortling the entire time.

The only companion of Princess Azla's who was sober was her lady-in-waiting.

Lady Esme was consistently a step ahead of the princess: moving a glass before the princess knocked it over, catching food before it toppled from her tray to stain her dress, warming the princess with her heat magic when a cooler breeze passed through. She was also the only one in their group who did not indulge in docüra.

Like the prince.

But Tanwen didn't want to think about the prince. And not only because her body seemed to betray her in his presence, but because of what else she had learned last night. That he could be gentle and inquiring and, worst of all, that he appeared to care for the princess despite their rather tumultuous family history.

Beneath his exasperated facade toward Princess Azla when she had appeared, Tanwen had seen the truth in his heart by the way he indulged her whimsy. Even with his scowl, she could see the amused warmth in his gaze.

It was a look Thol often gave Tanwen.

The thought disturbed her: that he could be so kind to his own family and yet so cruel to another's.

Tanwen cleared her throat, forcing away her unwanted musings and refocusing her attention on Huw. "But you were out just as late as I," accused Tanwen. "I saw you walk into the dormitory after me."

"Yes," agreed Huw. "But that had nothing to do with work."

Tanwen followed Huw's line of sight, to where it was hooked to a young footman two tables away. The young man regarded Huw with open desire, a curling grin to his lips.

"I'm glad some of us had a good time, then," she replied dryly.

"Oh, don't pout, my love." Huw turned to face her, leaning one elbow on the table. "You did splendidly last night. In fact, you rendered most of us atentés useless."

"That's not true." Tanwen shifted uncomfortably. "Everyone had empty bowls by the end."

Tanwen had wanted to stand out, but perhaps not by so much.

It was impossible to ignore the humming of whispers around her this morning. She, the atenté who had been beckoned by both prince and princess.

While some of the residual effects were pleasant, palace servants now greeting her kindly, even with respect, there were still the royal atentés who glared at her as though they wished to push her over a ledge.

Particularly *one* atenté.

"Don't pay Gwyn any mind," Huw advised, sensing where Tanwen's attention had traveled. "She's merely not used to being outshone. The princess is her charge. It's natural she'd feel threatened with how favored you were last night. To my complete delight to witness, of course."

Gwyn was seated in the corner of the dining hall, a royal of her own among her circle of admirers. And there was certainly much to admire. Gwyn's brown skin was flawless, smoother than worked stone, her figure voluptuous, while her chestnut hair was her highlighting feature. Her Pelkish horns artfully curled against her silky curls, all framing prominent cheekbones and full lips.

Though Gwyn's beauty turned sour as she noticed Tanwen's stare.

Gwyn leaned toward her companions, likely saying something insulting that made the whole table laugh and look at Tanwen.

Tanwen's cheeks grew hot, ire awakening in her gut, her old but never healing wound of being gossiped about breaking open once more.

Tanwen concentrated on her plate. "How do you know her again?" she asked Huw.

"She used to work at Sumora," he explained. "I was a greeny like you, actually, when I met her. Or, rather, was trampled by her. She doesn't long tolerate those who don't fall into line at her side."

"And she got promoted to the palace?"

"Mm-hmm." Huw nodded as he forked one of Tanwen's strawberries, then plopped it into his mouth. "After a party much like the one last night. Her goal was always to work in the palace, though. We were all glad to see her leave."

Tanwen considered this. "And you?" she asked. "Have you no desire to work here?"

Huw snorted. "The only ambition of mine is to live."

His answer disturbed Tanwen, only in that it mirrored her own. Well, before she was set with the task to reunite her family.

At the reminder, her stomach clenched.

"*Bogs*," she cursed as she stood.

Tanwen was meant to reconnect with Eli in the dormitory before they left. He had taken to searching the palace while she had been busy attending to the party. Tanwen had hoped he'd have found something of value for her to do some snooping of her own prior to their departure.

"Where are you going?" Huw's brows pinched in concern.

"What is the time?" She ignored his question.

"I'm not sure." Huw glanced to the view of the sky beyond a nearby window. "Early."

"I have to do something before we leave," she said, untangling from the table. "I'll see you at the gondola."

"But you haven't eaten anything."

"It's all yours."

Before Tanwen could take so much as a step away, she was stopped by a courier. "Madam Arini wishes to speak with you both," informed the man, his palace chiton pressed and immaculate.

"Us both?" questioned Tanwen.

"Yes, you and Mr. Lew."

"Mr. Lew?" Tanwen turned to Huw, unable to hold back her grin. "Your name is Huw Lew?"

Huw pursed his lips, less than pleased by this leaked information. "One of *many* egregious oversights by my parents," he muttered. "You don't have to look *so* very happy about it."

"But I think I do," countered Tanwen, her smile widening.

"What is it that Madam Arini wants with us?" Huw asked the courier, attempting to redirect the conversation.

"For you to see her." The man tutted. "Now come—she doesn't like to be kept waiting."

◆ ◆ ◆

Madam Arini's office was a reflection of herself. Neat, impersonal, and sharp. Tanwen stood with disquiet as she eyed the spilling bouquet of white-thorned roses atop her desk. Of which the marble top was carved into a sharp triangle, its tip pointed directly at where Tanwen and Huw hovered. A spear aimed at the accused.

"I'm going to get to this quickly, as I have other matters to attend to this morning," said Madam Arini from where she sat, poised upright in her chair. At her back, a large window framed her tall horns and thin frame. "You will not be heading back to Fioré today."

Tanwen blinked and then blinked again, not trusting her ears.

"It appears," she continued haughtily, "that you have pleased the proper guests from last night's celebration. You will be promoted, starting today, to serve in the palace as part of my royal atentés."

A ringing filled Tanwen's head as she floated for a moment above her body.

You will be promoted . . . to serve in the palace . . . starting today.

A bubble of deranged laughter nearly left her as Madam Arini's words finally sank in.

By the Eternal River!

She was to stay.

In the palace!

Where her father and Thol were being held.

Where she could search for them.

Find them.

And then set them all free.

Tanwen inhaled a stuttering breath, her chest feeling as though it might burst from her in shock and relief and gratitude. Her plan had *worked*. By the Low Gods, it had worked! She had bloomed and was being brought inside. She could not wait to write to her mother to tell her the news. At the thought, a punch of homesickness lodged between Tanwen's ribs.

But her moment of melancholy was robbed by Madam Arini's cool voice addressing Huw.

"Mr. Lew," she began. "As you know, finding quality male atentés has always been difficult. So while, yes, you were requested by a courtier to be pulled to the palace, you will still need to prove your worth to me."

"Of course, ma'am." Huw bowed, exaggeratingly too low. "I live only to serve you and the court."

Madam Arini sucked her teeth, unimpressed with Huw's mock deference.

"And you, Ms. Coster." She turned her shrewd gaze on Tanwen.

Tanwen stiffened.

"I'm sure you are pleased with how well you and your docüra performed last night."

It was a feat that Madam Arini could make such a statement sound so accusatory.

"Yes, ma'am," replied Tanwen.

"I will expect you to teach the others this prayer you say you use to enhance your mixture." She eyed Tanwen expectantly, fingernails clacking on her desk.

Tanwen kept herself from shifting, with a hard swallow in her throat. It was a test, of course. To learn if Tanwen was a charlatan or not. Could she reproduce what she had last night?

"I will certainly do my best to try, ma'am. Though it's not a tried-and-true method," she explained.

"I'm sure it's not," said Madam Arini, eyes narrowing. "Nevertheless, I will expect you to bring added value to my atentés; otherwise you are merely another mouth to feed, especially as you will be sharing the same duties with another of my staff."

"Same duties, ma'am?" Tanwen questioned.

"You now will be serving the princess as one of her personal atentés."

Tanwen's mouth went agape.

"A role that will be shared with Ms. Allyga," she explained.

Icy dread replaced Tanwen's moment of glee, understanding settling.

"*Gwyn* Allyga?" Tanwen asked.

"Indeed," Madam Arini confirmed, a knowing glimmer in her eye at Tanwen's unease. "You both will take turns looking after Princess Azla. You'll find that Her Royal Highness is a loyal sort, which is why she is keeping Ms. Allyga on. Usually atentés are replaced, but in this case, she has commanded for you both to see to her needs."

"As the princess wishes," said Tanwen with a bow, forcing herself to appear calm despite her racing pulse and growing terror.

This was not good.

"Any of your belongings still at Sumora, a courier will deliver later this evening," explained Madam Arini. "You will be fitted for uniforms upon leaving my office and shown to your stations within the atentés' quarters. Your responsibilities in your roles start now."

"Yes, ma'am," Tanwen and Huw replied in unison.

"That will be all."

Once dismissed, Tanwen shuffled out into the hall with Huw, her breaths feeling trapped in her lungs.

"Congratulations, little fawn." Huw wrapped his arm around Tanwen's shoulder, giving it a squeeze. "Look at the pair of us: me impressing courtiers, you a princess. Both getting promoted to work in the palace." He sighed. "Finally, I don't need to fib in my diary about living an exciting life."

Tanwen remained quiet, thoughts swirling.

"You don't seem pleased?" Huw observed before clicking his tongue in understanding. "Gwyn will learn to share."

"Will she?" Tanwen challenged, brows raised.

"No," admitted Huw. "She'll be wretched, but luckily you have me. I'll teach you how to deal with such sour grapes."

"I know how to deal with them," Tanwen conceded, the weight of exhaustion settling upon her. "I've spent my whole life dealing with them, actually."

Huw regarded her curiously, which made Tanwen regret her words. She needed to be more careful with what she shared.

Huw might be showing signs of loyalty, but there was no guarantee he'd stay that way if he found out the person he was currently embracing was Mütra.

Which was the precise danger of Gwyn.

If Tanwen couldn't trust a friend with her secret, how catastrophic would it then be to work so closely with an enemy?

For that's exactly how Gwyn would view Tanwen: as a threat to everything she had worked toward.

But the feeling would be mutual.

Tanwen had not come this far, gambled, and sacrificed so much to cower.

While in the palace, Tanwen had her own ambitions.

Her veins brimmed with anxious anticipation for her task ahead.

She *would* locate her father and brother, free them, and find a way off this island.

And Tanwen was determined to succeed, whatever the cost.

PART IV

LABYRINTH

21

The king was angry.

And regrettably, Gabreel was to blame.

"You have wasted my time, Heiro," boomed King Réol.

He was a rippling statue of muscle draped in white robes from where he stood at the head of the stone table. Gabreel was at the far end, having been brought to his council room, which was less of a room and more of a circular pillared temple on the west side of the palace. A lonely building surrounded by sky.

The only way in was to fly or climb a treacherous rocky wall. Gabreel might not have worn shackles, but his bonds were the perils of a deadly descent. As a light breeze blew through the columns, the scars along Gabreel's back burned, ghostly wings urging him to escape, to jump from the ledge and be free.

But he could not.

For more reasons than the brutal reality that he no longer had wings.

"You have wasted my time," the king repeated as his wintry gaze speared Gabreel. "And your own in your attempt to protect your offspring. These plans are unacceptable." He dropped the schematics on the table, the papers fanning out.

"Your Majesty," said Gabreel calmly, hands in fists at his back. "These are two viable and working options for the mine. More than what my predecessor could create."

"Yes, but they exceed our budget to erect," chimed in Lord Tezzos, one of the king's advisers. He was a trussed-up bird in his lavender-and-gold tunic, wings dyed to match. A theme, it appeared, for all in the king's council. The painted parrots were six in total, a colorful wall of fashion on either side of His Majesty.

"That's what it costs to build at this site," countered Gabreel. "The rock is unstable so close to the cliffs. The waves erode masses of dirt each year. We might be able to tap the ore for a time, but it would be short lived and extremely dangerous for both workers and overseers. We must fortify it properly, or you might as well throw every gem and ambrü you spend straight into the Aspero Sea."

There was a chorus of huffs and annoyed sputters from the council. They might have been displeased, but they knew Gabreel was right. Certainly, it was not the first time they had heard such an assessment. His predecessor's schematics were wrought with such findings. But where Bardrex had failed to finish the mine's design infrastructure, Gabreel had succeeded. *Twice.*

"And your other plan?" questioned one of the treasury chairs. Lord Artur, Gabreel thought his name was. He was a sprig of a man, pale, his brown wings seemingly too big for him to command with any real skill. *New blood,* Gabreel thought. *Primed to be corrupted.* "Is there a way to build from further away that will not take as long?" Lord Artur pressed.

If Gabreel were a cat, he would have hissed. These men were buffoons, children wishing for miracles.

A pounding throb had begun along his temples, sleep deprivation mixing with his desperate rage.

He had been working tirelessly over the past weeks to meet the deadline of this council session. Not sleeping, hardly eating.

The only soul capable of awakening him from his hypnosis was his son. Aberthol's torture had blessedly paused with Gabreel's progress, and with it his son had begun to stir, pieces of his old self returning in fractured light. He had even begun to sit beside Gabreel, watching as he worked. At one point, Thol had offered up a suggestion or two. It had nearly brought Gabreel to tears. But instead, he had merely nodded and scribbled down the note. Gabreel did not want to startle away whatever healing might have begun in his son.

Of course, Gabreel understood demons did not fade—pain became scars, forever marking minds—but with time he hoped Aberthol would return to a semblance of his old soul.

As had happened to Gabreel after he lost his wings.

It had taken nearly a decade to understand who he was, *what* he was, without them, but with the help of Aisling and the birth of his children, he understood his purpose lay in his mind, not his feathers.

Unfortunately, Gabreel feared time was not a luxury his son had for healing his wounds.

"Yes," said Gabreel. "I'm sure there is a way to build quicker. It's a matter of procuring, or inventing, the right methods to do so. If I am given another week or—"

"You have already been given many weeks," interrupted King Réol, wings snapping at his back.

"Yes, Your Majesty, I have." Gabreel bowed. "For which I am forever grateful, but I was unaware of how strict our timing and budget truly were. With my past services, there was always flexibility—"

"Your past services also produced more inspired solutions." The king's voice was a cracking of a whip.

Gabreel kept his head bowed, thumping heartbeat pounding against his ribs.

Time. I need more time.

The temple fell quiet, save for the subtle breeze running its fingers through the surrounding columns.

"Perhaps you have too many distractions, Heiro," began the king, a deceptive delight leaking into his tone. "Your spawn might inspire your speed, but it appears to deflate your usual inventive mind."

Gabreel's gaze met King Réol's, his lungs constricting with panicked fire.

No! he wanted to scream. *Do not touch my son!*

It took everything in Gabreel to remain quiet, biting the inside of his cheek until he tasted blood.

The king already knew he had him trapped with Aberthol, knew he could control Gabreel like a marionette. One simple pull of a string, and he'd bring him to his knees. It would not benefit Gabreel to give the king any more pleasure by letting him hear his pain. The High Gods knew he got enough by watching.

"Yes," continued the king, tone musing. "I believe I have been too lenient with you. If you want your week, you may have it, but in exchange you will give me your spawn for that time. I have no doubt you will find a better solution than what you have presented so far."

Gabreel was no longer standing in the room; he was shredded into a dozen pieces, ribbons of silent screams, strips of painful howls as King Réol gave a nod to the awaiting guards.

This monster will have my child, thought Gabreel, his lucidness slipping as hands gripped his arms. *He will destroy him.* Gabreel was pulled back, ushered toward the edge of the temple, only clouds and sky beyond. Soon he would be flown back to his windowless hole. *It should be me he takes. Me he destroys. Not Thol, not Thol, not Thol.*

"*Wait!*" Gabreel boomed, digging his heels into the marble floor, attempting to twist out of his captors' hold. His skin burned against their vise grip, muscles screaming. "Your Majesty! There is another way! I have another way! Please, it may be mad, but let me share it with you."

The temple fell quiet as the king signaled for the soldiers to halt, turning Gabreel back to him.

"Mad, you say?" inquired the king.

"Yes, Your Majesty," Gabreel breathed, desperate intakes of air. "It is an idea from a Gabreel of the past."

His words hit.

Gabreel was released, and with awkward, panicked motions, he demanded one of his leather-bound cases from the guards. He passed a scroll of papers to a councilman, who handed it to the king.

Gabreel watched, anxiousness swirling, as King Réol read through the proposal. It was a plan he had thought of during one of his exhausted sleepless nights. When reason gave way to make-believe, to dreams, to desperate fanciful hopes of how a problem might be solved. He had glanced to his son dozing in the corner, watched the gentle rises and falls of his chest, and had a mad slip of illusion they were back in their den in Zomyad. Aisling would be upstairs in her workroom, their children safe, tucked in. A sob nearly tumbled from him then. How angry was Aisling at him? How disappointed was she that he had brought such harm to their family? This was when Gabreel had written down his mad scheme, organized it as thoughtfully as any other probable solution. Aisling would have told him to do it, *ordered* him to.

Whatever is needed to save our child, do!

So Gabreel had.

After all, they had spent the past two decades tirelessly working to avoid Gabreel standing exactly where he was now, forced to create another design that would exploit the vulnerable for the gain of the powerful.

Gabreel had been naive to think he could ever escape his past, be gifted a life after his sin with the Dryfs Mine.

Why then fight fate further?

The king could have whatever plan of Gabreel's he liked. For as it was proved, he'd have it in the end anyway.

His Majesty met Gabreel's gaze from across the table.

A trickling of sickening, dreaded silence.

And then the king did something that was perhaps more terrifying than his wrath: he laughed, a rumble of thunder.

Gabreel held back a wince.

"And here is the man I remember," said King Réol, his blue gaze a reflective clear sky as he studied Gabreel. "Gabreel Heiro," he added, almost sighed. "The man who invents marvels from miracles." He passed the papers to the hungry men at his sides. They were vipers, lashing out to read first—at the very least, not wanting to be the last.

"Orzel?" whispered one of the councilmen in confusion.

"The High God?" another questioned with a frown.

"He controls the sea," said Gabreel matter-of-factly. "And the sea is our mine's issue."

"So it is," agreed the king. He was now looking at Gabreel as if a fond, proud parent.

"He will pull back the tides?" asked Lord Artur, who now held the plans, one delicate skeptical brow lifted.

"That is the idea," confirmed Gabreel. "If Orzel could calm the waters, permanently pull back the tide in that section, we can build the new mine twice as fast for half the price. It would be as if we were erecting a mine on dry land."

How easy it all sounded, how logical. But, of course, there was a snag.

"Your Majesty," began Lord Tezzos. "As you know, Orzel . . . is not the most cooperative of High Gods to . . . negotiate with."

Tezzos was being delicate. Orzel was the angriest, most disagreeable of the High Gods. Forever destined to live so close to the Low Gods, he was in a state of eternal displeasure, which showed in his constant rough seas. Orzel was in a permanent state of having a tantrum.

Which was exactly what made this plan so insane, so impossible.

"He'll certainly demand something of great value," said Lord Artur.

"A trade much worthier than what he is giving us," added another.

"Perhaps a gift that will connect him closer to the High Gods?" suggested Lord Tezzos.

"Yes," agreed the king, features turning pensive. "A gift is what he will desire. A gift that only I could give." A dangerous spark of understanding lit his gaze as it settled back on Gabreel. "Luckily, I know just the one to offer."

22

Zolya was irritated.

But being summoned at the first light by the king often left him in such a state.

Not even the quiet of the palace assuaged the tension radiating down his spine as he flew through the wide halls. The rising sun painted the white marble in pinks and yellows, yawning tendrils of gentle light cutting between the large columns. The morning was thick with the scent of jasmine, and the only others awake were the servants. No courtiers yet filled the palace. None were accustomed to rising before midmeal.

As Zolya curved around a pillar, the tips of his wings brushed the intricate carvings that ran up the spine, a familiar graze. He did not land until he approached the south wing, where the corridors became narrow, forcing him to his feet. His guards were forever in tow, silent shadows at his back.

He very much wished to shirk them.

It was too early to don his princely persona, but like any other time in his life, he hadn't a choice.

Just as he hadn't a choice to disobey his father's command.

Zolya was here to fetch Azla.

More reason for his current foul disposition.

King Réol hardly, if ever, took note of his daughter, and when he did, it was never favorable.

What could he want with Azla? It was the question that had weighed on his thoughts his entire flight over.

Zolya swallowed his unease as he approached the princess's chambers.

The two kidets stationed outside gave him quick salutes. The usher at the seam of her door bowed low.

"Your Royal Highness," said Emyr, his horns painted white to match his uniform, "I fear the princess needs a moment more to ready herself for your presence."

A flutter of panic filled Zolya's chest.

If one wished to anger the king, make him wait.

"I sent a summons before Ré had fully awoken," exclaimed Zolya, eyes narrowing. "How is she still not ready?"

Emyr did not so much as blink at Zolya's curt tone. As one of the ushers to the royal household, his duty was to intercept grievances. And being stationed with the princess, grievances he no doubt had aplenty. "Well, sire—" he began before he was interrupted by the opening of the door behind him.

"Sire," chirped Alys, the princess's lady's maid. She scurried out, giving a low apologetic bow, all while Emyr glared daggers at her for disturbing his post.

But the sight of Alys eased some of Zolya's tension.

If he wished for truth, she would be the one to give it.

Alys had been serving the princess for over four decades, but her age did not disturb her quickness or sturdy reliability. Originally hailing from the southern clan, her straight horns curved slightly inward to sharp points. As Zolya noted them, a vision of another flashed through his mind. Eyes like rich moss, onyx hair, and a bold fire even her polite words could not hide.

He blinked the image away, instantly disquieted.

Zolya had thought too often over the past few days of the meddyg turned atenté from the party. An oddity, for sure, for no stranger had ever occupied his mind at such length. Certainly not a servant.

"I hear the princess is still indisposed," said Zolya to Alys.

"She will not stir from her bed, sire," admitted Alys, cheeks an exasperated red. "I have told her you would be arriving posthaste, but she said if the prince was determined to summon her before even the High Gods deemed it acceptable, he could extend the courtesy of patience and wait."

Zolya raised a brow. "Did she now?"

Alys, looking horrified, nodded.

Emyr, on the other hand, was a gawking, bright-red splotch, no doubt appalled by a staff member sharing so much about their charge.

Emyr, evidently, was still put out by Alys's idiosyncrasies.

But Zolya had little time to help the two get on.

"Wait here," Zolya ordered his guards before marching past the usher and lady's maid.

The pair gave a useless, distressed plea, but Zolya did not hesitate as he pushed through the receiving room, then strode through the sitting room to swing open the bedroom doors.

The drapes had already been pulled back, the morning light covering the billowing puffs of pillows and blankets that made up Azla's bed in a honeycomb embrace.

Zolya was unfazed by the scene of his sister-cousin entangled in her lady-in-waiting's arms. A twisting of bare skin, hair, and feathers.

"Zolya!" Azla sprang up with a yip, white wings flinging around to cover herself and her lover.

"Sire!" said Lady Esme in equal dismay as she attempted to extend a gracious bow over the feathers.

If Zolya was in a different mood, he would have laughed at the absurdity of the moment.

But as it was, he was more terrified of making their father wait.

"Get dressed," he said to Azla. "The king wishes to see us."

"The king?" questioned Azla before repeating, "The king!" She jumped from the bed, no longer caring for modesty as she flew, bare arse and all, into her washroom. "Alys!" she cried. "You are needed at once!"

Her lady's maid hurried in, flowing gown in hand.

"Why did you not say it was for the king?" Azla demanded from the other room.

"I did not realize I needed to," replied Zolya from where he remained in the center of the bedroom. He eyed the trays of half-eaten meats and cheeses lying about, the multiple empty spirit bottles, and the remnants of a night indulging in docüra. "You two certainly appear to have had a fine evening," he said to Lady Esme, who had slipped on a silk robe. She stood by the foot of the bed, her pale complexion striking against her amber wings and hair.

"It was the eve of Lady Phiona's birth," she explained. "The princess is most thoughtful to celebrate each of her friends thus."

"Indeed," mused Zolya. "It is also most thoughtful if the princess's lady-in-waiting ensures she takes the summons from a royal relative more seriously next time."

Lady Esme had the good sense to look chastened, cheeks staining pink. "Yes, Your Highness. Of course." She curtsied. "I shall aid in preparing her now."

Zolya pursed his lips, showing a thin shred of satisfaction as Lady Esme disappeared into the adjacent room.

Only then, when alone, did he let out a tired sigh, his wings drooping at his back. He glanced to the connecting veranda beyond the tall pillars of the bedroom, to the endless azure sky.

It was another perfect day in Galia, but it brought little comfort.

Whenever Zolya was this ill at ease, he yearned for rain. He wished to gather the churning disquiet mixing within his veins and expel it. His magic crackled through his blood for him to make lightning, rumbled to let loose thunder. He was desperate to cover the sky in his storm.

Instead, he fisted his hands at his side, pushing away the temptation.

It was not Zolya's purview to disturb the weather in Galia. Least of all because of a sour mood. That was saved for the king.

At the thought of his father, Zolya's spine straightened further. They were certainly going to be late.

Frustration flared as he spun on his heels, preparing to dress Azla himself, but he was brought up short.

A servant had entered the bedroom, and the sight of her nearly stopped his heart.

"Tanwen," he heard himself whisper.

Her eyes went wide; evidently she was not expecting to find him standing there either. Or, at the very least, for him to be so informal as to call her by her given name. With the state of her shock, the tray she held rocked unsteadily, and before Zolya knew what he was doing, he shot forward, saving the delicate tonic from toppling to the ground.

A mistake.

Not only because he now found himself kneeling before her, a catastrophic role reversal that she alone would suffer the lashes for if seen, but also because at this proximity, he could practically drink her scent. An earthy vanilla that sped up his pulse on each inhale.

The world froze as Zolya looked up—or rather got pulled in by her rich green gaze, so much more vibrant in the morning light. The skirts of her simple peplos uniform were a finger graze away, the heat of her body pushing against his. Sunlight draped across her side, a shimmering to her dark hair and a spark against her gold-tipped horns.

He noted a line of four freckles along the underside of her jaw. Something about this new discovery pleased him. With each meeting there was more to collect, admire.

It was this precise musing, however, that snapped everything back into focus.

What am I doing? Zolya chastised himself as he stood.

The sudden height of him seemed to further knock her off balance, for she practically jumped to the other side of the room, as if he held the power of wind and blew her hence.

"Your Royal Highness." She bowed and remained bowing. "I apologize. I did not . . . please forgive my clumsiness."

"You may be at ease," he said. "No harm was done."

As she straightened, furtively meeting his gaze, it was as if they both knew he was lying.

Something harmful certainly had transpired, but with a sense of self-preservation, Zolya ignored what that something might be. He blamed his momentary loss in constitution on not getting enough sleep the night before and for his day having begun in a panic with his father's summons.

"Why are you here?" Zolya asked, an echo of the same question he had met her with the other night, but this time it came out accusatory. *Why are you here, again, taking up space in my thoughts?*

She straightened at his tone, the building of a wall.

But before she could respond, Azla returned to the room.

She was a burst of sea mist in her delicately wrapped green dress, silver laurel crown braided into her alabaster hair. Lady Esme and Alys were quick on her heels, looking breathless.

"Oh, thank Udasha," said Azla as she noted who else was in the room and rushed forward. "I am having the most dreadful of a morning, and your tonic is exactly what—wait, where is your tonic?"

There was a stretch of silence as the princess glanced from her servant's empty hands to Zolya, who held the missing tray.

"Why do you have that?" his sister-cousin questioned, hands plunking on her hips. "Were you being rude to my new atenté?"

My new atenté.

A rush of emotions spilled over Zolya, none of them pleasant.

"Why would I be rude?" he managed in an even tone.

"Because you are you," Azla reasoned.

"What does that mean?" He frowned, not at all enjoying such an accusation.

What am I? he thought mulishly.

"Never mind," said Azla. "We don't have time to discuss such matters. The king requests our presence." She floated to his side and, with a swig that was wholly unbecoming of a princess and completely revealing of her familiarity around strong drink, shot back the green tonic.

"What is that?" asked Zolya, still finding himself holding the tray as Azla set the glass down.

"My bleeding is coming," she explained, straightening her skirts. "Ms. Coster has been kind enough to make me something that helps with the . . . particulars a woman can suffer leading up to the affair. If I'm to face Father, I would prefer to do so feeling my best."

A surge of protectiveness coiled around Zolya at the reminder of where they were headed. He hated that he was dragging Azla into their father's lair; he particularly hated that he didn't know the reason why. It left no room for Zolya to plan, prepare as he was wont to do when it came to any interaction with the king. And because he despised feeling out of control, he directed his emotions at what he could.

"Your atenté is suggesting tonics to you?" Zolya turned from the princess to glare at Ms. Coster. She had remained, patiently awaiting her dismissal, by the threshold to the room. "Is that appropriate to your role here?" he accused. "We have the most skilled Volari meddyg in all of Cādra to service the royal household. It is not for you to suggest elixirs of any kind beyond your docüra to the princess."

Ms. Coster's eyes sparked with ire despite her reddening cheeks. "Of course, sire," she managed. "It will not happen again, sire."

Her compliance seemed to only further incite Zolya, as it made him perfectly aware of his ridiculous outburst. *But by the twin moons!* He was so very tired of working so very hard to keep everything for this palace, for Galia, for all Cādra, in order so his king—and, most importantly, their gods—would remain pleased. The least he asked from others was for them to not make it so damn difficult each and every day.

And Ms. Coster now being here—in the palace, working for the princess—only promised difficulty for Zolya. Her presence made him uncomfortable in that it made him feel at all.

"Well," huffed the princess. "If you needed further proof of why I had wondered if you had been rude . . ."

"*Azla*," he warned.

"*Zolya*," she mimicked.

Gods, he thought in silent frustration. He might as well have been arguing with his mother.

Which was probably why he put up with so much from Azla. The same freedoms the queen extended to him, he found he extended to the princess. But it was edging on enough.

"I am merely ensuring you are getting the proper care from the proper staff," reasoned Zolya.

"Then let me ease your woes by assuring you that I am," countered Azla. "Meddyg Hyrez may be skilled in many areas of healing, but to attend to the true ailments of a woman, he is most ignorant."

"How so?"

"He is a *man*, Zolya."

"And?"

"And he knows nothing about the intricacies of a woman's bleeding."

"If that is true, then why do no other ladies at court have the same grievances regarding Hyrez?"

"Because ladies are not meant to have grievances at all!"

The room hung quiet as Zolya hesitated with his response. He had inadvertently soared into a dangerous sky.

"Just as Volari women are not allowed to learn a trade," seethed Azla, seeming unable to stop herself now. "Or own a business. If we were, I would have *gladly* gone to the royal *female* meddyg for their aid. But as it is, we are only taught how to sit with poise and prune plants, marry well, and laugh at tiresome jokes. Even our magic is useless."

"*Azla*," hissed Zolya, fearing any High God who might be listening, not to mention the attending servants. This conversation needed to end. "Your blood has been blessed by our benevolent creators and holds a royal lineage. If anyone's magic has purpose, it is yours."

"Really?" scoffed the princess. "Then, pray tell, how is pushing colored sand into patterns with my wind for an entire day useful to our world?"

Zolya blinked, speechless. He had never witnessed this Azla. He knew she had complaints. Who didn't? But he hadn't known they were to such a fundamental extent.

It made him uneasy.

Mostly because he agreed with her.

But again, this was *not* the moment to share such sentiments, especially not when they had an audience.

He eyed Lady Esme behind the princess, caught the spark of admiration in her gaze, the love. Alys was the definition of a blush. Zolya did not dare look at Ms. Coster.

"I see you need time to collect your thoughts on the matter," said the princess, removing the tray from his hands and walking it to Ms. Coster. "While you do, sire, hear this. Yes, I implored one of my personal atentés for her services over meddyg Hyrez because, while Ms. Coster is exceptionally skilled in the making of her docüra, I was very pleased to learn she is also a talented meddyg, who comes from a lineage of meddygs. Unlike Volari, Süra woman are *allowed* to learn trades." The princess placed a gentle hand on Ms. Coster's shoulder, a sign of solidarity, of protection. "When she offered this tonic, I took it. And guess what? It *works*."

"Does it?" Zolya quipped, brows raised. Azla's disposition was anything but pleasing.

"*Yes.*" Azla glared at him. "So leave me, and her, be. You are obviously in a terrible mood because of who has summoned us. Do not be so predictable by taking your displeasure out on the help."

With that, the princess spun from her bedroom, strode to the veranda, and took flight.

Zolya's reaction was swift. He whistled for his guards as he chased the princess into the sky.

By the Eternal River, thought Zolya as he settled beside Azla, the warm wind pushing against his wings, *what just happened?*

He would not ask Azla, of course. Not now.

Not when they flew toward their father. Or while he still felt the sting from her earlier words and the gaze of Ms. Coster as he had run past her.

Ms. Coster . . .

A woman—no, a *servant*—who had literally brought him to his knees.

Zolya pumped his wings harder, attempting to work out his compounding frustrations and the unsettling chill of his and Ms. Coster's brief but private exchange.

This will not do, he thought. *This* certainly *will not do.*

As he flew toward the highest peak of the palace, Zolya thought how foolish he had been to believe his day could not get worse.

23

Well, mused Tanwen quietly as she hurried from the princess's chambers, *that was strange.*

Very strange, agreed Eli.

Her friend was curled within a small pouch tied along her waist. A carrying case Tanwen had constructed to blend in with her white uniform. If Eli insisted on accompanying her everywhere, he might as well travel less conspicuously. Tanwen surmised Madam Arini, as well as those in the palace, would not take kindly to him sitting atop her shoulder.

She certainly did not need to draw any more attention to herself, and not only because she was Mütra.

The prince doesn't seem to like you, stated Eli.

How convenient, returned Tanwen. *Since I do not like the prince.*

Which was the truth.

And yet . . .

Tanwen.

The memory of her name whispered from his lips trapped her heartbeat in an erratic pounding. He had been a shock to see, standing so stoically alone in the princess's bedchambers. And then when he had dived to save her tonic, bringing him to kneel before her. A mass of wings and muscle and glowing beauty. It had sent every alarm bell ringing within Tanwen.

Because she had enjoyed the sight.

Tremendously.

It had poured wicked imaginings into her mind. She the queen, he the imploring subject.

Tanwen commanding, him obeying.

Her family set free. Safe. Returned.

And then he had yelled at her.

Scolded her.

As if she were a child.

Tanwen's cheeks flamed once more, ire sparking as she quickened her pace. She needed to get to the lower level of the palace, where the servants roamed freer. There she could properly collect herself without the gaze of winged guards or strolling court members.

But it was not merely being in the presence of the prince that had dizzied her thoughts.

Princess Azla's speech had been revolutionary, inspired, and it had stirred awake precarious musing in Tanwen. If even she, a princess, could experience the injustices of their world, of being a woman, how many others felt the same?

Perhaps her argument around learning a trade was a bit . . . shortsighted, given Süra *had* to work to put food on their tables, whereas Volari were born into their idle privilege. But even so, Tanwen understood what it was to yearn for a purpose, wanting to work in something that brought her joy.

While the inequalities between women who were Süra, Volari, and especially Mütra were vast, at the end of the day, they each held the same shortcoming: not being born a man.

Rounding a corner, Tanwen was so lost in her thoughts that she hardly took in the group until she nearly ran into them.

"By the Eternal River," hissed the woman in the center, steadying her held basket. "Slow down, Weasel! If Madam Arini saw you running on the primary floor, she'd have you lashed. In fact, I see no reason why I shouldn't report the incident myself."

Tanwen's spine went rigid, her grip tightening on her tray, and not only because of who stood before her but because she eyed their gardening material.

Tanwen was going to be late to her next shift.

Bogs, she silently cursed.

Rats, squeaked Eli from her hip.

Hush! she warned him.

Her day was certainly starting out miserably.

"My apologies," said Tanwen, averting her gaze and taking on the meeker persona she had used all her life. While there was a time and place to stand up to Gwyn, currently she had little energy for it. Tanwen merely wished to be on her way so she could quickly change and get to the greenhouse.

Gwyn glared at her along with her two other atenté companions, Owen and Efa.

"You *should* report her, Gwyn," said Owen, a statue of chiseled muscle and rigid posture. His eastern horns were painted gold, contrasting against his short-cropped black hair and complexion. "How else will the Weasel learn?"

"We can take the burden off of the madam and teach her ourselves," suggested Efa, her grin slick and sharp on her pale face.

I will bite holes in their uniforms tonight, promised Eli within his pouch.

At Eli's threat, Tanwen suppressed a grin, though apparently not well enough.

"You find our threats amusing?" Gwyn's gaze narrowed, chin lifting.

"Not in the least," said Tanwen. "I truly am sorry to have gotten in your way. As you can see"—she waved to her general white dress—"I'm already going to be late to our gardening post, so my scolding from Madam Arini will be inevitable. You do not need to go out of your way on my behalf."

Gwyn sucked in her cheeks, as if she found anything Tanwen said to be repugnant. Her attention dropped to the tray Tanwen held, to the empty glass. Her eyes became slits. "You were with the princess."

Tanwen stood perfectly still, though her pulse galloped in fear.

They had been sharing duties to the princess for a week now, but it had become clear Tanwen was spending extra time with their charge. A development Gwyn was none too pleased about.

"Princess Azla never indulges in docüra this early," Gwyn accused, picking up the glass on Tanwen's tray and giving it a sniff.

Her nose wrinkled.

Gwyn was a talented atenté, to be sure, but she was no meddyg.

"What is this?" she questioned, accusing tone so like Prince Zolya's. "Answer me, Weasel! What have you been up to?"

Tanwen swallowed, eyes darting to see if anyone might be close, but the towering hall was annoyingly empty. Only the clouds beyond the columns were witness to their moment.

"I've merely been obeying the orders from our princess," said Tanwen.

"*This*"—Gwyn pushed forward the glass, as if she was resisting hurling it at Tanwen—"appears to be going beyond our regular orders."

Tanwen's temper momentarily flared. "You don't even know what *this* is."

Gwyn's brows lifted. "Well, it's obviously not docüra, *Weasel*."

Tanwen wanted to roll her eyes at the name. At least those in Zomyad had been more original. Weasels were amazing animals. Clever, playful, steadfast.

Gwyn could call her a weasel all she liked, but it would stir only amusement from Tanwen.

"No, it's not," admitted Tanwen. "The princess required certain services from me this morning, which I complied with, as every servant is meant to for their charge. I can say nothing more on the matter. It would be going against the code of—"

"Don't lecture me on the protocol of our roles," cut in Gwyn. "I have not risen in my rank by happenstance, you graceless farmhand."

That's it, declared Eli, offended. *I'm going to chew through not just her uniform but all the straps in her sandals. And I'm going to leave a nice trail of—*

"Of course," Tanwen said placatingly, cutting off Eli. She needed to get out of this tangle before it got worse. "Again, I apologize for disturbing your morning. I am only doing as I am told. Please, let me pass so I may prepare for our next shift."

Tanwen lowered her eyes, hands holding her tray subserviently.

Stay hidden, thought Tanwen, reawakening her mantra given by her mother. *Do not bring attention to yourself. Be small.*

The silence in the hall stretched painfully long—Gwyn, no doubt, measuring if Tanwen was currently worth the fuss. In the end, it appeared she was more than worth it, for Gwyn leaned in and whispered, "I see what you really are, Tanwen Coster. I see what you hide."

Tanwen's breath hitched, blood draining from her face as an all-consuming fear grasped her spine. *She knows? She knows what I am.*

"You are not a weasel," said Gwyn. "You are a snake, like the rest of us. But know this: *my* bite is fatal."

Gwyn dropped the tonic jar, sending it crashing against the marble floor. The glass's shattering was sharp, hundreds of pieces fanning out.

Gwyn bumped Tanwen's shoulder as she passed, as did Efa and Owen. A bruised knocking that pushed her back a step.

It would have hurt more if Tanwen was here to make friends.

But she wasn't.

She was here to save her family and return home.

Let them hate me, she thought.

They wouldn't be the first who did, nor the last.

Tanwen waited until she no longer heard their retreating steps to begin picking up the broken glass.

Her relief was instant despite the mess at her feet.

I'm safe, she thought. *I'm still safe.*

Yes, agreed Eli, *but you're definitely going to be late now.*

"That was rather the point of her dropping this," grumbled Tanwen, carefully gathering the sharp shards.

Should I get out of here, then? asked Eli.

"Might as well," sighed Tanwen, unclasping his pouch so Eli could scurry out. "Be safe."

Always, he replied.

Some of the tension in Tanwen's shoulders eased as she watched her friend slip through a crack along the far wall. If it wasn't for Eli, her search for her father and brother would have come to a standstill. Tanwen's days were too full, her nights always occupied, to roam about aimlessly. While she worked, Eli looked. The palace grounds were vast, to be sure, the maze of corridors underneath even more complicated than the wide-open buildings above. But Tanwen had faith.

They had made it this far.

Had gotten to the palace.

Tanwen *would* find her father and brother.

How she was to get them out of the palace and down from a floating island?

Well, that was a worry for later.

"I had wondered why you liked hanging out with me," came a familiar approaching voice. "But now that I know you keep mice as companions, your taste for the strange makes sense."

"Huw," squeaked Tanwen as she stood, heartbeats exploding in her chest. She had thought she was alone in the hall. "I . . . uh. That's not my companion."

"No?" questioned Huw, blond brows raised in disbelief as he stopped in front of her. "Then why were you talking to the critter like a dear old friend?" he challenged. "And why do you have a pouch perfect for its size on your hip?"

Tanwen stiffened. "It's for herbs," she explained.

"Herbs?"

"Yes."

"Because us atentés are in need of herbs often?"

"I have begun to need them often, yes," she said, her defensiveness flaring. "You know I've taken on other duties for the princess. I'm actually returning from giving her a tonic just now."

Huw eyed the empty tray in her hands and then the scattering of glass by her feet.

"I ran into Gwyn," Tanwen explained.

"Ah," Huw replied, features softening.

Without further questions, he bent down, beginning to collect the shards.

Hesitantly, Tanwen followed.

The silence stretched tensely between them, the sound of each collected piece of glass hitting her tray loud and taunting. Tanwen was a swarm of nerves, desperate to fix whatever Huw might have witnessed with her and Eli or, worse, come to surmise.

When they both stood, broken glass gathered, Huw met her gaze.

"I do not care if that mouse is your pet or not," he explained. "And I certainly won't tell anyone what I saw, but I am not like most." He looked at her earnestly, almost with concern. "You must be more careful, little fawn. I won't always be around to help clean up your messes."

Huw left Tanwen standing there and headed toward the greenhouse, his words sounding more like a prophecy than a warning.

24

A hurricane of panic raged inside Zolya as he stood before his king in the throne room.

His magic surged a protective wind through his veins, the beat of his pulse the heavy downpour of rain. Every instinct in his body screamed to grab Azla and fly.

Because the High God Orzel was present.

A god who was dropped into the seas from the heavens for a reason.

The immortal rose from a small pool of water that had been brought in, his wings a translucent waterfall, his legs surging waves. The rest of him was a weaving of barnacles and seaweed and snapping crabs, crustaceans, and puckering blowfish. His gaze was black, the ocean deep, his features sharp, though no less beautiful despite his patchwork form.

Zolya took note that his attention was pinned exclusively to Azla.

A rush of protectiveness filled Zolya, who wanted to take a step closer to the princess, but he stood still. Such a small movement would be noted by all and assuredly not well received.

What have you done, Father? Zolya wondered in terror.

His gaze moved to where the king stood at the base of Orzel's pool. Despite having already given the proper prostrations and greetings, the king still wore a smile.

A terrible omen.

If his father was happy, suffering soon followed.

"This is a fortuitous day, my children," boomed the king. He was fully adorned in his finest attire, including a beaded high-collared jacket with an open front revealing his muscular torso partly covered by a gold-laced chest plate. "Our mighty Orzel has agreed to aid us with the building of our new mine."

Zolya's confusion swirled. *The new mine?*

He chanced a glance at Gabreel, who stood obediently to the far side of the throne room, flanked by two kidets. The inventor had lost weight since his arrival, eyes hollow, a haunting. Zolya pushed away the rising guilt forming in his chest. He had wondered at his presence today, but now it made sense.

Azla's, however, still did not.

"You get ahead of yourself, Réol," said Orzel, his voice the lapping of waves against sand, a scratching hiss. "I have only agreed to such a favor if I am satisfied with my bride."

Zolya's gaze whipped to the god, then back to his father, blood freezing within his veins.

Surely he had heard wrong.

"Bride, Your Eminence?" questioned Zolya, determined to keep his tone even.

"Yes, our lovely princess," the king explained, gesturing to where Azla stood at Zolya's side. "She honors our family greatly with this binding. Come, my child, let me show you to your future mate."

My child.

Never had the king addressed her as such. The pageantry of this moment mixed with the reality of the situation made Zolya feel sick.

The princess seemed similarly afflicted, for she did not move, her brown complexion bleached of color.

Azla was a painting of terror.

A knife-sharp agony sliced across Zolya's heart at the sight of such fear in his sister-cousin.

But he knew the longer the princess remained still, the further his father's displeasure would grow at her insolence.

A solution to this nightmare would come later. The only action now was to comply.

"I will escort you, Princess," said Zolya, taking up Azla's hand. It was ice, her gaze a shattering soul as it collided with his.

Help me, brother.

Zolya's knees nearly buckled as he read what was so plainly etched in her features. But he was the prince of Galia, son of King Réol, and sole heir to the throne. This would not be the first time he had gone along with something he opposed. His father had ensured Zolya's disobedience was beaten out of him as a boy.

The most he could do to reassure Azla was to place another hand atop hers and squeeze.

He tugged them forward until they were mere steps from the king and Orzel.

The High God's power cascaded over them, an oppressive sting to mortal flesh.

"What is her age?" asked the god.

King Réol looked expectantly to Zolya, another punch to his heart, for he clearly did not know.

"She is five and sixty, Your Benevolence," answered Zolya.

"Still very young," said the king. "She will keep well under your waters."

Azla's nails dug into the top of Zolya's hand; he could sense her beginning to shake.

It took everything in him to remain calm. "If I may, Your Eminence," Zolya addressed his father. "What is this potential binding to do with the mines?"

"Ah, yes, my son, there has been so much to plan that I forgot to inform you. Our mighty Orzel and I have been in negotiations regarding his sea hitting against the cliffs where we need to build. In exchange for his benevolence to pull back his waters, I have humbly offered a favorite of the High Gods, a piece of the royal house of Diusé, the princess. A gift for his aid."

A gift.

Not a person.

Not his daughter.

A pawn for the king's gain.

A wave of ire awoke, hot and sharp, within Zolya, a deep-seated hatred for his father.

The sensation nearly rocked him back a step.

Zolya had taken special care to lock up tight such treacherous feelings.

But what was transpiring in this room was shattering the ironclad cage holding his emotions at bay.

If the king was willing to sacrifice his own flesh and blood, even if she was illegitimate, for the success of this mine, what wouldn't he do to ensure his crown remained securely in place?

Would Zolya be next?

Would his mother?

The king was talking, declaring more advantages of the pairing, but a ringing had formed in Zolya's head, blocking out his words. He forgot Azla by his side, forgot the immortal being hovering in front of him.

How has this happened?

How is this the solution?

Zolya's attention rose to the inventor beyond the king's shoulder.

When their gazes met, Gabreel quickly averted his.

Shame.

Guilt.

Both shadows Zolya knew well.

This is because of him, Zolya thought in fury.

The infamous inventor and his mad schemes.

Gabreel suggested this. Did this.

No, you did this, said another voice in his head. *You found him and brought him back. Because you are too weak to face your father when you fail.*

Zolya swallowed down a roar he felt surging up his throat, the room snapping back into focus.

"You will now have a favorite of the High Gods forever with you," the king was saying. "Or as long as you wish for her to be with you, of course," he finished with a humoring smile.

Orzel's features remained expressionless. The god eventually spoke to the princess, finally acknowledging her presence. "Your blood holds wind, yes?"

"It does, Your Benevolence," she answered, voice but a whisper, eyes remaining respectfully on the floor.

The throne room stretched in silence, the only sound that of the infinite churning waves that were Orzel's legs.

"Wind does well with water," the god eventually mused.

"It does indeed," agreed the king.

"I will have her," stated Orzel. "I will calm my waters in exchange for your princess as my bride."

With that, the god vanished into his basin of water.

And the princess vomited by the king's feet.

25

Tanwen was worried, but for the first time in a long while, it was not because of her family.

Princess Azla had taken ill.

Though it was a sickness not of body but of mind.

Tanwen knew, for she had seen it many times before from those in Zomyad: mourning widows, devastated beaux.

No longer did the princess entertain. Every meal she left untouched; she even refused the presence of Lady Esme. Evidently, the mere sight of her lady-in-waiting seemed to throw her into a deeper fit of despair. Or so the servants kept whispering.

It had been three days, and the princess had not left her rooms.

Normally, Tanwen would ignore such rumors swirling downstairs. To her the woes of aristocrats were hardly true suffering, but something had sparked in Tanwen's heart regarding Princess Azla.

She had been the first, and really only, Volari to ever show her true kindness.

She had taken the time to come to know Tanwen and her talents, even stand up for them. To the prince.

And Tanwen had understood the dangers of this.

Volari could bed Süra, but to defend them or show any loyalty to them . . . well, that was a road her father had gone down, and look where that had gotten him.

Süra sympathizers were not long tolerated, especially in Galia.

Which was why, despite the prince's reprimand, Tanwen found herself approaching the princess's chambers with a desire to help.

At least as much as she could.

"The princess has ordered not to be disturbed," said Emyr, eyeing Tanwen as if she smelled most foul.

If anyone was arrogant in their service, it was the ushers to the royal family.

"I have been told her monthly bleeding has begun," explained Tanwen, lifting her tray laden with meddyg supplies. "The princess ordered that she would need my services once they started."

"Meddyg Hyrez has already seen to the princess yesterday evening."

"Even so," countered Tanwen, forcing her confidence despite her wavering nerves. "Her Royal Highness was adamant that one of her atentés also saw to her in case she needed anything further. I would not like either of us to be punished for not obeying a royal command."

Emyr studied her, lips pursing. "Be quick," he demanded.

Tanwen obeyed, ignoring his and the two flanking kidets' scrutinizing gazes as she pushed into the princess's chambers.

The door shut behind her with a heavy click. Instantly, she was swallowed in darkness.

Every drape was closed tight; the only hint of the outside was the breeze that billowed beyond the silken folds that led to the stretching veranda.

"Your Royal Highness?" questioned Tanwen as she worked her way deeper into the opulent rooms. The ceilings were monstrously tall, the furniture large, made to fit a form with wings. "Princess, it is Ms. Coster," Tanwen tried again as she moved toward the bedroom. The hairs on the back of her neck rose, her sense of disquiet blooming as she eyed the doors partly ajar. There was no sound from the princess as she shouldered them open. "I've come to see if I can help ease any pains you may be suffering due to your course—" Tanwen gasped, nearly dropped her tray.

Sprawled on the carpet, halfway to the bed, was Princess Azla. She appeared as a bird shot from the sky. Her white wings were fanned out, arms at uncomfortable angles where she was flopped belly down, a mass of snowy hair hiding her face.

"*Princess.*" Tanwen rushed forward, sliding her tray along the rug as she came to kneel by her side. "Princess!" she urged again, heartbeat stampeding hooves against her ribs as her hands hovered over the princess's body. She was not meant to touch a Volari, let alone a royal—not unless given permission. Tanwen's panic spiked, her indecision made from the rules of her position clashing with her innate instinct to help.

In the end she bit out a curse as she delicately moved the princess's hair from her face. Her brown skin appeared sickly, lips a dangerous shade of purple. Tanwen placed her fingers to her neck, releasing a relieved breath as she felt a pulse. It was faint, but it was there.

Tanwen swung her gaze frantically about the room, looking for what might have happened. Then she spotted it: the broken pieces of a teacup beside the princess.

Tanwen jumped over to it, eyeing the brown liquid staining the carpet. She bent low, finding dark bits of flower petals among the spill. She sniffed them, took a small taste before spitting furiously. "*No,*" she croaked, recoiling as the licorice tang overwhelmed her mouth. "No, no, no, no. Princess, what have you done?"

Indigo Eclipse was a coveted bloom, almost as difficult to nurse as a Sun Orchid, but when it blossomed, it was deliciously fragrant as well as deadly poisonous if ingested. Tanwen had noted them scattered around the palace's exterior. Trophies of beauty, no doubt, over the precariousness of their nature.

In a flash, Tanwen was grunting as she tried rolling Princess Azla to her back, her wings making it difficult, but she eventually managed. Fear gave one unnatural strength.

Princess Azla's dress was twisted around her delicate form, her arms limp at her sides from where she remained cradled within Tanwen's embrace. Without thinking further, Tanwen angled her head to one side, forcing the princess's mouth open, and stuck her fingers deep into her throat.

The princess jolted with a gag, becoming semilucid as she released a splatter of liquid onto Tanwen's arm.

Tanwen cared not. She did it again and again, forcing out the contents of Princess Azla's stomach.

The princess groaned, attempting to push Tanwen away, but she held tight.

Only when the princess used her wind magic, blasting it into Tanwen's face, knocking her back, did she stop.

The princess was moaning, slurring incoherent words as she slumped back to the floor.

Tanwen was a ball of relief.

If the princess was making sounds, then Tanwen had gotten here in time.

Tanwen detangled herself, rushing to mop up the mess as best she could. She threw a blanket over where Princess Azla remained lying on the carpet, wings lifting and falling with her even but shallow breaths.

Tanwen's entire body shook as she stood, her mind racing.

This is bad, she thought, *very bad.*

And not only for Princess Azla.

If anyone was to walk in, observe the situation, Tanwen would assuredly be blamed.

"They will execute me," she whispered.

Panic clawed viciously through her veins.

Why did I come here? she chastised herself. *Why couldn't I keep to my regular duties and leave the princess well enough alone?*

Because you have a healer's heart. Her mother's voice eased into her mind. *Your duty is to help others.*

What about helping myself? Tanwen wanted to argue. Altruism was not a celebrated trait, certainly not in Galia, and it was *certainly* not a luxury for a Mütra to act upon. Her mother had taught her this as well.

Tanwen swallowed the frustrating scream angling up her throat as she stared at the princess on the floor.

Her fight or flight was a battle of wills in her chest.

But where would I go? she thought. *I'm on this godforsaken floating island.*

Running was not an option. Tanwen had been the last to enter the princess's chambers. If she did not fix this, and quietly, she might as well swallow the remainder of the wet Indigo Eclipse lying on the carpet and escape to the Eternal River in the princess's stead.

Tanwen balled her hands into fists at her side.

She had to fight.

Everything her mother had taught her about the deadly bloom surged forward. There was much still needed to tend to the princess, to ensure she was out of Maryth's grasp, but she required help.

Whose help? was the question.

Alys was the obvious choice, but there was no certainty she could keep secrets, especially one of this magnitude, despite the princess being her charge. She also held delicate nerves. She might instantly scream upon seeing the princess and bring every guard running.

Tanwen needed someone whom she could trust with such a sensitive matter. Who would do everything in their power to prevent anyone from discovering what the princess had attempted, as it would tarnish the royal family and jeopardize the crown's stability.

"I'm mad," mused Tanwen, knowing who alone fit such a description. "I'm mad," she said again as she rushed toward the door. "I will be back as quick as I can, Princess," she called over her shoulder. "*Please*, stay breathing," she finished to herself.

Everything became a blur as she slid from the princess's chambers, explaining to Emyr that she needed more bleeding rags. That the princess most *assuredly* did not want to be disturbed by *anyone*, least of all a man. He did not question her hurried steps away.

It was midweek, which meant she would find him on the Recreational Lawn.

Breathless, Tanwen wove through the pillared halls, wishing more than ever she had wings of her own to get there faster.

As she kept her head down, she skirted the columns, doing her best to disguise her panic.

But the birds who lived within the palace seemed to pick up on her distress. A chorus of tweets and calls followed her path. A few finches danced from candelabra to statue to banister's ledge as she passed, asking if she was all right.

I will be if you remain quiet, she pleaded, eyeing the court members who had begun to take in the odd display of fowl.

Please, she urged, eyes trained on the floor as she shuffled through. *I can't afford a scene.*

The hall instantly went quiet.

Tanwen cringed.

The sudden silence was perhaps more attention grabbing, but as she sped forward, she thanked the birds nonetheless.

Soon, she exited the main palace compound. The sun was dipping past midday, the evening light sending orange tendrils across the marble steps Tanwen ascended. The heat gripped her skin as she squinted into the far-off lawn, studying the amassing crowd settling around the base of a pitch. High above, in the center of the field, a flurry of wings zipped and soared and dipped through the air. It was the weekly games of pavol. A sport played by the kidets and kidars involving an oval ball and a lot of wrestling and sky magic. Tanwen had glimpsed the game once with little to recommend.

But she appeared alone in her disinterest, for the entire palace flocked to the Recreational Lawn once a week, servants included.

It probably didn't hurt that *he* played among his men.

As Tanwen rushed forward, she could instantly make out the prince against all the other players. He was like a drop of sunshine hovering in the sky, dazzlingly bright. A star. His white wings drank in the light as they were splayed wide, his immaculately sculpted torso bare and brown and beautiful. His pants clung to him as he twisted through the air.

Tanwen's cheeks felt flushed as she eyed his taut muscles, the grace of his movements, his strength.

It made her uncomfortable.

She wished to never look away.

Reason enough she held off on attending these matches with the rest of the staff.

That, and it was one of the only times the palace grew empty; even Madam Arini attended the games, giving Tanwen an opportunity to walk more freely, search for her father and brother along with Eli.

But today she had been foolish with her time, deciding to help a royal instead of looking for her family.

Guilt was a hammerblow to her chest.

One she forced aside as she dived into the mass of onlookers at the perimeter of the field.

The games had yet to begin, the shirtless players still stretching and idly passing the ball.

Tanwen's mind raced to piece together a plan as she pushed her way forward through the crowd.

The courtiers sat in raised stadium seats, while the servants stood along the lawn. This at least afforded her front-row access.

But once she squeezed her way between two disgruntled footmen, toeing the chalked line, the grass on the other side an immaculate rich green, she became paralyzed.

What now?

Tanwen's nerves continued to shoot across her body as she worried her bottom lip.

The prince hovered at the opposite end of the field. His wings were a terrifying pumping of power as he idly chatted with a kidar beside him. Kidar Terz, Tanwen had learned, the one who had held a knife to her brother's throat and was often seen with the prince.

A burning hatred filled her chest. In a stopping of time, she wavered once again on whether she should be doing this at all.

In the end, she came to the same conclusion: *My life is at stake, but also . . . I can't let the princess die.*

Her healer heart wouldn't allow it.

With a steadying breath, Tanwen stared full force at the prince.

Not the most sound of plans, but it had worked before; perhaps it would work again.

Look at me, Tanwen thought, urged, prayed, ignoring the pressing crowd at her back. *Please,* look *at me.*

He didn't.

Because of course not.

Tanwen was merely an insignificant speck among the pulsing assembly of fans, a servant made to blend in with all the others.

Argh! she wanted to scream. If only she could rush forward, yell his name.

In a flash of desperation, Tanwen grasped the gold clasp holding together one of her dress's straps, angling it so it might catch a spark of light.

Please, please, please, see *me!* she silently yelled. *See me!*

She felt like a fool standing there wobbling the metal, hoping that those beside her were too busy admiring the players to pay her mind.

She was about to drop her hands in defeat when a distant blue gaze landed on her.

Tanwen held her breath.

The prince—he had seen her.

Was seeing her.

She kept his stare, eyes wide to display her panic as she mouthed *Azla, Azla!*

The prince frowned as he regarded her, remaining entirely too far away.

Deciding she was already crazed, Tanwen leaned into her madness and beckoned him with her hands. A tight gesture, close to her chest.

Come, the gesture said. *Come now!*

Prince Zolya's brows rose, something passing through his features, but at this distance Tanwen could not make it out and didn't care to wait around to decipher. She turned and threw herself back into the crowd, heading toward the palace.

She hoped the prince's curiosity, or at the very least his offense, would cause him to follow.

Her steps nearly became a sprint as she approached the white pantheon of the west wing, but instead of ascending the stairs, she cut to the left, rounding a corner to tuck herself into a small grove of trees. Hidden.

With him hovering in the sky, he would have seen where she fled.

Her heart pumped wildly in her chest, her breathing uneven as she waited.

Did it work? Is he coming?

Too much time began to pass. Tanwen's desperation for the prince to show turned to worry about not returning to the princess in time.

But then a whip of wind pushed through the leaves above her; a dark shadow descended into the grove. The pebbles beneath his feet crunched with his landing.

Tanwen's pulse took a tumble.

At a distance he had been a sight, but at this nearness he was overwhelming. The prince was a vision of sculpted perfection, shirtless and gleaming. His hair was pulled back, leaving room for his angular features to be admired undisturbed. On his left pectoral were three vertical inked stripes, the symbol of his rain magic.

Tanwen's skin heated, and she swallowed hard as he tucked in his wings, approaching.

She gave a quick and clumsy bow.

"Ms. Coster," he began, his deep rumble stroking down her spine. "Your behavior is most untoward."

"Are your guards in tow, sire?"

Prince Zolya's brows lifted. From her question or from her directness, or both, she couldn't say. "Should they be?" he asked.

Tanwen glanced behind him, to the parting of trees, finding the space empty.

"I instructed my men to remain at the pitch," he explained. "Your covert summons had me assume this was of a delicate matter. Though why I felt the need to answer, I do not know." He said the last bit more to himself, a displeased murmur.

"It's the princess, sire," said Tanwen.

His expression froze. "What about her?"

"She . . ." *Oh gods, am I really going to do this?*

"She *what*?" His tone carried an edge as he took a step closer. "Ms. Coster, this—"

"She drank poison," Tanwen blurted out. "Indigo Eclipse. But I found her in time. I came to her chambers to see to her monthly bleeding, but she was just lying there—" Tanwen frantically waved at the ground between them. "I got her to dispel most of it. She lives," she assured, seeing his complexion pale, panic seizing. "But she still needs help. I—"

"Who else knows?" Prince Zolya was a calm storm as he gazed down at her, wings tense at his back.

"Only me," answered Tanwen before thinking, *Oh gods, only me.*
He can get rid of me.

Her rushed plan had missed this detail.

"I came to find you directly, sire." She tried to backstep. "I understood this to be a sensitive matter. Not even Emyr or her lady's maid or the guards beyond her door know how I found the princess. I came to you directly," she repeated, knowing she sounded desperate because she *was* desperate. Desperate for him to understand her value in keeping the princess alive. "As I said, I got what I could from her stomach, but she still needs tending to. I know meddyg Hyrez is of preference, but I did not know if he'd be obligated to tell the king, and

I wanted you to make that call, sire. I have been trained in how to heal from poisons. I can help, but I will need—"

Prince Zolya was upon her in an instant, a wall of muscle and wings, the scent of sunshine and wind, stopping her words.

Tanwen felt dizzy at his nearness, fought an overwhelming urge to close the last bit of distance between them.

"Do not make a sound," he warned.

"Sire?" she squeaked in disobedience.

But then the ground fell away as he scooped her up, as though she were as light as a reed.

Erratic heartbeat in her throat, Tanwen went rigid as she clung to his bare shoulders—warm, smooth, tempting—before he shot them into the sky.

26

The princess lay in bed, asleep. Her brown complexion had returned, and her lips were no longer purple, though the dark shadows beneath her eyes remained. A stain of endless shed tears.

Tanwen placed the decanter of medicine on a side table, then gently wiped Princess Azla's lips before bending to check the intravenous line that was attached to the inside of her elbow.

"She'll sleep for a while now," Tanwen explained, doing her best to ignore Prince Zolya's encroaching form. He sat close to the bed, attached to the other end of the tube, his blood being used to clean the princess's. "We can remove this soon, sire."

He remained silent, continuing to stare in the direction of the closed curtains. His expression gave nothing of his feelings away, a stoic statue lit by the nearby flickering candlelight.

When they had landed on the princess's veranda, he had let go of Tanwen so fast she nearly toppled to the hard stone. In quick strides he had entered Princess Azla's chambers, pausing for only a breath as he caught sight of his sister-cousin unconscious on the ground before scooping her up and laying her in bed.

Then came the demands.

Tanwen was to give him a list of what she would need to fix this. She was to reenter the princess's chambers from the outside while he went to fetch the items. All evidence of the event needed to be eradicated, cleaned, wiped away.

Tanwen had obeyed.

And the prince had returned through the veranda as quickly as when they both had left.

Tanwen didn't know how he had gotten everything she needed, if those he took from questioned why he would require such a plethora of medical supplies or a variety of herbs and hot water, but when he handed everything over wordlessly, Tanwen knew in that moment she had done what was right.

The princess would live, no one would know what had been attempted, and, Tanwen hoped, she would remain alive so long as the prince felt he required her services.

The only precarious spot had been their flight together.

"Sire," Tanwen began slowly. "Do you think anyone saw . . . that is, when you carried me here . . ."

Prince Zolya shook his head. "Mostly everyone was at the pitch," he answered. "And I skirted the side of the palace that is mostly wall."

Tanwen nodded, the tension in her shoulders easing slightly. She needed to remember that he had grown up here and assuredly knew the ground's idiosyncrasies better than most.

"May I?" she asked, gesturing to his arm.

He offered it up, watching as she extracted the needle.

Tanwen was excruciatingly aware of his attention, of his still-shirtless form and warm skin beneath her fingers. Her pulse became a restless sprint as the memories of him holding her flooded her mind.

Despite flying high above the ground, Tanwen had felt surprisingly safe in his arms. His grip had been sturdy yet gentle as he held her against his chest. The cool rush of air was a stark contrast to the warmth of his embrace. Tanwen had been oddly overtaken by the freedom of the moment, when they had soared untethered by gravity. With Zolya's mighty wings pumping at his back, his power seeped into her grip, the flex of his muscles, the subtle metallic tang of his magic lifting from his skin causing her own to burn with a strange, mad longing.

And then it was over, and they were back on solid ground.

Tanwen had been left unsteady on the veranda as the prince had hurried to the princess.

Tanwen blinked, the bedroom coming back into focus. She still held the extracted needle, Prince Zolya eyeing her questioningly.

She cleared her throat, hating the blush creeping onto her cheeks. "Press this against the incision point, sire," she instructed as she handed him a piece of cloth.

She turned to do the same to the princess, and after tying a bandage around her elbow, she moved to the end of the bed, where she had set up her meddyg table.

Tanwen meticulously cleaned her supplies as the room hung in silence.

"Thank you," came a quiet rumble.

Tanwen glanced up in surprise, her hands half-submerged in water.

The prince was bent over, studying the princess, his large white wings draped down his back, skimming the floor. A small worried pinch sat between his brows. It was the first emotion he had released since he entered Princess Azla's rooms.

"You saved her." His blue gaze lifted to meet Tanwen's. "Azla was right. You are a skilled meddyg, Ms. Coster."

Tanwen took an unsteady breath in, not knowing what to do with such gratitude from the prince. She certainly should not have enjoyed the way his compliment slunk down her body like warm honey.

"We both saved the princess, sire," she replied, removing her hands from the water basin and drying them. "She would not have recovered as quickly if not for your blood."

Prince Zolya glanced back at Princess Azla. "She will be mad we saved her," he said.

"If she is," said Tanwen, "I'm sure it won't be for long."

Tanwen still wasn't sure what had led the princess to take such action, but it wasn't her place to pry.

"This is my fault." The admission left the prince in a whoosh, a dam breaking as his features finally crumpled. He appeared haunted, devastated, young. He pulled the princess's hand into his own, stroking the top with his thumb. It was an affectionate gesture, loving, and in this moment Tanwen no longer saw a prince and a princess but the bond of a brother and a sister. Siblings. Family.

She saw herself and Thol.

A heavy weight pressed against her chest, an uncomfortable sensation that came from understanding his suffering, empathizing with it. "That could not possibly be true, sire," she reasoned.

"She's meant to marry Orzel."

Tanwen blinked. "The High God?"

"A recent marriage arrangement decreed by my father."

Oh dear, thought Tanwen, her attention settling back on the sleeping princess.

This was why she had sought Indigo Eclipse. Such a marriage was a death sentence on its own. The princess would be losing the woman she loved, taken far from her home, a creature born for the sky forced to be submerged into the deep, bound to the angriest of all the High Gods.

It appeared if she was to die, the princess wished to take her own life on her own terms.

A clawing guilt filled Tanwen. Had they done what was right?

"I still do not see how this is your fault," she said, watching as the prince brushed away a stray hair from the princess's face. "If it was the king who ordered the marriage."

Prince Zolya's frown deepened. "I brought him back."

"Who?"

"The inventor."

Tanwen froze.

The inventor.

Her father.

"It was his scheme which brought this upon the princess."

Tanwen's defensiveness flared, but she forced her tone to be even. "What do you mean?"

"It's a trade that's part of the building of the new mine. A favor from Orzel to pull back his waves at the excavation site in exchange for a princess bride."

This information settled like soured food to Tanwen's gut. "How do you know the inventor suggested this?"

"Because only Heiro would think up something so . . . barbaric." Prince Zolya nearly spit the last word.

Barbaric?

Tanwen's outrage was a surging wave.

Barbaric was cutting off the wings of those in love.

Barbaric was hunting down those whose only crime in life was their existence and then murdering them in broad daylight.

Barbaric was stealing back a man who already served his time, suffered his penance, while holding his son hostage.

Barbaric was this island.

This palace.

The king and the High Gods he so adored.

But certainly *not* her father.

"I do not know the relationship of the inventor and the king," Tanwen found herself saying, a chill to her voice, "but I would be amazed if Mr. Heiro felt comfortable enough to offer up the king's only daughter as a solution to any of his plans surrounding the new mine."

She instantly wished to swallow back the words as Prince Zolya's attention turned toward her, eyes narrowed. "Excuse me?"

"I . . . speak out of turn, sire." She averted her gaze.

"Yes, Ms. Coster, you do, but I ask that you explain your meaning. You obviously appear to have some passion on the subject."

"I do not, sire."

"And now you lie to me."

"No—" She glanced up, finding the prince watching her closely, as he had done at their first meeting in the fields outside Zomyad. As if he saw through what she presented. But this time he was half-naked in a bedroom. "I merely question the inventor's place to be so bold in his advisement to offer the princess," she explained.

"Indeed," agreed the prince. "But then who could be so bold?"

The king.

No one spoke the words, but the answer echoed through the room nonetheless.

A shadow passed across the prince's features, a dark understanding, as a frenetic energy filled the air, as though it were about to storm.

Every nerve ending in Tanwen was on alert.

Prince Zolya abruptly stood, wings fluttering at his back, making the bedroom—despite its immensity—feel entirely too small.

"I'm going to inform the staff that you are to remain with the princess," he said. "She came down with an illness due to her courses. You were here to see that she got the proper care. Alys will be fetched to assist in anything else you may need. I require to be notified when she wakes." He rounded the bed, approaching Tanwen. Her pulse quickened. "No couriers, Ms. Coster," he instructed, stopping an arm's distance away, glaring down. A wall of strength and bare skin and heat. "Anything to do with this particular matter and the princess, you will come to me directly."

"Yes, sire." She nodded.

"The king must never find out—do you understand?" His voice lowered, a warning. "It would only have him hurry the wedding further. If you truly care for the princess, you will never speak of what transpired here today. I will certainly know if you do."

His threat was a cold finger ringing her neck.

"Yes, sire. You have my word."

He studied her for a long moment, as though peeling back her flesh and bone in search of what else she might be made of. Despite her position, Tanwen forced herself to hold his gaze. *I am stronger than you may think,* she wanted to tell him. As their connection stretched, the space between them crackled and warmed, a traitorous pulling. Something dark and foreboding flashed through the prince's eyes. But neither of them dared step closer. Because why would they?

He was a Volari prince.

She was a servant.

When Prince Zolya spoke next, his voice was as rough as an uncut stone. "I have a decided sense, Ms. Coster, that you are good at keeping secrets."

Tanwen's heart was a pounding drum against her ribs.

"Yes, sire," Tanwen answered. "Kept secrets and I are very well acquainted."

27

Zolya did his best not to wince under the king's laughter.

It was not a sound he had ever enjoyed, even as a child.

The king's joy was only at the expense of others.

And as he stood before his father in his private chambers, today was no exception.

The king was laughing at Zolya.

"You are bold to come here with such demands," said the king as he handed his wine to one of his nearby mistresses.

She lifted it from his fingers, gracefully refilling it.

There were four with him this evening. Various ladies of the Sun Court, half of them married to others or, no doubt, promised to others, all fawning over the king as he reclined on his padded bench. They sat combing his feathers, rubbing oil over his bare arms and shoulders, or allowing him to graze an idle hand down one of their exposed legs. Since Zolya's mother had taken to her island, the king had grown less inconspicuous about whom he took to bed. But Zolya supposed there was no point in indiscretion after fathering a child with his aunt.

"I cannot fault your bravado, however," continued the king. "You *are* my son, after all. We are bold in our desires."

The ladies around him tittered, stroking the king's ego while flaming Zolya's ire.

"Bold, perhaps," said Zolya. "But I would never be foolish enough to demand anything from you, Your Majesty."

"And yet here you are." The king waved a hand toward Zolya, who stood by the foot of his pillowed dais.

The king's private rooms were unsurprisingly ostentatious. Bloated in their high ceilings and massive skylights. They were perfumed in honey this evening, the white marble warmed by dozens of flaming bowls.

"I am merely imploring we take a different tactic to secure our new mine," said Zolya.

"Are you saying I am mistaken in my decision?"

Zolya clenched his hands into fists at his side. He knew a laid trap when he approached one.

"I only wonder if there is a way that does not involve the princess," he reasoned.

"And what is wrong with involving the princess?" asked the king, a single brow lifting. "Her life now has a purpose. She should be proud to serve our family so honorably."

Zolya remained speechless for a breath, his father's coldness a slap. "Perhaps," he began, "but this marriage will kill her, Your Majesty."

The king huffed. "She will become immortal as the wife of Orzel."

"She will *drown* first," stated Zolya sharply.

The king eyed him, a cold flash passing through his azure gaze. "Leave us," he demanded.

Wordlessly, his mistresses obeyed. As they untangled from his side, their overfragrant forms slipped past Zolya and out a side door.

Zolya's pulse jumped with regret, as he now found himself alone with his father.

But he knew the only way to survive such a moment was to not cower. He tipped his chin up, drawing his shoulders back. As his father used to demand he do before he landed each of his blows.

"I had feared you might grow fond of Azla," began the king, running his fingers over the gold seam of his armrest. "If it had been up to me, she would have been sent away to Both Island, but it was the wish of your mother that I allow her to live in the palace. For you to know her. I would have regretted my choice to humor the queen if not for the advantage Azla's birth has afforded us today."

Zolya drank in this information, a stutter to his heartbeat.

It had been his mother's wish? The queen was the reason his sister-cousin had lived, despite the betrayal shown by her husband and sister.

Would his mother ever cease in her surprises?

"You may think I am cruel, Zolya," continued his father. "But this agreement with our almighty god of the sea is not only advantageous to the building of our mine. It will lay historic groundwork for any future business we might have with Orzel. Due to their roughness, the oceans have remained largely unexplored for centuries. With a Diusé below its waters, we have opportunity."

Only if Azla does not turn her back on all of us, thought Zolya, a chill running the length of him. He could not bear the weight of her wrath. She would certainly loathe him for eternity if he did not help her out of this.

"These are the nuances I need you to understand, my son," said the king. "When wearing the crown of our kingdom, you must always see the ripple of an action, not merely where the stone falls. It is how our people have been able to prosper so long under my rule."

"But what of our gods?" asked Zolya. "Have they blessed this union with Orzel?"

The king's gaze narrowed, a flash of displeasure. "They have not made their thoughts known otherwise," he stated, tone hardening. "Now, what *other* answers do you demand from your king?"

Zolya clenched his teeth together, understanding his father's patience was more than used up.

But he dared one last push.

"I am forever grateful for your time, Your Eminence," he appeased. "I, of course, see the wisdom of your words and decision. I only implore that I am allowed time with the inventor's other plans. Surely there is one which—"

"This is the *only* one which suits," interrupted the king, a decisive swinging of a hammer. "Your job was to retrieve Gabreel. It is mine and my council's to choose our next course forward. I am disappointed to learn you still do not grasp what is needed to be king, Zolya. Thank the High Gods I have a long way yet in my reign, lest our kingdom be at the mercy of your soft heart. This situation with Azla will be a good lesson for you, my son. A single life is hardly worth saving over the lives of many. Especially when it will afford us the solution needed for our treasury. She will become a legend in her sacrifice. Stories and songs will be spun from this momentous coupling. I am proud to call her my daughter, which is more than I can currently say regarding my son."

The king's words struck as intended, sharp and deep.

He was a disappointment. Always.

But Zolya was beginning to realize that earning his father's approval might require sacrificing more of himself than he was willing to give.

His father waved his dismissal, and Zolya bowed rigidly.

He left the king's chambers a tense coil, barking at his awaiting guards to remain behind as he took quickly to the skies.

Zolya's magic rumbled through his veins as he sped from the palace and then from Galia. He headed east, farther even than his mother's isle.

As his wings pumped, his thoughts raced.

He was unable to save Azla. Could do nothing to stop her impending marriage, which would tear her from the clouds and make her a prisoner of the ocean.

Zolya's magic crackled across his body, his breathing growing ragged.

Night approached, Nocémi's cool touch wiping awake stars, but he did not turn back.

As his wings screamed their exhaustion, Zolya was consumed with flying far from where he was a disappointment, from where he was powerless.

If he could not keep Azla safe, what strength did he possess to protect any of those he loved? Least of all his people.

I am disappointed. You still do not grasp what is needed to be king.

Zolya ran from his father's cold declaration, the slice of his taunting laugh.

He fled from the terrifying realization that he would never make his father happy or proud.

Yet, even more alarming, Zolya believed that maybe that was for the best.

It meant he was not a monster.

Zolya might not have grasped what was needed to be a king like his father, but he now knew he didn't want to be his father.

He didn't want to sacrifice his children for a business deal.

He didn't want to force his queen to flee to a distant island.

He didn't want to beat his son into submission.

Zolya didn't want to be a heartless ruler; he wanted to rule with heart.

He could hear his father's cruel laugh at such a sentiment, his condemnation of it.

Zolya's fury surged as he shot farther into the sky; he hated how his position under the king's thumb kept him paralyzed.

Only when the edge of eastern Cādra was far behind him, endless empty sky ahead and a dark ocean below, did Zolya give in to the crackling rage surging from his core.

He let loose a roar that drew a rumbling of clouds.

His magic pulsed from him, a potent ancient strength, as his frustration and anger and remorse lifted from his skin, channeling the lashing of rain and thunder and lightning.

Everything he had bottled up over the past weeks, months, years, he finally unburdened.

And it felt glorious.

Freeing.

Zolya flew, the eye of the storm, and screamed into the night.

PART V

Fallen

28

Two prisoners slept back to back.

Their floor mat tucked into a far corner.

The father lay without blankets, giving them all to his son. His child's nearness was the only warmth he required.

A single candle flickered on a center table, its wax tired and leaning, but its light burned bright against the heavy darkness in the windowless room.

The papers that had covered the table earlier were now neatly organized, complete. Even a decadent meal had been brought to both men, with wine. A gesture of a job well done. Though neither dared drink the dark liquid. The scent of poison was easily camouflaged under the strong fragrance of spirits.

Still, they had laid their heads down with full bellies and a rare slip of peace as they fell into their slumber.

With a ricocheting boom, the heavy door to their room swung open.

Instantly, Gabreel was on his feet, Thol, bleary eyed, crouching behind him.

Three kidets, a mass of dark wings and stern brows, shoved the inventor out of the way as they reached for his son.

"*No.*" Gabreel lunged, laying burning hands on the guards so he might free his child.

Wind knocked him across the room, his back smacking against the edge of a table.

He wheezed as he fell to his knees. "*Please!*" he pleaded, managing to push back to his feet. "I have done what the king has bid. I have done it!" He rushed forward to where the kidets were now dragging Thol toward the door.

His son's eyes were panicked. "Father!" he yelled. "Father!"

Gabreel's chest was ripped open, the fear in Thol's voice a dozen arrows to his chest.

"We had a deal!" Gabreel screamed as he fought his way forward, managing to grab a bit of his son's shirt. But a guard kept him from advancing farther. "We had a *deal!*" he bellowed.

"Yes," said a silky voice by the door. Kidar Terz now stood in its frame, a dark shadow on a pale face. "And the king wishes to remind you what will happen if you fail to succeed in this next part."

Aberthol's shirt was tugged from Gabreel's grasp as the kidets pulled him away.

Terz stood to the side as he was dragged past, features unmoved by Aberthol's agonizing pleas.

"No!" Aberthol cried. "Please, not again, not again, not again! *Fatherrrrr!*"

His son's screams faded as he disappeared down the hall.

Gabreel was feral as he flung himself at the remaining kidets, swearing and punching and kicking and screaming.

In the end it only left him the worse for wear.

Pushed to his knees, the door swung shut, a heavy bolt thrown.

Even so, he ran toward it, ramming into the hard wood over and over and over.

Only when the candle on the table had finally snuffed out, throwing the room into utter darkness, did Gabreel slide to the floor, breathless and bruised.

His throat was the jagged end of an old saw, rusted and coarse from his screams, but none of it mattered as he pitched forward and sobbed into the abyss.

So lost was he in his sorrow he noticed not when small paws were placed on his leg. Nor did he hear the squeaks filling the tomb of his prison.

Gabreel lay drowning in his grief as a mouse scurried from his lap to escape from the crack beneath his door.

29

It was another perfect night within the palace grounds. The twin moons sat full, the Kaiwi River bright and majestic as a warm breeze threaded through the open halls and walkways.

Tanwen had worked a full evening shift of harvesting jadüri in the gardens, their blooms bright and ripe under Maja's and Parvi's wide gazes. Her arms were sore, and her fingers were cramped from the delicacy needed when handling the sacred flowers.

Yet she had not retired to her bed like her peers.

Despite her exhaustion, sleep was not in her future.

Instead, Tanwen had slunk to a part of the palace she assuredly should not be.

Now, tucked behind a stack of barrels, she eyed a descending staircase at the far end of a pillared pathway. It sat like a yawning mouth of a giant, pitch black, as moonlight spilled between columns.

To her right, the flap of wings filled the air beyond the railing, the rambunctious laughter of men.

Tanwen was in the kidets' barracks, hidden within the main floor, which was mostly made up of a large courtyard and a few sparring grounds. The men's living quarters were above her. Below was a storage facility where training gear, uniforms, and various supplies were housed. Or so Eli had told her.

It was also where they were keeping very precious persons.

Tanwen's breaths came quickly as she stared down the dark archway in the distance, her pulse a flutter of anticipation and worry.

She had found them!

Or, rather, Eli had.

Her father and brother were here, together. Quite possibly directly below where she crouched.

Tanwen pressed her fingers into the cold stone at her feet, relief and excitement an impatient weight against her back. She wanted to rush forward, descend the stairs, and swing open the door despite the two kidets Eli had said stood sentry outside.

Tanwen swallowed the foolish urge, knowing she had not endured all she had to throw it away on an impulse.

But by the Eternal River, she had found her father and brother!

Her need to see them left her unhinged and desperate. She wanted to pull Thol into her arms and hold him and kiss him and yell at him for ever leaving her.

She rubbed at her sternum as a tugging pain gripped her chest, a sob threatening to spill from her lips.

Eli had found them last night before he had explained that Thol had been dragged away. From the sounds of her father's agony and brother's terror, it had happened before.

Dread was an icy clawing down Tanwen's skin, a queasiness to her gut.

She could not bear for Thol to be in pain. The horrors he must be enduring by being a known Mütra in the palace were unfathomable.

At least he lives. Tanwen attempted to placate her worry. *They live.*

And soon she would free them from this nightmare of an island.

Tanwen's attention swung back to the empty stairwell, catching a dart of movement.

Eli, she thought, pulse tripping forward as the mouse scurried along the wall's edge to slink into her shadowed corner. He jumped into her hand. *How are they?* Tanwen silently asked. *Did you see them? Did you give Father my note?*

Eli shook from her onslaught of questions. *Aberthol has been returned,* he told her, *but he doesn't look . . . well.*

What do you mean? Tanwen asked, back tensing. *Has he been beaten?*

Something has been done to him, Eli explained. *But it cannot be seen from the outside. I feel a sickness of magic within him.*

Tanwen frowned as this news worked uncomfortably down her throat.

I gave Gabreel your note, said Eli as he turned in her hands, displaying his back. *He gave me one in return.*

Tanwen's heart skipped as she eyed the small scroll tucked into the tiny canister she had outfitted to her friend.

Unrolling it, she squinted at the small words scrawled on the thin parchment.

Tanwen's lips pressed together with displeasure, her cheeks warming in ire as she read.

Oh, my wyrthia, you should not have come!

Tanwen resisted crumpling the note and chucking it over the nearby railing.

Should not have come?

These were the first words from her father for her risking everything to save them. For her suffering through all that she had so she could reunite their family.

I should not have come.

A lifetime of frustration awoke in Tanwen's gut.

She could never do what was right by her father.

Not even when it came to saving his life.

He is worried for you. Eli's thoughts entered Tanwen's. *He fell to his knees when he saw me, burst into tears when reading your note. I would not be upset by his reaction. They seem to have gone through much since coming to Galia.*

Her friend's reasoning was a chill breeze, cooling Tanwen's anger.

You are right, she replied before letting out a steadying breath.

I always am, squeaked Eli.

"I cannot believe we found them," Tanwen whispered, stroking Eli's fur. She allowed a bit of hope to touch her heart.

And now to save them, Eli replied.

"Yes," she said, a flutter of anxious anticipation passing through her veins. "Though there's much we still need to figure out in that department."

Like an actual plan, suggested Eli.

"One will come," Tanwen vowed. "Now that we know where they are, we can plan. We'll send them another note tomorrow after I post an update to Mother."

Tanwen had yet to write to Aisling since her first week in the palace, but given the progress in locating her father and brother, it felt time to pen another.

Tanwen removed Eli's collar and helped him into the pouch along her hip. After retrieving her tray of docüra she had tucked away, she stood.

With her senses on high alert, she glided from the shadows and into the torchlight, trying her best to appear calm. She hoped she resembled an ordinary atenté passing through the barracks, there in case a kidet wished for a drop of ecstasy. It was not an uncommon occurrence.

The difference was that Tanwen was doing it alone.

Atentés were allowed such nightly rounds within the barracks only when in pairs, if not groups.

Never by oneself.

But it had been a risk Tanwen unfortunately needed to take.

And so far, it had paid off.

As she strode through the central courtyard, the white stone was bathed in the glow of the full moons. Her leather-bound feet echoed softly with each step she took.

Tanwen felt the eyes of nearby kidets tracking her as they lounged against the far walls or sat on the ledge of a spilling fountain, either just getting off or about to start a shift.

Despite their lazy gazes, their attention felt predatory.

But so did that of most of Tanwen's clients.

Still, her low-neckline dress did not help in her desire to be inconspicuous. She loathed every form-hugging, silky drape.

I only need to make it to the receiving hall, she thought. Once she was there, other servants would be about whom she could hide beside.

As she stepped from the courtyard into a covered walkway, the hairs on the back of her neck stood on end. She chanced a glance over her shoulder, her heartbeat tumbling as she caught sight of stalking forms.

Dread gripped Tanwen as she met the leering gazes of two kidets, their wings like billowing capes at their backs.

We have company, she thought to Eli in a panic.

How can I help? he asked from where he hid in the pouch at her hip.

I don't know yet.

As she skirted a column, so did the soldiers.

Tanwen was an explosion of fear, wondering how far she could get if she decided to run.

"Oy, you there," called a deep voice from behind. "Don't run off too fast," said a kidet, as though reading her thoughts. "We seek your services."

Tanwen closed her eyes, issuing a silent curse, before she plastered on a smile and turned.

Because that was what she was meant to do when beckoned.

"Of course, sir." She bowed as the two soldiers stopped in front of her. "I have plenty of docüra left for each of you this evening."

"That's not the service we are interested in," said the taller soldier, his dark gaze running over her body.

Tanwen's grip hardened on her tray, terror rushing through her veins.

The kidets wore the lower-ranking uniforms, their gray coats short, with a cloud insignia adorning their lapels. This knowledge only had Tanwen's fear spiking. The greener soldiers were always the ones to watch. They had too much still to prove and were constantly looking for an outlet after being berated all day by their superiors.

"I fear docüra is all I have to offer at the moment, sir." Tanwen tried to appease with another grin. "My madam is unfortunately waiting for my return from my current rounds."

"Then lucky for you," said a soldier, moving a step closer, "we can be quick."

His hand snaked out, grabbing Tanwen and tugging her to his chest.

Her tray was knocked away, the jar of docüra crashing to the ground. The precious dark liquid spilled across the white marble and splattered the hem of her dress.

"Sir!" She tried to pull away, but his hold turned icy cold as he used his freeze magic. She cried out, her knees buckling from the pain surging against her wrist.

Tanwen was shoved from the covered passageway and into a shadowed alcove. Her vision blurred from her sudden tears, her wrist still smarting as her surroundings spun.

The other kidet was suddenly at her back, locking her against him.

Panic surged through Tanwen as his touch groped and tugged at her peplos. There was a ripping as one of her straps broke from its clip, a hard grip against her now-exposed breast.

Tanwen yelled as she scratched and kicked, but it was like attempting to shove off a pile of boulders.

"Fighting only makes it last longer," hissed the kidet behind her, his breath hot and rancid on her neck. "But perhaps that's what you want."

Tanwen rammed her head back, cutting his face with the tip of one of her horns. He roared a curse as he grasped the very horn that had maimed him. Her neck was yanked hard to the side, her spine screaming at the harsh angle as he wrapped his other hand around her neck.

Tanwen choked out a scream, a yell for help, but then her mouth was covered by a clammy hand.

Tanwen bit it, hard.

She was rewarded by a stinging slap.

"Know your place, *goat*," growled the soldier. "We seek euphoria, and you are meant to give it."

Tanwen became out of body then, her mind unbelieving that this was about to happen. She had heard such horrifying tales, of course—other atentés forced—but it was not something that was usually tolerated.

Plus, plenty of her peers already willingly bedded Volari.

But these men seemed to get off on the unwilling.

A howl filled their alcove, one that wasn't hers, as she was suddenly released. One of the kidets sprang back as he swatted at a gray mass of fur digging its teeth into his neck.

He tore Eli from his throat, sending him flying.

"No!" Tanwen lurched forward, toward where her friend had been flung, but she was snapped back by the other guard.

"Is that thing *yours*?" the bleeding kidet spit. His eyes were glossy, mind no longer lucid in his rage.

Tanwen froze, not knowing what to do. All she could think about was Eli hurt, but she couldn't bring any more attention to him. By some miracle, she remained rooted, gaze holding the monster in front of her as her body shook with her anger and terror and agony.

Please, be alive! she silently prayed, called to Eli in her mind.

I'm here, Eli replied. *I'm all right,* he assured despite his pained tone. Still, hearing him sent a rush of relief through Tanwen's veins.

The guards held her in place, their wrath palpable in their searing grips.

Tanwen braced herself.

But then a deeper darkness blanketed their shadowed alcove, a harsh gale as a towering mass of wings descended.

"If you value your lives," came a warning rumble, "you will remove your hands from the princess's atenté at once."

Blessed cool air replaced the press of bodies as the men sprang away from Tanwen, falling to their knees.

"Your Royal Highness," they said in unison, heads bowed.

"We did not know she belonged to the princess," one quickly explained.

Their intruder's wings were still wide, a massive cresting wave about to sink ships. He didn't waste time addressing them; his attention was consumed by Tanwen, who stood on shaky legs behind the prostrating kidets.

As Tanwen clutched her half-torn dress to her chest, she met the burning gaze of the prince.

30

Tanwen squeezed her eyes shut, angling her face away from the cool wind and into the warmth of soft cloth and solid muscle.

She didn't remember how she came to be flying within Prince Zolya's arms. She knew only that she now was, for the second time that week.

But unlike the first flight, he now held her as though a babe to his chest, fiercely protective.

His hands gripped her firmly, hers woven equally tight around his neck. Her fingers dug into his coat as his wings pumped an even but quick rhythm.

Tanwen had no idea where he was taking her, but she was eternally grateful that it was away.

Away from those men.

Away from the growing crowd of soldiers that had gathered with the prince's appearance.

Away from the memories of rough hands and foul breath.

The events following the prince's arrival came in dark flashes. A confusing mixture of gruff orders and movement. A clearing of bodies and a mouse hiding. Then Tanwen had stood alone. With him. Stunned when his rumble of rage had turned soft, gentle as he approached. There had been a question, an offering of assistance, which Tanwen must have agreed to, for she was no longer in the kidets' barracks but in the sky.

As the prince angled them to the left, Tanwen tensed, coiling further around him, but soon the wind stilled as they came to land on a veranda.

She began to untangle herself, but Prince Zolya kept her in place within his arms as he strode past billowing drapes and into a low-lit room.

Only then did he release her. Gently, as if she were glass that could break.

They stood at the threshold of a bedroom. An enormous one at that, with hints of multiple other connected rooms.

Tanwen's nerves skittered down her spine as she clutched a hand to her torn bodice, eyeing the large bed in the center. Pristine white sheets and plush pillows with the royal emblem sewn into their centers.

Her heart stilled. She was in Prince Zolya's chambers.

"Wait here a moment," he advised as he disappeared into an adjacent room. Low murmurs of orders were given before the soft clicks of far-off doors shutting. He was clearing away his staff.

Tanwen's pulse jumped as Prince Zolya reentered the bedroom, determined in his movements as he flung closed the tall curtains to the veranda. The light of the twin moons was snuffed out, throwing the space into a honey warmth made by the flickering candelabras. "Do not be alarmed," he said as he approached her, clearly noting her apprehension. "This was the most direct place I could bring you where you could regroup undisturbed. You are safe here."

Tanwen didn't quite believe that as she watched the prince run his gaze down her body, a pinch to his brow.

She clutched harder at the broken strap of her dress.

His frown deepened. "There is a warm bath through there." He gestured to a door in the far corner. "My staff always keeps one at the ready for me in the evenings. I offer it to you. I'm sure you wish to have a moment alone where you can also change."

Tanwen eyed him, unsure.

A bath certainly sounded incredible, but perhaps *not* in the prince's chambers.

Especially not when he appeared so . . . fierce.

She hadn't fully comprehended him in the barracks, her mind and body still thoroughly elsewhere.

But now, in the stillness of his bedchambers, she was able to take him in.

If Tanwen hadn't known better, she would have assumed he had just flown back from a battle.

Prince Zolya appeared wind torn; his white hair sat wild around his shoulders, there was a red flush to his brown skin, and a hint of bruising was beneath his eyes. She wondered where he had come from before he found her within the barracks.

Nowhere pleasant, she imagined.

Though despite his disheveled appearance, his gaze was steady, measured, as he awaited her reply.

"While I thank you for your offer, sire," she began, "I have nothing to change into."

He glanced at the state of her peplos again. "Leave that to me, Ms. Coster," he explained. "There is an anteroom you can dispose of your dress in before entering the washroom. A change of clothes will be waiting for you when you are finished. I understand this is all rather . . ."

"Illicit," Tanwen suggested, brows raised.

"I was going to say *unconventional*, but yes, I suppose *illicit* also stands," he replied. "But unless you wish to return to your quarters in your current state and explain to Madam Arini what has happened and perhaps why you were in the kidet barracks alone—"

"So your men attacking me is my fault?" Tanwen cut in, her rage spiking.

"Of course not," the prince quickly assured, brows pinching. "What those kidets attempted will be dealt with, *slowly*," he promised, his voice a dark rumble. "I am merely offering you my help, Ms. Coster."

"Why?"

The prince blinked, clearly taken aback. "Are you always this distrusting?" he asked.

"Considering what happened to me tonight, sire," she pointed out, "do you fault me?"

At the reminder, the prince's gaze flashed something deadly for a beat before his features softened. "I apologize," he said. "I can't begin to imagine how you are feeling. You can leave if you wish. Of course you can. My intentions are merely to assist where you may need it. It's the least I can do, given what you have done for my sister-cousin."

Tanwen's fight left her in a whoosh, the mention of the princess quickly diluting her anger. It felt unfair to bring her into this, especially because the prince and princess's relationship always awoke compassion within Tanwen and confusion toward the man standing in front of her. How the prince could show such adoration, gentleness, and love toward his sister while also being so coldhearted as to steal away her father and brother left Tanwen disoriented.

She was supposed to hate him, and yet she had been eternally relieved by his presence tonight.

These dualities left her frowning, not knowing how to be under these circumstances, especially when he acted so . . . kind to her. Dare she say, even generous.

Volari, let alone royals, were not meant to apologize to servants. Least of all offer up their warm bath that had specifically been drawn for them.

Suddenly, the vast gap between Tanwen's and the prince's stations pressed down on her again. Even more so, *what* she was—or, more aptly, what she was not supposed to be.

Mütra.

And here the prince stood, wanting to help.

If he only knew who he was offering to help, thought Tanwen, holding in a chill of terror.

"Please, Ms. Coster," urged the prince. "Will you allow me to assist you as you have assisted me?"

There was something desperate in his tone, a need that went beyond merely Tanwen and her current state. She couldn't quite place what it was, but she grasped that his intentions were pure.

"Very well," she said, tucking a spill of her hair behind her ear. "A bath does sound healing. Thank—"

Tanwen's elbow was snagged, her words cut off as the prince tugged her close.

"Did they do this?" he asked, his voice a gathering cloud of thunder.

Tanwen sucked in a breath, now finding herself practically draped against his hard torso as he glared down at her left wrist. There was an angry red welt ringing her pale skin, remnants of the freeze burn inflicted upon her by one of the kidets.

"Answer me," he demanded. Gone was the gentle prince, and in his stead stood the warrior.

His wings were half-spread at his back, his blue gaze a winter storm.

Tanwen was both terrified and mesmerized. "They did," she whispered.

The prince's lips were set in a hard line as he nodded, as though agreeing to a silent command within himself.

"Please," she said. "Your grip, sire, it's—"

"Forgive me." He sprang back, remorse flooding his features. "I should never have . . . especially not after . . ."

"No harm was done," she said, echoing words he had once spoken to her, though her body still vibrated from his touch, a traitorous yearning.

"What do you need to heal this?" he asked, expression still stern as he gestured to her injury.

"Aloe and a bandage," she answered. "But, sire, you don't—"

He didn't wait for her to finish as he brushed past her. Part of his wing grazed her arm, sending a warm shiver down to her core.

When Tanwen glanced over her shoulder, he was already gone. A ripple in the curtain was the only hint of him ever being in the room before he had slipped out to his veranda and back into the night.

◆ ◆ ◆

The bath had been decadent. Unlike anything Tanwen had ever experienced. The tub was also less of a tub and more like a small pond, constructed to fit a form much larger than hers and with ample space for wings. The water had been scented with bergamot, the mild spice clearing her mind while the warmth worked out the stiffness in her joints.

The memory of the kidets' hands along her body had slowly slid from her skin, her nerves settling. She had been eternally grateful for the opportunity to collect herself, dilute some of her panic from her attack into the suds. She also felt reassured that Eli was safe, somewhere tucked away and recovering in the palace. Tanwen could have stayed in the healing waters until morning if she hadn't been painfully aware of where she bathed.

The opulence of the marble washroom was too grand.

Too breathtaking was the mural of Nocémi's night sky, which spun a sparkling dark blanket across the ceiling, within it a depiction of the glowing Kaiwi River, the celestial home of the High Gods.

This space was not meant for the likes of her.

A reality that became only more pronounced with the clothing she now gazed upon.

Wrapped in a thick towel, Tanwen stood, in utter horror, eyeing the simple white tunic that had been laid out.

"He must be mad," she muttered.

A jar of aloe and bandages had also been provided, but she ignored them as she bent to lift the shirt. It was massive, soft, and unequivocally made for the prince.

"He *is* mad." Tanwen glanced to the other piece of clothing.

As if his shirt wasn't enough, there were also trousers.

His trousers.

A bubble of laughter worked up her throat, the feeling and sound foreign to Tanwen.

She couldn't recall the last time she had laughed.

Especially not like this, from a mix of exhaustion and grief and the utter absurdity of such a moment.

Perhaps she was mad as well.

Because in the end, after seeing to her wrist, the burn already going down, she slipped on his tunic.

It was either that or remain wearing a wet towel.

Her back was half-exposed from the large openings for his wings, but she buttoned up what she could reach.

"Sire," began Tanwen as she reentered his low-lit bedchamber. She had prepared a nuanced explanation for why she required different clothes, but her words were stolen by the current scene. "Are you . . . *sewing?*"

The prince looked up from where he occupied a wide plush bench within the center of his room. Draped across his lap was her white peplos uniform, within his large hands the delicate wink of a needle and thread. He appeared entirely ridiculous and unequivocally adorable all at once, such a large form as he carefully mended her dress.

Tanwen's question got further lost as she met his gaze. There was a darkening within his blue irises as they traveled over her. A muscle along his jaw flared, a hard swallow to his throat as his attention met her bare legs and feet.

Tanwen was nothing but flames, burning from his scrutiny.

Despite her swimming within his soft tunic and being far more covered up than she had been in her peplos, she was painfully aware of how intimate it was to be wearing his clothes, hair wet down her back. A detail she could tell the prince had not thought of until now.

Fool, she wanted to chastise.

"Where are your trousers, Ms. Coster?" The prince's words snapped her back to the room. He was no longer staring but glaring. That forever pinch between his brows.

"You mean *your* trousers, sire?" Tanwen countered, single eyebrow raised. "While I'm sure your intentions were . . . honorable in the lending of your clothes, you appear to have forgotten an important detail when it comes to you and me."

His frown deepened. "And what's that?"

Tanwen couldn't contain her snort of disbelief. "We are very *different*, sire." She gestured emphatically to herself. "Particularly in size."

His gaze traveled over her once more and, by the Eternal River, if she didn't feel as if he saw straight through her tunic. To every curve and swell of her nakedness beneath.

Tanwen resisted dashing back into the washroom to hide, her skin growing much too warm.

"Yes, well . . ." The prince cleared his throat. "I had nothing else that would suit," he explained before returning his attention to his task. "Your dress will be mended shortly. Though I can't do much about the stains. That is a task for the laundresses."

She watched his strong hands work the small needle in and out of the material.

"Where did you learn to sew?" she asked, approaching.

"It's a skill every soldier needs to master." He furtively glanced to where she now hovered over him. "Though I certainly prefer mending clothes over flesh," he explained.

"Easier to poke through," she offered.

"That, and it doesn't nearly whine as much as a kidet," he added.

"An ideal client."

He looked up at her then, a hint of a smile at the corner of his lips. "Precisely."

They remained connected for a breath, the room falling away as they shared a grin.

But then the prince blinked, seeming to recollect himself.

"How are you feeling?" he asked, gaze dropping to her bandaged wrist, which peeked from beneath his rolled-up sleeve.

"Better," she admitted.

The prince nodded. "I'm glad. In case you need anything to further settle your nerves, I poured you a glass." He leaned over to a side table, picking up one of the two drinks prepared. "It might help ease whatever else the bath did not."

"Thank you." She took the cup, painfully aware of when their fingers grazed, of every shift and breath the prince produced. He had changed since her bath. Or, rather, removed his heavy royal adornments and jacket. Tanwen noted how he seemed more relaxed in his simple gray tunic, no longer shouldering the garb of his responsibilities. His muscular form was also evident beneath the thin material of his shirt.

Why am I looking at his muscles? she silently chastised, sensing her cheeks flushing pink.

He was the definition of a distraction. And the Low Gods knew Tanwen couldn't afford distractions. She had more than enough to plan and prepare since locating her brother and father.

The last thing she should be doing was sharing a drink with the prince.

The very man who had split apart her family.

By the king's orders, another voice added in her mind.

Tanwen ignored it, allowing her animosity toward Prince Zolya to rise like a necessary shield, despite how battered it was becoming.

"I can do that, sire." She leaned forward to grab her dress.

"I'm sure you can." He elbowed her hand away. "But you won't."

"It's absurd for you to be sewing my dress, sire." She pressed a fist to her hip.

"It's also absurd for you to have bathed in my washroom and to be wearing my clothes."

Tanwen's face flamed hot, a sense of betrayal. "*Yes*, sire, it is, which was what—"

He cut her off, brows stern. "But tonight, propriety can go hang. You were attacked, Ms. Coster, by *my* men, who assuredly were trained better than that. All I care about is that you are well and healing. Society is not in this room. The palace may sit around us, but it is not currently with us. For a few turns of the stars, let us do away with all that. I want you to feel as if you can be yourself here. At least for tonight."

"That is a difficult order, sire."

"Zolya," he muttered.

She blinked. "What?"

"Please, call me Zolya. I'm blasted tired of the title of *sire* this evening."

"Sire, I cannot," countered Tanwen.

"Of course you can. Think of it as a request from a . . . friend."

Friend.

The word slid through the room, awkward and ridiculous.

Certainly illegal.

"You and I cannot be friends, sire."

"And why not?" he asked, a petulant child. "We have both helped one another. We share similar skills like . . . sewing." He lifted her dress as though it were an exhibit of proof in front of a council. "Are those not characteristics of a friend?"

Tanwen would have laughed if she wasn't so exasperated. "May I remind you that you are a Volari prince?"

"A wasted reminder," he countered.

"And I'm . . ."

The words got caught in her throat.

An abomination.

The prince was watching her closely, that insufferable inquisitive stare that told her he was noting some truth she wished for him not to see. "What are you, Tanwen?"

Tanwen.

Her name spoken like it already belonged to him.

Tanwen's pulse tripped into a sprint.

"I'm . . . me," she managed weakly.

The prince's gaze raked over her, sending a dusting of gooseflesh across her skin. She dared not breathe as his eyes lifted to meet hers once more, a center of a flame. "Yes," he said, a husky agreement. "You certainly are."

Tanwen's attention remained locked to the prince as she desperately attempted to ignore the pull she felt in her belly.

Ignore her torturous desire to know what his delicate strong hands could mend as they ran over her body.

He remained sitting, below her, as he had that one day when she found him kneeling at her feet. Similar wicked imaginings flooded her mind, but this time they took place in the bed mere paces away.

Tanwen spun on her heels, a burst of desperate clarity roaring through her chest.

What am I doing? she silently scolded before taking a full swig of her drink. The spirit burned down her throat, and she coughed.

"Are you all right?" Prince Zolya asked.

She dared a glance back at him, to where he remained on his bench.

"Yes," she assured. "The strength of the drink caught me off guard, is all."

She decided space was the safest next course of action.

He was too large, not only in body but in presence.

Yet despite the distance she put between them, despite the blocking of tables and chairs and pillars, Tanwen felt the prince's gaze following, a shadow she was unable to detach from her form.

Tanwen swallowed past the heat rushing through her body, her attention focusing on the various tomes and trinkets laid about the room. And tomes and trinkets the prince had aplenty. Books overflowed every surface. Stacked three or four high on side tables and benches and lounge beds. But what surprised Tanwen the most was the collection of toys, particularly children's. She stopped to study the various air gliders, rock spinners, and web catchers.

"Be careful with that one," said the prince as she picked up a miniature paper kite shaped like a hawk. "It was a gift from my mother," he explained.

"I wouldn't take you to be nostalgic, sire"—she took care placing the kite back on its shelf—"by still harboring childhood toys."

"To me they are less toys than interesting inventions," he admitted. "Did you know that rock spinner over there is what helped engineer wagon wheels and the making of flour? It's older than even my father and has outlasted generations yet still brings entertainment. To create something that could be loved for so long, that could inspire other ingenuity—well, I frankly find it astonishing."

Tanwen stood transfixed, his words echoing so much of her own passion for invention. Another added similarity between them that left her unsteady.

Which was why she focused, instead, on what else his admission revealed. "That was spoken like a well-studied future king," she said.

His brows slammed down. "What do you mean?"

"To become eternally loved." Tanwen repeated his words. "To inspire others. Are those not traits to admire in a great ruler?"

Zolya shifted with his discomfort, a nerve clearly struck.

"It is not something to be ashamed of, sire," Tanwen reasoned. "On the contrary, I admire your inclination to—"

"I am not ashamed," he interrupted, his features remaining brooding. "My fascination with invention has nothing to do with my future role as king."

Tanwen regarded him, confused as to why he would be upset if it did, but it was not her place to pry. "Of course not, sire," she eventually managed, moving away from the rock spinner. "You might find this . . .

amusing," she began, finding she was suddenly desperate to recapture some of the casualness they had begun to share. "I also have an interest in the art of invention."

"Why would I find that amusing?" Prince Zolya countered with a pinch to his brows.

"Because I am a woman and a servant," she reasoned matter-of-factly.

"I fail to see how either defines what you might find interesting. I'm a royal, born for an idle life, and yet prefer to train with my men and work with my hands."

At the mention of his hands, Tanwen glanced to where they delicately held her dress in his lap. A warmth blossomed across her skin, especially as she realized he was so much more than she had originally believed, filled with contradictions and nuances that went against the definition of his title or race.

Like me being Mütra.

Tanwen stilled, the thought shocking her.

"What exactly is it about the art of invention that interests you?" Prince Zolya asked, snapping her back to the room.

"I . . . well." She momentarily faltered, no one in her life ever having asked her such a thing. "I am fascinated by the possibility that we can make something from nothing," she began. "Or something good, better. I mean, take this room." She gestured to their grandiose surroundings. "People *made* this. What started as a simple need to live within walls and a roof, to have shelter, eventually was transformed into artistry and design. Right angles were able to become curved archways. Flat ceilings, domed. And it all appears so effortless. As if the required meticulous mathematics and constructed precision were mere magic rather than centuries of a dedicated pursuit by mortals."

The room stretched quiet, Tanwen realizing with growing unease that she might have spoken too freely, and certainly too much.

"Well," said the prince, a delighted glimmer in his gaze. "You certainly know your history of engineering."

Tanwen shifted her weight with discomfort. "Not really." She shrugged, attempting to deflect. "The practice of being a meddyg shares similarities," she reasoned.

"How so?" he asked.

"The constant advancing of medicine and instruments, for one," she replied. "While also utilizing effective methods that have been practiced for centuries."

"Indeed," the prince agreed, eyes alight with growing curiosity. "Azla mentioned you come from a lineage of meddygs, so I assume your mother . . ."

"Is also a meddyg," Tanwen finished for him. "She is one of the most skilled in my clan, actually," she added proudly.

"Is it she or your father who hail from Garw?" questioned Prince Zolya.

Unease worked through Tanwen. "Why do you ask?"

"Your horns," he explained. "You come from the western clan in Zomyad, yet your horns are of eastern heritage."

Tanwen hesitated as she turned to study an arrangement of flowers. This line of questioning was getting too close to her father for comfort.

"I apologize," the prince began, obviously noting her change in temperament. "I did not mean to overstep."

"It is fine," she said before taking a sip of her drink. "You wish for us to be friends, do you not? A friend would wonder such a thing."

But it was also a friend's prerogative if they wished to divulge an answer. Tanwen certainly did not.

"You say the queen gave you some of these toys?" She worked to change the subject, continuing her stroll about his room.

"If not exclusively," he admitted. "My mother has always nourished my curiosities. Most of the books are from her as well."

Tanwen could note the admiration in the prince's voice, the love.

"You must be close," she observed. "You and the queen."

Prince Zolya's lips pressed together as he continued pulling and pushing with the needle. "We are as close as I suppose we are allowed," he eventually answered. "Despite her living outside of the palace, her isle has become . . . a safe place for me to visit."

Something warm and unwanted unfurled inside Tanwen, hearing the prince discuss his place of safety. She knew too well the desire for a sanctuary.

And the prince had shared his with her, of all people.

"Do you see her often?" she couldn't help asking.

"As much as I can, though I'm sure she would say it's not nearly enough," he admitted with a slight smile.

"Will you . . ." Tanwen hesitated with her next question.

"Will I what?" he urged, looking up.

"Will you tell her about the princess?"

Prince Zolya's brows furrowed, a darkness overshadowing his relaxed features. "I'm not sure yet."

"Oh goodness!" Tanwen gasped, hand covering her mouth.

"What? What has happened?" Prince Zolya was nearly on his feet, searching Tanwen to find the cause of her sudden distress.

"No, sire, I apologize. I'm fine." Tanwen raised her palm, attempting to assuage his worry. "I merely forgot to tell you that she woke up this morning. The princess. I had gone looking for you, but your usher said you were not on palace grounds and then . . . well, my duties and—"

"All is well," he placated, settling back in his seat. "I was away from the palace since yesterday afternoon, so it is no fault of yours."

Tanwen wondered if where he had gone was why he appeared so ruffled.

"How is she?" asked the prince, pausing in his work.

"Despondent," Tanwen admitted. "And mad," she added.

"I'm sure her anger is exclusively saved for me," said Prince Zolya, his brows furrowing.

"I thought we agreed it was not you who arranged her marriage," said Tanwen.

"Still," replied Prince Zolya, gaze growing out of focus.

"Still what?" pushed Tanwen.

A muscle along his jaw ticked before he met her question with one of his own. "Do you want to know the ficklest part about being the next in line for the throne?" His gaze held hers, a steel blade of ire. "You must *act* in line."

Tanwen remained silent, not knowing how to reply. For a flash she could see the prince as a young boy, his childhood stolen because of who he had been born. By no choice of his own, responsibilities and expectations had been saddled onto his shoulders, gilded weighted epaulets. An anchor to his wings.

How strange for Tanwen to understand him so viscerally in this moment—perhaps not the royal part, but certainly remaining in line. The necessary comprehension from a young age that one's life was not like others and there would be dire consequences if rules were not followed, obeyed.

Prince Zolya's discomfort around his future role as king grew clear. Perhaps he had not wanted this life, just as Tanwen hadn't wished for hers. Maybe his destined role was not a blessing from the High Gods but a curse for him to unwillingly follow in the footsteps of his father.

I'm blasted tired of the title of sire this evening.

His words from earlier now rang as an exhausted plea.

A pressure bore down on Tanwen's chest, an uncomfortable compassion filling her heart.

Compassion for the man who helped the king capture her father and brother.

"I went to see my father yesterday," said the prince, as though he had the power to know the subject of her thoughts. "After you saved the princess."

"*We* saved, sire," Tanwen corrected yet again.

"Yes, well, *we*, *you*, it's all for naught." Prince Zolya glowered at her dress in his lap. "No amount of pleading could alter his decree regarding the princess's fate. I may command an army, have blood blessed more powerfully than all other Volari, yet *still* I can do nothing to save Azla."

The room vibrated in the following gloomy silence.

Tanwen had a sudden mad urge to go to him, smooth his frown, hold him in her arms, and tell him all would be well.

Despite both knowing it would not be.

"I'm sorry," she managed instead, her gut clenching in anguish for what this meant for the princess, for knowing what it was to feel useless and lost in wishing to save someone you loved. "I can understand that is a maddening position to be in, but you mustn't discredit your attempt in fighting for her. Though I have not met the king, I imagine it takes courage to openly oppose one of his decisions."

"Or idiocy," murmured the prince.

"Yes," mused Tanwen. "I do suppose they are often synonymous."

The prince gave her a wry, amused look, and a strange sense of accomplishment filled Tanwen's chest.

She could tell he was not a man who smiled often, least of all at staff.

"The way I see it," she added, now unable to stop herself, her drink indeed making her foolishly brave. "You could have done nothing at all, sire. A greater offense in my opinion than offending a king. Though it might feel impossible, I would not yet give up on your campaign. Nothing of importance ever manifests without work. Surely you know this from all your tomes on the history of invention." She gestured to the scattering of books. "Greater miracles have transpired in our world than His Eminence changing his mind."

Prince Zolya's stare was unyielding, a flash of wonder in his blue depths as he drank her in. "Yes," he said. "I suppose greater miracles have."

Tanwen's cheeks grew flushed, her skin uncomfortably heated. "Precisely," she managed, tearing her gaze from his to once again study a nearby flower arrangement. She had set out to lift his mood, but in her attempts the air had turned thick with a new tension, one that had nothing to do with her family, his sister-cousin, or the king.

For Tanwen's own preservation, she needed to get them back on course.

"In the meantime," she said, playing with the lip of her glass, "the princess will have Lady Esme as company. She asked for her before I left," she explained. "If anyone can cheer her, it's her lady-in-waiting."

"Indeed," said the prince, features turning pensive. "Though I suspect Azla will tell Lady Esme what was attempted."

"Yes," agreed Tanwen. "I'm sure she will."

"I will visit the princess tomorrow," he said with a nod, "before discussing the importance of discretion with Lady Esme."

"A sound plan," replied Tanwen before sipping her drink.

Prince Zolya continued looking at her, and Tanwen really wished he'd stop doing that.

It was becoming much too enjoyable.

"Thank you," he said.

It was Tanwen's turn to frown. "For what?"

"For listening to the ranting of a prince." He shook his head, as though embarrassed. "I appreciate your counsel."

Tanwen was knocked unsteady by his words.

I appreciate your counsel.

The counsel of an atenté in matters of the royal household.

Greater miracles, indeed, thought Tanwen.

"Of course, sire. I am here to serve."

The prince watched her a moment longer, an inquisitive stare, as if trying to solve a complicated puzzle, before he blinked, seeming to catch himself. "I believe your dress is done," he said, lifting her peplos.

Tanwen came to sit beside him, leaving her glass on a nearby table. She leaned over, studying his work.

"Well, sire," she breathed. "You might have another profession waiting for you if being a prince doesn't work out." Tanwen slid the dress from his hands, pulling gently at the strap that had been twisted and tucked and sewn back around the gold holder. One would never know it had been ripped off, so exactly did it match the other.

When the prince did not reply, she chanced a glance up.

A mistake.

He was intimately close.

Or perhaps she was.

Tanwen hadn't noticed how near she had shifted to admire his work.

Her fingers gripped the forgotten material in her lap, her breath hitching as her pulse hurried. Their thighs were touching, pressed together as his scent of bergamot and night curled around her. It mixed with the heat of his body, a delicious pulling as she glimpsed a swath of smooth brown skin peeking from beneath his shirt, the collar loose around his neck.

Tanwen should move, push up and away.

She didn't.

Because she was trapped.

By him.

His gaze was a tightly wound rope holding her still.

Hungry.

Pained.

Resolved.

A cacophony of emotions swirled within his blue depths as he remained looking at her.

"I fear you may have been right," he rumbled.

"About what?" she dared to ask.

His attention dropped to her mouth, his features darkening. "About us not being friends."

Tanwen's skin was on fire, melting in rivulets to the floor.

"Sire—"

"Zolya," he corrected.

She remained quiet. Terrified. Burning to move closer. Desperate to push away.

But again, she did neither, for in that moment the prince slowly lifted his hand to her cheek. A soft, aching caress down to her neck, a river of lava following his touch. He paused at her clavicle, where the collar of her shirt, *his* shirt, covered the rest of her. It was as if he was branding her, a scorched imprint.

Her quick breaths had his hand rising and falling, rising and falling against her chest.

He watched the connection for a torturously long moment, let the rhythm of them sync before he met her gaze once more. "Who are you, Tanwen Coster," he breathed, "to make me this way."

Tanwen Coslett, she wished to correct, was desperate for him to know.

"And what way is that, sire?" she asked on a shaky exhale.

"To wish I wasn't . . . me."

Pain was a tight lacing to her heart.

"But you are you," Tanwen reminded.

"And you are you," he echoed.

"I am," she said, a cold despair clinging to her words.

The prince's brows pinched, pained and angry. A deep inhale lifted his shoulders. "Despite who we are, I need to know, do *you* want this?" he asked. Tanwen's heartbeat stuttered as he gathered her hand and placed it on his solid chest. They now mirrored one another. "Do you want *me*?" he clarified.

This.

Him.

What shouldn't be possible, what was forbidden.

Like Tanwen's existence.

But in both instances remained real and breathing, alive and wanting.

Do you want me?

Did she?

Could she?

Her desire for him was treasonous, the inexplicable pull in her heart blasphemous.

He was her enemy, was he not? He was born to rule. She was born to hide.

And yet . . .

There was a ringing in Tanwen's ears as chaos swirled within her veins, a swarm of pushing and pulling, of emphatic yeses and weak noes. He was so very warm and solid and *there*, beneath her fingers. So many differences made up the weaving of their blood, yet the marrow within their bones felt the same, a meeting of reflective souls. They were shared contradictions.

"Do you?" Tanwen redirected, unable to be the first to admit to such a shattering truth.

"More than I know I should."

His reply was a blow, but *gods* if she didn't understand, didn't feel the same.

"Then we share more than a knack for sewing and a passion for invention, sire." She managed a small smile.

Lucidness began to rear its ugly head as she attempted to pull back her hand.

The prince held it firmly in place.

"Zolya," he reminded, urged, his quickening heartbeat felt beneath her palm. "Please," he whispered. "Will you say my name, Tanwen?"

She hesitated as the ache in her chest intensified, but in the end, she gave in. More from her own need than because of any request of his. "Zolya," she sighed.

His grip on her tightened. His breath was coming out ragged, his desire clear in every stern angle of his beautiful face. "I will move away," he promised, his voice a low rumble. "I will let you go. You only need to say the words, Tanwen. You only need to command me—"

Tanwen cut Zolya off as she tugged him down to her lips.

31

He was everywhere.

A stretching of endless sky that blanketed Tanwen.

And it felt devastatingly right.

Perfect.

Inevitable.

His lips were soft, encouraging, skilled as they worked against hers.

He tasted sweet, like his drink, his tongue brushing hers as he groaned into her mouth.

Tanwen loosened a surprised breath as Zolya gathered her into his lap. Her atenté dress slipped, forgotten, to the floor as she straddled his strong thighs. His hands ran down her back, gripped her waist through her shirt as he all but feasted on her.

"You are my devastation, Tanwen," he growled, pressing her closer against his chest.

And you are mine, she thought as she fought her rising guilt, ignored how it judged each kiss and touch and groan.

She could feel Zolya's need beneath her—powerful, hard—and knowing that *she* was the one stirring his desire only inflamed her own.

His attention slid from her mouth to the curve of her neck and exposed shoulder.

Tanwen was no longer tethered to this existence but blown into a million particles.

To consume every shred of pleasure Zolya poured over her was her sole purpose.

And pleasure he gave in abundance.

Gently, he cupped one of her breasts, sucking at her nipple through the material of her shirt.

A spike of euphoria flooded her core, and she angled further into him.

He groaned his approval.

His fingers slid dangerously low to cup her backside, lingered where her tunic flared open, bare skin revealing where no undergarments separated what yearned the most for his touch.

Tanwen, rubbing against him, moaned for him to keep going.

"By the Eternal River," he cursed, meeting her with a thrust of his own.

Tanwen cried her bliss, Zolya grazing exactly where she needed him.

His wings had curled around them, a white wall of safety as he slowed their kiss.

He drew back, forcing her to meet his liquid topaz gaze.

She squirmed in his lap, desperate for more, and he rumbled a low, pleased laugh.

"I want to ease your aches, Tanwen," he said, running a hand up her neck to cup her cheek. "May I taste you?"

His question slid like fire down her spine. Tanwen let out a ragged breath as she found herself on another precarious ledge. She had already fallen far with their kiss. Could she crawl her way out if she fell any further?

"If your answer is no, I will go no further," he assured, no doubt noting her hesitation. "We can stop."

Stop.

The action felt impossible.

Tanwen certainly didn't want any of this to end, though she understood it would. Must. The consequences of tonight inevitably loomed, but by the Low Gods, she was desperate to fight that reality for as long as she could. Her need for a reprieve from her responsibilities, a slice of her own euphoria after doling out so much to others, raged through her veins. Zolya had said she was safe here, that society remained outside these walls. Let them test that theory.

If only for tonight.

"Taste me," she ordered.

Zolya's grip tightened, his eyes pooling with untamed desire. "As you wish," he replied.

Tanwen's stomach dropped, a dizzying of movement as Zolya lifted them into the air.

With her next breath she was lowered onto his bed. The sheets were silken clouds, puffs of perfection beneath her body.

Zolya was above her, leaning one elbow onto his bedding as his weight deliciously sank against her. His wings were a wide, magnificent snowy canopy. He angled her chin, claiming her mouth once more.

If their first kiss had been a storm, this one was a languid summer's eve, a slow dip of sunset over warm grass.

Tanwen slid her hands around his taut shoulders, grazed where his wings met skin.

She paused.

"You may touch them," he whispered, studying her as she tentatively stroked his plumage. His feathers were soft but strong, magnificent.

She felt Zolya shiver under her ministrations. His eyes fluttered closed for a breath, and Tanwen became transfixed by the peace that slipped across his features, the letting go.

A rare occurrence, surely.

"You are beautiful," she said.

A clear blue sky blinked open, Zolya looking down at where she lay beneath him.

A frown briefly marred his brow, but then he was sliding down her body, pressing kisses to her breasts through her shirt, across her belly.

Her nerves spun with anticipation as he raked sure fingers along her bare legs, slowly, achingly spreading them wide.

Tanwen had experience with kissing. Despite growing to become a pariah in Zomyad, she had been kissed before, stolen ones, sweet ones by village boys or girls.

She also knew how to pleasure herself, but never had her touch felt anything like that of the man who now grazed his teeth along the inside of her thigh.

Her breathing was quick, her pulse racing as his warm breath lingered on her skin as he settled between her legs.

It was a strange and heady sight, the prince in all his strength and size and grace bowing by her opening.

Tanwen felt her cheeks grow pink as he ran his gaze over where she rested, aching and wet. A small groan purred from him before his eyes rose to meet hers, a consuming hunger shimmering in their depths. "You are beautiful," he said, echoed, before he pressed his mouth to her and licked.

Tanwen arched, a cry escaping at the delicious sensation, her ache finally touched.

But it wasn't enough, and Zolya understood this, for he was excruciatingly thorough in tasting her, finding where she needed him most and generously lingering.

Gently, she felt the pressure of his finger, a teasing graze before he pushed in. There was an exquisite building as he worked in and out, in and out.

Her groans lifted from her as she tangled her fingers into his hair, keeping him connected.

There was a rustling of clothes, which drew Tanwen's attention to Zolya loosening his trousers, freeing himself. Tanwen sucked in a breath at his magnificence, mouth growing dry when he took his hard shaft in hand and began to pump long strokes.

As he pleasured Tanwen, he pleasured himself.

The view of him commanding them both was too much. Tanwen felt herself building, tipping over the crest of euphoria. And then she was falling, diving, before floating blissfully down into softness.

A guttural moan had her fluttering her eyes open to find Zolya, now kneeling by her feet, sliding his hand in a quicker rhythm over his hard length. His gaze was a swirling of untamed lust, completely pinned to where she lay, spread wide and wet and satiated.

Tanwen had never witnessed anything so glorious.

With another grunt, Zolya bent forward, spending himself on the sheets between her legs.

And then he was curling himself around her, fitting her back to his chest, a cradle of warmth and protection. It was too easy then for Tanwen to close her eyes and drift to sleep.

◆ ◆ ◆

When she awoke, the soft yellow glow of sunrise was pressing against the closed curtains.

A heavy arm was draped over her waist, a comforting press of heat at her back.

Tanwen's eyes widened.

Oh gods, she thought. *The prince and I—*

"Don't," mumbled Zolya from behind her.

Tanwen froze in her task of sliding from his hold. "I must go, sire," she said.

She squeaked as she was pulled back, Zolya suddenly above her, pinning her wrists beside her head. "So I am *sire* again?" he challenged. There was a glint in his eyes, an amused but dangerous spark.

Tanwen took in a stuttering breath. The weight of his body against hers stroked alive yearnings she no longer could entertain.

"I fear today you must be," she said.

It was as if she had poured cold water over them both.

Zolya slowly released her, sitting back on his heels. His hair was gloriously tousled from sleep, his clothes needing a good pressing, but he remained no less impressive, ethereal in his beauty.

The sight of him was more painful than it ever had been.

Because no longer was she free to touch such perfection, to feel him touch her.

That was last night: a strange stopping of reality as they each gave in to their desires.

Now it was morning, like the beginning of all other mornings in Galia, where the chasm of their rankings, their births, her forbidden existence, and his sin against her family ripped across the space between them.

Tanwen slid from the bed, chest aching as she retrieved her peplos from the floor.

With her back to him, she pulled off her tunic. Her moment of nakedness elicited a hiss from behind before a gale of wind.

Zolya was at her back, not touching her, but there.

Tanwen closed her eyes, an agonizing tug in her belly as his heat caressed along her exposed skin. His scent a delicious inhale.

"Please," he implored, a husky whisper as he took her dress from her hands. "May I help?"

No, she thought.

"Yes," she said.

It was torture, his gentle touch to her arms as he raised them, his delicately slow easing of her dress down her body. Tanwen held her breath as Zolya brushed her hair to the side, fixing the straps of her peplos before tightening the wrap along her waist.

"This is clever," he said, noting Eli's pouch. "Is it for your herbs?"

Tanwen stiffened. "Yes, it is to help in my daily tasks," she explained.

As she spoke, the true reality of where she stood came crashing down. *Whom* she stood with.

And Eli. *Gods*, Eli. She needed to find him. Make sure he was properly all right.

A knife of guilt slid between her ribs.

Because despite what transpired in the kidet barracks, who remained hostage within the palace, Tanwen had still enjoyed herself last night.

Which was the problem.

She *enjoyed* him.

The prince.

Entirely too much.

The son of the man who had torn the wings from her father, who had been among those who hunted her mother. The one who had threatened her brother's life, broken apart her family. Who would turn his back on her as soon as they stepped beyond this room.

He came to your rescue last night, said that incessant contrary voice within her mind.

Tanwen ignored it, knowing such a truth did not change, or help, her current situation.

"I must go," she said, stepping away from Zolya.

"Tanwen," he began.

"How would you suggest I leave?" She cut off his next words, glancing around. "I fear it's too bright to fly from your veranda unnoticed, and striding from your quarters is, of course, out of the question."

"Tanwen," he tried again. "We should discuss last night."

"Why?" she challenged, finally meeting his gaze. "What is there to discuss that would change who we are today? Who *you* are, sire."

Zolya grew still, stiff, at the use of her formality.

Good, she thought. *He needs to remember himself.* It was certainly impossible for Tanwen to forget.

"You indulged yourself last night," she found herself explaining. "Which is perfectly understandable. I have been told that to bed a servant can feel exciting. Enough Volari at court do it to prove such a theory. And I'm not delusional to think I'm the first you've entertained within your rooms. I willingly engaged and enjoyed myself. Let us leave it at that, sire."

Zolya's wings drew taut at his back, his gaze growing dark as a cold energy collected in the room. The brewing of a storm. "Leave it at that?" he rumbled.

Tanwen swallowed, a slip of fear entering her veins.

"Leave it at that?" he repeated, taking a step toward her.

Tanwen met it with a step back.

"You think *I* am accustomed to taking servants to my quarters?" he posed, his tone a blade's tip. "To offer them my bath and clothes as I sew their garments and share with them my innermost thoughts? That I would wish to taste them as I tasted you? You are to believe that last night was a ploy to obtain a dalliance of forbidden entertainment for an evening? I am the prince of Galia." His shoulders drew back, chin lifting. "If I wished for taboo pleasure, Tanwen, I merely need to snap my fingers."

His words were thrown knives, and she was useless in blocking their slicing pain.

"Then pray tell, Your *Royal Highness*," Tanwen challenged. "What *was* last night to you? What else can *I* be but my station and you yours?"

He opened his mouth before closing it, a fury painting his features.

Tanwen's heart broke: he was now, finally, grasping the truth of today. Of every day that would follow last night.

As he had said, he *was* the prince of Galia.

And she was too low, too horned, to even entertain the title of *the prince's mistress*.

"I need to leave," she said, pleaded. "Please, Zolya, I *need* to leave."

Tears were threatening to spill free as her desperation echoed through the room, touched the forgotten drinks from last night, pressed against the rumpled sheets of his bed.

Tanwen had to get far from the scene of their crime. And fast.

Zolya studied her an excruciatingly long moment, his shoulders tense, gaze blazing, but in the end, he said, "Follow me."

Tanwen held in her wince from his cold command as she shadowed his steps into his washroom.

Zolya stopped at a marble wall in the far corner. As he pressed a nearby carved tile, a panel slid open, revealing a dark tunnel. A musty breeze flowed out.

"Not even the staff know of these passages," he explained. "Each royal has one in their rooms, in case we ever need to escape unseen."

Escape.

His choice of word was not lost on her.

"But you have wings," she reasoned.

"The sky is not always safe," he explained, avoiding her gaze. "This will have you exit just below the western wall of the palace."

Tanwen glanced into the darkness, her nerves skipping down her spine.

"Take this." Zolya pulled free a candle from a nearby holder.

"Thank you," she said, making sure they didn't touch as she took the flame.

Zolya seemed to notice, for his brows drew in, annoyed.

"And thank you for your help . . . in the barracks," she added. "I truly am grateful that you found me."

Eternally so, she finished to herself.

Zolya only nodded, his expression severe.

Tanwen hesitated for a moment, not knowing what else to say.

If anything further *should* be said.

"Good day, Ms. Coster," said Zolya, his clipped dismissal like a tight fist around her throat, suffocating. But she knew it was what was right. What was needed.

"Good day, Your Royal Highness," she replied, meeting his icy stare.

And then she was fleeing into the lightless tunnel, running from the pain blooming in her chest.

But as Tanwen stepped into the dark, it wasn't lost on her that the prince guiding her toward this exit was also him providing her a pathway back in.

32

Within her office, Madam Arini clicked her long nails against her desk, a portrait of displeasure as she scrutinized Tanwen. The air was heavy with tension as her piercing gaze dissected every strand of Tanwen's hair, the folds of her peplos uniform, and finally her bandaged wrist.

From where she stood, Tanwen's unease only grew. Despite her best efforts to erase any remnants of last night—bathing again before acquiring a new uniform—there was not much she could do to disguise what had happened to her wrist.

"Your absence was noted in the dormitories yesterday evening," said Madam Arini, her voice firm yet composed. "Not an unusual occurrence for my atentés, of course," she added, blond manicured brow raised. "But what *was* untoward were the reports of your appearance when you returned this morning. Evidently, you looked quite in a state. Your hem was said to have been stained, and no tray of docüra was on your person. Not to mention the clear injury to your wrist."

The room filled with an expectant silence as Tanwen's disquiet raced through her veins. *Damn Gwyn*, she thought, for she held no uncertainty about who had been the informant.

"I apologize, ma'am." Tanwen lowered her gaze. "I will ensure it does not happen again."

"I am not seeking your apology, Ms. Coster," said Madam Arini. "I am looking for an explanation."

Tanwen hesitated, not expecting the building pressure of tears behind her eyes. It appeared it would take more than bathing and clean clothes to eradicate the trauma inflicted in the barracks. It did not help that she also still reeled from her night with Zolya, desperately grasping back emotions that were plucked free. Tanwen stood a raw, confused mess.

An odd expression reshaped Madam Arini's features as she likely noted Tanwen's hesitancy. As if she saw the shadow of what Tanwen held. When she spoke, her voice was uncharacteristically gentle. "Ms. Coster," she began. "You are safe here."

The words ricocheted against Tanwen, both true and false, and yet still allowed her to draw in a much-needed breath. Her tears now ran unchecked, as did her embarrassment. Tanwen might not have cried since her attack, or since her argument with Zolya, but she had hoped when she did, it would not be in front of the head of the royal atentés.

A less empathetic soul she had yet to meet.

Madam Arini remained sitting, poised and quiet, as Tanwen sniffed and sniveled, trying her best to pull herself back together.

"I apologize," Tanwen found herself repeating, wiping at her eyes. "I'm not sure what came over me."

"I do," said Madam Arini, brows drawing in, though her frustration was not aimed at Tanwen. "If you are unable to share details, Ms. Coster, I understand, but I still must know some of what transpired. Otherwise, I cannot help."

Help.

How odd a word to hear her speak.

Tanwen took in a steadying lungful of air. She knew Madam Arini would eventually find out some version of the truth. It was not as though the incident had been without witnesses, the prince's arrival and their joint departure less than subtle. It would only behoove her to control as much of the narrative as she could, especially regarding any of her interactions with Prince Zolya.

"I was attacked," Tanwen blurted out, her words as shaky as her resolve. "By two kidets near the barracks." Her story then came in fits and starts as she worked around *why* she was in that part of the palace to begin with as well as how the night ended. Or rather her morning. She opted for omissions rather than lying. She had just finished her rounds near the edge of the barracks when she was attacked; the prince intervened, then helped see that she got the proper medical attention for her wrist before Tanwen had taken solitary time to calm and recollect herself before returning to the atentés' quarters.

When Tanwen was done, her pulse thundered as a sense of queasiness churned in her gut.

Her fate now lay like a skewered fish, raw and exposed, flopped onto Madam Arini's cold marble desk.

And her madam allowed it to lie there an excruciatingly long time, though when she spoke, her response was not the anticipated reprimand.

"You said there were two kidets?" she asked, voice as rough as sand.

"Y-yes, ma'am."

Tanwen watched an unusual stillness settle over Madam Arini, her blue eyes glossing as if she was hurtled back to a haunting chapter of her own past. Shared scars and untold stories. But then it went as quickly as it had come. Madam Arini's expression returned to sharp points.

"You are fortunate the prince was near," she said. "Many are not so lucky."

I was not so lucky, Tanwen could tell she meant to say.

At the realization, Tanwen's chest constricted, a new understanding illuminating the reasons for all of Madam Arini's harsher angles. How brutal a chisel was the injustices of their world.

Tanwen resisted a frown as a snapping of ire awoke in her veins along with her sympathy. Though she could tell Madam Arini certainly didn't wish for anyone's compassion, least of all hers.

"I have faith Prince Zolya will see to the consequences of this incident properly," said Madam Arini. "If any of our kidars demand etiquette from their soldiers, it is he. Still, I will have a word with His Royal Highness. The safety of my royal atentés *cannot* be in question."

Tanwen remained silent, unsure what to do with this rare moment of support by her madam.

She certainly didn't want to ruin it by sharing her gratitude.

"In the meantime," continued Madam Arini as she reached into a drawer beneath her desk, "I want you only serving the princess this week. All other atenté duties, you will be excused from."

"Yes, ma'am," agreed Tanwen, nearly buckling from her wash of relief.

She had been dreading needing to suffer through the unwanted grazes from courtiers tonight.

"Put this over your bandage." Madam Arini held out a decorative leather cuff.

Tanwen stepped forward, taking the accessory and turning it over. It was finely made, the leather soft, the stamped floral design intricate. It felt like a gift from an admirer. Tanwen furtively glanced to Madam Arini as more questions surrounding her past bloomed.

"I require you wear this until your wrist heals," she explained. "I can't have my atentés sporting injuries as they serve the court, least of all the princess. For your sake, you should send prayers to Thryn that your wound does not scar." She arched a brow.

"Yes, ma'am." Tanwen nodded, grasping the cuff. "Thank you."

"Mmm," replied Madam Arini dismissively before adding, "Learn from this, Ms. Coster. I hope not to see you in my office again."

With that Tanwen was waved away.

As she stepped from Madam Arini's chambers, she had barely let out a relieved sigh before she was accosted by another's presence.

"Huw," Tanwen gasped, hand clutching her chest. "You really need to work on making yourself known."

She had not seen her friend leaning against the wall by their madam's entrance before he had reached out a hand to stop her.

Huw's blond hair glinted in the morning light coming through the open-column walkway, his horns painted with rings of gold. "Apologies," he said. "I didn't mean to scare you, but I have been waiting out here for an age. The atentés have been all up in a chatter about how you returned this morning. I was desperate to find you to see for myself, as you didn't come to morning meal." He raked his gaze over her body, brows knitted. "You look fine, though. Perhaps tired around the eyes. I didn't want to believe the gossip, but when I heard you were summoned by Madam Arini . . . well, little fawn, you have me *worried*. What has happened? Why did the dragon wish to speak with you? *Are* you all right?"

"Please." Tanwen settled a hand on Huw's shoulder, her mind reeling. "You are interrogating me more than Madam Arini."

Huw, appearing unmoved, plunked a fist on his hip in a *Well?* gesture.

"I'm fine," she explained on a sigh. "I merely had a . . . bad run-in with some kidets last night, but the prince arrived before anything—"

"The *prince*," hissed Huw, now drawing her farther down the hall before tugging them both between two columns. The wide-open sky loomed, both breathtaking and terrifying from the nearby ledge. "You must tell me *everything*."

Gods, how she wished she could.

"I can't," said Tanwen. "At least, not right now."

And not only for her own safety but because she truly couldn't relive what had happened. Not after recently exposing everything to Madam Arini. Tanwen had no desire to cry again, be so vulnerable again, despite the more welcome company of Huw. She merely wished this all behind her. *Especially* her moments with Zolya. Everything inside her was hurting, most of all her heart.

What else can I be but my station and you yours?

Her own words lashed out in her mind, an unforgiving sting.

Tanwen caught Huw regarding her, a meddyg studying a patient, clinically. He must have read the exhaustion in her features, her pain, for he straightened, brows softening.

"Of course," he said, gentler. "I'm sorry, of course—you don't have to tell me a thing. I'm just glad you're all right . . . you *are* all right?"

"Yes," she assured. "At least, I will be. Madam Arini was surprisingly . . . understanding."

His brows rose. "Are Süra flying?" he questioned as he searched the sky beyond their pillars. "Madam Arini capable of being understanding?"

A soft laugh escaped Tanwen, the sensation a welcome lightness to her somber mood.

"Yes, a miracle, to be sure," she agreed.

"Well, I won't ruin it by doubting." He took her arm, walking in step as they traveled down the hall. Tanwen found herself leaning into his supportive warmth, relishing having found a real friend here amid the chaos of her life.

"Oh, what's this?" Huw lifted her cuffed wrist, admiring the accessory.

"A disguise," Tanwen explained, shifting the leather to display her bandage, the flesh beneath still sensitive despite healing. "One of the kidets was a freeze wielder," she explained. Despite her attempt to sound nonchalant, her body betrayed her by stiffening, a phantom sensation flooding her of the kidet's hard grip.

"Oh, little fawn," Huw whispered, slowing them to a stop. "You have been through it, haven't you?"

Tanwen swallowed, unable to respond as the blasted pressure of tears squeezed behind her eyes once more.

"I'm sorry." Huw brought her into a hug. Tanwen rested her chin on his shoulder, biting her lip to stop the wobbling. "I know you said you didn't want to discuss it," he said softly into her ear, "but whenever you do, know I am always here."

"Thank you," she managed.

"No thanks necessary," he replied, stepping back.

Arm in arm, they continued their stroll down the corridor.

"You know," began Huw. "If we want to find some light in all this, your home visit couldn't be more perfectly timed. I'm sure now more than ever you are looking forward to putting space between you and this island."

Tanwen halted. "Excuse me?"

"Your home visit," he repeated, eyeing her with confusion. "That starts at the end of the week. Did you not see the bulletin in the dining hall?" Huw questioned. "You're listed with the next group of palace staff who have been granted leave to visit their loved ones."

"But . . . I thought those were saved for veteran servants," said Tanwen, still attempting to find her footing with this news.

"They are, with the exception of the recent palace recruits," explained Huw. "Like you. Though, it's all pretense, of course." He waved a hand. "A way to keep families happy, thinking they made the right decision, being able to see loved ones so soon after their departure. The next visits usually don't come back around for six months, at least."

Tanwen stared at her friend as her insides went to war. Doubt, confusion, desperate hope.

Could this be real? Was she truly able to see her mother? Her home?

And after locating her father and Thol.

She'd be able to tell her mother how she had succeeded. In person.

Feel Aisling's strong arms around her, breathe in her calming scent, ask for her help.

Tanwen wouldn't have to plan this next part alone.

An anxious, elated fluttering filled her chest as she gripped Huw's shoulders. "Where did you say this bulletin was?"

"In the dining hall."

Tanwen cared little for etiquette as she spun, nearly running toward the servants' quarters, down the steps, snaking the tighter corridors, passing affronted staff to skid to a halt before a large scrawled-on sheet of paper pinned along the far wall of the dining hall.

"By the Low Gods," Huw wheezed as he came up behind her. "My fine form is not meant to exert itself so."

She ignored him as she slid her finger down the list of names, her heartbeat galloping.

Tanwen Coster.

Her breath hitched as she stared at her name in disbelief. "That's me," she whispered.

"Of course it's you," harrumphed Huw, attempting to right himself despite still being out of breath. "Did you think I'd lie?"

"But . . . that's me," she repeated, still stunned as she glanced to her friend.

Huw appeared to drink in her shock before flashing her a grin. "Yes, little fawn," he said. "You get to go home."

Home.

The word dangled, bright and precarious, in her mind.

A blessing and a terror, for despite a Low God's promise, Tanwen was unsure what sort of home she'd find waiting.

33

"I *hate* him," seethed the princess as she reclined against Lady Esme in her private rooms. "I knew Father to be cruel, but I didn't think him capable of selling off his own offspring!"

"I did," replied Lady Esme coolly as she ran soothing fingers through the princess's white hair. "The king's only prerogative is to keep his crown secure and to please his court. I fear he sees you as a tool he's free to wield however he wishes."

Princess Azla was committing treason, yet Tanwen couldn't blame her for it.

From where Tanwen stood, mixing a tonic, her arm slowed. It was impossible to ignore the women's conversation.

As ordered by Madam Arini, Tanwen was exclusively seeing to the needs of the princess. And needs Her Royal Highness had aplenty.

Since waking from her perils with Indigo Eclipse, she had constantly been ringing Tanwen for tonics to calm her nerves, an elixir to help alleviate her ever-present headaches, or docüra to silence her swirling melancholy.

Tanwen didn't fault her demands, of course. Nor did she question why the princess avoided talking about that day or how Tanwen was the one who found her. She could only imagine what the princess must have been going through since the public announcement of her nuptials with Orzel.

Tanwen only wished she had a moment between summons so she could pack. She was set to leave for Zomyad tomorrow, and she had yet to prepare a scrap of clothing.

You hardly have a scrap to worry about packing, reasoned Eli from the pouch at her hip. *You won't need long to gather what you need for the morning.*

Tanwen pursed her lips. *If that was meant to be reassuring,* she thought to her friend, *you failed.*

Since the incident in the barracks, Eli had wanted to remain tucked by Tanwen's side as much as possible. And she was all too happy to comply. Well, until he became a nuisance, as he was becoming now.

To travel light is an advantage, explained Eli. *Look at myself. All I require is the fur on my back.*

Tanwen nearly scoffed. *That's because I carry all your soft comforts. Or do you forget how you spent most of our travels to Galia asleep in my pack?*

Eli quietly squeaked his indignation but otherwise remained silent.

"What am I going to do, Essie?" The princess's distress pulled Tanwen's attention back to where she was nestled against her lady-in-waiting.

Despite her current fervor, the princess still wasn't eating much, her withering form an added blanket to her despair.

"What are *we* going to do," corrected Lady Esme. "You are not in this alone, my love," she reminded. "And as we discussed, we have options."

"The only option that would change my fate is if Maryth claimed my father," said the princess, aggressively plucking at the beadwork along her chiton. "Before she claims me."

Tanwen stilled, spoon forgotten in her hand, upon hearing such sedition from the princess.

"*Hush,*" admonished Lady Esme, attention sliding to where Tanwen suddenly rebusied herself with her task, heartbeat in her throat. "Let us discuss this later. Getting worked up will not help matters." She turned Princess Azla's face up to meet hers. "I need you to stay healthy." She pressed a gentle kiss to her lips. "I need *you*."

"You have me," said the princess before she frowned. "At least for the next two months. The king has decided on a date, did you know? I will be wed to Orzel by the second full moons. Once the mine's construction is proving stable. The announcement will be made this week."

Tanwen furtively watched a shadow pass over Lady Esme's features, her grip tightening on Princess Azla, who swam in her arms.

Unwillingly, Tanwen's thoughts skipped to Zolya, having witnessed his similar despair and rage for his sister-cousin's fate. How powerless he had admitted to feeling.

And then, as if her mind was a masochist, everything else poured in.

Their kiss, his touch, the feel of him hard and hungry beneath her, his mouth everywhere before *there*, perfect, pleasuring—

Please, enough, cringed Eli.

Tanwen blinked back to the room, skin burning.

Stop listening, she admonished.

I can't help it, he defended. *Just as it appears you couldn't help yourself with—*

Eli!

Instantly his internal musings were cut off as Tanwen swallowed her embarrassment. She glanced to the nearby ladies, thankful to find that neither seemed to notice her distress.

She released a breath.

Tanwen and Eli hadn't officially broached the subject of the prince, despite Eli clearly understanding what had transpired. After all, Tanwen felt as if she were being haunted. Her mind was cruel in how often it decided to replay her and Zolya's evening together, despite her better efforts to concentrate on what mattered. She had located her father and brother. She was set to visit Zomyad, see her mother, and come back with a plan for how she could free all of them. Tanwen didn't need any other distractions.

Zolya certainly seemed to agree, for the prince had made himself scarce. Tanwen had not seen or heard of his whereabouts since that morning.

All for the better, of course.

"Tanwen."

Tanwen jolted back to the room, finding the concerned gaze of the princess.

"Are you all right?" she asked. "I've been calling your name for a spell."

"I apologize, ma'am." Tanwen flushed. "I was absorbed with the mixing of your tonic." She approached where the princess and Lady Esme lounged, then placed the drink on a side table. "When you wish for it, Your Royal Highness. It will help you sleep."

"Thank you, Tanwen," said the princess. "I'm not sure how I will manage while you are away. When do you leave again?"

"Tomorrow morning," said Tanwen, her stomach fluttering with impatience at the thought.

She hoped to send one last note to her father and Thol before her departure. Their correspondence was forced to be economical, given their carrier's limitations.

Eli could handle only so much weight on his back at a time. Still, Tanwen prayed her father might have become inspired to find a way to get them out. Thus far, Gabreel had remained steadfast on Tanwen taking her leave from Galia as a chance to run. For her to get Aisling and head north to the Low Gods' territory, as they had always planned.

But that, of course, was out of the question.

"Must you leave?" protested Princess Azla. "Can you not wait until your next home visit?"

"I will be back soon enough," Tanwen assured, more than flattered at the extent to which the princess had come to rely on her. Though saving her from being poisoned no doubt helped. "In the meantime,

"I can show Gwyn or Alys how to make some of your tonics while I'm gone," she suggested, despite how she loathed the thought of sharing any of her meddyg secrets with Gwyn. Tanwen had been able to avoid her nemesis as of late, and no part of her wished to change that.

"Show Alys," instructed the princess. "Despite her better efforts to hide it, I know she misses being the only one to fuss over me."

"As you wish, ma'am," complied Tanwen, relieved.

"But do ensure you only teach her the simple mixtures," said the princess. "I may trust Alys with dressing me properly, but my confidence wavers on her abilities around the nuances of being a meddyg such as yourself."

Tanwen couldn't help her smile. "I'll pre-prepare your favorite elixirs, ma'am. All Alys will need to do is add tea or water."

"Bless you," the princess breathed, pleased. "If only *I* held a skill half as useful as yours."

"You are highly skilled with your wind, my love," reassured Lady Esme.

"Yes, to play music or make art," scoffed Princess Azla. "But what is useful about that?"

"If I may, ma'am," interjected Tanwen. "That shows you have extreme control of your magic. Not every Volari can successfully pluck strings with their wind or channel it through holes in a flute to produce music in key."

The princess arched a single white brow at Tanwen. "And?"

"*And* precision is a very sought-after skill for anyone to master," explained Tanwen. "As for usefulness, perhaps it's about applying your talent to something that might serve you other than your art."

The princess blinked, as if she were seeing through fog for the first time. "You have me intrigued," she said, sitting up. "What might you suggest?"

"Well . . . ," began Tanwen as she looked around the large room. "Let's say you wish to nap but don't feel like getting out of bed to close the curtains. Do you think you'd be able to move them closed with your wind from here?"

"But I have staff to do that," argued the princess.

Tanwen couldn't help giving her a dry glance. "For the sake of this experiment, let's say that you don't."

"All right," Princess Azla conceded as she turned toward one of the open drapes that framed the entrance to the veranda. She took a deep breath in before making a quick and fluid slice through the air with her arm.

A funnel of wind burst from her hand to run along the curtain rings, sending a panel to flow shut. The light in the room dimmed.

"By the High Gods!" exclaimed Princess Azla. "I did it!"

"Well done, my love," said Lady Esme, clearly pleased by the princess's happiness.

"What else can I do?" Princess Azla turned expectantly to Tanwen.

Tanwen couldn't help but laugh. "Dare I say that is now for you to experiment with, ma'am. I'm sure your capabilities are unending. You merely need to flex your imagination."

An invigorated spark shone in Princess Azla's blue gaze, and for a flash Tanwen had a vision of standing before the prince, their features so similar. Same azure eyes, alabaster hair, and smooth brown skin along angular features. Their relation was inarguable.

So was the fact that Tanwen was beginning to care for each of them.

Truly an unwelcome realization.

"How enlightening this day has become," said the princess, strangely echoing Tanwen's thoughts, as she turned to Lady Esme. "Let us see what we can do with your heat."

"I think we both already know what I can do with my heat," said Lady Esme, her grin wicked as she held the princess's stare.

Princess Azla blushed.

Tanwen cleared her throat. "Do you need anything further from me, Your Royal Highness?"

"I do not," said the princess, reluctantly tearing her gaze from her lady-in-waiting to address Tanwen. "Your services today are, as usual, above and beyond. I hope you enjoy your visit home."

"Thank you, ma'am." She bowed.

After collecting her supplies, Tanwen was too glad to leave the lovebirds, but as she reached the front door, she was stopped. "Ms. Coster," called Lady Esme. "May I have a quick word?"

"Of course, my lady." Tanwen turned, a slip of unease entering her stomach as she noted the seriousness in Lady Esme's features. "How may I help you?"

Lady Esme furtively checked their surroundings, her red hair catching the sunlight streaming through the columns and into the grand receiving room where they stood. Despite them clearly being alone, she still guided Tanwen away from the front door to an alcove filled with wild foliage.

"I wanted to discuss what transpired with the princess last week," said Lady Esme, her delicate brows drawn together. "Or, more specifically, *your* help with what transpired with the princess. No, please, do not yet reply." She quickly raised a hand, stopping Tanwen's poised interjection. "Princess Azla shared what she could remember about your presence there that afternoon, but the prince filled both of us in on the rest of the details. He explained what you did, and I . . . well, I want to thank you."

"My lady," began Tanwen, "you do not—"

"I *do*," she interrupted again. "I *really* do. Azla feels the same, of course. But she is in the denial stage of her grief. She'd prefer we not discuss that day or what she attempted, despite how it looms around us. I have left offerings to Udasha every day, however, thanking her for such fortune in having it be you who found Azla. I can only imagine the outcome if it had been someone else . . . if it had been someone who hadn't acted as you had . . ." She stopped herself, a thickness in her voice as she momentarily looked away. "We both truly appreciate your presence in our lives. All the help you've given. And, well, I want you to know that to the princess, and to myself, you are more than her atenté. You are a . . . friend," she finished in a whisper.

Friend.

There was that word again.

Now spoken twice by those not meant to speak it.

Behavior that could never leave closed doors, lest one be labeled a Süra sympathizer.

And it was clear Lady Esme understood this, or she wouldn't have ensured their current privacy for such a conversation or have said the title in such a hush.

Which only tainted her sentiment.

Let us be friends, but in secret.

And then between Tanwen and Zolya.

Let us be lovers, but no one must know.

Tanwen suddenly felt centuries tired.

Was this to be the curse of her life?

Forever hiding, blending in, keeping secrets. Living, but only when behind shuttered curtains and locked doors. She was her father in Zomyad, but her being Mütra could not so easily be removed like his band of horns.

A tightness encircled Tanwen's throat, her desperation to leave this bloody island stronger than ever.

"I thank you for your words, my lady," said Tanwen, forcing her tone to be even, professional. "It is, of course, my honor to serve you and the princess. Your gratitude is not necessary. If that is all, I do have much to prepare before my leave tomorrow."

Lady Esme frowned, a hesitation in her gaze. "Just one more thing," she eventually managed. "The princess's earlier words regarding her father—"

"What words?" Tanwen interrupted, face neutral.

Lady Esme studied her a beat, weighing Tanwen's act of ignorance. "Indeed," she replied. "Once again, your discretion is appreciated. If ever you find yourself in need of such a favor in return . . ."

Tanwen plucked up the offering. Despite her wavering trust, she would not ignore leverage for future use. "I will be sure to seek your counsel, my lady."

"Please do." Lady Esme placed a gentle hand on Tanwen's arm, a sudden determined spark in her gaze. "The gods are fickle with how they move us around their celestial board, Ms. Coster, but I believe we knock against one another for a reason. Zenca, our goddess of destiny, has a plan. If the princess was meant to die that day, Maryth would have claimed her. Instead, there you were."

Lady Esme's grip on Tanwen tightened, a hint of her heat magic simmering in her touch. Tanwen's nerves skipped down her spine. "Your presence here is not happenstance," said Lady Esme. "And I recognize that."

Tanwen couldn't speak; she could hardly breathe.

Because Lady Esme was right.

Tanwen being at the palace *was* a carefully orchestrated, carried-out plan.

One she had believed was of her own doing, but she now was beginning to think it, in fact, could have entirely been inspired by Bosyg and dusted with Udasha's luck: her being placed at Sumora instead of any other den in Fioré, then being chosen to work the palace party before being promoted to the role of atenté to the princess.

Tanwen had been given more access to the royal household and palace quarters than she had ever dreamed of acquiring, all aiding—she had thought—in her endeavor to find and free her family.

But perhaps such access was for another reason.

Unease coursed through Tanwen's veins.

The gods are fickle with how they move us around their celestial board, Ms. Coster.

Lady Esme's words swam in her mind, foreboding. Tanwen did not enjoy the idea of being a pawn in someone else's divine game.

A time will come when I will need a favor of my own. Bosyg's promise sprouted in her thoughts then, an unwanted reminder.

Tanwen swallowed her rising disquiet.

Up until now she had worried only about succeeding in her mission, a daunting task on its own, but as she left the princess's chambers, she began to fear the validity of Lady Esme's words.

Could divine scheming be afoot in Cādra?

If it was, Tanwen hoped only that the endgame still included her and her family's survival.

34

From the southern roof of the palace, Zolya watched her leave.

Tanwen was but another speck among the crowd shuffling toward the awaiting gondola, but even at his distance, he could pluck her apart from the others.

She shone differently, her energy a magnetic draw despite how she attempted to blend in with the surrounding mass that waited to board the transport.

Zolya knew the subtle curve of her horns and the way her raven locks melted into liquid around her shoulders under Ré's light.

She was an agile creature, Zolya had come to observe, moving as if used to avoiding the notice of others. Or, at the very least, understanding how to traverse around them, through them, to get where she needed.

Disquiet filled Zolya's chest as Tanwen disappeared into the gondola, doors shutting.

His wings twitched along his back.

Follow, they seemed to urge.

Zolya did not.

He kept still as he tracked the gondola's descent toward the town of Fioré, where it would reunite some of the palace staff with their family there before lowering the rest to Cādra.

Tanwen would be heading to Zomyad for her home visit.

Which meant she would be gone from the palace long enough for Zolya to regain his sanity.

Thank the High Gods, he thought.

He still was reprimanding himself for what had transpired the other night.

What *more* he had wanted to transpire.

What he still wished he could do every evening since.

But, of course, he could not.

What else can I be but my station and you yours? Tanwen's plea awoke, angry and unwanted, in his mind, her words that had done their job of clearing the euphoric fog in his head.

How annoyingly correct she had been.

Still was.

While others at court were given allowances for their desires behind closed doors—within reason—Zolya was the crown prince. Sole heir to the throne. Every action of his was a statement, a decree, a representation of his bloodline and his father. If any were to learn he favored one of the staff . . .

Zolya's shoulders stiffened.

It would not be only he who suffered.

Tanwen would be at the mercy of the king's retribution for a prince who had misbehaved.

A slip of panic settled into his gut, stirring awake his ever-present frustration.

How could I be so careless? he chastised.

The only excuse Zolya could think of was the state he had been in when he had found Tanwen cornered by those kidets: groped, dress torn, and nearly forced.

He had still been coming down from his tantrum in the sky, his emotions raw, exposed, when he had realized *whom* his men had within their grasps. All hope of logic and reason had then been devoured by his rage. Zolya had once again found himself untethered.

The next he knew, she was in his arms, shaking but gripping him tightly. As though his warmth was the only way to thaw her chill.

Zolya's thoughts had been only on getting her safe, getting her well.

He'd had no foresight around what would happen if others saw them soaring into his chambers so late at night or how she would look in his shirt, freshly bathed, flushed, nipples hard and nearly visible beneath the thin material.

Zolya shifted as heat traveled to his groin.

This is madness, he thought with annoyance, eyes still trained on the now-distant gondola, soon to be swallowed under the canopy of trees along the mountainside.

Zolya couldn't afford to be out of control.

In fact, he had worked hard to avoid it.

Chaos and uncertainty were what his father had brought to his life.

And Tanwen—Ms. Coster—she was an utter enigma that threatened his decades of learned and cherished composure.

She had pulled his curiosity despite his best efforts to look away.

Zolya was not used to noticing staff.

Had been raised not to.

Yet there she had been, over and over again, utterly engrossing. Dangerously tempting. Helpful. Healing. Listening.

The care she had taken with Azla, her shared concern that had nothing to do with her required duty—it had melted a layer of his armor. And then her attention to him in his rooms, her encouraging words, shared faith in his abilities, despite *her* being the one he had originally intended to console. He hadn't been prepared for any of it. Least of all meeting another who shared his passions, echoed thoughts he held only in his heart, and understood the burden of shouldering secrets that could alter another's life.

Zolya had then found himself afloat on an unknown island, his blood pooling with desires he hadn't felt for anyone in his near century of existence. He hadn't *let* himself feel. And yet there he sat, wanting, wishing, praying that Tanwen would kiss him. For that decision to be *her* own, and not by any pressure of his.

Which she had.

And everything he had ever believed, thought, assumed about their world had been shattered apart. Zolya was now left desperately attempting to fit the pieces back together.

But even if he could, he knew the fractured cracks would always remain, marks that proved life could be different.

Life could be lived.

"Enjoying the view of your kingdom?" said a deep voice through a whip of wind.

Osko landed on the roof beside Zolya, tucking in his black plumage.

"Something like that," Zolya replied, attention traveling to the distant town that hugged part of Rhada Lake. *She will be in Fioré soon,* he thought.

"Galia does look fine today," admitted Osko, gaze taking in the lush and manicured greenery. "Though, thanks to our gods, she shines thus most days."

"Mmm," Zolya absently agreed, a gentle breeze carrying the scent of jasmine and the cawing of macaws flying nearby. "Tell me, Osko." Zolya turned to his friend. "How many at court and of our soldiers do you suppose have bedded staff?"

Osko scoffed, his black hair reflective ink in Ré's morning light. "All of them at one point, I'm sure," he replied.

For some reason this surprised Zolya. "Have you?" he questioned.

Osko met his stare, a suspicious pinch between his brows. "Why do you ask?"

"Curiosity." Zolya shrugged. "I hadn't realized how common it was."

"Well, I suppose it's not *so* common," Osko backtracked. "The risk is certainly still there to be labeled a sympathizer if affairs stretch too long. As for myself, despite the rarity of Volari reproducing, I'm not keen on the possibility of an abomination."

Abomination.

Zolya clenched his teeth together. He never could tolerate that word.

"Is this about what happened the other night with the princess's atenté?" asked Osko. "The barracks are still up in a chatter about it."

Zolya remained very, very still as his magic hissed and kicked in his veins. "Those kidets were out of line," he said.

"Yes," agreed his friend. "Though not the first to have been."

"That still doesn't make it tolerable," Zolya snapped. "Nor will it ever make such behavior allowable."

Osko watched him for a beat, head tilting inquisitively. "No," he agreed. "It does not, which is why those soldiers have been dealt with as you've mandated. A good beating will knock their behavior back in order."

"Let's hope," said Zolya, wishing he could have been the one to land the blows, but to further involve himself in the incident would not be wise.

"I've never known you to be so concerned with these matters before," reasoned Osko, still studying him.

Zolya resisted shifting under the scrutiny. He needed to be careful. Osko might have been his oldest friend, but he was undoubtedly a purist. Despite how Zolya's chest burned to share what he wrestled with in his heart, he could not trust Osko with such a confession.

The realization left Zolya rather deflated. The truth of his loneliness covered him like an eclipse, cold and foreboding.

Which was the temptation of Tanwen.

She had proven to be trustworthy, a rarity in this palace, in Zolya's life. Which had allowed him to share bits of his childhood and his relationship with his mother. When he had seen no judgment from her, no collection of leverage, only genuine interest and compassion, it had nearly been as arousing as her standing there, bare legged in his tunic.

"Yes, well," began Zolya, ignoring the heat coursing across his skin as he refocused on Osko. "As you said, the atenté was part of the princess's staff," he explained. "If Azla learned of what happened, she would be incensed. I have little patience to add calming her constitution to my plate. Attacks on servants also don't bode well for morale. Madam Arini made that and many other thoughts clear when she sought an audience with me after the incident. We can't have her worried over her atentés' well-being while in the palace, nor the other staff. It would only hurt the Recruitment."

"Yes," said Osko. "That is true. Though enough Süra join the Recruitment knowing they might be sent to work the mine or fill lower services in Fioré," he explained. "The opportunity they get in Galia is still beyond the Kaiwi River better than what they might find on Cādra."

A circumstance only we have perpetuated, thought Zolya darkly. "Nevertheless," he replied. "The last thing we need is a reduction in recruits. Especially with the building of the new mine." Despite how Zolya loathed this truth, it remained. Their treasury was continuing to bleed, his father refusing to curb palace spending for fear of losing face in front of his court.

"Speaking of which," said Osko, "that is why I came to find you. The king wishes for us to inspect the build. We're to report on the delivery of materials and ensure the promise of labor is well on its way." Osko flattened a lapel on his gray coat. He was dressed in his full kidar regalia, no doubt in preparation for their official visit to the mine. "The king is demanding to see significant progress by the next full moons," he went on. "So it can be on track to be operational by the eve of Princess Azla's nuptials."

Zolya breathed out his frustration at both the mention of Azla's death sentence disguised as a wedding and his father's notorious impractical expectations. To have an up-and-running mine in two months' time would be backbreaking work. But Zolya supposed that was fine by the king so long as it was Süra backs breaking.

That will change when I'm king, he thought before stopping himself, disturbed by his musing.

He had never allowed himself to imagine being in his father's place on the throne. Despite doing all he could to live up to the title, knowing he was next in line. Such a future forever felt improbable, at the very least centuries away. But lately that daydream had begun to take hold.

That was spoken like a well-studied future king. Tanwen's words arose like a warm, supportive press to his shoulder. *To become eternally loved. To inspire others. Are those not traits to admire in a great ruler?*

Could he really be such a king?

But then the intruding words of his father slithered awake in his mind, a viper's bite knocking him down. *I have a long way yet in my reign, lest our kingdom be at the mercy of your soft heart.*

That ever-present flame of ire surged within Zolya's chest, his gaze landing on the distant white sprawling city of Fioré, his mind tipping to the woman who was now there.

Soft heart, indeed, he thought, his frustration rising before he unfurled his wings. It was a relief, stretching his plumage to allow the sun to warm each of his feathers.

"Whatever the king demands," said Zolya, "we shall obey."

He then took to the sky, Osko quick to join.

Zolya flew toward his responsibilities and away from the view of his fantasies.

PART VI

Favor

35

Gabreel had all but given up on the High Gods years ago, but it appeared Udasha still remembered his decades of service. The goddess of luck was shining on him that morning as he and Aberthol were transferred from their windowless room to an old groundskeeper's cottage on the northern edge of the palace grounds.

Blessed fresh air pushed its way through the small open panes. Dust motes danced within the sunbeams as Gabreel and Aberthol were shown into the abandoned space.

What might have appeared as squalor to those on Galia was a haven to the inventor and his son. After their weeks spent locked in their cramped and lightless prison, the multiple-room home felt extravagant. Gone were the shared floor mat and musty blankets. In its place was an actual bedroom with two beds and down mattresses. There was even a small kitchen with a kettle and provided herbs, bread, cheeses, eggs, and fresh water.

But what Gabreel took note of immediately were the windows. Every room had one. Even the shed—now a converted workshop—that was connected to the kitchen and where they were currently being shuffled.

Three rooms total.

Three windows.

Three views that teased their freedom.

Teased, not promised. Because though their surroundings were an enhancement, the cottage was still very much a prison. Guards were stationed by the front door, while the entire back of the building skirted a steep cliffside. To climb out was a perilous journey, and one would still find oneself stuck on a floating island high in the sky.

And yet even a sliver of blue expanse was a welcome sight compared to the dungeon they had been suffering.

"We will finish transferring the rest of your materials tonight," explained the gruff voice of the kidet who loomed in the workshop's doorway, his wings barely fitting in the frame. "As requested by the king, you'll be able to oversee the build of the mine from this new location day and night." He gestured to a large telescope protruding out the far window.

Gabreel approached it, bending to peer through the lens. The magnification was impressive, as he could clearly see the northern edge of Cādra. And there, hugging the coastline before spilling over its ledge, was a skeleton of the new mine. It appeared fragile with its naked beams and scaffolding. But where once rough sea pounded rock, assuredly bashing and breaking such a structure with a simple cresting wave, the rock wall now sat dry. Orzel, as agreed, had pulled the tides, allowing construction to begin.

"Once you're settled," said the guard, "let us know if you need anything further to outfit your new workroom."

"I will still need to have visits on site," explained Gabreel, turning back to the kidet. "To ensure all of my schematics I'm creating up here are properly installed down there."

"Prince Zolya and Kidar Terz will be your liaisons for that," he replied, eyes tracking Aberthol, who was inspecting their new workspace.

Don't look at him, Gabreel wanted to seethe, the heat in his blood thrashing against his skin. He hated any notice the kidets took of his son.

Scorched Skies

"No offense to His Royal Highness and Kidar Terz," said Gabreel, stepping forward so he could redraw the attention of the guard, "but neither is an engineer."

"Engineers are stationed at the mine," the kidet explained coolly. "Those who were Bardrex's assistants. They are on the ground for His Royal Highness to confer with and will be sending the king, his council, and you weekly reports to review."

How thorough of the king to ensure I never have need to leave this place, thought Gabreel darkly.

"And in the meantime?" asked Gabreel. "What exactly does His Majesty wish of me?"

"To do what you are meant to," said the kidet, gesturing to their surroundings. "Invent."

With that the soldier left Gabreel and Aberthol, seeming too eager to escape the small cottage. Their front door was pulled shut, metal lock bolting into place.

The descending quiet echoed with the guard's last words.

Do what you are meant to do. Invent.

Gabreel refocused on the workroom as a creeping unease slithered awake in his gut. Everything now shone with new light. From the fresh parchment and balsa wood and ink along the stretching table to the far wall, which was fully stocked with a variety of new tools and instruments: T squares and straightedges, dials and circumferentors, adzes and calipers. Even their stocked kitchen and new sleeping accommodations were no longer fortuitous.

This was not merely a transfer for Gabreel to oversee the building of the new mine. It was the foundation of a permanent residence.

The king was settling Gabreel in to stay.

Them to stay.

Such a realization should be a relief, prayers answered that they were then to live.

But no joy came to Gabreel. Only panic as he met Aberthol's gaze from across the table.

His son had continued to wither despite the latest reprieve in his torture. His cheeks were sunken, his once-lustrous dark curls now limp and matted around his horns. The dark smudges under his eyes were a forever reminder of his fitful sleeps, his screams in the night and quiet sobs. And there Gabreel had lain beside him, unable to console him, comfort him. His touch still causing Aberthol to recoil.

The only hint of light in his son had come when they had learned Tanwen was in the palace. It was like a shooting star, hope there and gone in his gaze before Aberthol's features grew dark. As he, no doubt, came to the same conclusion as Gabreel.

Tanwen was just as trapped as the two of them.

"They will collect me tonight," said Thol, his despondent tone refocusing Gabreel's attention, "for him giving us this place."

Him.

The king.

Their monster.

"I will not let them," Gabreel promised.

"You have no power to stop them," stated Aberthol. It was said not in anger, merely in resignation—pity, even.

His father could not protect him.

His father could not protect any of them.

And Aberthol had accepted this. He stood in their defeat.

A painful chill wrapped around Gabreel as he understood his son had lost all faith in him.

But the worst of it was, he could not blame Thol.

Gabreel had lost faith in himself. In the entire world and every cursed god who tricked mortals into worshipping them for the hope of their favor.

Which was why Tanwen being here was not fortuitous.

It was to be his family's final tragedy.

A parable to teach others: look what will transpire if you dare defy your almighty king—you will be made to watch all that you love die.

"Thol, I—" began Gabreel before stopping himself. He didn't know what he could say to his child to ease his pain, lessen either of their suffering.

Everything he had done since they arrived was for Aberthol, for Aisling, and for their family. Every moment he spent ensuring the success of the mine—gladly accepting the future suffering of thousands of Süra and standing silently by when the princess was offered up as chattel—was all to keep his son safe.

For them to have one more night where he would not be taken.

And yet . . .

Failure.

I am a failure.

The mine was underway, and Thol's future still loomed uncertain, painful. Once the mine was complete, how quickly would the king shrug off his promise to Gabreel and begin to play with Aberthol based on his whims? More than he already had been. His Mütra pet.

Gabreel dug his fingers into the table he leaned on, his useless rage roaring through his veins.

He was stuck.

Trapped.

In body and in mind.

"Do you think Wen will return?" Aberthol asked, picking anxiously at a scab on his arm.

"For her and her mother's sake, I hope not," said Gabreel, brows furrowing.

A pensive quiet stretched between them.

"If she does," began Thol, "how will she know where we've been moved?"

"We were very publicly paraded through the upper halls to get here," said Gabreel. "But I also dropped a scroll by the crack in the door to our old cell for Eli. She will know."

Thol worried his bottom lip, gaze unseeing as he stared out the window to Gabreel's right.

"She cannot end up like me," Thol eventually whispered.

"Like you?" questioned Gabreel.

His son met his eyes, the shadows swimming in their green depths a haunting. "If there is a promise you wish to fulfill, Father," he said, "let it be that Wen will *never* become like me."

Like me.

Broken.

Hollow.

The king's plaything.

His request was said like a desperate command, hoarse and terrified and determined.

"Thol," choked Gabreel, stepping toward his son, but Aberthol merely stepped back, shaking his head before dashing into the kitchen.

Gabreel winced as the door slammed shut.

He was left standing alone in his workroom.

The wind from the cliffside howled through the open pane at his back. The stark reality of his solitude bore down on him as he closed his eyes. He took a deep breath, gathering the fortitude he needed to survive another day.

Aisling, he thought, *I need your strength. I need you.*

But despite his plea to his wife, who remained half a world away, Thol's command continued to bear down on him.

Wen can never *become like me.*

No, thought Gabreel, his breaths growing painful. *Nor can she become like me.*

A soul full of regret.

36

Tanwen's bottom held more bruises than a rotten apple. The days of endless sitting within the covered wagon mixed with the overwhelming scent of body odor had made for a rough journey home.

But despite her discomforts, Tanwen had never been so happy.

She was back in Zomyad.

The city of Ordyn rose up and around them like a giant interwoven garden. Moss-covered branches twisted to connect bridges and footpaths high above, while warm glows emanated from the hundreds of dens and businesses built along the giant trunks and protruding roots.

Tanwen angled forward, between the others sitting beside her, to get a better look out the back of the carriage.

The road along the forest floor was clogged, a bustling of travelers coming and going. Hardly any paid mind to the caravan of returning recruits.

As their cart rolled to a halt beside the Recruitment Office, Tanwen nearly tripped over the other passengers in her desperation to place booted feet to soft soil.

The fresh, cool air was a heady slap. One that caused her to take large, hungry inhales.

Tanwen couldn't get enough of the woody richness. Gone were the dry, overperfumed florals and constant jasmine breeze.

No longer was the sky a bright and intrusive blue, but it was now a glorious green. A canopy of shaded safety stretched high above. Ré's light was only allowed fingers of sunlight to stream through the fanned-out leaves; the rest was a soft, covered jade illumination.

Tanwen realized then how long she had truly been away for this to all feel so . . . different yet blessedly right.

The biggest change, however, was no longer finding herself flinching from the endless passing shadows made by massive wings. Absent were the sudden gales from Volari landing nearby.

Tanwen was home.

Tanwen was safe.

An ache worked up her throat at the realization as she hitched her pack to her back. As soon as she was able, she had changed into her leather boots, trousers, and sturdy green coat. It had been a liberating moment for all the recruits once they descended to Cādra. A rush of stripping their servant garb for that of their clans before they crammed back into the awaiting carriages and headed west.

"Oy," called one of the Recruitment guards from the office's entryway. "Make sure you sign out over there"—he pointed to a nailed-up piece of parchment—"before you leave. We'll expect your return in three days' time for the journey back to Galia. And don't, some of you, get ideas about not showing. That'll only allow Volari to come searching in our woods."

Tanwen distractedly signed her name with the others, her mood remaining high despite the reminder that she was still very much tied to her contract.

"Wen!"

Tanwen turned, her heart stopping as she spotted Aisling pushing her way through the throngs of people. She looked thinner, smaller, but Tanwen ignored her sense of worry and ran.

"Mother!"

Tight arms wove around Tanwen, the scent of gardenia filling her lungs on an inhale. She let out a relieved sob, which her mother echoed as they stood embracing for what felt like an eternity.

"Oh," laughed Aisling, drawing back. "Hello, Eli dear."

The mouse had scampered from Tanwen's pouch, up and over to her mother's shoulder to nuzzle her cheek.

He was squeaking his delight, whiskers twitching in telling glee.

"All right, Eli," said Tanwen, lifting her hand so he could scurry to sit on her shoulder. "We'll have plenty more time for that once we are back at our den."

Our den.

The words nearly provoked more tears.

A gentle hand was placed on Tanwen's cheek, her mother studying her with a soft but pained smile.

"I cannot believe you are here," she said. "You look so much older."

"I haven't been gone that long, Mother," Tanwen teased.

"A day has the power to age us a century," Aisling answered, dropping her arm.

Tanwen's stomach fell with it.

It was clear, despite her mother's letters saying otherwise, she had not been well during Tanwen's absence.

But whatever melancholy hung in the air was cloaked with Aisling's smile. "Come," she said. "I borrowed Rind to quicken our trip home."

Tanwen's pulse fluttered, pleased, as she eyed the cart and mare on the other side of the road.

"How have you been, girl?" Tanwen grinned at Rind as she came to hold her bit, stroking her brown nose.

Tired, Rind said, *but very glad to see you.*

Same here, my friend, replied Tanwen, touching her forehead to Rind's muzzle.

"Are we ready to go?" asked Aisling.

"Yes," said Tanwen, giving Rind another pat before swinging herself and Eli up into the cart.

As their buggy lurched forward, Tanwen felt a wash of relief, a sting of happiness as they traveled down the stretch of road promising home.

◆ ◆ ◆

Their tea sat cold and forgotten.

Afternoon sunlight streamed into the kitchen, where Tanwen and Aisling huddled together. Eli was fast asleep beside his buttered bread roll on the table, the smattering of crumbs serving as his bedding.

"By the Low Gods," murmured Aisling, sitting back. "I still can't believe you found them."

Tanwen had finished retelling—as best she could—what had transpired on Galia since her arrival. She had written bits and pieces to her mother, of course, but it had been difficult to get it all down on paper. Now, face to face, she could unburden the lot of it. Though she took special care to leave out certain details, mainly around Thol's torture and what had happened between her and the prince.

There was no reason for Tanwen to share the first, given Aisling's worry was clearly already affecting her health. Her pale skin had grown more ashen, and the dark circles under her eyes had Tanwen assuming she wasn't sleeping.

As for the situation with Zolya, well, she already knew that was an egregious mistake. One that would *never* be repeated. She didn't need to send her mother into a catastrophic spiral of panic and, no doubt, fury at her daughter.

Tanwen had done enough chastising of herself for the both of them. Her visit home needed to have a singular focus, and that was how to get her father, Thol, and herself off Galia and somewhere safe.

"Well, Eli technically found them," clarified Tanwen. "I have yet to figure out a way into their holding cell. But we've been able to communicate through short notes, which Eli has carried back and forth." Tanwen glanced at her furry friend asleep by her arm, smiling as his legs twitched. He no doubt was dreaming of more loaves of bread he could burrow into.

"I really didn't think it possible," said Aisling, redrawing Tanwen's attention. "You found them," she repeated.

Tanwen's chest grew tight as she noted her mother's shocked relief. She leaned forward, placing a reassuring hand atop Aisling's. "Yes," she said. "We found them."

And then her mother burst into tears.

◆ ◆ ◆

The light outside had dimmed by the time Aisling was able to compose herself.

Tanwen had rebrewed their tea, their mugs releasing curls of steam as the candles along the kitchen table had been lit. A flickering warmth draped across the kitchen.

"I'm sorry," sniffed Aisling, wiping her nose with her already damp handkerchief. "I've become rather blubbering since you've all left."

"Mother," said Tanwen, squeezing her arm from where she sat across from her. "Never apologize for having feelings."

Aisling let out a choked laugh, dashing away more falling tears. "Gods," she said. "Who is parenting who now?"

"I *have* always been the mature one out of Thol and me," argued Tanwen, sharing in her mother's grin.

Aisling scoffed, but her smile remained. "A statement your brother would gladly argue."

"Which shows his immaturity," countered Tanwen as she and her mother shared a laugh.

But then their grins faltered in the wake of their unspoken worries surrounding her brother and father.

Beyond the kitchen window, the chirps of birds had been replaced with the buzz of nightlife, the tepid air growing cool. Tanwen's animal friends had come to poke their heads in from time to time, welcoming her return. It had warmed her tremendously, painting her visit as a true homecoming. She could almost forget everything that still loomed ahead. Almost.

"There's been news in Zomyad of the king's new mine," said Aisling after a beat, absently running a finger along a groove in the tabletop's wood. "That it is projected to be operational by winter."

"Yes," confirmed Tanwen. "That is what they are saying."

"So your father truly has met the king's demand."

Tanwen wasn't sure if her mother was upset by this. Surely, she had to understand *why* he had complied.

"I fear Father had as much of a choice in the matter as he did when he and Thol were abducted," reasoned Tanwen.

Her mother remained quiet, features pensive, pained.

Tanwen was hesitant to pry into her thoughts, not wanting to possibly knock loose a new fit of tears. She was worried another bout would only release her own grief, and she was *really* trying to hold it together for her mother.

"Orzel is helping the king," said Tanwen, attempting to change course. "King Réol has given Princess Azla to Orzel for his aid in pulling back the tides by the mining site."

Her mother's eyes widened. "The princess is to be given to Orzel?" she breathed. "That poor soul."

"Yes," agreed Tanwen. "She's as unwilling a bride as one could be."

Visions flashed through Tanwen's mind then, of the princess collapsed on her floor, her sickly complexion and shallow breaths, the poisonous tea leaves splashed across the carpet. Then to the prince sitting sentry by her bed. Shirtless and powerful as his concern and rage overtook the room before he asked Tanwen for her discretion and trust. Then, much later, when she had felt his strength as his hands slid across her body, pulled out her pleasure in delicate—

"*Tanwen?*" said her mother, the concern in her voice snapping back her attention.

Tanwen blinked, her skin burning with embarrassment. "Sorry," she said. "What did you say?"

"I asked about your experience as the princess's atenté," Aisling said, continuing to eye her critically.

"It's going well," admitted Tanwen, clearing her throat along with any last remnants of her traitorous fantasies. "At least, more enjoyable than when I was at Sumora. She's a much better companion than having to suffer through serving the court and Volari aristocrats. In fact, the princess is . . . not what I had expected."

"How so?"

Tanwen considered her response. "Well, she's kind, for starters," she explained. "And . . . generous. She seems to genuinely wish to know her staff."

Aisling leaned back in her chair, studying Tanwen. "Be careful there, my wyrthia," she warned.

Tanwen frowned. "What do you mean?"

"Princess Azla may have those traits in private," she explained, "but she is still the princess. A Volari beholden to the laws set by the king, more so than most."

Tanwen tensed, her mother's reprimand hitting too many exposed nerves.

You are more than her atenté, Lady Esme had said. *You are a friend.*

A painful tease and utter delusion.

One that matched the night she had experienced with the prince.

"I know that," said Tanwen, perhaps a tad too defensively. "I'm not oblivious to my position on Galia."

"I never said you were," placated her mother.

"You insinuated, however."

"Tanwen—"

"I will *always* remember my place, Mother," she interrupted. "You and Father have certainly made sure of that. Thol and I could never forget who we are and what we're not supposed to be."

"Tanwen," attempted her mother again, though softer. "That is not—"

"Let us not speak further on the topic." Tanwen drew the conversation to a halt as she glanced out the window to the darkening forest. "For us to argue will waste my visit home."

Aisling was quiet for a breath. "All right," she appeased. "Then what shall we discuss?"

"How about a plan to get Father, Thol, and me off that blasted island," Tanwen suggested with a frown. "Aside from figuring out a way past the guards, the biggest obstacle I can't solve is how to get us off after I do. The only way down from Galia is the gondolas," explained Tanwen. "But those are heavily guarded and require the proper paperwork for a servant to use. They also are riddled with tedious checkpoints. There is the one from the palace gondola to Fioré and another for the gondola to Cādra before a final checkpoint once on the ground."

"That is complicated," said her mother, brows furrowed. "And even if we could get the papers, who knows how much time you three would have before someone took note of Thol's and Gabreel's absence. You might not even make it to Fioré."

"Yes," agreed Tanwen, her frustration rising with how impossible this next task was. "Galia really is a prison for anyone without wings."

The quiet that filled their kitchen was deafening. Empty air that represented the chasm they needed to cross.

"Then perhaps," mused her mother after a moment, "we need to give you all wings."

Tanwen stared at Aisling, concern for her mental health growing. "Mother," she began slowly. "Did you slip spirits into your tea?"

Her mother gave her a measured look. "I'm completely sober and serious."

"To give us wings?" repeated Tanwen dubiously.

Aisling nodded, her long brown hair shifting around her shoulders. "And how, in all of Cādra, would we do that?"

Her mother rubbed her lips together, a nervous tic, as her features grew pensive. "Come with me," she eventually said.

Her chair's legs scraping against the floor woke Eli.

What's happening? he asked blearily as he sat up.

Mother appears to have lost her mind, replied Tanwen silently, reaching out so her friend could scurry up her arm to her shoulder. *She's evidently going to give me wings.*

Eli squeaked out a laugh.

My sentiments exactly, said Tanwen as they followed Aisling out of their den.

"Where are we going?" she asked as they descended to the forest floor.

"Your father's workshop," answered her mother, setting off down the familiar small footpath.

Tanwen's pulse quickened, a surge of anticipation building.

They were going to her father's workshop.

A place she had thought she'd never see again, where she used to find joy sneaking in alone at night.

Now she walked there with her mother.

Tanwen had never been in her father's workshop with her mother.

As they traveled toward the small glen, Tanwen's excitement was momentarily pulled elsewhere as she took note of the air around them. It felt thicker, an odd clinging of humidity. There were still the familiar woody fragrances and purring of insects and animals that made up her home, but it all now seemed . . . muted—cloudy, even—as if she had stuffed her nose and ears with a layer of wax.

"It feels different around our den," said Tanwen as she kept pace behind her mother.

"It is Bosyg's favor," Aisling explained, pushing away a branch in their path. "She must have put some sort of enchantment on our home, for I have gotten no visitors since you left. And when I do go to town, those in Unig seem only to remember me, but none of you."

Tanwen's brows rose. "Not even Father?"

"Not even him."

"Well . . . that is good, right?"

"I suppose," said her mother, though Tanwen noted the hint of melancholy in her voice.

As they crested a small hill, the glen came into full view beyond the final line of trees. The glow of the crescent moons bathed the field in a cool blue. And there, tucked into the side of the trickling waterfall, was her father's workshop.

Tanwen held her breath as her mother pulled a key from her pocket. As they pushed through the door, familiarity hit her like a wave.

The scent of balsa wood, ink, and parchment filled the cool, dark air.

With the striking of flint, her mother lit a nearby lantern, sending a bubble of light to brush against their surroundings.

Her father's workshop sat in disarray, the pillaged remnants of when it had been invaded by kidets. Tanwen's ire slid hot in her veins as her footsteps crunched against the scattered papers on the ground, and she eyed the broken bits of once delicately carved wooden models.

Another crack fissured across Tanwen's heart. The reverent space now sat tainted from the intruders. Ransacked. Soiled.

She followed her mother to a long worktable in the far corner. Aisling set down the lantern, the light feathering out along the worn wood. Tanwen frowned as Aisling reached under the table, and with a small click, an endless cascade of scrolls spilled out.

Her mother had activated a hidden false bottom.

Tanwen's pulse jumped. "What are those?" she asked.

Aisling gathered the scrolls atop the table, then shuffled through each before she stopped on one. "Wings," she answered before breaking its seal and unrolling the parchment.

Her father's handwriting filled Tanwen's vision, as did an illustration of a kite. Though this one seemed large and a lot more complicated than the child's toy she had played with in Zolya's rooms. It was also drawn in proportion to a body, the person's arms raised to mimic the kite's wingspan.

"After your father lost his wings," began her mother, stroking the inked lines as if they were Gabreel himself, "he became obsessed with figuring out how to fly again. This is a glider he created that could be worn."

"Worn?" Tanwen questioned, stepping closer as her heartbeat stopped and started before it ran. "Did he ever make it?"

"Yes," said Aisling.

"By the Ré's light," breathed Tanwen, meeting her mother's gaze. "And did it work?"

"Yes." Her mother nodded. "But not as he intended."

"What do you mean?"

"It could glide from jumping from a high point, but for it to be able to fly, to be able to soar back up, well, it needed magic."

"Magic?"

"Yes."

"But where is there magic—" Tanwen stopped herself as the answer slid into place. "Jadüri?" she questioned.

"Yes," replied Aisling. "I worked with your father to produce an elixir from the gods' nectar that could help power the wings, but not indefinitely. Once the solution is used up, the only direction these can take you is down."

"Is that what this is?" Tanwen pointed to a drawing of a canister that was attached to the spine of the glider wings.

"Yes. Suction points adhere to your spine, sensing your desired flight path."

"Mother, this is . . . incredible!"

"It is," Aisling agreed, though her brows pinched in. "But perhaps still foolish to suggest."

"Not in the least," countered Tanwen. "This can get us off Galia. The material to build doesn't look complicated. Father can even construct it within his holding cell. He says it's outfitted like a workshop. The material can easily be disguised as something he's inventing for the mine. He could construct it in pieces, something we pull together when we need to." Tanwen's thoughts were in motion now, her veins filling with hope, possibility. "We can fly right from a ledge of the palace. Disappear into the clouds below and—"

"Fly where, though?" challenged her mother. "It's a long way from Galia to one of Cādra's coastlines. The wings also require training to operate, otherwise you might go plummeting straight down."

"It's still the best option we have, the *only* one at the moment," argued Tanwen. "We will figure out the rest later, once I get these plans to Father—"

"But what of the elixir?" asked her mother, now seeming to backtrack, her tone revealing her rising worry. "It takes two jadüri blooms per canister. Another reason your father gave up on this design. It's too hard to find the necessary ingredients."

Thoughts of the rolling endless jadüri gardens in the palace filled Tanwen's mind. "Luckily it is not so hard on Galia," she said. "I can get the jadüri," she assured. It would still require stealth, of course, but Tanwen would succeed. She had to. "The next full moons are a month away, enough time for Father to build these and for me to acquire what we need for the elixir."

"I don't know, Wen." Her mother looked back at the drawing of wings. "There's too much that could go wrong."

"There's too much that already *will* go wrong if I don't return to Galia with a plan to get us free. Thol . . ." She stopped herself.

"Thol what?" Her mother's attention snapped back to her, features contorting into a panic. "What about Thol, Tanwen?"

Tanwen pressed her lips together, regret already surging in her heart, but she needed her mother to understand what truly was at stake. What little time they had on their side. There was no telling what the king would do to Thol once the mine was complete.

Nausea ripped across her gut.

"Thol is a known Mütra in Galia," Tanwen reminded her mother. "A Mütra that is being kept at the palace by the king. Every day he remains alive there is a miracle. I do not want us to press Udasha's luck with waiting for another plan."

Beside her, Aisling paled, her understanding seeping in like a sickness. "Oh gods," she breathed, shaky hand going to her lips. "My Thol, my baby." Her lips trembled, and for a moment Tanwen braced herself for another collapse of grief, but then Aisling's features cleared as a rising rage pooled into her gaze. "I will *kill* him." She slammed a fist on the table. Tanwen, as well as the flames within the nearby lantern, jumped. "I will have Réol burn beneath the sun he loves so much," she seethed. "I will watch with glee as his flesh melts from bone."

Tanwen's brows rose.

She had seen her mother angry but never consumed with revenge, with fantasies of hurting rather than healing.

It was both frightening and satisfying.

Her mother was no longer hiding; she was fighting.

"Yes," agreed Tanwen. "That is a lovely thought. One we can certainly elaborate on later. But perhaps for now," she continued delicately, "we can concentrate on our escape plan?"

Aisling nodded, though her gaze was still glazed with her ire. "Yes," she said. "Yes. Your escape." Her attention dropped to the schematics. "Wherever you fly to will need to be direct," she explained. "Somewhere nearby enough so the elixir doesn't run out on your journey, and where Volari couldn't easily follow once you land."

"Perhaps I can aid in that." A rippling of a dozen voices filled the workshop as the space began to bend and warp. Moss and leaves and blooming branches unfurled in every direction as Bosyg grew up from the floorboards.

Tanwen choked out a gasp as she and her mother quickly fell to their knees, heads bowed. Tanwen's heartbeat raced as a cascade of ancient power pressed against her shoulders.

"Almighty goddess of our home," said her mother. "It is an honor."

"I am glad to see you returned, child," said Bosyg, a branch coiling out to lift Tanwen's chin. She was forced to meet black, depthless eyes. Her pulse was a rapid beat through her veins as the goddess studied her.

"I see you have learned much in your time living within the clouds," said Bosyg, releasing her hold on Tanwen. Her vines curled back into her torso.

"Yes, almighty Bosyg," she replied. "My time on Galia has been most educational."

"And productive, it seems." Bosyg's roots were a constantly shifting creature, moss growing and melting along with her bloom of leaves. "Your father and brother have been found, and now you wish to find a place of sanctuary."

"If I can free them," clarified Tanwen.

"You will," said Bosyg as a flutter of butterflies took flight from her bark.

Tanwen's breaths quickened at such a prophecy.

The gods are fickle with how they move us around their celestial board, Ms. Coster.

Lady Esme's words awoke in Tanwen's mind, both a reminder and a warning.

Why would Bosyg care for Tanwen's success? Or perhaps a better question: What was the goddess hoping to get out of it?

"Drygul has always been a place of sanctuary for those seeking asylum," Bosyg explained. "I invite you there. You will be safe to enter by way of the Cactus Forest. No wings would risk being ripped apart by following you through."

The Cactus Forest, of course, thought Tanwen. Though it did butt up against the eastern checkpoint on Cādra. They'd need to ensure their flight was at night, skirting its perimeter. And Drygul . . . the Low Gods' territory, where her mother and father had planned on taking them before they'd been split apart.

Tanwen shared a glance with her mother kneeling beside her, trying to work out what her mother was thinking, fearing, but her expression held only a burning determination. She gave Tanwen a small nod.

It was as if she placed an encouraging hand on her shoulder. *You have this, my wyrthia.*

Warmth bloomed in Tanwen's chest; her mother was finally showing her faith.

"Thank you, our almighty goddess." Tanwen bowed before Bosyg. "We are humbled by your continued offered hand in this matter and graciously accept the place of sanctuary within Drygul."

"Do not thank me yet," said Bosyg. "I will open the way for you to enter Drygul so long as my favors become repaid."

Trepidation gripped Tanwen's spine.

A time will come when I will need a favor of my own.

And here they stood on the precipice of such a request.

"What do you wish of me?" Tanwen forced herself to ask.

Bosyg extended her branched hand, unfurling her vine fingers to reveal an innocuous black stone. "For you," she said.

Tanwen hesitantly plucked up the pebble. Its hard surface was a kiss of freeze to her fingers. "What is it?"

"A gift from Maryth," explained Bosyg. "Poison."

Tanwen nearly dropped the rock, heartbeat tripping. "Poison?"

"It is safe to hold," assured Bosyg. "Though to drink it is most deadly. It is a collected tear of our almighty mother, Maryth. It is scentless, tasteless, and colorless. Untraceable once dropped and dissolved into liquid."

By the Eternal River, thought Tanwen, her meddyg and inventor side completely fascinated. She studied the glint of reflective dust coating its dark surface. *This is a tear of Maryth.* And then—*Holy Gods, this is a tear of Maryth!*

The reality of what she held came crashing down.

Panic seized as Tanwen resisted throwing the rock across the space, the skin of her hand already feeling sickly, dead from the contact with the tear. "And . . . what exactly am I meant to do with it?"

"You are meant to fulfill your favor to me," explained Bosyg. "You are to kill the king."

37

Zolya stood in disbelief at what he was witnessing.

The ladies at court had gone mad.

Or at the very least were in their cups to be fighting one another.

"What is going on here?" he boomed, pausing the scene of chaos.

The wind and rain and ice shards dissipated as everyone froze, glancing his way. A lady in the corner gasped with relief as the silken scarf choking her fell to the ground, and the small cyclone of air made by her opponent disappeared.

"Please, carry on, ladies," urged Princess Azla from the center of the fray before gliding toward where Zolya and Osko stood by the front of the glass atrium. "Sire." She bowed. "Kidar Terz," she acknowledged. "What an honor it is for you both to visit us."

"*Azla,*" hissed Zolya, brows furrowed. "What is the meaning of this?"

"What?" She glanced to the view of her ladies, who had slowly resumed their fighting, though with less vigor now that they had an audience of the prince and Kidar Terz. "We are practicing our delicate magic, as we are meant to each afternoon."

"There is nothing delicate about what is taking place in this room," he admonished.

"Of course there is," she argued. "We have our painting corner over there." She gestured to where a group of women were working together to make razor-sharp shards of ice from a combination of their rain and freeze before the third woman flicked out a gust of wind, sending the shards to puncture a large stretched canvas. The collection of holes was making an impressive image of a flower. "Then we have Lady Beatrice and Lady Esme practicing their sculpting." She pointed to where the two women were heating up balls of wax and lobbing the pellets at an ice block, the creation a sizzling, melting monstrosity. "Their style is quite avant-garde, wouldn't you agree?"

Zolya lifted a brow sardonically. "And what is happening there, then?" He inclined his head to where one woman was commanding her wind to send strips of silk to tie another to a column.

"Fashion designing," offered the princess.

Osko barked a laugh beside Zolya, not helping matters.

"Oh, come now, Zol," said Osko, catching his disapproving glare. "This is all rather cute, is it not?"

"Cute?" managed the princess, eyes narrowing at how not cute she found such a comment.

"Yes," said Osko. "You ladies attempting to do combat."

"Attempting?" Azla's brows shot up this time, along with her voice.

"There's no need for you to learn to defend yourselves, Princess," he placated. "That's what we are for."

"But then, pray tell, Kidar Terz," Azla managed through a tight smile. "Who is there to defend us against you?"

Osko blinked, confused, before Zolya stepped in.

"Azla," he tried again, though softer. "Do you think it wise to be practicing such . . . different uses of your magic so publicly? Lord Drumel rushed to inform me the princess and her ladies had gone round the twist. Evidently, he was almost hit by a rogue splattering of hot wax?"

"Then I suppose he should have had a kidet present to protect him, right, Kidar Terz?" She grinned sweetly at his friend.

Osko's cheeks reddened, his evident rising indignation soon to leave his lips, but Zolya tugged Azla away before the two could start a proper row like the rest in the room.

"What has gotten into you?" Zolya asked, bringing his sister-cousin to a secluded corner. The afternoon sun streamed through the glass panes at their side, adding warmth to her white hair and brown complexion.

She crossed her arms over her chest, a defiant posture she had often taken as a child whenever she found herself chastised by Zolya. "I'm merely spending my final days as I wish," she argued.

The fight left Zolya in a whoosh.

"Azla," he managed as an unfurling of pain filled his chest.

"Don't," she warned, sensing his changed mood, his pity. "This marriage merely has me realizing how much I haven't learned, haven't *lived*, despite my age. I am in my sixties yet have never been off this island. Did you know that? I have never actually *seen* Cādra besides what I can view through a telescope. Ever since I was a child, Alys has told me stories of the Pelk Forest, of her life and family in her clan, and yet I have never been allowed to see it. I have no real sense of where our staff come from or why they might want to live up here with us."

"Alys should never have discussed her home with you," said Zolya, frowning.

Azla glared at him, incredulous. "*That* is what you took from all that I've said?" She tried to shove past him, but he snagged her arm.

"Wait," he said. "I apologize. I did not know you wished to see Cādra," he reasoned. "I can organize an outing for you and I to—"

"That's *not* my point," she shot back. "No Volari women have been allowed to leave this island."

Zolya absorbed this information, his brows drawing together with discomfort. "That cannot be true."

"It is." Azla lifted her chin. "And if any have been, it's only with a walled entourage of soldiers. While the men are allowed to fly wherever they wish whenever they wish, *unaccompanied*."

"That is because it isn't safe."

"Isn't safe for who?"

"For you, of course," he snapped.

Her gaze was pure flame. "And why do you suppose that is?" she challenged. "Perhaps because we have never been taught to defend ourselves."

Zolya let out an impatient breath. "You are the princess of Galia. The ladies at court the blessed descendants of High Gods. You are born into privilege to not need such training."

"Privilege has nothing to do with it."

"It has *everything* to do with it."

"Then why, *sire*, would you, the very definition of born privilege as the direct descendant of our king and queen and next in line for the throne, have been raised with sword in hand?"

"Because to hold a throne is only made possible by one's ability to defend it," argued Zolya. "If I couldn't protect myself, how could I protect my kingdom? I have no other choice but to be who I was born and to obey my inherited responsibilities. Same as you and same as all in this room."

Azla's chest rose and fell, rose and fell as his words settled around them. A look of disappointment weighed on her features.

"And that is precisely my point, brother," she said.

Brother.

The title pierced Zolya's heart, pressed against his ever-present childhood longing to have been free to be more of a brother to Azla, for her to be more of a sister.

"What point?" he dared to ask.

"Choice," she answered. "What good is privilege if having a choice is not included?"

Zolya remained silent, the question causing a suffocating panic to encircle his neck. Because the answer would not release either of them from the realities of their lives or their destined paths.

"You above all must see the truth in what I say," implored Azla. "Both of us have been constrained by the laws of society, of titles and bloodlines. My whole life I have desperately followed those rules, Zolya, foolishly hoping that my obedience would grant me freedoms, grant me acceptance from our father—and perhaps even his love. But despite my efforts to be a 'good princess,' I merely remained his property, remained *Galia*'s property." She blinked quickly as if to eradicate the building of her tears. "And there lies the difference between us. You are meant to own, and I am meant to be sold. Just as every woman in this room is meant to be. We are *property*, Zolya. Property in that men can dictate who we are allowed to spend our time with, how we spend it, and who we marry. We may have been born with wings, same as you, but we have been grounded our whole lives. Even our magic is clipped and controlled. It is forever meant to remain *delicate*, unintrusive, a gentle spectacle. It might have taken me being sentenced to the sea to realize this, but I am over living by others' rules or opinions of how *I* should behave to please and benefit others. I will not take these final days topside in vain. I am going to fly, Zolya," she declared, her features pinched in determination. "Before my wings can no longer catch air, and there's nothing you, or anyone, can say to change that. After all, I've already been given a death sentence—what more could I possibly lose?"

Zolya was pressed against the wall by Azla's speech, her words pinning him like daggers, a searing sharp pain. He knew there were injustices in their world, but never had he realized just how oppressive they could be for some, for *them*. His attention fell to the women in the room, the scene unfolding in a new light.

The ladies were not fighting; they were flexing, stretching after being forced for decades, if not centuries, into a tight, contained box of decorum. Their skin was flushed, gazes exuberant, smiles wide, wings rustling as they learned just how capable they were by exploring a new use for their delicate magic. Zolya's soldier sense noted how utterly terrifying and impressive their precision was, more so than many of his kidets.

Perhaps then you will learn how dangerous delicate can be. The words of Naru rose, taunting, in his mind.

Zolya looked back at Azla then, at the fire burning in her gaze, her radiating resolve.

Jealousy flooded him.

Not at her forced marriage, of course, but that she found herself in a unique position where she could confidently do whatever she bloody well pleased, and everyone else could go hang.

"You are right," said Zolya.

Azla drew back, brows slamming down. "What?"

"You are right," he repeated.

"About which part?"

"All of it."

"I—" She stopped herself, clearly not having expected Zolya's reaction.

"While I know I cannot begin to make up for the decades which you, or any of our ladies, have suffered through," he began, "I hope you know you have an advocate in myself. If you wish to invite more ladies from the Isle and Sun Courts to these lessons, I will not stop you," he explained. "Though I'm sure you'll be hearing from many displeased parents soon," he added sardonically. "As for seeing Cādra, I will work on organizing routine trips for whoever wishes to visit. I cannot promise them to be unchaperoned, but the biggest changes—"

"Thank you!" Azla surprised him with a hug.

He stood there for a moment, arms awkwardly at his sides, before he wrapped them around her waist. For as far back as he could recollect, never once had he or Azla ever embraced. A cold, forgotten part of his heart thawed as he breathed in her calming scent of cherry blossoms.

"You have no idea what having your support means to me," Azla whispered close to his ear. "What it can mean for the future of Galia." She stepped back, keeping her hands on his shoulders. "You will be a great king, Zolya."

Pain filled his lungs on a quick inhale, Azla's decree a well-aimed arrow piercing a lifetime of longing. It might not have been said by his father, but it still resonated deeply when said by his sister-cousin. His sister.

Zolya cleared his throat. "Yes, well," he began, forcing a neutral tone. "There's a long way yet until I sit on the throne."

Something sharp danced through Azla's gaze. "Perhaps," she said as she turned back to take in the room.

Zolya frowned, a chill of unease stroking down his wings.

"Ms. Coster will be excited to learn she was right," said Azla with a smile, quickly distracting him.

"Ms. Coster?" he asked, ignoring how his pulse began to race.

"Oh!" Azla glanced at him with chagrin. "You mustn't punish her, Zolya."

Punish? Now he was beginning to worry. "That wholly depends on what she did," he replied.

"She didn't *do* anything, really," Azla backtracked. "She only suggested that my skills in delicate magic could hold purpose beyond making art."

"Did she now?" His gaze narrowed.

"Yes, but it was *I* who experimented with what that purpose could be," explained Azla. "And isn't it marvelous what I found?"

Zolya regarded the room, taking in the madness.

"Marvelous," he echoed sardonically.

Here was more evidence of Ms. Coster's influence. He wasn't quite sure how to feel about it.

The fact that she wasn't even presently *on* Galia and yet had been able to fundamentally disrupt its centuries-old way of life was impressive if not terrifying.

Zolya dared to wonder what would happen when she returned.

38

Tanwen climbed into the covered wagon, praying to the Low Gods no one took notice of the crinkle emanating from her coat.

Her father's wing schematics had been sewn into the lining.

It's as loud as a tavern in here, assured Eli from the pouch at Tanwen's waist. *No one is paying us mind.*

That wasn't exactly true.

A few men sitting farther down in the carriage she recognized as fellow palace staff, and they evidently recognized her. Their gazes slid to her chest, which was properly covered by her tunic and coat, but she knew what they saw. It was hard to forget the low cut and revealing garb of an atenté, as was intended.

Annoyance flickered awake in Tanwen's gut as she turned her back to them. She was already tired; to add on needing to be aware of her leering companions pushed her to exhaustion.

As she forced a calming breath, Tanwen refocused on the crowd of loved ones forming around the Recruitment caravans.

Though the scene was just as tearful as when they had arrived in Zomyad, the mood had changed. Their earlier excitement had been replaced with a heavy sense of mourning. Children cried as they reached out to siblings or parents waving goodbye, caregivers holding them back as their features pinched in anguish.

Tanwen swallowed her own grief as she met the gaze of her mother in the middle of the fray.

Aisling stood stoically still.

Her brown hair rested around her shoulders, her eastern horns setting her apart from most of those around her.

She looked lonely standing there, and it caused a painful grip to encircle Tanwen's heart.

We'll be reunited with her soon, said Eli from within his pouch at her waist.

At the reminder of their next tasks, Tanwen absently touched the necklace that sat under her shirt.

The stone pendant pressed to her chest, an unnatural cold digging into her skin. Even after she and her mother wrapped the pebble and wove it into an intricate leather casing to pass as jewelry, it still held a supernatural chill.

A gift from Maryth.

Bosyg's raspy voice dug into Tanwen's mind.

Poison.

Tanwen loosened her grip from the pendant, a clawing of unease climbing up her throat as her thoughts tipped to the past.

"You are to kill the king." Bosyg's decree had stopped time.

"What?" Tanwen's attention had shot up to meet the goddess's black gaze.

"This is the trade of favors," said Bosyg. "A life for a life. The saving of your mother's life, of your family's, for the taking of the king's."

Tanwen knelt in disbelief, her reality collapsing inward, burying her alive.

"Almighty creator of our home," began Aisling, who had remained crouched beside Tanwen. "This task may be achievable by a god as mighty as yourself, but for a mere mortal to—"

"If the Low Gods could have removed Réol from his throne," interrupted Bosyg, a sprouting of thorns along her bark skin, "we would have by now. This matter is delicate, nuanced, and exactly a task for one such as your child."

"But why?" Tanwen couldn't help asking.

Bosyg's gaze pressed down on Tanwen, a seeing that went further than what was visible. "You have gained favors within the royal family," said the goddess, sending prickles of unease down Tanwen's spine. "Favors grant access, young one. You also have the proper motivation to succeed."

A snaking of vines whipped out, curling around her mother.

Aisling gasped her pain as Tanwen lurched forward, but another of Bosyg's branches knocked her back.

"Stop this, please!" implored Tanwen, fear spiking through her veins.

"My intent is never to hurt," reasoned Bosyg, though she did not let go of her mother. "Only to teach. I have taught you I can keep your family safe," she explained. "Do you need to learn what happens if you're unwilling to pay your dues?"

"No," said Tanwen, a sob working up her throat as she watched the vines tighten around her mother. Aisling's complexion turned purple, her lungs compressed. "Please, no, almighty goddess." Tanwen fell to her knees, a desperate prostrating as her forehead kissed the dirt floor. "I will do as you ask. I will kill the king."

Her mother was released. Tanwen flew to where she crumpled to the ground, helping her sit up, take in gulps of air.

A searing hatred filled Tanwen's chest, a maddening desire to lash out at the goddess.

"Your anger is understandable," said Bosyg, clearly sensing Tanwen's emotions. "Though misguided. Remember who put you in this predicament, child. Who took your father and brother. Who keeps them captive still. Who suppresses all who call Cādra home. Who has forced you to hide your entire life and who wishes for your kind to be eradicated. It is time for King Réol's rule to end and with it the claim our celestial cousins have had on our soil. They have already taken the sky; why then should they also own the land?"

Understanding slipped, cold and unwanted, through Tanwen.

This was the game that was being played.

A war of the gods.

Tanwen knew the myths, the stories of the celestial ripping. Maryth, mother of the Low Gods, was finally taking retribution for her brother Ré's betrayal all those millennia ago, when he clipped her wings and banished her to the ground.

And Tanwen was to be their sacrificial pawn.

The one to remove Ré's precious king from the board.

"I shall remind you that the stone is a gift," said Bosyg, revealing the black pebble once more. Tanwen had dropped it rushing to her mother. "Use it however you wish." She placed it back into Tanwen's palm.

The cold surface bit into her skin, the chill of death.

Tanwen swallowed her disquiet as she closed her fingers over it. "What of after?" she asked. "You say you can keep my family safe. How will we be safe once the king's death is on my hands?"

"I suggest you leave Galia before anyone knows," reasoned Bosyg. "You have your father's plans for his wings. Use them," she instructed. "Fulfill this debt, child, and our agreement will be complete. Your mother will be waiting for you in Drygul."

A loud ripping tore through the room as the Low Goddess gathered her forest and disappeared into the ground.

Tanwen and her mother had found themselves returned to her father's workshop, the only proof of Bosyg's visit the cold kiss of the pebble clenched in her fist.

Poison for the king.

Tanwen was bumped, causing her to blink back to where she sat in the stuffy wagon as more recruits were shuffled in.

Her skin was dusted in a cold sweat; the memory of being with the Low Goddess slowly dissipated.

Soon their wagon lurched forward. Everyone's attention turned toward the crowd of loved ones huddled around the opening at the back.

Within the mass, Tanwen met her mother's gaze once again, a new suffocating pressure in her lungs.

Neither of them waved their goodbyes as the wagon pulled away.

A pact they had agreed upon on their ride back to Ordyn.

After all, this wasn't a goodbye. They would see each other again.

They had to.

She will be safe in Drygul, assured Eli from his pouch. *Many animals in Zomyad have skirted Drygul's borders. Despite its strangeness, they say it is safe.*

Eli's words only slightly reassured Tanwen.

She studied the other recruits sitting around them. All were just as quiet, just as pensive and somber.

None were glad to be returning to their lifetime of service to the children of gods.

Not a new realization, surely, but nonetheless still not comforting.

More than just her and her family wanted to be free of Galia.

The stone lying against Tanwen's chest pulsed, a chilled whisper in her mind that perhaps killing the king would help more than the Low Gods.

Tanwen shifted uneasily on her bench.

Yes, perhaps, she thought, but she was in no position to take on anyone else's problems.

The Low Gods certainly knew she had enough for three lifetimes: bargains to complete, a king to somehow murder, and a family to free.

Despite the growing warmth in the carriage from the packed-in bodies, Tanwen pulled her jacket more tightly closed, her anxious worry for what lay ahead sending a chill through her bones. The impossibility of it.

But she *had* to succeed. Faltering now would be perilous. For herself, her mother, and her father and Thol.

Tanwen touched the lining, feeling for her father's plans, now reassured by the crinkling.

Tanwen might be wearing the mad scribblings of a man who had been desperate to replace his wings, but she was now his mad daughter, just as desperate to fly.

39

Zolya knew the moment she was back in the palace.

He had told himself it was happenstance. That he found himself returning to the southern rooftop ledge each morning so he could see the sunrise paint Galia in a spill of honeycomb. A necessary moment of respite before he started his exhaustive list of royal duties.

It was certainly *not* because this was also when the first gondola lift would arrive from Fioré.

Nor was it a relief when he finally caught sight of Tanwen's familiar dark hair and horns as she stepped from the cable car.

It was in fact a hindrance, because now any chance of him remaining productive that day was consumed by his palpable desire to find a way for them to be alone.

He wished to ask of her visit home.

If her family was well.

If the trip to and from Zomyad was met with any hardships.

Did she think of him half as much as he found himself unwillingly thinking of her?

Zolya breathed out his frustration as he slipped beneath a shadow made by a nearby decorative portico.

This needed to stop.

He needed to stop.

He was bordering on obsessive.

An oddity for himself, surely.

He had had plenty of mistresses in his lifetime, plenty of bed partners and lustful, torrid nights. So why could he not get their evening together out of his head? Get *her* out of his head?

Because she promises more than mere pleasure. An unwanted voice slithered up and out from his chest, warmed the cold, empty corners of his heart.

Zolya shifted, ill at ease. *Yes,* he thought. *Promises to be an utter disruption to my very delicately balanced way of life.* After all, she was already proving thus if Azla and the ladies at court's behavior was anything to go by.

Zolya pressed his lips together, thoughts churning, as he watched Tanwen and a handful of staff stroll toward the servants' entrance at the base of the southern wall. Despite the heat, Tanwen was still dressed in her western clan's garb of sturdy green pants and a long-sleeved coat. He noted how her strides seemed more confident, more fluid than when she wore her atenté uniform.

This observation, of course, only fueled his annoyance. He should not notice such details, should not find himself yearning for her comfort.

A gust of wind briefly drew him from his souring mood, a guard landing nearby.

"Sire," said the kidet after giving a curt bow. "A situation has arisen in which the king needs your presence most urgently."

Zolya let out a tired sigh. "Of course one has."

The kidet looked unsure of how to reply, his wings shifting nervously at his back.

"Show me the way, soldier," Zolya instructed. "There is nothing out here that I desire more than serving the needs of the crown."

As he followed the kidet, he held in a derisive snort at his own words.

Zolya had always been good at lying to others, but he'd had little success lying to himself.

40

The palace was in an uproar.

Confusion engulfed Tanwen as she found herself an unwilling sheep in the flock of servants being corralled upstairs. Hardly had she finished drying off from her bath and slipping on her atenté uniform before all staff were hurrying toward a southern courtyard.

Tanwen's only reprieve was knowing Eli remained in the atenté dormitory, sparing him from the stampede.

"What's going on?" Tanwen asked, finding Huw in the fray.

His blond hair gleamed in the sunlight streaming through the corridor, his chiton a pristine, pressed white.

"There's to be a public sentencing," he answered breathlessly.

"Sentencing?" she repeated, brows pinching as her nerves soared.

"A lady of the Isle Court has been accused of being a sympathizer."

Tanwen's steps faltered, causing impatient staff to nudge past them.

Sympathizer.

The hairs on the back of her neck rose, unease a cresting wave through her veins.

"Are you all right?" Huw asked, holding on to her elbow. "You should stay here if this is too much after your day of travel."

"No," she managed. "I'm fine."

Huw looked unconvinced, but his desire to move with the rest of the group won out, and soon he turned back into the stampede.

Tanwen followed blindly, her pulse a rushing beat.

Despite understanding the shortened term *sympathizer* was connected to *Süra sympathizer*, and the danger it possessed, never had she witnessed an actual trial. Though, of course, Tanwen had lived through the repercussions of what happened when those on trial were found guilty.

Visions of her father's large angry scars along his back flashed within her mind. The jagged, puckering skin from his wings having been broken and severed. His wincing in pain anytime he suffered the phantom sensation of his plumage still being there.

Nausea rolled within Tanwen's gut as she and Huw were pushed and pressed into the open marble courtyard, the staff a claustrophobic horde.

The sun was punishingly bright, forcing her to squint as Ré's light hit and heated every marble surface. White stone made up each column, tile, and balcony, causing the space to merge into one large reflective sheen. If not for the people filing in, it would have been difficult to determine its dimensions and length.

While the servants were the ants on the ground, the five levels of wraparound galleries were overflowing with winged court members, their collection of animated whispers louder than if everyone were shouting.

Tanwen had never been to this part of the palace. Assuredly a blessing, given the raised executioner block in the center.

Tanwen stared at its pristine surface, finding the dark bloodstains caught within the tight veins. No amount of cleaning appeared capable of erasing the history of pain the stone had endured.

Her heartbeat stuttered just as the crowd fell silent.

A wave of kneeling as the king arrived.

The quiet was oppressive, the sun burning as it pressed on the back of Tanwen's neck and exposed shoulders.

"Rise," King Réol finally commanded.

The mass obeyed.

As Tanwen stood on shaky legs, she drank in the king for the first time.

Her breath hitched.

It was like looking at a star, his presence so brilliant the edges became lost. His wings were large, perhaps the largest she'd seen despite them remaining tucked in at his back; his gilded breastplate was an intricate layering of white and gold across his broad chest; his brown complexion was warm under Ré's light; his snowy locks rested in waves on his shoulders; and his laurel crown was sharp—a threatening reminder of his rule—as it sat atop his head.

And she was meant to murder him.

Ice filled Tanwen's veins, a nauseating dread of how impossible such a task was.

I will fail my family, she thought with a panic. *How will I ever be able to kill such a demigod?*

Tanwen's pulse surged as her gaze slid to the prince, standing just to his father's right.

His father . . . *gods, I've agreed to kill his father!*

Tanwen was paralyzed by her fate as she stared at Zolya, an austere replica of the king. Mouth stern, gaze hard, shoulders broad, his presence intrusive and powerful. But Tanwen was relieved to note the important difference between the two.

The king, though undeniably beautiful, held a brutality to his aura. A trait Tanwen could tell ran straight to his soul. A heart that might beat, but not with life.

Zolya's mask, while cold, was still a mask. A veneer that she knew could be thawed. His hard gaze could be softened and warmed. His brutal strength was still capable of delicacy, a gentle caress, a reverent gaze.

Tanwen swallowed down the ache rising from within her throat, not having expected the flood of emotions that would come from seeing him again after so long. Her skin tingled recalling his skilled touch, her lips warming as if his mouth still pressed to hers, the taste of him before he had lowered himself to taste her.

You are my devastation, Tanwen.

Tanwen shifted from the blossoming of heat between her legs.

This is absurd, she chastised herself. *It was one night!* A mistake not to be repeated.

Though even she could hear the lie in her thoughts. Seeing him again made her realize that nothing about what they had shared that evening felt wrong. On the contrary, it felt entirely too right, too necessary. Despite their vast differences, despite who Zolya was and the command he had obeyed for his father, Tanwen had felt irrationally safe with him. A forbidden attraction of souls that eerily echoed her parents' past.

As if he sensed he was the focus of her thoughts, Zolya's attention lowered, and he spotted her in the crowd.

Tanwen's heart stuttered to a stop.

His blue gaze penetrated through her, a shadow passing over his features, a remorse, but then Zolya looked away, severing their connection.

Cold plunged across Tanwen's skin, a shaky exhale.

"Bring in the accused." The king's demand boomed through the space.

All eyes looked up as the quiet courtyard was abruptly engulfed in jeers, hisses, and vicious shouts as two shackled forms descended from the sky.

A group of kidets encircled a Volari woman, her wings tightly bound, and a male Süra, guiding them to a marble block. Both were attired in plain tan garments—she in a peplos, he in a tunic and trousers, the uniform of the accused. Despite their shackles, as they were forced onto their knees, they still strained toward each other.

Tanwen's chest constricted in anguish.

It was the desperate act of separated lovers already resigned to their fate.

A simple touch, an embrace, remained their ultimate and final desire.

But before it could be granted, they were pulled apart.

The courtyard erupted in louder heckles and ridicule. A rock was even thrown, hitting its mark as the man's head whipped back. The woman cried out, imploring hand reaching as a vicious cut now marred her lover's cheek, blood sliding down his pale skin.

"Enough," boomed the king, his tone a resounding hammer, commanding obedient silence from the assembled onlookers. King Réol waved a hand, a gesture that said, *Get on with it.*

A herald stepped forward within the royal box. He was the very definition of a twig, his chiton hanging loose over his belt, his wings minuscule compared to the king's. As he unfurled his scroll, the crinkling of paper filled the tense quiet. "Brilyard Mendi," he began, voice haughty, "of the northern clan of the Pelk Forest, and Lady Eonya Heeba, of the eighteenth house of the Isle Court, you have been accused of breaking the fifth code of conduct decreed by our almighty king and chosen son of our High Gods, King Réol Ajno Diusé the Fourth, ruler of the Sun and Isle Courts, protector of the kingdom of Galia, and lord of Cādra: the continued cavorting of relations between Volari and Süra beyond what is professionally acceptable. Do you deny these accusations?"

From where the two remained kneeling, Brilyard poised to respond, but Lady Eonya's defiant response rang out first. "I do not." She held the king's stare as she spit on the execution stone.

The crowd erupted just as her kidar handler landed a backhanded slap.

Lady Eonya fell to her side, Brilyard wrestling within the other soldiers' grips, his rage and despair palpable. "Eonya!" he called.

Tanwen was jostled from all sides, the energy heightening around her, but she was unsure if the staff was cheering or jeering. The courtyard was a dizzying chaos of emotion.

A loud clap of thunder sounded, a vibration of energy barreling through the open room.

Everyone froze.

The king had approached the edge of his balcony, his skin emanating a soft glow from his quick use of magic. More disconcerting, however, was the sharp smile marring his lips as he held Lady Eonya in his sights.

"I thank you for your honesty, Lady Eonya." He spoke calmly. "It only helps in the simplicity of your sentencing. By disregarding my orders, you have not merely ruined your life but also shamed your family's name."

A breathless sob drew Tanwen's attention to a woman on an upper gallery. She held a hand to her mouth, her face sallow, grief stricken. The look of a mother who had lost a child. The man beside her, however, held only contempt as he gazed down at his daughter.

Tanwen's rushing heartbeat was a loud pulse in her head.

"To be in love should not be a law to defy," declared Lady Eonya, her voice strong.

"A simple statement made by a simple mind," said the king. "Your sin is not your so-called love but the repercussions of what it can grow within your womb."

"And here is our king's truth." Lady Eonya turned her attention to the crowd. "Scared of a baby."

Her head whipped back again, another blow from the kidar. "No one disrespects our king," he seethed.

Eonya spit red but rose back to her full height from where she knelt, features almost appearing satisfied.

"Your insolence grows dull," barked the king, quieting the growing whispers. "By the throne, I find you guilty," he declared.

There was a hush as the reality of his words settled like ash from a pyre, a burning understanding.

"As law decrees of the guilty," announced the herald, "you will be stripped of your wings, Lady Eonya. Your Süra coconspirator executed."

Lady Eonya's strength faltered then, her gaze meeting that of her lover.

Tears slipped down both their cheeks, chests rising and falling with their anguish, but in the end Brilyard smiled. A gentle *I will love you always* smile that ripped open Tanwen's chest to witness.

It appeared to similarly affect Lady Eonya, for she let out a frustrated scream, sending a burst of chill into the air. It pummeled over the crowd, momentarily stealing Tanwen's breath. But more importantly, and perhaps intentionally, it slapped against the two soldiers, causing them to loosen their holds.

She and Brilyard leaped toward one another, blessedly reunited for a heartbeat. Their kiss was violent, desperate, before they were once again dragged apart.

"If you wish to make a scene," said the king, unmoved by the tragedy taking place within his courtyard, "then do it with your punishment."

Lady Eonya's hatred was etched into her creased brows and dagger glare. Her breaths were giant puffs as she looked up at her king. "If you will take my wings, sire," she said, "then take my life."

"No!" shouted Brilyard. "No, Eonya, no!"

She ignored his plea; no doubt his one solace in entering the Eternal River was knowing that she still lived. But it seemed the lady had no desire for a life that did not include him.

A thousand blows punched through Tanwen's chest, her thoughts consumed by her parents, to the lengths to which they had gone to remain together, all that their love had defied.

And then to Zolya, to their fleeting night of perfection, what she could feel growing between them—unable to be born.

She didn't know which was worse: knowing such intense love only to have it ripped away or never allowing oneself to experience it at all.

Both seemed ripe in tragedy.

The king eyed Lady Eonya from his great height, a calculation in his gaze. "As you wish," he replied.

Tanwen could not look while their throats were cut.

As those around her stood riveted by the cruelty taking place, Tanwen met the hard stare of the prince.

Her skin ran cold.

Zolya's expression was unreadable, distant, masked, but Tanwen didn't need to know his feelings to understand her own.

With her pulse stumbling, she held in her flinch from the sound of a blade slicing through skin, the splattering of blood across stone, and then the heavy thud of one lifeless body before another.

Two souls had been ripped away, added to Maryth's Eternal River.

All because of love.

Throughout the execution, Zolya's stern expression remained pinned to her, his features slowly growing darker, more withdrawn.

Here was Zolya's world.

Beautiful and cruel.

What he was born into and what he was meant to inherit and uphold.

And then there was Tanwen: worse than a servant, she was the defiant creature that her mother had grown in her womb.

Mütra.

The only future they had was the execution in front of them.

Tanwen tore her gaze from Zolya, pain a lacing around her lungs as she fought for each of her breaths.

Despite what they had shared that night, despite the yearning she felt in her heart to have found another with the same beat, it needed to remain in the past. Locked tightly away. Ignored.

This execution was the reminder she did not need, but it certainly cemented her resolve.

If she held any hope of survival, Tanwen had to get as far as possible from this palace, this island, and assuredly this man as quickly as she could.

After all, even if the prince could come to care for a Mütra, he certainly could never love someone who planned to kill his father.

41

The wind battered against Tanwen as she clung to the rock face. The gust lamented a terrified howl as though just as distressed as she to find itself blowing at such a deadly height.

With no moonlight, Tanwen maneuvered along the northern cliffside of Galia by the illumination coming from the Kaiwi River. It was slow, painful work of feeling her way over the jagged slab's surface. Tanwen sucked in a breath, stomach jumping to her throat as one of her feet lost purchase. She caught another lip with her toe, digging her fingers in for dear life as a scattering of falling rock was swallowed by the looming clouds below. It was a soft mirage that hid the great distance between herself and the angry, churning Aspero Sea.

Tanwen momentarily closed her eyes, nerves like a cluster of swooping swallows. Her biceps strained from her desperate grip on the cold, sharp stone, her thighs and calf muscles screaming.

Tanwen was seriously beginning to doubt her decision to attempt this climb.

But it was the only way.

A stubborn fire awoke in her gut as she glanced up, gaze holding the gentle glow coming from the back of the groundskeeper's cottage, still a precarious distance away.

I will get there, she promised herself. *I will get to them.*

With a steadying inhale, Tanwen continued sliding her way across and up the rock.

She and Eli had been quick to learn her brother and father had been moved from the kidet barracks during their absence.

Despite the overwhelming chatter surrounding that morning's execution, Huw had been all too pleased to fill her in on what had transpired while she was away. Which included the inventor being paraded through the great hall, his son shuffling in shackles at his heels, toward their new quarters. It was a statement by the king once they had celebrated successfully breaking ground on the new mine. *Pay attention, my subjects, I do keep my word for those who obey the crown's commands.*

It had been the only promising development since Tanwen's arrival.

That was until Eli scouted the cottage's location.

It was situated on the northernmost lip of the palace grounds, and two kidets stood sentry at the front while one took purchase on a nearby temple's rooftop. Their coverage was thorough except for the raw, wild cliffside that hugged the house's back wall. But no one in their right mind would approach from there, least of all survive if they tried. And if one flew in from the north, they would be seen by the aerial guard.

But Tanwen was no longer sane; she was desperate.

So she approached from the cliffside like a lunatic.

A shot of jealousy edged between Tanwen's ribs as she thought of Eli already inside the cottage. He held no desire to remain with Tanwen given she might very well plummet to her death. Much easier for him to scurry in from the various cracks in the cottage's foundation so he could give her father and Thol warning to expect her by the back window.

Tanwen let out a grunt as she pulled her way to the next handhold before the next and then the next. It was a snail's pace, but it was progress as the wind continued to slam her from every angle.

Her only protection from the harsh gale was her clothes.

Tanwen was back in her clan garb, having changed into the dark pants and coat before she had descended over the cliff. She hoped that if any Volari were flying nearby, she would blend in with the shadowed rock. Also, her father's wing schematic was still hidden in the lining of her jacket.

Gradually, the light above grew brighter as she neared the cottage. Her heartbeat fell into double speed as the kitchen window came into view.

And then she was pulling herself up, breaths labored as she twisted to press her back to the wooden slatted wall, her heels against the small lip protruding from beneath the house. She dared not look down as she gently rapped her knuckles on the window's pane.

Almost instantly a creak sounded by her head. The window opened. A warm, strong hand grabbed hers before she was hauled up and in. The cold wind was traded for heat, orange light from a fire, and the scent of chamomile tea.

Tanwen awkwardly maneuvered over the marble basin, the stone pressing uncomfortably into her hip, before she planted feet on solid floor.

She was met with silence as her eyes adjusted to her new surroundings: a small table tucked to one wall, two chairs, a modest-sized iron hearth, and a—

"*Oof.*"

Tanwen was pummeled into a hug.

"Sister," Thol's hoarse voice declared as he buried his face into her shoulder. She could feel his sobs racking his body, his hot breath on her neck. Tanwen's chest blew apart with pain and relief as her arms encircled a torso that felt more like bones than flesh and muscle.

Worry engulfed her, and eventually, she delicately detangled herself so she could regard her brother.

Or what was left of him.

Aberthol was skin stretched over a skeleton.

His emaciated form punched her with guilt and grief.

Here she had been, sleeping comfortably and eating plenty within the palace, while her brother was . . . becoming this.

Thol's hair had grown long, to his shoulders, exaggerating the sallowness of his pale skin. His horns now looked much too heavy atop his head.

Tanwen stood paralyzed, unsure how to digest this new brother, this withering one.

Her hatred for King Réol awoke like the heat of ten thousand suns. The poisoned pendant beneath her shirt pulsed, as though sensing her ire, and whispered, *Yes, yes.*

"Wen."

Tanwen's pulsed skipped upon hearing the familiar voice, and she glanced behind her brother.

Her father slid into the fire's light. His face was shaved, revealing the oddity of his youth despite his age. Proof of his Volari blood. His hair was still in tight brown curls, cropped short, and maintained. But what revealed the truth behind his polished veneer was the exhaustion that swam in his green eyes and the bruises beneath, proving sleepless nights.

In that moment her father was both familiar and like a stranger, deepening the ache in Tanwen's chest and intensifying her uncertainty about this reunion.

But then Gabreel took two long strides before pulling Tanwen into his arms.

It was a bone-crushing, soul-healing hug.

"*Wen*," her father said again, almost reverently, his voice thick with emotion. "My wyrthia."

Tanwen released a shaky breath as she inhaled his familiar fragrance of ink and parchment and wood. Even here, so far from their home, his scent remained the same.

"Father," she returned, tears now spilling down her cheeks as she melted into his arms.

She turned to find Thol watching their embrace from a distance.

His features were hard to discern behind her blur of tears, but all Tanwen cared to take in was that she had found them.

Was *with* them.

A tremor of relief and terror and desperate hope took hold of her. Tanwen was at last surrounded by the family she had sacrificed so much to find.

◆ ◆ ◆

The wind continued to howl around the cottage, where Tanwen, Thol, and her father sat within their workroom.

The wing schematics were spread across the table in the center, candlelight pooling warmth across the parchment as each of them remained quiet. Tanwen had just finished explaining the plan she and her mother had come up with. Even Eli was silent, attentive, as he rested on a nearby notebook, whiskers twitching in anticipation.

"I had nearly forgotten about these," her father eventually said as he ran his fingers over marks he had made over two decades ago. "Your mother certainly liked to indulge me back then."

"She said you constructed a pair that worked," explained Tanwen, hopeful.

Their reunion had been hurried, each of them understanding time was not on their side. Too soon Tanwen would be due back in the atenté dorms, lest her absence be noted, and evidently the kidets liked to poke their heads in the cottage before they changed shifts at midnight.

This could be the only chance the three of them got to figure out their escape plan.

"I did make one that could fly," admitted her father, brows pinched. "But I never used it at this high of an elevation; the wind behaves differently here." As if the wind wanted to prove this, a gust rattled against the window along the far wall.

"Then rework your design based on what you do know of this elevation," said Tanwen, tone hard. She didn't need excuses; she needed solutions. "You are one of the greatest inventors in Galia," she continued, "and have made the impossible possible before. You *will* make this work, Father, because our lives depend on it."

Gabreel's brows rose as he met her gaze, surprise clear in his features.

Tanwen couldn't fault his reaction; she was just as astonished by her speech. Never had she spoken thus to her father. Nor would she have dared to in the past.

But no longer was she the same daughter he had raised, just as he and Thol were not the same father and brother she had parted ways with in Zomyad.

Tanwen furtively glanced to Thol across the table, the sight of him still painful.

Though they hadn't discussed what he had endured while on this island, Tanwen knew Eli had been right—a sickness was growing inside her brother. One made from living through excruciating pain and cruelty, anger and fear, over and over and over again.

It made her nauseous to think about, to witness, her guilt overwhelming. She also noted the wide berth her brother now gave their father, Thol's hesitancy to meet his gaze.

The change was a blow to her chest.

The Thol who had idolized their father, hung on his every word, was no more.

Further proof that whatever had transpired for these two while in Galia had broken them both.

The necessity for their escape wrapped tighter around her throat, suffocating.

Tanwen *had* to get them out of here, and soon.

Her father was studying the plans again, slowly nodding. "Yes," he said. "You're right. These can work." He pressed his palm to the parchment. "They have to."

Tanwen barely hid her sigh of relief. "Do you need my help in acquiring any of the needed material?"

Gabreel's gaze remained pinned to his schematic, mind clearly churning. "Not currently. We can disguise most of this as model building around efficiencies with the new mine."

"Good," replied Tanwen. She had hoped for such an answer.

"What of you and the elixir?" asked Thol. "By these calculations we'll need six jadüri blooms between our gliders."

"Yes," answered Tanwen, brows furrowing. "But I can take care of that. As an atenté, I have access to the gardens."

Tanwen noted the worried crease appearing between her father's brows. Clearly, he understood the business of atentés and the risk they faced, but he held back whatever thoughts filled his mind on the matter.

"This leads us to our timeline," said Tanwen, already anticipating an argument. "We must leave the night of the next full moons."

"The next . . . ?" began her father, incredulous. "But that's in one month's time."

"Yes," said Tanwen. "But as you know, the jadüri's nectar needs to be bloomed to activate the ingredients in the elixir. The longer we wait to use it after it's made, the less powerful it is. We'll need all the power we can get to fly from here to the edge of the Cactus Forest," Tanwen explained. "Plus, the princess's prewedding celebration is planned for that night. The palace will be fully distracted. No one will be thinking of you and Thol, and I'll be able to walk more freely to make my way to you."

Tanwen had gone over this plan again and again since leaving her mother.

It was a good one, if precarious.

Every step had to be flawlessly executed, and there were still many unknowns. Like how exactly she'd be able to steal jadüri.

But she'd find a solution, just like her father would find a way to build their wings while under constant supervision. Because they had no other choice.

Which was probably why Tanwen had omitted mentioning one major part in all this: killing King Réol.

At the thought, the stone pendant shivered a cold kiss against her chest.

Use me, it whispered, reminding her of her debt to a god.

Tanwen shifted with unease beside her father.

His success in the building of these wings was their only hope. She couldn't afford to distract him with this added burden. He had already been disturbed to hear Bosyg's involvement. He didn't need to know precisely *how* involved the goddess was in them succeeding.

After all, Tanwen was the one who had made this agreement; she would be the one to fulfill it.

"All right," said her father, clearly not pleased by the reality of their timeline but resigned, nonetheless. "By the night of the next full moons, we will plan to fly from Galia."

A heady anticipation filled Tanwen's veins, her heart racing. She glanced between Thol and her father. "It will work," she said.

While neither echoed her sentiments, she understood that doubt was a luxury none of them could afford.

42

Beads of sweat slipped down Tanwen's neck as she dug her gardening shovel into the rich soil.

Despite the setting sun, the heat remained thick and oppressive within the royal greenhouse, her wide-brimmed hat offering little reprieve from the suffocating warmth. But so was the necessary atmosphere for jadüri to thrive, especially when transplanting their seedlings.

With her brow puckered in concentration, Tanwen took care when lifting the small, frail plant from its container—gloved hands cupping its roots—before lowering it into the larger gardening box.

She released an anxious breath, pushing off her hat before wiping at her brow.

She stepped back, admiring her day's work.

Tanwen's row now housed dozens of young jadüri, soon to be fully grown buds that would bloom, ripe and ready to be plucked under Maja's and Parvi's wide gazes.

It never ceased to amaze Tanwen, the sight of the royal gardens. The botany that was cultivated outside the greenhouses was just as fragrant and rare as the vegetation within the large conservatory. However, nothing compared to the glass-covered field of jadüri where she currently stood. Under the full moonslight, the blossoms opened to create a radiant blue sea, emitting a sweet and pure fragrance that could make one weep.

Working in the garden was the one enjoyable part of Tanwen's atenté duties, reminiscent of her tasks at home with her mother. Though their own plot was minuscule compared to the royal gardens, it still boasted a variety of herbs and vegetation crucial for their tonics, ointments, and elixirs.

At the thought of her mother, Tanwen's chest grew tight, the tasks she had yet to accomplish for them to be reunited forever looming.

As Tanwen's gaze ran over her row of adolescent jadüri, her thoughts tumbled forward, wondering if these would be the very plants she'd collect to enable her escape. A hum of anxious anticipation fluttered awake in her chest. The other ingredients for the elixir were thankfully less precarious to acquire. Most could be found around the palace's grounds or rummaging through the royal kitchen.

What Tanwen needed to figure out was how she'd eventually get past the guards with extra jadüri in hand. Kidars were peppered throughout the greenhouse, bored and overheated, which made them prickly to interact with. Especially when it came time for them to count their blooms after a full moons' harvesting. Each atenté was meant to leave with only a dozen for their allotted mixture of docüra that they'd be making later that evening. Tanwen would need to be quick and clever with how she collected the additional six buds.

Though it was not merely the soldiers she'd need to elude.

Her fellow atentés worked around her in the various rows. Huw was stationed closest but thankfully at her back. He'd need to turn fully around to eye what she was doing.

A laugh drew her gaze to Gwyn and her friends posted up in a far corner of the greenhouse. They preened and tittered from where the glass windows gave way to one of the soldiers' training grounds.

Tanwen frowned.

Now, *they* were who she would need to look out for.

Always.

Gwyn had been less than pleased with Tanwen's return, seeing as they were once again splitting their services to the princess.

But Tanwen didn't care to appease Gwyn or any of the palace staff. She'd be gone from here soon enough, and the problems they posed would be in the past.

Tanwen blew out a tired sigh, fingering off her gardening gloves before taking a sip from her canteen.

The water was warm but relieved the dryness building in her throat, though it did nothing to ease her aching joints.

She had not been sleeping well since the day of the execution in the palace. And not just due to the burdens she carried but also because the sounds of the two lovers' throats being cut replayed in the darkness as she lay in bed.

Tanwen couldn't shake the feeling that the sentencing happening on the eve of her return to Galia was an act by the Low Gods to give Tanwen more evidence why the king was unfit to continue his tyrannical rule.

It definitely reinforced her belief that he needed to be removed as king, but being the one tasked with eradicating him . . . well, she was in the business of healing and saving lives, not ending them.

Killing the king, no matter the motivation, would mar her soul.

A rock of nausea hit Tanwen at the reality of her circumstance, the impossibility of carrying out such an order—to murder a man who was quite arguably the most powerful being in Cādra.

She would have laughed at the absurdity of it, but as it was, the reality of her predicament she didn't find funny in the least.

Tanwen still had no plan for how to use Maryth's tear, which she had now sewn into the lining of the pouch at her hip. Madam Arini had made it clear that her atentés could only wear jewelry she had approved.

Tanwen's necklace had been "too crude" for the palace, she had informed her.

Eli hadn't been pleased with his new cold companion, but Tanwen had been too frightened to leave it anywhere else but on her person.

Tanwen. Her name shouted in her mind caused her to jump. *Tanwen,* Eli called again.

By the Low Gods, she silently breathed, finding the gray field mouse by her shoe. *You nearly stopped my heart.*

So long as I succeeded in stopping your chaotic brooding, I can live with that, he said, whiskers twitching as she bent to pick him up.

I was not brooding, she replied, offended.

Eli jumped from her hand to the ledge of the gardening box. *Worrying?* he offered instead.

Can you blame me if I was?

No, there's much we must do, he agreed.

We.

The word provided the supportive embrace she hadn't realized she desperately needed.

She wasn't in this alone.

She would always have Eli.

Even if he was only a mouse.

A mighty *mouse,* Eli added emphatically.

Tanwen smiled just as a distant bell tolled.

Her shift in the greenhouse was done.

Tanwen readied to place Eli into his pouch when a tingling of awareness prompted her to look up, finding Gwyn's attention.

Two rows away, Gwyn's gaze caught on Eli cradled in Tanwen's hand.

Tanwen's heart stilled, fell, fled.

Go, she ordered Eli, her panic surging as she moved her hand so he could jump into a bed of soil.

What's happened? he squeaked in concern.

Go! Tanwen urged again, pulse stumbling and fumbling as it restarted. *Gwyn saw you. Hide!*

Eli did not question her further as he disappeared into the maze of raised garden boxes.

Tanwen worked hard to keep her expression neutral as she concentrated on gathering her supplies before heading for the door.

"Are you all right?" asked Huw, who had fallen into step beside her. "You look pale."

"I merely need some fresh air," she replied, just as another voice sounded at her back.

"And here I thought they were silly rumors," said Gwyn, "that the princess's favorite pet had a pet of her own."

Tanwen closed her eyes, chest constricting with her dismay. *Fool,* she chastised herself. *Fool. Fool. Fool.* Why hadn't she been more careful?

Gwyn sidled up to her other side, Efa and Owen close at her back.

"What are you on about, Gwyndolen?" accused Huw.

"Oh, just wondering what Her Royal Highness will say once she learns the hands that make her precious tonics are tainted with vermin piss and scat?"

Tanwen could sense Huw's concerned gaze on her as she clenched her teeth, grip tight on her basket. He had warned her of being careful regarding Eli. What had she been thinking by so publicly interacting with him?

An unhelpful voice sounded in her mind. *You needed the comfort.*

As their group exited the greenhouse, the other atentés gave them a wide berth, clearly sensing drama was afoot. None cared to intervene when Gwyn and her gang came out to play.

"And here I thought I'd have to find another way to get my position back serving the princess," mused Gwyn.

"You never lost your position with Princess Azla," Tanwen reminded her curtly before immediately regretting her words. She needed to stay quiet and fade away. To provoke Gwyn further was the definition of idiotic.

Gwyn's brown eyes lit up, a pleased lioness regarding her prey. "I might not have lost my position," she said, "but don't you know by now? I loathe sharing."

Owen and Efa chuckled at their backs.

Tanwen's annoyance flared.

Gods. She had no time for this.

"In fact, I was reminded how much I hated sharing during your absence," continued Gwyn as they shuffled from the greenhouse to the cool open air of the pillared walkway.

Despite the relief the breeze left on Tanwen's skin, she would have gladly remained in the hot glass garden if it meant she could escape her current companions.

"The princess even stopped mentioning you while you were home. Thank the *gods*," huffed Gwyn. "Seeing as I am just as capable, if not more, of keeping her in her comforts as *dear Ms. Coster*," she finished in a mocking tone.

"If that is true," said Tanwen, unable to stop herself from facing Gwyn, "then I see no reason for you to be threatened by my presence."

It was as if she had slapped her. Gwyn's chin pulled back, her eyes widening. "*Threatened?*" she seethed. "There is *nothing* about a rodent-loving straight horn that threatens me."

If Tanwen hadn't been called many other slandering names since she was young, Gwyn's words would have hit their mark, but as it was she merely scoffed, flashing an amused smile.

A gesture she'd come to regret, for Gwyn took a threatening step toward Tanwen, but whatever cruelty she readied to set loose was interrupted by the booming voice of a nearby herald.

"Make way for His Royal Highness!"

Heads turned, breaths caught. Gwyn and her friends jumped to the side as all came to a bow.

Tanwen's pulse thrummed as she staggered back with the rest of the group.

The air was snatched from her lungs. *By the twin moons,* she thought.

Zolya approached like a sleek jungle cat, grace and power and beauty, his backdrop an enormous entourage of kidets, along with Kidar Terz keeping pace at his side.

But what made heartbeats falter and the servants' stares linger beyond propriety was that they were all entirely without shirts.

The soldiers stomped through the hall in their uniforms for their weekly game of pavol.

Tanwen swallowed hard, a fevered blush erupting across her skin as she drank in Zolya's chiseled perfection. His tucked-in white wings framed his broad shoulders. His rippling of abs drew her attention to where they dipped into his trousers. His tawny skin was smooth and luminous against the midday sun. As he walked forward, the clouds beyond the hall seemed to shift directions so they might follow along with him, but these all became blurry details as the prince's azure gaze collided with Tanwen's.

It was an arrow to her chest.

A flood of heat between her legs.

A rippling of awareness to her skin.

With her breaths getting lost somewhere in her lungs, Tanwen dutifully lowered her eyes. She concentrated on the woven blue thread making up the rug beneath her feet, held tightly to her gardening basket as Prince Zolya and his procession of soldiers passed.

Despite not looking at him, she could sense his lingering attention. Her cheeks burned, neck growing flushed. Her body was forever a traitor, reacting, heating, desiring his whenever near.

And then he was gone, his entourage turning a corner, heading for the Recreational Lawn.

The silence of the hall was replaced by excited chatter.

Tanwen took an unsteady step back, Gwyn and her companions having forgotten her existence. Their giggles erupted as they followed the rest of the staff, who were now headed to watch the games.

The entire palace would be redirected for a few dips of the sun.

One benefit from His Royal Highness's sudden appearance.

But Tanwen's relief was cut short as she noted the watchful eye of Huw, who remained at her side.

"Are you all right?" he asked, head tilting curiously as he, no doubt, took in the flush along her pale skin.

Tanwen cleared her throat, feigning poise. "I fear the heat of the greenhouse has gotten the better of me," she explained.

"Yes," he mused wryly. "It must have been the greenhouse's fault for why you're as splotchy as a sun-scorched fruit."

Tanwen shot him a sardonic glare. "As always, Huw, your colorful observations remain unrivaled."

He flashed her a charming grin. "It's why I'm so good at my job."

"Indeed," Tanwen placated. "Now, if you'll excuse me, I'm clearly in need of a drink."

"But the kitchens are the other way," Huw called to her as she practically fled from his side.

Tanwen ignored another of his unwanted observations as she hurried from their hall to turn a corner into the next. It was blessedly empty, more proof that everyone had been drawn like moths to muscular torsos, following Zolya and his company of soldiers toward the games.

All the better for Tanwen.

She finally released her breath. She needed to calm the chaotic flutter of her pulse. Between her row with Gwyn and the sight of Zolya, Tanwen's nerves were a mess. Something the nearby fowl of the palace appeared to pick up on. Parakeets danced and flittered along the capital of each column she passed, a tweeting, anxious canopy.

Please, she begged of them. *I thank you for your concern, but I am well.*

They didn't appear to believe her as they continued to chirp and flutter, following her hurried footsteps.

Tanwen's frustration soared.

Now of all moments, she couldn't afford a scene. Not after Gwyn had seen her with Eli. Or after yesterday's execution. The palace hummed with distrust.

A gust of wind pressed against Tanwen, the tell of a Volari landing nearby.

The corridor plunged into silence as the parakeets dashed away.

Fear leaped up Tanwen's throat, the fowls' terror not reassuring.

But as she turned, eyeing who approached, she understood their desire to flee.

Tanwen would have as well if she had wings.

Instead, she remained rooted in her panic, watching the prince approach.

Shirtless.

43

"Sire," Tanwen breathed, her pulse a roaring beat as she gave a quick customary bow.

Zolya stopped a pace too close for what was appropriate.

It took everything in her to not take a step back. The scent of wind and bergamot wafted from his exposed skin, dizzying her senses. Tanwen became captivated by the three lines of his rain tattoo adorning his left pectoral. Considering her height reached only his chest, it was positioned directly in her line of sight.

If Tanwen blushed any further, she'd become a ripe tomato.

"Aren't you meant to be headed toward the Recreational Lawn?" she questioned, eyeing the empty promenade.

Zolya didn't reply right away; he appeared preoccupied with raking his gaze over her, as if searching for something beyond what could be discerned on the surface.

"Sire?" Tanwen questioned, her concern growing.

"Are you not a fan of pavol, Ms. Coster?" he asked.

Tanwen blinked once, twice. "Excuse me?"

"I notice that you are not headed with the others to the games," he explained.

Tanwen opened her mouth before closing it, thoughts stumbling. "You left your entourage of soldiers to come find me, all so you could ask why I'm not participating in your fanfare?" she asked, incredulity clear in her tone.

The edges of Zolya's lips twitched. "No," he replied.

"No?" she repeated, confused.

"I forgot my charm of Udasha in my rooms," he explained. "I never play without her luck beside me on the pitch. And, as I'm sure you are aware, this *is* the path back to my chambers."

"Oh," Tanwen stammered, embarrassed. "But . . . surely a servant could fetch that for you?"

"Are you offering your services, Ms. Coster?"

Tanwen tripped over her response as visions of the last time she had been within his rooms rose like a heated mirage. Except this time, Zolya was bare chested as he lay atop her.

It was as if he sensed the direction of her thoughts, for he suddenly grew very still, his gaze searing.

No, Tanwen silently chastised, a desperate command. *No. This is wrong. I cannot want him. And he certainly cannot want me.*

She forced herself to think about her brother and father, guarded and trapped. Forced herself to think of Zolya's involvement, which had brought them here. To yesterday's execution and her agreement to a god to kill the king, Zolya's father.

If he knew any of these truths, especially the latter, he would not be looking at her thus, as if he wished to slowly devour her with pleasure.

Instead, he'd have a knife to her throat before quickly slicing it open.

Tanwen's resolve steadied. "If that is what you wish of me, sire," she forced out amicably.

Zolya appeared to wrestle with his response. "My dear Ms. Coster," he began, tone rough, "you do not want to know what I wish of you."

There went her balance, her resolve.

His words were hot liquid down her skin.

Gods. This was too much. Too tempting.

And incredibly dangerous.

"Zolya," she managed, though it came out breathier than she had intended. At the use of his name, Zolya's attention clung to her, a precarious glint. "We can't do this," she explained, nerves on high alert as she once again eyed the long corridor. Save for the fingers of sunlight streaming between columns, they remained unaccompanied.

"Do what?" he challenged. "Am I not allowed to walk about my own palace?"

"You know what I'm referring to." She gave him a measured look.

"I don't think I do," he replied, brows lifting in feigned ignorance. "I came this way to fetch my charm. I didn't want to hold up the games by having staff get it for me when I can acquire it quicker. Plus, as you can see"—he waved to the empty hall—"there are none about to ask anyway. Everyone is nearing the Recreational Lawn. Well, all besides you, of course."

"I was in search of some water." Tanwen felt the need to explain. "My work in the greenhouse has left me rather parched."

Zolya slid his gaze down her body, as though he wished to drink her.

It was bordering on cruel.

"Aren't the kitchens the other way?" he asked.

Tanwen's annoyance flared, his observation echoing Huw's. Was her every move to be so scrutinized?

"I decided to go the long way round," she managed. "The fresh air is good for health."

"I see." Zolya arched a brow, mouth fighting a grin. "Just as further exertion helps eradicate thirst."

Tanwen blinked. He was teasing her.

And *gods*, it felt wonderful. Light and easy.

Everything her life currently was not.

Neither of their lives could be.

Not with each other, at least.

Tanwen needed to end this before she had no strength left.

"Yes, well, if that satisfies your curiosities, sire." She gave him another quick bow, fingers tightening around her gardening basket. "I will leave you to retrieve your charm and wish you all of Udasha's luck in your games."

"Tanwen, wait." Zolya grasped her arm, keeping her from backing away.

She stared at his grip, a fissure of heat erupting and cascading across her skin from where they touched.

"Sire?" She frowned, heartbeat thundering in her chest as she glanced up.

Zolya's brows similarly knitted as he released her. "And now we are back to *sire*."

"That is how servants are meant to address you," she insisted. "I was out of line earlier."

He raked a hand through his hair in frustration, causing his stomach muscles to ripple. "I can't stand this."

"This?"

"This charade." He gestured between them. "This forced propriety."

"Then perhaps you should take your plight up with your father," Tanwen reasoned, tone harder than she had intended. "For it is his law, is it not, which enforces it. Or shall I remind you of yesterday's execution?"

His features grew sharp as he took a predatory step closer. This time she did follow it with a step back, but her retreat was brief as she found herself pressed against the cold marble wall.

"It might be his law," Zolya ground out, voice a rumble of ire, "but it would *never* be mine."

Tanwen inhaled her gasp.

It was sedition of the highest degree.

And spoken by the king's own son: his wish to break centuries-old law, his open opposition of it.

A heady hope filled Tanwen then.

What else might Zolya wish to change once king?

Mütra, a voice whispered. *Would he free Mütra?*

But she forced herself from wandering down that fruitless daydream.

"Do you mean that?" Tanwen asked softly, heart pounding beneath her ribs.

"I am not one to say things I do not mean," Zolya answered. "To rule with fear is not a tactic I find as constructive as my father does."

Tanwen understood she was receiving a rare gift, something not many had access to, a glimpse at the ruler the prince intended to be. "And what tactics do you find constructive?"

"Listening," he replied easily as he slid closer. "Understanding motivations." His attention fell to her lips. "Desires and, of course, the power of persuasion." He leaned a hand on the wall beside her head.

Zolya was a gasp away, the heat from his exposed skin sliding across her front. His muscles flexed as his magnificent wings slowly spread and curled around them, shielding her from any eyes but his own.

The gesture was possessive, but she didn't feel cornered or trapped. Tanwen felt safe, as though he were offering himself as her armor.

She wanted to fold herself around him, press naked flesh to naked flesh.

Gather his heat and drink his power.

She also wanted to scream.

Because this was utter and complete madness!

This uncontrollable pushing and pulling that seemed to always fate them to collide.

Despite the known risks and understood inappropriateness, here they were, *again,* breathing heavy and daring the other with their gazes. *You first.*

But she couldn't.

Not again.

Not with everything she had on the line to ensure her family's freedom.

Freedom that had been taken by the very man encircling her.

The man she would betray with a promise to a Low God.

"Tanwen," Zolya whispered, begged.

"I know," she replied, closing her eyes, her longing a palpable pain across her skin. "I know."

"Please, look at me."

"I can't."

"You can."

Tanwen pressed herself further into the wall, longing to be as solid as its surface. With a shaky breath she opened her eyes, finding Zolya's gaze a crystal blue lake of yearning.

"You should go," she croaked.

"I should," he agreed, though he did not move. He remained, angling every part of himself around her, as if that might lessen the painful desire for them to touch.

If we are near, it is enough.

But, of course, it wasn't.

Never would be.

It only made the suffering of what they couldn't have even worse.

"If you will not go," Tanwen managed, "you must allow me."

Zolya worked his jaw, displeased. "Only when you allow leave of my thoughts," he replied in a frustrated rumble. "Gods, Tanwen"—his muscles grew taut with his clear aggravation—"you have consumed me. Completely. I can't stop wondering where you might be each day, what you might be doing, or what your brilliant mind might be thinking or solving. Every night I lie imagining you beside me in bed and atop of me." His gaze darkened, a gathering of energy humming around them. "I thirst for the taste of you on my tongue, for the feel of you beneath my palms. In all my years, I have never been so bewitched. You are the brightest constellation in my sky, and I forever find myself searching for a way home, to you."

Tanwen could not breathe.

She could not speak.

She was no longer tethered to the ground. She was only aching desire and stubborn resistance. Because even in the midst of her yearning after his confession, cursing herself for feeling the same, the sharp reminders of her responsibilities and burdens flashed before her. The truth of her and Zolya's two worlds remained present, a cleaver to their union.

Zolya might have wished to be a different king, a ruler who allowed the coupling of two races, but it was still his father who sat upon the throne. Still his laws that threatened her existence. And still her layers of secrets she could never expose.

"Zolya," Tanwen whispered, pleaded. "Please. You know . . . this cannot happen." The words tasted sour as they left her tongue.

"But it already has," he declared. "*You* have happened, Tanwen. To me."

He lifted his free hand. Tanwen dared not move. His palm hovered beside her cheek.

Touch me, she wanted to beg.

Leave me, she prayed instead.

Zenca must have been listening, for fate intervened in that moment.

Approaching footsteps echoed down the hall.

Like the ripping of wax from skin, Zolya tore himself away, vanishing in a painful blink. His wings flared as he leaped between two columns, disappearing into the wide-open sky.

Tanwen was left behind, clutching both of their exposed hearts in her hands.

PART VII

Storm

44

Gabreel stood in the corner of his workshop, watching his daughter try on her wings.

The candlelight within the room pressed its warmth against Tanwen's pale skin and flickered against the gold caps accessorizing her horns. Her brow was knitted in determined focus as she adjusted the straps and tested the mechanism.

She appeared more capable and assuredly older than he had remembered.

But perhaps she had always possessed these qualities, and he had simply failed to recognize them. Too often, Aisling had been beside his daughter, occupying his sight and thoughts. And many of his days and nights in Zomyad had been consumed with teaching Thol or passing solitary hours in his workshop. With this realization, an uneasy weight pressed against Gabreel's spine.

He had neglected his daughter.

Failed to see the strong, intelligent woman she had grown to be.

One who had single-handedly found her way onto Galia, then into the palace, to free them.

Guilt dug into Gabreel's chest for any moment he might have doubted her.

"We should put some padding around the joint holds," suggested Tanwen, flexing one of her arms, which were both strapped to the glider. "Once we are in the air, our weight will quickly drag against them, especially when we angle to change directions. I'm not expecting the flight to be comfortable, but I'd rather not grow distracted by the pain of rubbed-raw skin when I'm meant to be concentrating on not spinning out."

"Yes," said Thol thoughtfully as he bent to eye the parts Tanwen mentioned. "We can add another layer of leather before some fur lining, especially around the wrist straps. It will only help with its durability too."

Tanwen nodded her agreement. "I was also thinking, because of the length of our flight, we should make footholds we can slip our feet into by the glider's tail. It will help control our steering, not having to worry about dangling legs."

Thol grabbed his notebook and started to jot down their thoughts. "Good idea. I'll add that to our list of improvements."

Gabreel resisted a grin, watching his children working together, a lump of pride forming in his throat. While Thol would never be his old self, with Tanwen's visits, his energy had picked up, a bit of light shining once again in his gaze.

It was a glimmer of hope Gabreel had not dared believe still existed.

But then Tanwen had arrived with her plans and determination. Her sure words and access beyond their confines.

Despite his previous skepticism, Gabreel found himself convinced this escape could be possible.

A dangerous thought, he knew.

The gods did not grant reprieves without sacrifice.

But Gabreel was forever prepared to lay down his life for his children to live.

"Show me how these come apart again," requested Tanwen to Aberthol.

Aberthol left his notebook beside Eli, who watched from the worktable, before helping Tanwen unclip and unclasp the wings.

Gabreel's attention returned to Eli, whose whiskers twitched from where he sat observing on his hind legs. The mouse had become a strange comfort to him and Aberthol, his nearness usually meaning Tanwen was also nearby. In their cottage prison, Eli had become their small beacon of reassurance.

"And then you can easily fold them down like this," Aberthol was instructing as he collapsed the various parts of the glider.

Gabreel scrutinized the fluidness of the motion, looking for any potential flaw, but the wings appeared sound. It was a relief, given he and Thol had spent countless nights perfecting the design. Thus far, they had constructed one glider, requiring it to be flawless before proceeding with the construction of the other two.

His original schematics, while successful, were—as he had suspected—outdated.

Many new materials and advancements had been invented in the past twenty-odd years. A benefit, given the number of additional alterations that needed to be applied: a stronger skeleton to withstand their longer journey, a more insulated canister to keep their power supply from freezing as they fell from such a high elevation, and a design that could be easily disassembled and reassembled so their wings could become innocuous when laid about his workroom.

Gabreel's recent influx of requested materials had, unsurprisingly, piqued the king's interest. What must his glorious inventor be inventing now? The kidets toured his workshop often to collect reports for King Réol. So far, Gabreel had been able to disguise what he built as a device that was meant to redirect the strong winds coming off the Aspero Sea near the new mine.

Any advances in the productivity surrounding the new mine His Eminence appeared pleased to support.

"This is spectacular," breathed Tanwen, staring at where the wings were now split into two neatly folded piles. "How long will it take to make the other two?"

Aberthol turned expectantly to Gabreel, and the gesture nearly knocked him unsteady. His son had not looked at him like that in an age, with a need for guidance.

Gabreel's response was momentarily stuck in his throat. "They will be operational by the next full moons."

Three weeks.

Tanwen nodded, determination hardening her features.

The following silence was disrupted by their cottage door banging open.

Eli scurried under a pile of tools as each of their gazes went wide, snagging on to one another as their joint panic froze time.

And then their workroom filled with movement.

Tanwen and Aberthol hurriedly stashed the glider and schematic while Gabreel hissed for Tanwen to hide. He then sprinted toward the kitchen door.

"How may I help you?" he asked the two kidets who loomed near the front door, soft night air filtering in. Gabreel did his best to mask his panicked breaths. He prayed they were here to check on him and Aberthol before their shift change.

But when they didn't answer him and instead pushed farther into the cottage, his fear spiked.

"Have you come to see progress in my wind shifter?" Gabreel asked as he backed his way into his workroom. The guards' wings tucked in tight as they pressed their way through the doorframe. "I just finished up for the night," he explained as his heartbeat slammed against his ribs. He furtively glanced around the room, but thankfully Tanwen was nowhere to be seen. Gabreel chanced a relieved breath, though his muscles remained tense. "I can give you an oral report for the king, however," he went on.

"The Mütra is to come with us," one kidet declared as the other stepped toward Aberthol.

The room fell silent as the request was absorbed within the space.

"Wait," Gabreel called, a rising hysteria filling his lungs. He wedged himself between the kidet and his son. "I've been working, inventing. I do not understand. My son is meant to remain with me so long as I'm working." He hated the desperate plea in his voice, the fear, but he'd prostrate himself any way necessary to stop this madness.

"Our king does not need reason for his demands," stated the kidet, a look of disgust in his gaze as he attempted to force Gabreel out of the way.

"*No!*" Gabreel dug in his heels, his heat magic surging to his hands. *I will set you all on fire!*

"Father."

His name said softly from behind paused his retaliation.

"It's fine," Aberthol added, voice hollow as he placed a reassuring hand on Gabreel's shoulder.

Fine.

It's fine.

Nausea swelled in Gabreel's stomach, a cold sweat awakening on his skin.

Nothing about this was *fine*.

He met his son's eyes, caught the meaning in his hard gaze, the worry that had nothing to do with his own future pain.

Tanwen.

She was here, hiding.

And needed to remain hiding.

Wen can never *become like me.*

Thol's plea to Gabreel all those weeks ago.

Gabreel clenched his teeth, the agony of the moment too much.

He stood paralyzed.

The longer the guards remained in their cottage, the more at risk Tanwen became of being found. But if he merely stood aside . . .

"I will come," Aberthol said to the guard, stepping around Gabreel.

"Thol," he whispered, disbelieving.

But his child did not look back as he was absorbed by the large men and shuffled out.

The front door of their cottage shut with a gentle click.

The wind rattled the workroom window.

Gabreel stared at the doorway his son had fleetingly occupied.

His son, who had gone willingly to his own suffering.

And Gabreel, like every time before, could do nothing.

Aberthol had endured more than all of them and still had the fortitude to walk toward his nightmares.

A racking sob escaped Gabreel as he fell forward, but a strong, steadying grip kept him from hitting the floor.

Tanwen.

He met her wide green gaze, her eyes red from unshed tears.

Her features mirrored his own, displaying a mix of terror, fury, and grief. But there was a strength there that he no longer felt within himself. His daughter, who had come to save them, remained propping them both up despite the agony he knew she shared.

Gabreel took a moment to marvel at her.

To marvel at his son.

His children, who were braver than him.

"Father," she whispered, pained.

He could hear the question in her tone. *What now?*

But Gabreel no longer held answers. He held only facts.

"It's happening," he said.

"What is?" Tanwen asked, brows furrowed.

"The king is growing bored of his promise."

Gabreel watched Tanwen's expression grow panicked with her understanding.

It didn't matter if Gabreel behaved, listened, and obeyed.

King Réol had a Mütra within his palace, and he wished to play with him.

Our king does not need reason for his demands.

Though he and Tanwen remained quiet, their unspoken fear hung heavy within the workroom.

For Thol, waiting until the next full moons to escape could prove to be too late.

45

Tanwen hadn't intended to linger so long outside Princess Azla's sitting room door. Nor had she meant to overhear so much.

Yet she had.

"We have already discussed this," sighed the princess to her companion, her voice muffled from beyond the door. "If we ran, my father would never give up hunting us. And we wouldn't merely be hiding from him but from any High God allied to Orzel."

Tanwen could hear the princess's tiredness, her frustration in her looming fate.

"No, we need something more permanent," Princess Azla continued. "Something that would ensure the ending of my marriage contract."

"Besides the king annulling the agreement," came Lady Esme's voice, "which we both know will not happen, the only other solution would be to eliminate one of the signatories."

There was a slip of tense silence, the meaning of Lady Esme's observation filling the space.

Since Orzel was immortal, that left only one possible target: the king.

From where Tanwen remained on the other side of the door, her heartbeat kicked into a sprint.

"Yes," the princess ultimately agreed.

"But it's impossible," reasoned Lady Esme, her worry clear in her tone as she walked back her suggestion.

"Nothing is impossible," replied the princess.

"This nearly is."

"He's a king, not a god, Essie. He *will* die eventually."

"Yes, eventually, but he's ruled for over two centuries and has, no doubt, evaded numerous attempts on his life."

"I don't understand why you're fighting me on this," said Princess Azla tersely. "Especially since we've already debated this back and forth and always end up at the same conclusion."

"Because I do not want this sin on your hands," said Lady Esme.

The princess's responding laugh was cold. "*Is* it a sin to kill a tyrant?"

Tanwen's blood continued to pump a hungry, anxious rhythm in her veins. She gripped the tray in her hands as her breaths came fast and uneven.

Could she trust her own ears?

Were the princess and her lover really discussing murdering the king?

Yes, hummed a tempting voice, which slithered up from the rock hidden in the pouch at her hip. *And isn't it glorious?*

Tanwen's skin chilled as a wicked daydream pressed into her mind, but whether it was her own or that of a vengeful god, she could not tell.

Visions flooded her: The lifeless body of King Réol. His eyes wide, unseeing, as his mouth was frozen in a silent, painful scream. His magnificent white wings limp and useless, splayed across a marble floor. His power gone. His threat removed as his soul was now in the grips of Maryth in her Eternal River.

Tanwen snapped back to the princess's chambers, her lungs fighting for air.

As the dark fantasies dissolved, only one thought prevailed—a thought that overshadowed all others: with the king dead, Aberthol's monster would be slain.

Tanwen's veins filled with a mix of agony and hot vengeance, as they had last night when she was forced to remain crouched in the shadows within the cottage as her brother was taken to be tortured. It had left her in a trembling fury, reliving her past, when Tanwen could do nothing to help her family but hide.

Tanwen couldn't bear it.

Quickly had her resolve hardened then, her mind becoming clear.

King Réol *must* die.

And not because of a promise to a god or to save a princess from a tragic marriage.

But because of Thol.

For Thol.

If it was the last thing Tanwen did on this godforsaken island, she would exact revenge for the injustices inflicted upon her brother.

"We might understand what needs to be done"—Lady Esme's voice pulled Tanwen's attention back to where she hovered outside their sitting room—"but we still don't know how to do it. He is guarded always, his food and drink tasted and tested, not to mention his own godly strengths."

"A solution will present itself," reasoned the princess.

Had Eli been by her side, he surely would have cautioned Tanwen against her impending actions, persuading her not to succumb to the malevolence she felt toward the king. However, at present, her friend was conspicuously absent. In fact, she hadn't laid eyes on him all morning. But that concern would have to wait for later.

Without further thought, Tanwen knocked.

There was a beat of a startled hush before, "Enter."

Balancing the items on her tray, Tanwen pushed into the sitting room. She gave a quick bow to the princess and Lady Esme, who sat close on a plush bench. Their gowns were made of silk, their wings drawn tight at their backs. They were positioned in such a way that would inspire a painter's brush, save for the closed drapes behind them, which blocked the view from the large windows.

"Tanwen," addressed the princess.

"Ma'am," replied Tanwen.

Neither of them said anything further as they held each other's stares.

A silent assessment.

What is it that you might have heard?

Plenty to be dangerous.

Though Tanwen was not there to be a threat.

She had made herself known to play a hand.

One she hadn't known she had until now.

Your discretion is appreciated, Lady Esme had once told her.

Well, Tanwen was prepared to continue her discretion so long as she could call in Lady Esme's promised favor.

With her pulse thrumming fast in her veins, Tanwen threw further caution to the wind as she fingered out the black pebble from the pouch at her hip. The surface was colder than she remembered, almost frostbite inducing. She placed the black stone onto the table between them. It sat like a dark void on the white surface.

Tanwen held her breath.

"What is this?" Princess Azla asked, single brow raised.

"A captured tear from Maryth," Tanwen answered, attempting to keep her tone even, confident.

Princess Azla's gaze widened with her surprise as she looked back at the stone on the table. Meanwhile, Lady Esme's features furrowed with her concern.

"A captured tear?" questioned Lady Esme. "From Maryth?"

Tanwen nodded, trying her best to hide her rising panic for what she had done, was doing. But there was no going back now. Her faith lay in their mutual desperation.

"Poison," Tanwen clarified.

The princess snatched her hand back from where she had been reaching out to pick up the rock while Lady Esme grew stiff, stance ready to protect, fight.

"You can touch it," Tanwen assured. "Only when dropped into liquid does it become the deadliest of its kind. More so than Indigo Eclipse," she added pointedly, holding the princess's stare. "It is scentless, tasteless, and colorless, making it untraceable once dissolved."

The tension within the sitting room compounded as the ladies appeared to absorb her words.

"You have forgotten yourself, Ms. Coster," said Lady Esme, her fury clear. "It is a crime punishable by execution to bring such a thing near the princess."

"I know," replied Tanwen.

She was no longer in her body but floating overhead, an observer to whatever fate handed her next.

"Then why *have* you brought me this?" asked the princess, her brows knit in a mix of horror, hurt, and a dangerous spark of intrigue.

Tanwen did not answer for a long moment, allowing the question to stretch and warp, slowly becoming answered.

Because you need it.

"Because it was given to me," Tanwen eventually said, "and I now believe it was meant to be given to you. A tear from the goddess of death to claim someone godly. A solution," she added meaningfully.

In the resounding silence, the truth of her words unfolded.

Yes, I heard what you are plotting. Yes, I support it.

This is for the king.

"You should not be forced to marry anyone but who you wish, Princess," said Tanwen.

You should not be forced to marry Orzel.

Tanwen's loyalty sat on display between the three women, innocuous but very real.

The princess and Lady Esme shared a furtive glance.

"You do understand that what you have suggested is treasonous," said Lady Esme. "If found out, you'd be executed."

"I understand that what I have done is extend another act of service to help a need of the princess," Tanwen clarified, her heartbeats pounding against her ribs. "As for whether I'm found out, well, my lady, that is up to your discretion."

Lady Esme held her stare, an understanding passing between them, the memory of their past conversation hovering in the air.

Your discretion is appreciated, she had said. *If ever you find yourself in need of such a favor in return . . .*

Tanwen was now calling in that debt.

"While I would like to believe my staff are this loyal to myself," began the princess, "I am not so delusional. What do you wish to gain from this offering?"

Tanwen regarded the princess—her poise and grace retained while discussing the murder of her father. "It is not only you, ma'am, who the king suppresses," said Tanwen. "There are many others who could be freed by such an . . . outcome," she finished carefully.

A flash of curiosity shone in Princess Azla's blue gaze.

"And if I may continue to be so bold," Tanwen added, because if she was doing this, she might as well get it right. "The night of your prewedding celebrations could pose a perfect time to address your . . . solution."

The princess almost laughed from her clear shock at Tanwen's inappropriateness. "And why is that?" she asked placatingly.

"There will be many distractions that evening," reasoned Tanwen. "And many potential guests to carry the blame, if blame is required."

It will also help with my and my family's escape if attentions are turned elsewhere.

Plus, if the king was killed before the party, who knew the heightened levels of security that would be in place in the palace, making it even more difficult for Tanwen to move around unnoticed. It wouldn't make their escape impossible but just that much harder.

As tension filled the room, Tanwen steadied herself and grabbed the tonic she had prepared for the princess.

She set it beside Maryth's tear.

Your choice, the gesture said.

The princess recoiled from the drink, clearly now distrusting of anything Tanwen might prepare.

Her reaction hurt, even though Tanwen understood.

Whatever the princess decided to do after this moment, her relationship with Tanwen would never be the same. For Tanwen had revealed just how dangerous she could be.

"I leave you with this decision, Princess," said Tanwen. "For you to maneuver as you wish." She gave a departing bow, then exited the sitting room without waiting for a formal dismissal.

Tanwen walked slowly despite wanting to run, her lungs unable to draw any relief even after leaving the women's company.

But before she closed the doors to the sitting room, she saw Princess Azla ignore her tonic and reach instead for the stone.

46

Tanwen was going to be sick.

With each retreating step from Princess Azla's chambers, her rush of adrenaline faded, and the weight of her actions crashed down on her like an avalanche of uncertainty and regret.

What have I done? What have I done? What have I done?

Tanwen had gambled with the riskiest hand of her life. She had placed a bet on each of her family members' lives. She had given away the only poison that could guarantee the king's death and was now a conspirator in sedition.

But it had been such a clear-cut path at the time. The princess wanted to get rid of the king.

Tanwen had the tool to do it.

This also saved her from having to do it herself. Bosyg had never specified that it needed to be Tanwen to kill the king, only that he needed to be killed. An act that seemed more impossible by the day.

And days Tanwen no longer had the luxury to give.

Her brother was withering, her father was a step behind him, and the approach of the next full moons was edging ever closer.

What access did Tanwen have to the king?

None.

Scorched Skies

But the princess and a lady of the Sun Court had plenty.

They also could be calling the guards right now, reporting Tanwen's insolence in having been so bold to offer up a poison to kill King Réol, the princess's father.

Oh gods. Tanwen hurried behind a nearby column, dry heaving over the corridor's ledge.

Tears sprang to her eyes from the pain of only bile rising. She hadn't yet eaten today.

As she leaned against the hard stone, she gripped her empty tray in one hand while wiping at her mouth with the other. She tried taking in steadying breaths, but the breeze carried only the perpetual sweet scent of jasmine, worsening her nausea.

She was beginning to loathe the smells of Galia.

She now understood the perfume's purpose: to hide the sour rot growing from within the island, the dead hearts of the aristocrats and their king.

Reluctantly, Tanwen thought again of the princess and what she had overheard before entering the sitting room.

In contrast to her courtiers, the princess's heart was very much alive. Fighting for her life just as Tanwen fought for her own, fought for her family's.

Which, Tanwen reminded herself, was exactly the reason she had done what she had.

Her insurance in giving Princess Azla the stone was that she was clearly just as determined to win in a similar high-stakes game.

If the princess didn't want to sacrifice herself and her happiness, the king *must* die.

A wriggle of guilt twisted in Tanwen's gut then at the thought of Zolya.

It was clear Zolya had a complicated relationship with his father, admitted to not agreeing with the way in which he ruled, and openly despised his maltreatment of his daughter, but did that equate to him wishing for his death like the rest of them?

Nausea rolled through Tanwen once more.

No, Zolya was too honorable in his duty to the crown to ever support such treason.

Even if this would free his sister and finally allow him to be king.

Allow him to rule as he believed just.

It might be his law, but it would never *be mine.*

Zolya's declaration still prickled down Tanwen's spine. Her mind spun at what else he would change, improve.

Stop it, a voice hissed within her mind.

This was not the time to daydream.

Her reality was that Zolya could never find out what she had done or helped try to achieve.

If he had been out of her reach before, this would set their fates even further apart.

Zolya would never forgive her this sin, and even if he could, his father would then be dead, and he'd be king.

And a Volari king could *never* be with the likes of her.

Heartache awoke like sharp knives blossoming in Tanwen's chest, but she resisted crumpling under the pain.

Instead, she held tight to her purpose in coming to Galia: to save her brother and father. King Réol still sat on his throne, and her family's lives were still in danger.

As Tanwen straightened, her resolve for what had transpired with the princess found its footing again.

It was done.

Her move had been played.

Only time would tell if it would work against her.

◆ ◆ ◆

Tanwen made her way to the servants' quarters beneath the palace. After leaving her tray in the kitchens, she headed to the atenté dormitories, seeking a brief reprieve before her next shift. But upon entering, a commotion near her bed caused the hairs on the back of her neck to rise. Noting her arrival, the other atentés fell silent.

Dread pooled, acidic, in Tanwen's gut as she worked her way forward, the crowd parting, but before she could see what they had been looking at, Huw intercepted her.

"Hey," he said softly, too softly. "Let's go for a walk."

"What's happened?" asked Tanwen, attempting to sidestep him.

"I'll tell you, but not here." His grip grew painful as he tried to turn her around.

"Stop." She pulled her arm free, her concern rising. "I want to know why everyone is—"

Tanwen's words faltered as she caught sight of Gwyn's sinister smile from where she leaned in a nearby doorway. She stood removed from the crowd, Efa and Owen close by, but they looked less confident in their sneers. In fact, they appeared frightened, guilty, swiftly averting their gazes when Tanwen made eye contact.

Unease worked like claws down Tanwen's back, terror pumping with each beat of her heart.

She shoved past Huw, ignored his pleas for her to stop.

As Tanwen reached her bed, she drew up short.

Eli.

Pinned to her sheets.

The white-handled docüra knife gleamed, pristine against the pool of his blood. Eli stared unseeing up at the ceiling.

A silent scream tore from Tanwen's throat as she gripped her chest, pain eviscerating.

Her heart.

Her heart.

Her heart.

Ripped.

Severed.

Destroyed.

Eli.

My Eli!

Dead.

Devastation was a cresting wave, an engulfing surge that dragged Tanwen down into its depths. She barely registered a soft touch to her shoulder, a weak tether to life above. Huw was nearby. Somewhere.

But Tanwen was drifting further beneath the ocean, lost in an incomprehensible despair as the gruesome scene overtook her vision.

"Eli," she whispered, sobbed, before crying out, "*Eli!*"

A lashing hate snapped Tanwen back into the room, surging her above the bleak darkness as a vicious growl tore from her throat. She turned and lunged toward Gwyn.

"You monster!" she thundered, vision stained red. Tanwen held no doubts as to who was responsible for this.

A strong grip snagged Tanwen, keeping her from reaching Gwyn. "You soulless beast!" she bellowed as she fought against whoever held her captive.

Gwyn's eyes widened, revealing her flash of terror. She had the good sense to take steps away.

But the distance didn't matter.

Tanwen would reach her. She was feral, frothing, and desperate for blood.

Gwyn's blood.

"It will not bring him back." She heard the urgent cruel words of Huw, who held her, was containing her. "Madam Arini will not side with you attacking Gwyn over a mouse," he reasoned further, his words a vicious truth. "But she *will* get what's coming," he promised, a fierce whisper in Tanwen's ear. "Though not like this. You need to go, Tanwen. Go!"

His shove was hard, a command.

Tanwen had no idea why, but she obeyed.

She turned from the cold silent room and fled.

47

Tanwen did not recognize her surroundings.

But she hardly cared.

As she collapsed into the cool dirt, she understood only that she was outside of the palace, alone.

Trees shaded where she gripped her stomach, bent over sobbing into the ground.

Snot rolled from her nose into her mouth, her vision gone as her tears endlessly overflowed down her cheeks.

In the far recesses of her mind, she understood her dress was now dirty, smudged from where she knelt, but they were scuffs that could be cleaned, removed.

Unlike the stain of blood forever pressed into her memory.

Eli's blood.

Tanwen screamed into the empty woods, the sound hoarse and broken. She pounded her fists into the ground, sharp rocks breaking apart skin as she tried to release the pain that was poisoning her veins.

Dead.

He was dead.

Eli.

Murdered.

Taken.

Her friend.

She had failed him.

Left him alone.

Brought him into danger.

Tanwen's renewed surge of despair robbed her of breath, her weeping unceasing as her heart continued to be cut and pulled and shredded.

It wasn't until she was on the verge of slipping into an inescapable darkness that they appeared.

The animals emerged from above and below, diverse shadows moving in Tanwen's blurry periphery.

Soft fur burrowed beneath her hands, covered her arms; cold scales wrapped around her torso; wings pressed supportively along her shoulders; beaks nuzzled into her neck; bugs hummed soothingly beside her ear.

We have you, the creatures told her. *We have you.*

Her magic had called them, brought them. Her only companions that had ever consistently carried her through the dark. Their loyalty remained, even here within palace grounds.

Tanwen's skin hummed as her magic surged through her veins, a pulse of recognition, of gratitude for their offered support.

We have you, their chorus repeated. *We will always have you, friend.*

Tanwen's cries intensified then, but the arrival of animals did not cease.

They continued to gather until she did not know where she started and they began.

They encircled Tanwen, their feathers, fur, and scales intertwining to cover her like armor, as if to contain her shattering soul.

48

Something strange was occurring in the orchards.

Though Zolya would hardly have noticed if it hadn't been for Tanwen running into the grove of trees a few moments prior.

He saw her hurrying out of the palace from where he was hiding beneath the shadow of a pediment on the western rooftop. After a recent meeting with the royal treasury, Zolya had been desperate for a reprieve. The conversation had concluded as they always did: poorly.

But those worries dissipated as a panic seized him. Zolya leaped into the air, wings splayed wide, rushing to where Tanwen had disappeared.

Was she hurt? In trouble?

His unease grew as he neared the edge of the palace grounds.

Above the canopy of trees, an odd array of fowl gathered in the sky. Like vultures they circled, though their pattern of flight seemed protective rather than predatory.

As he approached, a few dived at him, a screeching and flapping attack.

Zolya banked to the left before the right, dodging the usually docile macaws and parakeets.

What is going on? he thought, his concern rising as he landed at the edge of the tree line.

He eyed the entrance, uncertainty rooting his feet.

The day was slipping into evening, Ré's light painting the trunks a burnt orange while pushing shadows into the bowels of the grove.

The royal orchard was a place very few Volari roamed. And for good reason. The short fruit trees gave little berth for wings such as his. In fact, Zolya couldn't remember if he had ever been inside.

Because why would he ever want to be?

But now Tanwen was in there, somewhere, and potentially in trouble.

A mournful scream echoed from within.

Zolya's heart stilled before racing.

Tanwen!

He tucked in his wings and dipped beneath the trees.

The air instantly grew cooler, his surroundings quiet. The sweet scent of ripe fruit filled his lungs.

The orchard had been planted in neat but tight rows, leaving the view of the sky nothing but a thin line above reaching branches.

He would not be able to take flight from here, not without the threat of injuring his wings.

Claustrophobia pressed down on Zolya, but he forced himself to hurry down the path, his footfalls purposeful, eyes on alert.

"Tanwen?" he called into the fading light. "Tanwen?"

He was met with no answer, his worry growing.

Since their encounter in the hall, Zolya had made a conscious effort to avoid crossing paths with her. He had gone as far as to avoid visiting Azla and disregarded his usual attendance at evening court functions in case Tanwen would be present among the staff.

It had become clear it was dangerous to be anywhere near Tanwen, especially when in public. He couldn't help but be drawn to her whenever they were in the same vicinity, and he worried about how long it would be before someone else noticed where his focus lay—the wrong someone.

Scorched Skies

But currently, Tanwen was clearly in distress, and this he could not ignore.

As he ventured deeper into the orchard, his pace faltered as he noticed who else traveled alongside him. Animals—a strange mix of foxes, hares, chipmunks, lizards, and snakes—wove forward within the forest. Birds darted from tree to tree or flew down the path, all seemingly driven by a singular purpose, headed toward a specific spot in the middle of the grove.

Their behavior was disconcerting, unnatural, and reeking of magic, of possession, yet there was no lacing of celestial energy filling the air, no hint that a High God might be present.

With his ever-rising disquiet, Zolya's defenses flared, his hand coming to rest at the knife hilt along his hip.

He followed the procession of animals, continuing to search the trees for any sign of Tanwen, but still there was no trace of her.

Where are you? he thought. *Where did you go?*

As he ducked beneath a low branch, he stepped into a new lane before coming to a halt.

There, not ten paces away, was where the animals gathered.

They collided, creating a single chaotic swarm, a rising and moving mound of scales and fur and feathers. Overhead, additional birds collected within the treetops while other creatures fanned out along the ground, a carpet of life encircling a monstrous form.

Zolya's heart stopped, the air robbed from his lungs.

He had no idea what he was witnessing, but it was all at once frightening and mesmerizing.

As though the creature knew it was no longer among kin, the mass moved, shifting to face him.

Zolya took a step back, muscles tense as he tightened the grip on his sheathed knife.

But then his surroundings blew apart, and beneath the tapestry of animals, familiar green eyes met his.

Zolya stood a statue, frozen, unbelieving.

This was not happening.

This was not real.

Slowly she stood, and as she did, the animals slid from her as though rainwater, pooling by her feet. There they remained, a pedestal of support as every eye became trained on him, watching, guarding, warding off.

But the only gaze Zolya cared for was hers.

Tanwen.

Uncovered.

Revealed.

A goddess standing amid her loyal subjects.

She looked wild. Her dark hair was a mass around her shoulders, her white peplos and pale skin stained and dirty. Devastation was etched into her features, tearstains disturbing the smudges on her cheeks, which sent a slashing pain through Zolya's chest. But even in her despair, she held her head high, her horns appearing regal as she looked at him with a dangerous defiance.

Zolya was transfixed, consumed.

She had never been so breathtaking, so powerful, so perfect.

But within Zolya's awe came a quickly forming realization as he eyed the creatures encircling Tanwen's feet. Her connection to them was unnatural, a godly gift.

Understanding solidified like a sick lump in his gut, a dreaded truth.

Tanwen appeared to read his thoughts, for she waited, gaze unwavering, forcing him to say it.

"You are Mütra." The words were rough and finite as they left his lips.

"I am," Tanwen replied.

The world crumbled beneath Zolya's feet.

From where he remained under a canopy of leaves, hidden from the watchful gazes of gods, he fought a silent war within his heart; decades of molded obedience, fundamental teachings, collided with personal beliefs and wants and desires.

Tanwen was Mütra.

Her existence was deemed wrong, evil, by society, her magic a mutiny against the crown.

And she was on Galia, had somehow escaped detection to serve within the palace.

Serve the princess.

Act as her healer.

And then there was Zolya.

Who had kissed her, tasted her, *wanted* her. It was beyond intolerable to his people.

To be a Süra sympathizer was one offense, but that of Mütra . . . Unfathomable.

Especially for Zolya, a Volari prince, next in line for the throne.

There would be no leniency shown to him if it ever became known, only a clear-cut punishment of death for such sedition against his father, the king, and his kingdom.

But with a terrifying clarity, Zolya realized he did not care.

All he cared for in that moment was Tanwen. Tanwen, who was obviously in distress, hurt, broken. By whom or what, Zolya was desperate to know, to fix, to avenge.

She may have been Mütra, but she was still *her*, still the woman he loved.

The realization rocked him back a step, a shock vibrating down his spine.

He loved her.

Tanwen noted his retreat, misunderstood it, for pain shone in her gaze before hardening her features. "Will you kill me here?" she asked, tone eerily calm, "or have the slitting of an abomination's throat be a spectacle?"

It was as if she had plunged a knife through Zolya's heart. "You are not an abomination," he said.

Her green eyes flashed, incredulous. "And yet your kind says I am." *Your kind.*

Another cleaver between them.

"You are *not* an abomination," he repeated.

"Then what am I?" she challenged. "What is the product of a forbidden union?"

The answer came to him easily. "A miracle."

And gods, was it true.

Zolya had been surrounded by power and beauty his entire life, but none of it was as real or as pure as what he was witnessing now, with Tanwen. She was a marvel. What should be impossible made possible. Her magic was unique, her blood a mixing of soil and sky, of two pantheons of gods. She was a miracle because she represented the unity of a millennia-old divide.

Tanwen drew in an unsteady breath, her gaze widening with her shock from his answer.

Zolya witnessed her hard veneer crack, and with it she revealed a delicate, raw woman beneath.

His body was seized in agony.

Let me hold you, he silently pleaded.

Instinctively, Zolya stepped closer, but Tanwen's protective barrier of animals reacted swiftly. Snakes lunged, fangs bared; foxes growled; and birds swooped down.

Zolya found himself in a rare situation, shielding himself from danger.

As if a silent whip had been cracked, the grove stilled, the creatures severing their attack.

Zolya met Tanwen's gaze, apprehension and admiration filling his chest. He knew she had commanded them, controlled them. Told them to stand down.

Incredible.

"Tanwen," he began gently, a tentative outreach so as not to scare her away. "Tell me what has happened. Are you hurt? Why have you been crying?"

Surprise momentarily danced across her features. "That is what you wish to know right now? After what I admitted to."

"It's the only thing that matters."

Silence stretched as Tanwen wrestled to take in his reply. It was evident her trust in others was nonexistent—no doubt for good reason—but *gods* how he was desperate for her to trust him. Believe him.

Her being Mütra was inconsequential in this moment.

"Don't do that," she eventually warned.

"Don't do what?"

"Be kind." Her voice wavered, emotion thick.

"Why?" he asked, brows furrowed.

"It makes it worse."

"I don't understand."

"No, you wouldn't." It was less an agreement than an accusation.

I don't understand.

No, you wouldn't.

Their exchange echoed through Zolya, his comprehension finally settling. Despite her menagerie of guards, Tanwen appeared alone then, lonely in the growing darkness creeping into the orchard.

Just like when he had found her unaccompanied outside the forest of Zomyad.

Alone walking the halls of the palace.

Removed from the other servants heading toward the pavol pitch.

Her life must have been a solitary one, filled with constant suffering, continued suffering, knowing that what she was—what she could not help being—was considered an offense, one to be eradicated. Did she have anyone whom she could confide in? Trust?

Not many, he assumed, especially when a heavy payment of gem was tied to revealing her secret.

Kept secrets and I are very well acquainted.

Tanwen's words, which had been an oath at the time, now rang out with new meaning, the tragedy of them for her survival.

A pain surged through Zolya's veins as he realized that Tanwen had been forced to bury her true self her entire life.

Like me.

The startling thought came quickly. Zolya would *never* have said he suffered like Mütra—roaming a world that hunted them—but he knew inherently the need to disguise one's truth. The necessity of it for self-preservation.

He was the heir to a kingdom that was bloated with privilege and vile behavior, abided laws he silently abhorred, and wished for a future for Cādra that looked nothing like its present. He was ashamed of his father and the legacy of oppression he was to inherit.

But none of this he could openly share or act upon, not as a prince still beneath the mighty thumb of a tyrannical king. The Volari ways were centuries deep and tied to the desires of selfish, fickle gods.

"Tanwen, please." He tried again. "I know I cannot make right the challenges you've faced in life, but I need you to understand, I am not your enemy."

A cold laugh escaped Tanwen, her green eyes shining with incredulity. "You, sire, are the very definition of my enemy."

"No," he rebuked, his frustration rising. "That is my father."

She stiffened, a dozen thoughts flooding her features. "Perhaps, but it is still you who obeys him."

"I am not obeying him now." Zolya kept his gaze tethered to hers, allowed her to see the truth of his words. He would not hurt her. He could *never* hurt her.

"You are cruel." Her statement was barely a whisper, but it still punched through Zolya's chest.

"Excuse me?" He drew back.

"How dare you say such a thing to me," Tanwen seethed, her ire rising. "How dare you promise me this false sense of security."

"It is *not* false."

"No?" she challenged, chin tilting up. "Then tell me, what sanctuary do I have beyond this moment here with you? What protections can you promise me tomorrow? Or the next day? What will happen when someone else learns of what I am? Will you be able to stop your father's decree? Or will you remain as silent and still as you did for Lady Eonya and Brilyard's execution?"

It was a low aim but still met its mark.

Zolya was a powerless prince.

"That is unfair," Zolya rebuked.

"Unfair?" Tanwen's brows snapped up. "What is unfair, *sire*, is that since my birth I have been made aware of what I am and what I am not supposed to be. For my entire life, I have watched Mütra be slain. Their only guilt to have been born, as I was born—at the mercy of others' decisions. I have watched their throats be cut, their bodies beaten and hung as they fought for their final breaths. And do you want to know the worst part of those moments? Every single time I found myself ashamed to be grateful it was not me. So you say I am a miracle"—her gaze was searing as it clung to his—"and yet I know of no other miracles who grow up terrified, regretful of their existence, and constantly aware of the bounty on their heads. You say I am a miracle, but the only miracle I see is that I was able to survive for as long as I have."

Zolya held no reply.

He was lost.

Drowning.

Her agony was palpable, penetrating.

How dare he think he understood her pain.

Tanwen had said he was cruel, and she was right.

Zolya had done terrible things.

Obeyed unjust orders.

Remained silent, compliant, when he instead wished to scream his protest.

His cruelty lay in his inaction to erect change for what he believed was right and wrong.

He had been preoccupied trying to survive his own dangerous game played against his father, maneuvering in a world meant to please his king and his High Gods.

Shame was a hot branding to his chest, one that burned further when he saw the curling resentment growing in Tanwen's gaze.

"So I beg of you," she went on, "do *not* promise me safety when I know there is none for Mütra, *especially* here. Or have you forgotten about the inventor's son who you offered up to the king? You knew he was Mütra, yet *still* you stole him away to Galia knowing what torture would await him. If you held any empathy for my kind, you would have left him behind in that glen in Zomyad."

Her voice broke on the last sentence, a wavering of fury and further despair.

Zolya frowned, a cold slip of unease down his spine. "How did you know I found them in a glen?"

"I—" Tanwen hesitated, realizing her misstep. Her complexion grew paler. "The story of you tracking and trapping the inventor is famous," she reasoned quickly.

Zolya regarded her a long moment as his creeping sense of disquiet continued to slither awake in his veins. In an odd flash, he was back in the field outside Zomyad, Tanwen kneeling by his feet, her features now uncannily familiar. In a blink, a different face was suddenly in front of him. Same green eyes and dark hair and complexion. Same defiant glint and bitter resolve.

Gabreel.

Zolya took a sharp breath in, heartbeat storming against his ribs.

No, he thought desperately. *No.*

But then he drew forward the image of the Mütra Tanwen spoke of, the inventor's son, who, he realized now, had an uncanny resemblance to Tanwen.

Like a broken bone resetting, the connection forcibly snapped into place. Agony barreled through Zolya.

How had he not seen it sooner?

Gabreel. Aberthol. Tanwen.

Tanwen Mütra.

Tanwen being his connection to finding Gabreel.

Gabreel in Zomyad, standing within the open glen, glancing back into the forest as though to find another who might have been watching.

She was that someone.

And then, soon after, Tanwen's sudden appearance on Galia.

Why are you here? Zolya had asked her that first night at the palace party.

Because I must be.

With the same ability Zolya held for knowing lies, he saw with certainty this truth.

Tanwen was Gabreel's child, his *other* child, his daughter, Mütra, and she had followed him here.

But why?

Because I took them. Zolya's answer was clear and horrifying.

He had taken her father and brother.

Had taken a Mütra to the king.

To be studied, tortured.

Zolya stumbled back, legs growing unsteady.

A flash of concern shone in Tanwen's features, but she quickly recovered, mask of ire back in place.

And Zolya could not blame her.

How could she stand to be near him?

How could she allow him to touch her, kiss her, after what he had done? What he was still allowing to *still* be done to her father and brother?

Or had everything between them been pretense? Get near him to get near them.

Zolya would not fault her if it had been, and yet it did not dull the eviscerating grief tightening around his heart. Zolya's magic surged, chaotic, in his veins, a gathering of confusion and anger and regret.

"I must go," Zolya said in a rush, a suffocating force bearing down on his chest.

He no longer trusted himself here, with her. He was a brewing storm wishing to destroy the sins of his past, the tragic reality of his present.

He was in love with a woman whose family he had imprisoned, who was clearly here with ulterior motives, and who, in his mind, could not possibly love him. Which should be a blessing, should be a relief, because under no circumstance could they be together.

Zolya turned and fled.

Tanwen did not stop him.

49

Tanwen was numb as she gazed down at Eli's open-air pyre. The small flames flickered in the night's warm breeze from where she and Huw stood alone along the outskirts of the palace grounds.

Eli's tiny body had been wrapped in white cloth, purified, and prepared to meet Maryth in her Eternal River. His form was no bigger than a pine cone where he rested atop the sticks, the fire quickly devouring and charring everything black.

Tears welled in Tanwen's eyes, blurring her vision, the rise of her grief finally returning as the weight of her loss settled heavily upon her heart.

Her friend was gone.

Her constant comfort.

Eli, who had been such a joy in her life, who had been integral in finding her father and brother and planning their escape, would now never see it through.

Which only added to the pressure for her to succeed, for his sacrifice to have not been in vain.

But in vain it might certainly be after what she had revealed to Zolya.

Tanwen bit her lower lip, keeping at bay the sob she felt rising.

She had cried enough today. Enough for a lifetime.

The only relief to her agony had come with Huw.

He had prepared everything.

It had been dark by the time Tanwen had returned to the palace, the servants' quarters thick with whispers as she entered. What had transpired in the atenté dormitory clearly had made its way to the entire staff, her disheveled return not helping matters. But it was easy to ignore their stares and soft mutters when nothing mattered.

Everything Tanwen had held tightly to her chest was now cleaved open, revealed, leaving her fatally bleeding out. Her moment with Zolya in the orchard was but a distant haze in her memory. Another arrow lodged in her pincushion of despair. Tanwen knew she should have been more frightened, worried, regretful, but currently she was empty of caring.

Tanwen had walked like a specter through the halls, no hint of Gwyn or her gang nearby. A blessing, given Tanwen no longer felt in control of her reactions or her words.

Eventually she had found herself returned to the scene of the crime.

But it was now pristine, no evidence of the earlier nightmare. Tanwen had stood by her bed, staring down, unblinking.

"I got you a new mattress." A soft voice had come from behind her. "And changed your bedding."

Tanwen had turned, finding Huw.

In his palms he cradled a small wrapped form.

Eli.

Tanwen's stomach had clenched, her breath stolen with her flash of agony.

"Let's get you cleaned up," said Huw. "And then we'll give him a proper send-off."

Tanwen had allowed Huw to bathe and re-dress her, his ministrations gentle and caring, before he shuffled them outside.

Tanwen blinked, finding herself back where she stood behind a large hedge with Huw beside her, watching as Eli's small pyre cast a warm glow, filling the somber air.

With trembling hands, she placed a small buttered roll onto the fire, a final tribute to Eli's favorite food. The flames licked hungrily at the added fuel, as if Eli himself were devouring the offering.

It was both reassuring and painful.

In the following quiet, Tanwen whispered a silent farewell to her friend, thanking him for everything and apologizing for all of it. She did not know if a soul continued to feel when within the Eternal River, but Tanwen hoped he was at peace.

She would carry their pain for them both.

Eventually, Eli's pyre faded to dying embers, and with it Tanwen turned.

"Where are you going?" asked Huw, who remained behind.

"To bring closure to another loss," she answered.

Tanwen pressed into the night and headed toward the tunnel that would lead her to the prince.

50

Cautiously, Tanwen slipped through the hidden door.

The small glow from her flickering candle barely illuminated the empty, dark marble washroom. The only other light was that of Maja and Parvi, which streamed in, white and gold, from the skylight overhead.

Before Tanwen could fully adjust to the dimness, a sudden force pinned her against the cold stone wall. Her candle fell from her hand, snuffed out, as a sharp gasp escaped her.

In the shadows, Zolya's eyes glinted with ferocity as he pressed a knife against her throat, his grip firm and unyielding. For a moment, panic surged through Tanwen.

This is it, she thought.

This was how he would right his earlier wrong, how he would kill the Mütra. But then recognition dawned in Zolya's gaze, and he recoiled as if stung by his own actions, releasing her from his grasp.

"Tanwen," he breathed. "What are you doing here?"

His open robe revealed his shirtless torso and low-slung trousers, his white wings half-expanded at his back. His hair fell to his shoulders, tousled as though he had been disturbed from slumber. Zolya stood before her, a temptation.

"I need to know what you'll do," said Tanwen, forcing her voice to be steady, unmoved by the vision of him.

"Do?" he questioned, brows pinched.

"About me being Mütra."

Zolya regarded her a long moment, a dozen thoughts dancing within his gaze, before he sheathed his blade, then laid it on a nearby table. "I'm not going to do anything," he said.

Despite his response, Tanwen felt no relief, only more confused dread. "Why not?" she asked.

Zolya looked at her evenly. "Would you like me to do something about it?"

"No," she replied quickly. "I just don't understand . . . why you won't."

"I already told you why," he said, his tone carrying an edge of exhaustion. "I am not your enemy."

She hesitated, wishing, *wanting*, to believe him, but her years of watching what happened to the Mütra who were exposed left her in a state of perpetual distrust.

"Though I understand why you would think I was," Zolya added after a beat, features pained, "after I took your family from you."

The room warped and bent, his words knocking the air from Tanwen's lungs.

"I know," Zolya continued, gaze penetrating. "I know that Gabreel is your father."

Tanwen shook her head with disbelief, taking a retreating step toward the hidden pathway at her back. "How?" she breathed.

"You rather gave it away in the orchard," he replied.

Her hand involuntarily went to her mouth, trapping her gasp. *No,* thought Tanwen, grief and guilt clawing through her gut. *No. I've ruined everything.*

She had not meant to say so much earlier in the grove, but her anger and agony regarding Eli and everything else weighing her down had overwhelmed her. Tanwen had been desperate for a release, and lashing out at Zolya had been the only nearby option.

"I don't know how I didn't see it earlier," Zolya admitted, redrawing Tanwen's attention to where he studied her beneath a stream of moonlight, his white wings and hair aglow. "You share an uncanny resemblance with them, especially your brother."

"Aberthol is my twin." The words were out of her mouth before she knew what she was saying.

Stop it! Tanwen silently scolded herself. *Haven't I done enough damage?* She couldn't bear the thought of giving Zolya any more leverage. And yet . . . deep down, a part of her held on to the belief that he wouldn't exploit such information against her.

And in all honesty, it was a bloody relief to cling to such faith, to finally release all she had kept hidden. Zolya now knew everything, all parts of who she was and was not supposed to be. No one besides her family and her animals had ever known her truth.

Zolya now did, and he had laid down his knife.

Sheathed it and set it aside.

I am not your enemy, he had told her.

But then what was he to her? What could he be?

Tanwen was Mütra and the daughter of the inventor he had stolen away for the king, for his father.

"Tanwen," said Zolya, her name a whisper echoing in the quiet room. "I'm so sorry."

As she noted Zolya's clear pain and guilt etched into his features, haunting his blue gaze, her breathing grew shallow.

His apology pricked open the well of grief Tanwen had desperately been attempting to smother. Everything she had been trying to contain regarding the loss of Eli, her brother's torture, her withering father, her mother alone and so far away, overflowed.

Her family, the only safety net she had ever claimed, was splintering.

Tanwen's throat tightened, tears gathering behind her eyes.

"What I have done . . ." Zolya paused with his hard swallow. "It's unforgivable. But I will do whatever I can to make it right."

"Free my father and brother," she challenged, begged.

The groove between Zolya's brows deepened, a look of remorse. "You know I don't have that power."

Tanwen scoffed, incredulous. "You are the prince; you have power."

"Yes, but not enough to reverse a king's command."

"Then how could you *ever* make this right?" Tanwen seethed, turning from him. Her chest felt cleaved open.

I will not cry. I will not cry. I will not cry.

Tanwen cried.

She let loose loud sobs that she tried muffling with her hands.

A breeze drew her attention to Zolya, now a graze away; he hovered, unsure, the heat of him pressing against her exposed skin along her back. She could sense his need to embrace her, but she understood that given the nature of his apology and the things he couldn't change, it would be completely inappropriate. He had kidnapped her family, put their lives at the mercy of the king, a king who tortured her brother, who forced her father to erect a new mine despite what it would cost future Süra.

And yet still . . . while Zolya had committed his sin, Tanwen *hated* understanding it had not been done by his own desires or beliefs. He had been compelled to follow orders beyond his control.

You are my enemy, she had accused him.

No, he had corrected, *that is my father.*

Gods, why was this so bloody complicated?

Tanwen drew in a steadying breath, forcing her composure as she wiped at her eyes.

Zolya was right.

The king was the problem. For many.

But not for long, she thought, though a sting of guilt followed.

Since losing Eli, she had nearly forgotten what she had done that morning.

She had helped in a plot to kill the king.

As she had agreed to do for a Low God.

Obeying orders, just like Zolya.

Tanwen's hands weren't exactly clean either.

But she had already accepted her involvement. Had been firm that Zolya could never know the sin she was part of.

Tanwen was already treading a precarious edge with what Zolya did know about her. This could send her toppling over, with Zolya being the one to push.

Hesitantly, she turned.

Zolya loomed over her, a wall of contained power mixed with clear worry. His muscles were taut beneath his open robe, as if he struggled to keep himself from touching her.

Tanwen fought her own desire to fold into his offered strength, allow herself to be warmed by his heat. Despite the chasm of their circumstances, there forever appeared a stubborn bridge, connecting them, inviting them to cross over toward each other.

"I must ask," Zolya began slowly, "was that your intention in coming here, then, to the palace? To free your brother and father?"

Tanwen's silence seemed to give him his answer.

Zolya frowned. "You know it's impossible to escape Galia."

"It's hard," she corrected. "But not impossible."

Zolya shook his head, almost pityingly. "Even so, my father will not stop hunting you."

"I have hidden my entire life," Tanwen reasoned, chin lifting. "I have no issue hiding for the remainder of it."

A shadow played across Zolya's features. "Do you even know where your father and brother are being kept?" he asked.

"In an old groundskeeper's cottage along the northwest perimeter of palace grounds."

"So you have a plan," he said, a statement, not a question.

"I do."

Zolya remained quiet, pensive, which only drew Tanwen's uncertainty.

"Will you stop me?" she asked.

His gaze bore into hers. "No," he said, "but I also cannot help you."

"Not stopping me is helping me," Tanwen explained.

Zolya allowed her declaration to fill the washroom, the truth of it heating the small gap between them.

Yes, his silence seemed to say. *I know.*

Tanwen's pulse rushed, her skin aching with her longing.

If she leaned a breath closer, they'd touch.

By some miracle she remained still.

"When will you attempt this?" he asked, gaze dipping to her lips.

"Soon," she exhaled, heat rushing through her body. She wavered on whether to share more, but it was as if a dam had been broken and all her truths were pouring free. "During the evening of the next full moons."

Zolya's surprise visibly flared. "That is at week's end."

"Yes."

"The princess's prewedding celebration is that night."

"It is."

Understanding dawned in his features, of how perfect the opportunity was, given the palace would be thoroughly preoccupied that evening.

Zolya's jaw set along with his nod. "While I cannot be the one to physically free your family, I can do what I can to help make your escape easier."

A shock of disbelief washed over Tanwen. "How?"

"I will find ways."

Tanwen regarded him for a beat, a warmth of gratitude filling her lungs.

I can do what I can to help.

"So you are helping me," she said.

Zolya's gaze did not waver from hers. "Tanwen." Her name spoken on a gruff whisper. "If you needed me to tear down the stars from the heavens, I would. Your safety and happiness are all I care for. To not be able to fly your family from Galia myself is maddening, but you must understand, having my involvement known would not help either of us after you . . . leave." He forced out the last word as if it were an unbearable thought. "I can better keep you and your family safe if the king believes I am still loyal to his demands of Gabreel. So what I *can* do, I will do quietly."

Tanwen worked to keep her expression neutral as a waterfall of emotions cascaded through her: humility for his clear devotion toward her, desire to ease his worried brow, and guilt that soon the king would not be of issue.

So long as the princess uses your stone, said a niggling voice of worry in Tanwen's mind.

At the intruding thought, she resisted shifting.

While Tanwen did not know if the princess was going to use the poison, let alone use it when she'd prefer her to—at the night of the prewedding celebration—those were worries for another time. Preferably a time when Tanwen was not standing before the prince, so raw and wanting and seen.

"Thank you," she managed. "Your help . . . it proves what you have said."

"And what is that?" asked Zolya.

Tanwen held his stare. "That you are not my enemy."

Zolya's features twisted with clear remorse. "Tanwen . . . ," he started before stopping himself.

"Yes?" she pushed.

"I'm sorry this could not be different."

This. Us.

Tanwen swallowed past the lump forming in her throat, did her best to ignore the renewed pain raking across her heart. "Yes," she agreed. "But perhaps one day it will be."

When you are king.

Zolya seemed to hear her unsaid words, a determined spark lighting his gaze.

"Yes, perhaps," he repeated, eyes running the length of her.

Tanwen was on fire, her nerve endings burning, screaming for her to reach up and touch him. For him to reach down and touch her.

"We could . . . ," Tanwen ventured before pausing, her fear of how intense her feelings were for this man becoming overwhelming.

"We could what?" questioned Zolya, swaying ever closer, ever tempting.

"We could allow things to be different tonight," Tanwen forced out.

Zolya grew still, unbreathing, as his eyes darkened with his mix of desire and uncertainty. *Are you sure?* he seemed to ask.

Tanwen had never been more certain of anything in her life.

Amid all the pain of today and what surely awaited them tomorrow, Tanwen wished only to have one last slip of reprieve. And have it with the man who had embraced her for who she was—Mütra—and had not cared. Who knew what she was planning—to free her father and brother—and would not stop her. Who would do what he could to help. To protect. Despite the threat Zolya might represent as the prince of Galia, a kidar, and Volari, she had never felt so safe in her entire life, standing here, alone with him in his chambers.

Zolya was the sanctuary she had longed for all her life.

The home she had fought to build and keep.

He stood gazing down at her, seeing all of her, and remained marveling.

Tanwen reached up and dragged Zolya down to her lips.

51

There was nothing sweet or tender in the way Zolya kissed her.

It was an act of letting go, giving in to what they each knew was forbidden.

Tanwen was on fire as Zolya's hands left trails of heat as they wrapped around her waist, forging them together, possessing.

She had never felt more powerful, emboldened by the way he desired her.

Tanwen let out an encouraging groan as Zolya pressed her back to the cold stone wall. It was a shocking contrast to his blanketing warmth.

His mouth worked over hers like that of a parched man finally finding water, greedy.

Tanwen let out a startled breath as he effortlessly lifted her legs to wrap around his hips. Zolya's grip on her backside was supportive and kneading. Tanwen moaned as waves of pleasure pulsed from her core, his need palpable as he pressed against her.

Tanwen's dress had spilled open, leaving his trousers their only barrier. It was cruel and maddening and delicious.

"*Gods*," Zolya muttered. "Kissing you again has consumed my thoughts."

He claimed her lips once more, took long drags that sent Tanwen spinning. If he hadn't been holding her upright, she would have collapsed to the floor, his ministrations weakening her strength with each caress.

Tanwen splayed her hands against Zolya's chest, slipped fingers beneath his silken robe to grip his wide shoulders. Zolya curled his wings around where he held her against the wall. The shelter of his feathered canopy heightened Tanwen's sense of security, enabling her to surrender herself, kiss by kiss.

Zolya slid his mouth to her throat, and she angled her head away, allowing him better access. He hummed his approval before lifting one of her breasts to spill over the neck of her dress.

"You are perfection," he groaned, admiring her fullness, his gaze the deepest blue.

As he kept her lifted in one hand, he massaged her breast with his other before bending to take her nipple into his mouth.

The hot pinch shot straight between her legs.

Tanwen called out his name, fingers tangling in his hair as she arched deeper into him, rubbing, squirming, wanting.

"By the twin moons," Zolya growled, spinning them around and quickly carrying her from the washroom into his bedchambers.

The curtains to his veranda were closed, the only light coming from a flaming bowl in the far corner, which sent a warm glow across the room.

Gently, Zolya laid her on his bed, the sheets cool and silky and promising against her skin.

In an impatient rush they both gripped and pulled and tugged at each other's clothes, soon both bare for the other to appreciate.

And *gods* was there much for Tanwen to appreciate.

Zolya was carved perfection where he stood at the edge of his bed. His brown skin smooth, his shoulders broad and strong from his command over his wings. His waist was tapered, stomach chiseled.

Tanwen's gaze slid lower, anticipation building in her belly as she drank in his fullness, ready, aching.

She watched him watching her, admiring her as she lay stretched out in his bed. His gaze was liquid heat, glazed with desire as he met her stare. Slowly, he took himself in hand, working long pumps over his shaft.

Tanwen nearly came undone right then.

She squeezed her legs together, trying to quell the painful throb building.

She wanted him.

Badly.

Summoning a boldness she hadn't realized she possessed, Tanwen gradually parted her legs until they were splayed wide open.

A maddening groan slid from Zolya before he was above her.

Bare skin was deliciously pressed to bare skin as he kissed her and licked down her throat before sliding down to suck one of her nipples and then the other into his mouth. He then continued lower, dipping himself between her legs.

There Zolya hovered, waited, his hot breath teasing her opening.

His searing gaze collided with hers. "May I?" he asked.

Tanwen almost laughed. "Gods, yes."

His grin was pure evil before he pressed his mouth to her.

Stars erupted in Tanwen's vision, and she collapsed against the mattress. She moaned as ecstasy coursed through her veins, her fingers gripping his sheets.

There was pressure of a finger sliding inside her before another, Zolya unceasing in his attention to pull out every sliver of her bliss. In a dizzying swirl of groaning his name and tangling her fingers into his hair, keeping him exactly where she needed him, Tanwen came undone. It felt like an eternity until all the pieces of her finally gathered, collecting to re-form where she lay panting on his bed.

As she blinked back to the room, she caught him watching her, looking very pleased with himself. Zolya pressed gentle kisses to the inside of her thigh. "Welcome back," he rumbled, his smile making him even more breathtaking.

Tanwen mirrored his grin with her own.

Then she was pushing herself to all fours, guiding Zolya back to stand at the edge of his bed. He eyed her curiously before he let out a hiss as she took his length into her mouth.

Tanwen was resolved to bring him as much pleasure as he had brought her.

She cupped his balls as she worked over him, drawing back to lick around the tip of his shaft.

"*Tanwen*," he gasped. Zolya tore her away, lifting her into his arms. "I need you," he said, features almost pained with his yearning.

"Then take me," she demanded.

A dangerous and delicious glint sparked in his eyes.

Zolya eased her back to his bed, draping himself atop her. His weight was a poultice, his kisses a tonic to fight away the years of loneliness that had chilled her heart. Zolya was giving her a memory to keep her warm when she would soon need to disappear, forever.

But those darkening thoughts were pushed aside as Zolya slowly, achingly entered her.

Tanwen held her breath, fingers gripping his shoulders as he stilled, allowing her to grow accustomed to his size.

The sensation was sharp and full at once, until it became a pleasurable pressure before a maddening one. Tanwen squirmed impatiently, but Zolya did not move.

He held her gaze, a wondrous expression softening his features. "This is your first time." Another of his certainties, but she could hardly lie given what he no doubt felt being inside her.

"Yes," she whispered, a sliver of uncertainty. Not in wanting to lie with him but for what he might think of her never having done this before.

"Tanwen." He said her name reverently as he ran a gentle hand against her cheek. "Why did you not tell me?"

"I want it to be you."

Zolya searched her features, a severity to his stare. "I am honored."

An ache bloomed in Tanwen's chest, one that came from realizing her heart was no longer her own. Zolya now claimed a piece of it. In that moment she understood she was in love with him.

"Zolya," she whispered, nearly begged. For what, she wasn't certain. She knew only that she needed him to move, to distract her from the depths of her feelings that were surfacing.

Zolya appeared to understand, for he began to rock his hips, gently, as he took her mouth in his. It was a tenderness that was almost heartbreaking.

Here he lay with a Mütra and cherished her like a god.

Tears slipped from the corners of her eyes as Zolya worshipped her with every gentle touch of his lips and caress of his fingers.

It was too much. Too devastating in how right she felt, with him.

Tanwen wrapped her legs around Zolya, urging him deeper, faster, as she clung to his taut shoulders. He pulled back so he could look at her as he continued to move, his blue gaze the hottest center of a flame.

Tanwen lay in her tumultuous mix of heartache and arousal, captivated by the sight of him moving above her, thrusting. Zolya's wings were partially unfurled, his brown skin glistening in the dim glow, his white hair falling around his face. His expression brimmed with intense desire as he focused solely on her and her needs. In this moment he was a descendant of Ilustra, come to pleasure her to the near brink of her life.

Tanwen gladly offered herself up as a sacrifice.

Zolya ground into her in deep, long strokes, filling her over and over and over until she felt that glorious building again. Somewhere in the haze of her passion she heard herself moan his name. "Please," she panted. "Yes, *there*," she pleaded.

"Gods," Zolya cursed, grunted, before leaning back down to suck one of her nipples, hand cupping her breast. She whimpered at the delicious sensation.

Tanwen became untethered.

Zolya was everywhere, his heat and scent and sounds.

But still, she needed more, needed him never to stop.

With a cry, Tanwen crested into her euphoria, soared into the sun that was Zolya's claim over her body. Tanwen became nothing but light and heat until she fell, liquid fragments hitting his sheets.

Zolya pulled himself free, and she ached with the sudden absence of him.

But then his warmth was felt on her belly as he spilled his seed, the low grunts of his pleasure vibrating through the mattress.

Zolya collapsed at her side, each of them panting, satiated.

He laced their fingers together, his mouth pressed to her shoulder. A soft kiss.

Tanwen smiled, chest swelling with her happiness.

Until a crack of pain splintered the moment, reality setting in.

This is temporary, she had to remind herself. No matter what they felt for each other, they could never be together. And not merely because of who they were but because Tanwen soon would be gone. The next full moons were in a week. Princess Azla's wedding neared and with it her and her family's escape.

Zolya slid from the bed, momentarily distracting her thoughts. Tanwen watched him disappear into his washroom, then return with a soft towel he used to clean her. As he did, he met her stare, an endearing smile playing on his lips.

Tanwen was suddenly struck by the strangeness of the moment. Here was a prince attending to a servant. But when they were together like this, alone—no world to shove them into societal roles—Zolya made her feel not just equal but superior.

He rejoined her in the bed, pulling the covers atop them. Tanwen turned and nuzzled into his warmth. They lingered in the tranquil silence of the night, Zolya gently tracing his fingertips over her collarbone.

"Will you tell me about your magic?" he asked, eventually breaking the quiet.

Tanwen shifted to meet his gaze. Zolya's features were open, calm. He was the most relaxed she'd ever seen him. "What do you want to know?"

"How does it work, your connection with animals?"

Tanwen rolled to her back, looking at the distant ceiling, the intricacies of the carved design. "I can communicate with them," she answered. "Not only with thoughts but with feelings. I can sense them, and they can sense me."

"Incredible," he breathed.

She scoffed. "Despite it being forbidden."

Zolya slid a hand to her stomach, a touch of reassurance. "Mütra magic is unique in that no two kinds are alike, and my father fears anything he cannot control," Zolya admitted, drawing her stare. "That is Mütra. The unpredictability of what you each can be is his greatest nightmare, especially when he has maintained power for so long by keeping Cādra exactly as it has always been."

"But nothing truly ever stays the same," Tanwen argued. "Life *is* change."

Zolya regarded her, adoration filling his gaze. "To Volari that is a radical concept. Change terrifies many of us whose lives move not by years, but by decades."

Tanwen had never considered that perspective before. Reluctantly, she understood it, though she still didn't approve of the prejudices it brought. "Does it terrify you?" she asked.

"No," Zolya replied easily, lifting a hand to tuck a lock of her hair behind her ear. "It excites me."

Tanwen couldn't help her smile, her chest filling with an odd sense of pride. This was why she loved him, why he was different from other Volari, and why she knew for certain he would make a great king.

He will bring change, she thought.

But then a prick of uncertainty creased her brow.

"And the High Gods?" asked Tanwen.

"What about them?"

"Don't they also condemn my kind?"

Zolya was quiet for a long moment. "If they do, I have never personally heard their disapproval."

Tanwen drew back, blinking at him as shock vibrated through her veins. "So, you mean . . . this law against Mütra was solely your father's and not handed down by the divine like others say it was?"

"The law was made before my birth," he explained. "The exact genesis of it is unknown to me."

Tanwen was quiet for a long while, absorbing this information. For her entire life she had been persecuted under the belief that no god had wanted her existence, that it was a form of defiance.

What about you would scare a god? Bosyg had wondered.

But here Tanwen was now told she in fact scared only a man—*one* man, the king—because of his fear of the unknown. Though perhaps that was what kept the High Gods quiet regarding King Réol's acts of genocide toward Mütra: they were creatures who thrived on traditions, and Tanwen represented the possibility of change.

"Can I ask you a question now?" Zolya inquired, returning Tanwen's attention to him.

She drank in his beauty as he leaned up on one hand.

Tentatively, Tanwen nodded.

"What happened today?" Zolya asked softly. "Why were you crying in the orchard?"

Tanwen pressed her lips together as her sorrow slowly resurfaced. "I . . . lost a friend," she confessed. "Who was very important to me, but . . . I would rather not talk about them right now."

Concern creased Zolya's brow. "Of course," he said, bringing his arm around her waist. "I'm so sorry for your loss."

"As am I," replied Tanwen.

"What would you like to talk about instead?" Zolya asked, drawing circles around her navel. It sent a warmth feathering over her skin.

"I don't want to talk at all," she admitted.

His mouth curled sinfully as his gaze darkened. "That can be arranged."

Zolya leaned in and kissed her.

It started slow, a languid swim in a lake, before they each gave in to their quickly ascending desire. Tanwen was eternally grateful. She didn't want to think about Eli, or her looming escape, or the uncertain future that awaited them.

She simply wanted to lose herself in Zolya, enjoy him for as long as she could have him.

Zolya seemed of the same mind.

In that moment, they surrendered to each other, forgetting their burdens and responsibilities. Even as Ré's light began to seep through the curtains, casting an unwelcome illumination on their inevitable paths, neither of them acknowledged the new day's approach.

They continued to explore one another, committing to memory every sweet exhale and taste and touch.

As if they both understood this could very well be their final farewell.

52

Zolya decided he was cursed.

All the women whom he cared for in his life were suddenly growing reckless.

"You promised you'd remain calm," Azla protested from where she sat on a settee within her chambers, watching as he paced.

"That's because I didn't think you'd be telling me something so . . . so . . ."

"Imperative," she offered.

"Absurd!" he corrected, spinning to face her.

Zolya was beyond outraged; he was appalled. Or perhaps he was merely stunned.

Stunned that Azla could scheme up something so mad.

And then confess it to him!

"Azla, what you wish to do is"—he lowered his voice—"*treason*. And worse, *murder*. Of our *father*."

"You think I do not understand that?" she retorted, annoyance marring her brow.

The midday sun streamed in through the open veranda at her back, casting a radiant glow on her white wings and braided hair. She sat calmly in a mauve wrap dress, looking poised and innocent.

A farce.

Here lounged a princess who wished to kill the king.

"But it's the only option I have," she reasoned.

Zolya widened his gaze, incredulous. "Is it?"

"*Yes*," Azla pressed before sighing. "Zolya, will you *please* come sit? You must allow me to explain."

He shook his head. "There is no world in which an explanation will condone this thinking."

Gods, he had finally come down from his panic over Tanwen's planned escape, and now this!

His sister-cousin appeared to wish him a heart attack.

Azla pursed her lips, frustration flaring. "*Sit*," she demanded, violently patting the space beside her.

Begrudgingly, Zolya sat.

He had been lured to Azla's chambers under false pretenses. She had sent him an urgent summons, only for him to find an overly sweet yet anxious Azla standing beside a decadent spread of his favorite desserts.

Zolya should have fled right then. He knew a laid trap when he neared one.

But because Azla was Azla and it was difficult to deny her anything, especially his company, Zolya had stayed.

And now he was an accomplice to potential patricide.

Insanity.

Zolya would have laughed if he wasn't so terrified.

"You must understand," Azla began. "We did not come to this conclusion lightly."

"*We?*" Zolya countered, swiveling to look at her. "Wait, no." He held up a hand, stopping Azla's reply. "Never mind. I can assume who your accomplice may be."

Lady Esme—the woman Azla had been with for three decades.

Of course she would be in favor of this plan, a coconspirator. Lady Esme was on the brink of losing the love of her life. To not fight such a fate would be a betrayal to their union and everything they had built together.

People took drastic actions for the ones they loved.

Zolya tensed, an uncomfortable understanding pressing against his chest.

His thoughts briefly drifted back to Tanwen—as they were wont to do. She had sacrificed everything to make her way to Galia in the hope of freeing her father and brother. Was still risking her life in the attempt.

And he was going to help her. Had already begun to in subtle, deft ways.

Despite such action clearly being an act of mutiny against the crown, given their end goal, Zolya had switched out the guards stationed by the cottage where Gabreel and his son were being kept. The soldiers were now his personally trained and loyal men, who would do whatever he asked without question. And his first order had been to show the inventor respect while leaving his child well enough alone.

Zolya doubted he could ever make up for Gabreel's and Aberthol's suffering, but he'd do everything to help Tanwen and her family escape. For he should never have brought them here in the first place.

At the thought of Tanwen leaving, pain plucked with each beat of his heart.

He was going to lose her. If Tanwen succeeded, she would be gone. If she was caught . . .

A shiver ran the length of him, nausea a punch to his gut.

He didn't want to imagine what would happen if she was caught.

Since yesterday morning, Zolya had been in a chaotic swirl of fear and heady daydreaming. His and Tanwen's meeting felt fated, albeit destined for a tragic end. She was quite possibly the *worst* person for him to fall in love with, and yet here he was—transfixed and consumed in his wonderment. The completeness that settled within his heart as he held her, kissed her, listened to her tell him stories from her life and share with him more details of her magic—it left him breathless.

And terrified.

Because he no longer held agency over his emotions.

Tanwen held that power now.

"I *can't* marry him, Zolya." Azla's desperate tone redrew his attention, reawakened the genesis for his wandering thoughts. Azla wished to kill their father to escape from an arranged marriage to an angry god and save her love.

While it was a wildly inappropriate solution, Zolya held compassion for her motives. He himself was committing treason for someone he loved. Of course, without such a drastic outcome.

He hated his father for what he had condemned Azla to, had wished every day since that moment with Orzel in the throne room that he could fix it, save his sister-cousin, but never was *murder* an option in his mind.

"And running would not end the contract of my marriage to Orzel," Azla continued, her features pained. "It would only prolong the inevitable once Father found me and dragged me back. To get rid of one of the signatories is the only guarantee of voiding the agreement. According to our laws, it would make it annulled. The only way to bind it again would be by my next-of-kin guardian." She looked at him pointedly. "Which is you, brother."

Brother.

A well-aimed shot.

Zolya tensed, despising that her manipulation was working. The armor around his heart cracked, but with it came another rise of ire.

"Is this why you summoned me?" he asked coolly. "Confided in me? To have me promise not to re-sign your marriage agreement?"

"I summoned you here because you have always been good to me, Zolya," she explained, features earnest. "You have cared for me when others in your position would have shunned me. I know what my mother did. How her actions were a betrayal to your mother and our queen. I have always wanted to do right by you, Zolya. Have always wanted to make up for the sin of my birth."

Shame deflated a bit of Zolya's rage. "You never needed—"

Azla raised a hand, cutting him off. "I wanted you to know what I am planning," she continued, "and what I intend to go through with because I owe it to you. You are going to be a great king, Zolya." She placed a hand atop his where it rested on his thigh, a resolute gleam in her eyes. "I did not want your moment of ascending the throne to be overshadowed by my actions. I want you to be prepared."

Zolya shook his head. *This can't be real. This can't be happening.*

"I have already thought a great deal about what options I have," she admitted, "but with the wedding at week's end, this is the only one that promises my freedom. *Our* freedom," she added meaningfully. "Also, the way in which it will be done . . . guarantees success."

Zolya held in his wince. "Please." He lifted a hand. "Spare me the details. I already know more than I'd like about this ridiculous scheme."

"It's not *ridiculous*," she argued, sitting back. "It's a necessary action."

Zolya sighed, a heavy weariness pressing against his wings. "Azla," he began slowly, holding her hard stare. "I do not fault you in your desires for retribution. In fact, I understand them, but you have not seen clearly past your own end goal. There are *many* ramifications that will follow such an action and none that help in either of our 'freedoms,' as you say. Our father's rule has been with the support of many at court and that of our gods for centuries. To"—he lowered his voice to a whisper, hating to utter what he would next—"*assassinate a king* will create much instability. Instability and distrust that *I* will have to deal with. You say you do not want my rule to be overshadowed by your actions, but with this path it will be more than overshadowed. A murdered king will be an eclipse to my ascension. It will be questioned and scrutinized beyond a normal passing of a crown. I do not wish to sit on our throne by default," he added, a tight shame filling his chest. "I wish to sit on it because I have earned it."

"And you *have* earned it, Zolya," said Azla, recapturing his hand in hers, a fierceness to her gaze. "You deserve to be king far more than the monster who currently claims the title."

"*Azla,*" Zolya warned. Her boldness was bordering on madness.

"You might not like what I am saying"—she held his hand firm—"but you know, deep down, I am right."

Zolya sat stiffly in his discomfort. Years of trained obedience to his king kicked and snarled at Azla's words. Despite coming to accept that he, indeed, disagreed with many of their father's ways of ruling and that, yes, their father was clearly not a good man, did that still justify his murder? A plot against him from his own children?

You deserve to be king far more than the monster who currently claims the title.

Azla's declaration turned over in his chest, an absorption into his marrow.

Zolya understood that to be a great ruler, his responsibilities went beyond his own desires. The very nature of a king's position was sacrifice—for his people, for the betterment of others.

What sacrifices did his father ever make?

For eight decades, Zolya had witnessed his father sacrifice only others.

At the realization, fury worked like flames over his skin.

And not merely because of how he and Azla had been mistreated by the king. Thoughts of his mother and aunt swam forward. The inventor and his son. All Mütra and every Süra. Those who worked the mines. And even his own people, Volari whom King Réol quickly condemned as Süra sympathizers if they stepped out of line.

King Réol might spout harsh ideals about how a few must be offered up to satisfy the needs of many, but it was only ever his court, Volari aristocrats, who benefited from his brutality. A minuscule number compared to the ocean of souls he'd used to prop them up.

I am not your enemy, he had said to Tanwen. *That is my father.*

And it was true. So much of the suffering in their world *was* because of his father and his endless centuries of oppressive rule.

Zolya was unsure what to make of his turning thoughts, the reasoning he was finding to back Azla's actions. The worst, of course, being that this *would* help his sister as well as those like Tanwen. Mütra, whose lives were blasphemous under his father's rule.

Could this be what the gods wanted for King Réol? If not, surely they would have intervened by now. If they were not stopping Azla and Lady Esme's plans, did that mean they condoned it?

Historically, tyrants had been removed from power before.

Zolya's unease buzzed as he glanced to the open veranda, to Ré's light spilling along the marble tiles.

It was a very risky gamble to assume.

"Despite how fit or unfit I may be as a future ruler," Zolya finally replied, looking back at the princess, "I *do* know this is a very dangerous game you are playing, Azla. What if you get caught? I won't be able to protect you from the consequences."

"Then I suppose I can't get caught," Azla reasoned. "But I am at peace with my fate from whatever outcome occurs. At least this way, I'll be the one responsible for my future rather than at the mercy of another's decision for what they believe it should be. Father has forced us both into a corner for too long, Zolya," she explained, voice hardening. "Into his cage. It is time we break free. We are not his helpless children any longer."

"There is a difference in breaking free from our father and plotting his death," reasoned Zolya.

"The *only* freedom we'll ever have from him is when he's dead."

Zolya stopped breathing as Azla's cold declaration lashed against him.

My gods, he thought, *she really does hate him.*

The silence stretched as he sat assessing the princess, drank in her calm confidence, her unwavering stare, and finally grasped her position.

In Azla's mind, she had nothing to lose. Whether she married Orzel or faced the consequences of her intended actions, her fate was sealed. Her life as she knew it would be over.

She had endured decades of neglect from the king to finally be given the proof that he did not love her and clearly never would. She was a pawn to be played and then discarded.

Why should she not then play her own game?

"There really is no convincing you against this," said Zolya.

"No," replied Azla. "We will go through with this the night of my prenuptial celebration."

Zolya froze.

The night of my prenuptial celebration.

The same night Tanwen was planning her escape.

Zolya's ears began to ring, his breathing growing quick. Depending on when everything happened, this had the potential to help Tanwen further. The chaos that could follow Azla's plan would divert attention from activities at the edge of the palace grounds.

Of course, that chaos was the death of his father.

Zolya held back an aggravated growl. *Why?* he thought, pleaded to any High God who might be listening. *Why are you colliding every part of my life on this night? Why do you test so viciously where my loyalties lie?*

"Zolya," the princess said with concern, seeming to mistake his visible panic for another emotion. "Unless, of course . . . you're thinking of stopping me?"

Azla's words were an eerie echo of Tanwen from the other night.

Will you stop me?

Zolya almost laughed at the cruel irony.

Once again, he found himself trapped in a moral dilemma, torn between his loyalty and love for Azla and his duty to the throne. To his king.

And, yes, just like with Tanwen, he *could* easily stop Azla, throw her and Lady Esme into a holding cell until the day of the wedding. Chain Azla to his arm as he dragged her toward her betrothed. *But then that would kill her,* a voice reasoned in his mind. *You want to save her. This way does.*

Frustration surged through Zolya's veins, his magic a crackling storm in his blood. Like with Tanwen, he realized that to do what he believed was right, he would have to resort to doing something wrong. To free Tanwen's family, he was allowing sedition. To save his sister's life, he was condoning his father's death.

Every decision held loss.

I'm sorry this could not be different, he had said to Tanwen. The sentiment of his regret now extended beyond just the two of them.

Yes, Tanwen had replied. *But perhaps one day it will be.*

Perhaps one day Azla would be free of her nightmares.

Mütra would not need to hide because they no longer were being hunted.

The treasury would not be bleeding because palace spending would be better regulated.

Volari and Süra would not be condemned for caring for one another.

The queen could return to Galia.

Zolya would finally be able to act, *do,* rather than remain compliant and silent.

Perhaps, perhaps, perhaps . . .

When I am king.

The statement swirled through Zolya's blood, settling into his heart. A declaration.

His magic now buzzed with a different energy, a hum of dangerous longing, a resolve that might have been mad, might have been the biggest sin of his life, but he now knew was the only way to save those he loved and push Cādra toward a better tomorrow.

An opportunity for change had been handed to him. He needed to decide if he would reach out and grasp it.

When wearing the crown of our kingdom, his father had once said, *you must always see the ripple of an action, not merely where the stone falls.*

Zolya saw every ripple that would follow allowing this plan, but any that held consequences, he would own, for he'd then be king, and that would be his duty.

Zolya met Azla's gaze, his pulse a chaotic thrum. "I will not stop you."

53

Tanwen's heartbeat skipped as she reread the note. The parchment was thick between her fingers, the penmanship elegant and refined.

It was a message from the princess, delivered a moment ago by a palace courier.

The words were brief but did their job of robbing her of breath.

> Thank you for my gift. I look forward to using it during the festivities tomorrow evening.

Tanwen's grip tightened on the note, nervous anticipation flooding her veins.

Tomorrow evening.

The same night she planned to escape.

Princess Azla was going to poison the king during her prewedding celebration.

She was listening to Tanwen.

Despite the severity of what this meant, how this would disrupt the entirety of Cādra, create a further chasm between her and Zolya, Tanwen's breaths came out even. Sure.

It was happening.

Her favor to Bosyg would be complete.

But perhaps most importantly, her brother's monster would be eradicated.

No longer would Aberthol suffer.

Calmly, Tanwen folded the note promising the king's death and smiled.

54

Tanwen's fingers slipped on her shears, her grip clammy as she concentrated on clipping each stem of jadüri. Not even the beauty overtaking the greenhouse could distract her from her task. And the beauty was indeed luminous.

The large glass ceiling was propped open, allowing silvery and golden beams of moonlight to spill in and over the ethereal blooms. Jadüri petals were parted, emanating a vibrant blue glow as if they were absorbing the very essence of Maja and Parvi themselves. The night was early, warm, and blessed with the full glowing eyes of the twin High Gods.

Perfect for an evening of palace revelry.

Tanwen, however, felt no sense of celebration coursing through her veins.

She felt only nerves and a slip of nausea.

Tanwen forced her hands not to tremble as she delicately clipped free the jadüri flowers from their plot. They'd be used to make her docüra for that evening's celebration—and more.

Today marked the day of Princess Azla's prewedding festivities, and simultaneously, it was the day of Tanwen and her family's planned escape and, evidently, when the king would be poisoned.

It was perhaps too much to anticipate.

Tanwen paused in her work to wipe a slip of sweat from her brow. The heat of the room was making her feel lightheaded, though her anxiety didn't help her feel grounded either.

Tanwen may have been warned what the princess intended to do this evening, but she did not know exactly *when* she was going to do it. And that uncertainty, amid the anticipation of everything else she had to get right, was leaving her rather overwhelmed and agitated.

"Are you all right?" asked Huw, who stood a few paces down her row.

"I'm tired," Tanwen admitted as she gently laid another of the jadüri blooms into her basket.

"You're too young to be tired," Huw countered.

Tanwen cut him a glance. "You and I are the same age, and you complain practically every morning that it is too early to be awake."

"That is because I don't go to bed as early as you, elda Tanwen."

"Maybe if you did, the morning bell wouldn't offend you as much."

"*Or*," Huw argued, "I'd end up like you, still tired in the prime years of life."

"That logic makes absolutely no sense," said Tanwen, rolling her eyes. "It's a good thing an atenté is judged on their looks over their intelligence, or you'd be out of a job, my friend."

"Is that a jest, little fawn?" Huw raised his brows, fighting a grin. "And here I thought you had permanently lost your sense of humor. I'm glad to see there's still an ember of your wit alive."

"Well," began Tanwen, a slip of annoyance entering her tone, "I apologize if life lately has left me unamused."

A thick silence fell between them, and despite the truth of her words, Tanwen regretted them.

Huw was only trying to help.

He was *always* trying to help.

"I'm sorry," said Tanwen. "Tonight's event has me on edge. I didn't mean—"

"I understand." Huw lifted a placating hand. "You only lost your friend a few days ago."

Her friend.

Eli.

Tanwen resisted shifting under the reminder.

Despite still grieving Eli, Tanwen was desperate to compartmentalize his loss. She'd certainly be losing a lot more after tonight.

Despite all she had endured on Galia, she would miss Huw. With Eli she had lost one friend, and soon she would lose Huw too.

And Zolya, an intrusive voice whispered.

Tanwen swallowed past the rising grief working up her throat.

She had tried not to think about her and Zolya since their night together.

Which was, of course, impossible.

When Tanwen was not consumed with thoughts of her escape, she was consumed with thoughts of him. His touch, his taste, the way he had held her all night, as if she were a dandelion seed and he feared she might scatter the moment he let go.

Zolya was the rarest soul she had ever met, and he wanted her, was helping her, despite how it went against his loyalties to the crown. He wanted to atone for his actions toward her and her family, be a ruler who could change the centuries-old prejudice poisoning Cādra.

And Tanwen loved him desperately for it.

Ilustra was cruel in fating them together.

Only for them to be forever apart.

For this time tomorrow, if Tanwen was lucky, she and her family would be far from Galia, hiding under the protection of the Low Gods.

Tanwen pressed her lips together, forcing down her swirl of emotions. How horrible that her success tonight also meant the breaking of her heart.

Tanwen turned back to the glowing buds, her anxiousness forever churning as she worked. She needed to stop moping and concentrate on what needed to be done.

The final piece of her plan rested on gathering six extra jadüri for the mixture that would power their wings, another task fraught with risk.

In the distance, a bell chimed; their shift had come to an end.

Methodically, Tanwen gathered her tools before making her way toward the exit.

Concealed within the bottom of her basket lay the extra jadüri, carefully hidden in a secret compartment she had crafted herself. Tanwen's pulse quickened as she approached the checkpoint, where the guards stood inspecting each basket.

Her clothes grew suffocating as she waited anxiously.

"*Gods*, it's so hot in here," muttered Tanwen, attempting to fan herself with her hand.

"Well, it *is* a hothouse," reasoned Huw.

"Still, it feels worse than usual."

Huw eyed her with concern, but their line moving forward redrew their attention.

Tanwen faced an awaiting kidet.

As she held her breath, she presented her basket for inspection. The guard fingered through her jadüri, brows furrowed in concentration as he counted. He felt along the sides of her basket as Tanwen's heart hammered in her chest.

And then he was handing back her basket and, with a quick gesture, waving her past.

Once outside, Tanwen exhaled deeply, relief flooding her.

Tanwen fought to steady her trembling hands.

She had done it!

Her smile felt inappropriately wide.

"You weren't kidding," said Huw as he reclaimed his spot by her side, eyeing her grin. "You really must have needed out of that greenhouse."

"You have no idea," she muttered.

With the extra jadüri safely concealed, Tanwen had what she needed to make the mixture for their wings.

A step closer to freedom.
Though her elation was short lived.
The daunting task of navigating the evening's events lay ahead.
Tanwen still had to survive tonight.
And leave behind the man she loved.

55

The royal banquet hall was bloated with opulence and grandeur.

Elaborate flower arrangements adorned every swath of the open-air room, petals dyed blue and green, with flecks of diamonds to mimic a midnight ocean—an homage to Orzel.

The soaring columns gleamed under the warm glow pulsing from large burning bowls. Food and wine overflowed from passing trays, allowing half the mingling guests to already be in their cups. Their laughter and chatter filled the air, their painted wings a kaleidoscope of colors complementing draped satin and organza and silks, courtiers reveling in the ambience of a royal celebration.

Zolya stood at the head of the room, unmoved.

In fact, he was offended by the entire charade.

Tonight was not a commemorative occasion—it was the beginning of many ends.

His magic swirled in an anxious rhythm through his veins, his body so tense he might shatter with the next light breeze.

How was he to survive this?

Zolya looked over the crowd, searching for her, but the atentés had not yet been let loose within the party.

A mountain of unease rose within his chest.

Was Tanwen going to come? Or was she already making her way to her father and brother?

No, thought Zolya, restraining himself from abruptly flying from the party to verify. Madam Arini would immediately note Tanwen's absence. She would need to make an appearance first. The madam always did a final check of her staff, her approval necessary before each was ushered into an event.

A blessing, for Zolya *had* to see Tanwen one last time.

For the past three days, they had been overwhelmed with their separate duties. Apart from passing glances in the hall, he and Tanwen hadn't found a moment alone.

Zolya clenched his jaw, despising the idea of *this* being how they spent their final time together, their final farewell.

A night in which he could not kiss her and elicit her beautiful moans or laughs or hold her in his arms as they drifted off to sleep.

That moment had come and gone much too quickly.

Zolya hadn't been able to confide in Tanwen, either, regarding Azla and Lady Esme's plans, despite wishing very much to unburden his worries with someone he trusted, really the *only* person he trusted. But Zolya knew Tanwen had enough to get right tonight, that they *each* had to get right. Zolya feared telling her about the princess's plan for the king would unsteady her footing.

Especially since it was still thoroughly unsteadying his.

I can't believe I've condoned this, Zolya thought with further disquiet, gaze surveying the room, drinking in the crowd of ignorant guests.

Though, like every day since his meeting with Azla, he remained unchanged in stopping her.

As if on cue with his thoughts, the arrival of the princess drew the hall's attention.

Heads turned and conversations ceased as a wave of bows trickled down the center of the room.

Azla glided toward the front dais, where Zolya stood, her head held stoically high while her entourage of ladies and guards trailed behind.

Zolya's heart skipped.

Despite the occasion, Azla was resplendent.

Her dark skin was luminous, her alabaster hair and wings adorned with precious flecks of gold as her seafoam dress cascaded down her lithe form. She met Zolya's gaze, a ripple of determined energy jolting forward.

She was a warrior disguised as a bride.

As she reached him, Zolya stepped forward to take her delicate hand in his before they faced the room together.

The court bowed once more, the view of the massive prostrating crowd sending an uneasy twinge to Zolya's wings.

Will they still bow to me after tonight?

Will they accept me as their new king?

Zolya forced himself to ignore his rising doubts as he and Azla settled onto their plush benches.

The prince and the princess sat, a royal spectacle, allowing the court to resume their revelry.

"How are you?" Zolya leaned in to gently ask Azla.

She kept her gaze forward. "As good as one can expect given the circumstances," she answered before fervently glancing his way. "I couldn't sleep last night," she admitted and then, after another pause, asked, "How are you?"

"As good as one can expect given the circumstances," Zolya repeated.

He felt Azla's continued focus on him.

"You look angry," she observed. "Are you angry with me?"

"Do you want the honest answer?"

She paused as though thinking. "No."

"Then I am not angry with you."

"*Zolya*," she admonished, though it came out more like a plea. "I cannot suffer the guilt of your scorn, *especially* not this evening," she finished on a whisper. "You *know* I clearly am not happy with either of our situations, but this is the fate the gods handed us. Or would you rather I go through with tomorrow and be pulled into the ocean's abyss for eternity?"

Zolya let out a long-suffering sigh, sitting straight. "No, of course not."

"Then smile," she demanded. "Or, actually, don't. Your scowl is perfect. It will draw less suspicion, as you rarely are a jovial participant at parties."

Zolya sucked in the side of his cheek, annoyed. "This is hardly an appropriate time for wit," he countered.

"If we can't laugh tonight," Azla offered, "then when can we?"

"Ask me in a decade," he muttered. "After this evening is thoroughly behind us."

The gentle touch of her hand to his momentarily startled him.

Zolya met Azla's blue gaze. The same blue as his, as their father's.

"We *are* doing what is right," she said softly. "And you know it. Otherwise, you would stop me."

"Who says I still won't?" He arched a brow.

Azla studied him a beat, a wavering shadow passing across her features, but then she regained her poise, lifting her chin. "You won't," she assured. "Your passion for fairness and justice is too great. Plus, you love me too much and loathe *him* enough."

Zolya stiffened.

Him.

The king.

Was that why Zolya was allowing this all to happen? Not because he knew it was a necessary, albeit tragic, outcome to create a better Cādra, to free many of those he loved, but to satiate the hatred he might have for his father?

The thought didn't sit well. It made the circumstance feel spiteful and vindictive. Well-known traits of the king.

Zolya frowned. *No, I will never be like him,* he silently vowed. *I'm doing this to set others free, not myself.* For Zolya knew that the role he

Scorched Skies

would take on tomorrow would restrict his thoughts and actions even further. No freedoms would he enjoy.

"Will you at least do me a favor?" Zolya asked.

Azla glanced at him, her expression wary, but she waited for him to continue.

"Will you warn me before you . . . do what you intend to do tonight?"

Azla's features softened. She looked as if she wished to comfort him with another touch of her hand, but they remained in her lap. "If I am able," she replied. "Yes."

Despite her answer, Zolya didn't feel any more relieved.

But their conversation was put on hold as Osko approached.

"Your Royal Highnesses." He bowed low between them. "What a beautiful night for a celebration. I wanted to congratulate you again on your upcoming nuptials, Princess." He inclined his head to Azla. "You honor us with this divine union. Never has our kind been elevated to such illustrious ranks. You will be a beacon to aspire to for all ladies of court."

Zolya inwardly cringed. Osko was laying it on rather thick, and he didn't need to look at Azla to know her gaze was searing. Neither of them had ever truly cared for each other.

"Thank you, Kidar Terz," Azla replied, honey sweet. "I do hope you are right. I would be *honored* if my actions regarding this union inspire others. We ladies must know what we can achieve."

Zolya cleared his throat, her meaning more than clear to himself, while Osko merely preened, oblivious.

A dramatic hush swept through the hall as a herald announced the arrival of the king.

Azla and Zolya stood from their bench before sinking to their knees, mirroring the reverence of the entire room.

The king's promenade took forever, Zolya's heartbeat a pounding drum against his ribs from where he remained prostrating. A coiling of fear and dread, a common affliction whenever his father was near.

"You may rise," boomed the king as he took his place at the head of the room. Zolya and Azla now flanked his sides on the royal dais.

King Réol's authority loomed over the great hall, his power unfurling in a heavy current.

I am greater than you, it seemed to say. *Stronger, blessed, chosen.*

Zolya forced his breaths to be even, forced away the rise of overwhelm surging through his veins, kicking against his magic.

Now as he stood beside his father, their intentions for tonight seemed not just foolish but impossible.

The way in which it will be done guarantees success, Azla had promised.

But what could possibly guarantee the killing of practically a demigod?

Zolya fisted his hands at his sides, his annoyance with himself flaring.

He should have asked more details, should have allowed Azla to tell him exactly what she was planning to use and how.

But Zolya had been too stubborn in thinking if he knew less, he'd have less sin on his hands, less of their father's blood, less to hide when standing before his subjects as their new king.

Now he realized his foolishness, as this had left him only ill prepared.

"My devoted patrons," said the king, his voice a rumbling storm through the hall. "Tonight marks a momentous occasion. It is the eve of one of our own ascending to the rank of goddess. Historical in its union, this symbolizes a fortuitous future for us all, with our mighty Orzel as an ally." He extended his hand to Azla, which she accepted, though Zolya noted the tension along her jaw. This perhaps was the first time their father had ever touched his daughter. Zolya's own physical contact with the king had only been from hard blows.

He swallowed his sudden spike of protectiveness toward Azla.

"You honor me, daughter," the king proclaimed, a show of adoration for his child as he smiled. "You honor us all." He turned back to the room. "Dear guests and loyal subjects, I thank you for attending tonight to celebrate this joyous occasion. Let us hope that all my children can make us this proud. Now feast!"

The banquet hall rose with cheers of delight while Zolya stiffened at his father's last statement, a purposeful public lashing.

Let us hope that all my children can make us this proud.

Because Zolya still had not.

But despite how in the past such sentiments from his father would have knocked him down, tonight they helped Zolya regain his footing.

He was nothing like his father, and never did he wish to be.

He glanced at the king, who appeared content and bloated after selling his only daughter to an angry god. All so he could sustain his court's lavish lifestyle.

One of his many transgressions.

We are doing what is right. Azla's earlier words now echoed a steady beat in Zolya's heart.

For the first time all week Zolya felt a sense of calm.

She was right.

Their father's cruel rule *needed* to end.

And Zolya would help see that it did.

As the soiree bubbled around them, their royal dais slowly filled with familiar faces. Osko reclaimed his spot beside Zolya while a few of the king's close advisers slid into their circle as well as Lady Esme.

Zolya had acknowledged her arrival but couldn't bring himself to converse with her.

There was too much meaning in each of their shared glances, too much radiating between her and Azla, too much anticipation.

Are they going to do it now? Zolya wondered, his anxiousness compounding. *Right here, where everyone can see?*

His swirling thoughts were interrupted, however, by the king addressing Lady Esme.

"My lady." King Réol turned his icy stare on her. "I must compliment you on your years of service to my daughter," he stated. "It is rare that a lady-in-waiting would so long stay with their charge.

Usually, your position is used to make an advantageous marriage match. And yet you have remained with my daughter for decades, unwed."

It was a purposeful undercut, for King Réol knew perfectly well why Lady Esme remained a charge of the princess as well as unwed. Ire flashed like lightning through Zolya's veins.

"It has been my honor to serve the princess, Your Eminence," said Lady Esme with a bow, deftly ignoring his other statement.

"I would assume so," replied the king. "Which is why I have been thinking a great deal about how untethered you'll be once Princess Azla is married and living in her husband's domain. It would be cruel of me to allow you to fall from ranks at court after how loyal you have been to my family."

No one spoke, a thickening of tension in the air.

"I have decided that you will serve in my personal entourage," he announced, eyes lingering a beat too long on her bosom. "You are young, with much still to learn regarding the ways in which you can be valuable. I will see to it personally that your continued royal service is an educational experience that will benefit your future."

Zolya had stopped breathing, his rage a quick boil to his blood.

I have decided that you will serve in my personal entourage.

He was claiming Lady Esme as one of his mistresses.

In front of his daughter.

Zolya clamped his teeth together, his wings stiff at his back, as he glanced to Azla.

Her brown skin had been sapped of color, her gaze a flash of unchecked animosity and grief.

Osko met Zolya's gaze, his eyes wide in shock; even his dutiful friend saw the wrong of this moment.

Yes, thought Zolya, *this is the monster we are meant to serve.*

But the true warrior of their group was Lady Esme.

She hardly faltered as she produced a demure blush to her cheeks. "You honor me tremendously, Your Eminence," she replied. "It would be my privilege to continue serving your family."

King Réol's triumph was vile in how his eyes darkened with pleasure, his grin sharp. "You are a good girl, aren't you?" he purred.

Princess Azla hastily waved forward a servant, then snagged a flute of spirits from his tray.

She finished it much too quickly.

Zolya's rage surged with his wave of helplessness, wishing he could knock his father to the ground, a shockingly new emotion. But he held steady, knowing his sister's retribution would come.

Now more than ever, it *needed* to.

In a change of energy, the arrival of the atentés distracted the party.

The hall filled with murmurs of delight as the provocatively dressed servants wove through the crowd, their promise of euphoria sparkling in their bowls.

Zolya's heartbeat raced as he frantically searched the crowd.

And then his pulse stilled as he caught sight of Tanwen, toward the middle of the room. She was alluring and graceful as she slid through the guests, her sheer chiton clinging to her curves.

Tanwen's hair had been pulled into an intricate weaving, her horns capped with gold, matching jewelry glittering from her pointed ears. Her beauty seemed to cast a spell, drawing admiring glances from all.

A protective flame caught light in Zolya's lungs.

None of them were worthy of her presence, deserving of her smiles and wit.

As if sensing his attention—despite being across the room—she turned, meeting his gaze.

At the contact, Zolya nearly shivered from the heat traveling the length of him.

His desire to go to her was overwhelming, his want to shield her from this looming madness. But before he could do much of anything, events unfolded rapidly.

The king began to select guests and various servants to join him in his private receiving room, a customary practice at such gatherings.

He only ever graced the full court with his presence for a moment before shutting himself away with a chosen assembly of guests. A privilege that invariably stirred envy among those left behind in the grand hall.

Disturbingly, Lady Esme was among the chosen few.

Zolya watched a flash of panic shoot across Azla's features as she pulled Lady Esme quickly aside. Their heads were bent low as hurried, worried whispers were shared.

But then Lady Esme grabbed the princess's hands, an assured grip that said, *I've got this; do not worry.*

Something passed between their hands, small, dark, and round.

Zolya's pulse raced as understanding dawned.

Their plan . . . it had begun, but he sensed something was amiss.

It wasn't transpiring as intended.

Unease surged through him as he worked his way toward the ladies, but when he got there, Lady Esme had already departed with the rest of the small party.

He and Azla stood watching her disappear. "Is it happening?" he asked.

Princess Azla nodded before a hard swallow. "It wasn't meant to be Essie," she said, her voice a scratchy whisper.

"Who was it meant to be?"

Azla met Zolya's gaze, a haunting in her blue depths. "Me."

Zolya was poised to respond when another commotion caught his attention: Tanwen among the staff being ushered into the king's private gathering.

Zolya's wings half unfurled, his pulse stopping as a madness overtook him.

No! he silently screamed, his body a fight of wills. Every muscle battled his heart, which demanded he fly forward and snatch her back.

The idea of Tanwen being anywhere near the king, within his cruel eyesight, left him shaking with fear and dread.

"Zol?" questioned Azla, who he had forgotten was still standing beside him, suffering a similar torment. "Are you all right?"

But Zolya couldn't respond, couldn't breathe, as—for a pause in time—Tanwen glanced over her shoulder, finding him through the buzzing crowd.

Their eyes locked, held, her dismay evident in her gaze.

Then she was gone.

The doors closed behind Tanwen with a finite whisper.

56

Tanwen learned that terror had a taste.

It was a metallic flare across her tongue as she stepped into the king's private receiving room.

"This is insane," whispered Huw at her side, his eyes wide as he drank in the opulent space. Neither of them had ever been inside these grand chambers. They were usually saved for official use: greeting esteemed guests and meetings with various aristocrats.

But tonight, they had been decorated to honor the theme of the evening.

The towering columns were draped in blue and seafoam fabric, the cavernous space illuminated by flickering bowls. The effect created a secretive, if not lurid, atmosphere.

The night sky peeked through the large skylights above, offering a glimpse of freedom beyond, though Tanwen noted the guards stationed around the room. Their austere expressions and sheathed blades didn't help her growing unease.

"I would have preferred to stay in the public gathering," Tanwen muttered, her eyes darting nervously to every alcove and tucked-away exit.

There had been more ways to escape in the grand hall.

More ways for her to blend in and disappear.

Not to mention, Zolya was out there, his devastated expression as the doors had severed their connection seared into her mind.

In here, Tanwen was at the mercy of the guards to allow her leave. Nothing about this situation spoke of remaining innocuous. Especially since the entire gathering was perhaps thirty in total, including atentés.

With Tanwen's worries compounding, her thoughts went to her father and brother, who waited for her.

How will I get to them now? she thought with dread.

She moved in a fog, following Huw and the other servants deeper into the room, eventually fanning out to service the various courtiers, who lounged on low settees and padded benches.

Tanwen became automated as she cleaned skin and offered up a knife before dropping docüra into fresh cuts. Over and over and over.

But in her periphery, her attention hovered at the head of the room, where King Réol reclined in regal repose as wine and refreshments were continually brought forth.

While Tanwen bandaged her most recent satiated client, her stomach churned as she watched Süra servants meticulously test each dish and drink that was brought into the room, their solemn expressions betraying the gravity of their task.

But amid everything, Tanwen's gaze fixated on Lady Esme, who sat nearest the king.

She was clearly his preferred companion for the night.

His hands lingered a beat too long on her knee or against her wrist as they remained locked in conversation.

Inwardly, Tanwen recoiled at the thought of being touched by the king, but Lady Esme's composure was a marvel.

Tanwen didn't know how she could so gracefully endure the unwanted attention of a man she despised. Though perhaps her poise stemmed from the looming prospect of the king's death.

At the thought, Tanwen's nerves buzzed. Was this where they planned to do it? Within this private gathering? She glanced around the room once more—no sign of the princess.

Tanwen frowned.

If the princess wasn't here, would they wait?

Who held the stone?

And what would happen if an opportunity didn't arise?

Would they lose their nerve?

No. Tanwen tried to assuage her worries. *They* have *to do it tonight, soon, otherwise the princess is as good as married, as good as dead.*

They couldn't back out now. Certainly not Lady Esme.

Tanwen knew too well what someone would do to save the ones they loved.

Forcing calm, Tanwen discreetly slipped from the group of guests she had finished servicing, seeking solace within a column's shadow.

The atmosphere in the room had grown increasingly debauched. Clothes slipped away, revealing breasts and chests, chatter turning to moans.

Tanwen did her best to ignore the scene as she concentrated on Lady Esme, who had motioned for a servant to bring more wine.

Tanwen watched with rising disquiet as Lady Esme took the full decanter, gesturing that she would like the honor of pouring for His Eminence. But before she could, one of her dress straps slipped from her shoulder, diverting the king's gaze to her more exposed bosom.

Lady Esme laughed demurely, a flutter to her lashes as King Réol's expression darkened with his desire. Slowly, she worked the strap back up with one finger.

And that's when it happened.

Tanwen caught the subtle sleight of hand with Lady Esme's other.

Tanwen's breath held as Lady Esme deftly slipped Maryth's tear into the red wine decanter resting in her lap.

Scorched Skies

Tanwen's grip on her tray tightened, her pulse fluttering with anxious anticipation in her veins.

She waited for someone else to have noticed, guards to come running, but the room continued in its oblivious revelry.

Poison churned innocuously in the wine Lady Esme poured for the king.

She offered up the tainted cup to King Réol, her smile concealing her deadly intent.

But then everything took a turn when he gestured for her to partake as well.

"My cup is already full, Your Grace," Tanwen could hear Lady Esme reply.

"Not nearly full enough," he urged, gesturing for her to obey.

Lady Esme faltered for a moment, but because no one dared to defy the king, quickly she was forced to recover.

Lady Esme topped off her glass with the soiled wine, her gestures stiff.

"To you," the king declared, raising his cup, "and your new honor of your services to me."

This was the only time all evening that Lady Esme's smile broke.

From over the king's shoulder, she briefly met Tanwen's gaze.

A flash of regret and sorrow and grief filled her features, but then her expression shifted to a steely determination.

For my princess. Tanwen could imagine Lady Esme altering the king's salute. *For my love.*

Tanwen's heart stopped, her mind screaming, *No!*

Horror and tragedy enveloped the room as Lady Esme lifted her cup to her lips and drank.

57

Tanwen's breaths came out as ragged gasps as she raced toward the cliff near the old groundskeeper's cottage.

Her quick footsteps echoed in the night, the grass beneath a hissing beat filling the tepid air. High above, the eyes of Maja and Parvi glowed bright and full, lighting Tanwen's way.

Despite the evening's stillness, panic surged through Tanwen's veins.

Lady Esme had drunk the poison!

Lady Esme was going to die.

She might already be dead.

Princess Azla would be destroyed.

Tanwen picked up her speed, as if she could outrun the thought, as if the farther she got from the palace, the further the tragic truth would recede.

But no one could outrun such fate.

The goddess of death would be waiting to claim the souls who tasted her tear.

Lady Esme and King Réol.

King Réol, whose death currently held no joy for Tanwen, nor did it bless her with relief.

Would the princess blame Tanwen for Lady Esme's death? Given she was the one who provided the stone.

Would she tell Zolya what Tanwen had done, what she had encouraged?

Devastation barreled through her chest, causing her pace to momentarily falter.

Her thoughts tumbled backward, to when Lady Esme had swallowed her demise.

Tanwen had been rooted in her shocked horror before the reality of the situation pummeled into her like a winter freeze.

Her actions had then been swift.

Tanwen had fumbled with her tray, spilling the rest of her docüra on her dress, disheveling her appearance.

An unacceptable state to be in in front of the king.

A guard by one of the side exits promptly granted her passage to clean up. A thousand blessings, for Tanwen's urgency to flee the room had compounded.

She had no idea how long before the poison would take effect.

But she refused to wait around and find out. The palace would soon be in an uproar, and she needed to reach her father and brother before it happened.

Tanwen immediately descended to the servants' quarters, but instead of heading toward the atenté dormitory, she veered in the opposite direction until she reached the outdoors.

That's when she had run.

As she was now, before she came to a low shrub grove.

She dropped to her knees beside the roots, frantically digging at a pile of rocks and dirt.

Soil pressed into her fingernails, her breaths loud in her ears as she pulled forward her buried backpack. Inside were the three elixirs for their wings and a change of clothes.

Tanwen quickly shed her atenté dress and donned her sturdier and warmer clan trousers, tunic, and coat.

As she fitted her pack over her shoulders, she spun to continue her ascent up the hill when a gust of wind pushed her back a step.

Zolya landed in her path.

Agony tore through Tanwen's heart at the sight of him.

He glowed like a god beneath the full moons' light, his features severe, his wings pristine white, his gaze eviscerating—tortured.

For a moment neither spoke before they rushed forward, colliding.

Zolya's scent of rain engulfed her, his mouth warm and demanding against her lips, his chest impenetrable from where he held her against him. He curled a hand against the nape of her neck, a possessive hold securing Tanwen exactly where he needed her. Tears slipped unchecked from the corners of Tanwen's eyes, the anguish of each palpable as they clung to one another, feasted like they were each other's last meal. Neither cared that they were in the open, Nocémi's night watching from above. They *needed* this. They needed each other. They needed one final taste, smell, touch to hold within their hearts.

Eventually, Zolya drew away, ending their kiss.

Tanwen held in her distressed whimper, kept herself from reaching out to pull him back.

Zolya's gaze was searing, a pooling of desire and pain as he looked down at her.

An appropriate distance now yawned between them.

A canyon of heartache.

"You were able to escape my father." Zolya's voice was the deep abyss of night, his words not a question but a marveled observation.

"Yes," Tanwen scratched out.

"You weren't going to say goodbye." Another statement, but she caught the hurt in his tone.

Guilt slid like a knife down Tanwen's spine. "I'm sorry," she began. "I couldn't risk it."

Zolya's expression remained hard, though eventually he nodded.

They stood in silence, Zolya's attention raking the length of her, as though he wished to commit everything about her to memory.

It forced another dagger into Tanwen's heart. She didn't want him to need to remember. She wanted him to forever be a part of her now. But such a fate was never theirs.

"There are no guards outside the cottage," Zolya announced.

Tanwen blinked. "Excuse me?"

"I allowed the kidets a reprieve so they may join in the palace festivities for a spell," he explained. "The front door to your father's cottage remains locked but unguarded."

Tanwen was momentarily robbed of a reply. Zolya had removed the soldiers. Her father and brother were unwatched. Tanwen's last obstacle to her family was gone.

Will you stop me? she had once asked him.

No, but I also cannot help you.

Not stopping me is helping me.

Never were her words truer than in this moment.

There was so much Zolya believed he was powerless in, incapable of because of his father's looming presence, but he was the most capable, courageous soul she had ever met.

What he had done would save her family, allow them to escape, and was a direct action against his father, an atonement for an order Zolya had once obeyed.

At the thought of the king, Tanwen's chest constricted in a mix of guilt and dread.

"The king drank poison," she blurted out, as if sharing this news could somehow match his gesture, absolve her from everything else she would never be able to confess.

"He what?" Zolya stiffened, brows furrowing.

"He drank . . . poison," Tanwen repeated. "As did Lady Esme."

"Lady Esme?" Zolya's eyes widened, his shock clear. "How do you . . . ?"

"I saw it happen," Tanwen explained. "Lady Esme, she—" Tanwen stopped herself, not knowing how to share what she knew without outing the princess and her lover. She could not betray their trust, not even to Zolya. Not after they clearly had kept her involvement a secret.

A thunderous blast interrupted their moment, sending a wave of energy surging out from within the palace. Tanwen reached for Zolya, steadying herself as the ground shook beneath their feet.

Everything then fell silent. Still.

Tanwen's gaze locked with Zolya's. A ripple of uncertainty, of fear, stretched like a taut rope before snapping back.

Screams rang into the night. Winged guards poured in toward the palace.

Panic erupted in Tanwen's veins.

The king.

It had happened.

"You must go." Zolya's deep rumble snapped her back to where her hands still gripped his forearms.

His blue gaze was wild, an austere swirling of concern and determination. She could sense his magic rising beneath her fingertips, a cool vibration of power, like the creeping of fog at dawn. He looked every bit a warrior readying for battle.

Tanwen stepped back but then hesitated, torment raking through her veins.

"Go!" he bellowed, a king's command.

Tanwen pushed past Zolya and fled.

58

The wind coming off the cliffs swirled and howled, mirroring the chaotic turmoil taking place in the distant palace.

"What's happened?" Gabreel asked, eyes wide as he surveyed the scene.

The sky was erupting with Volari courtiers streaming out of the palace. Their colorful garments billowed, painted wings flashing under the moons' light while guards evoked their sky magic, attempting to restore order amid the chaos.

Tanwen and her brother knelt at the cliff's edge, ignoring the madness as they hastily assembled their gliders.

"The king's been poisoned," Tanwen replied in a rush, cursing her shaking hands as she feverishly worked to attach each of their power elixirs.

"*What?*" Gabreel swung around to face her. Thol froze in his task of snapping together joints.

Tanwen momentarily met each of their startled stares. "The king's been poisoned," she repeated. "He's dead." Tanwen knew how absurd it sounded, how impossible, but they *really* couldn't afford to dwell on her words. They needed to finish building their gliders. They needed to leave—now!

"Oh gods," Thol breathed as he clutched his chest, falling back on his heels.

"*Thol.*" Tanwen caught her brother, hating the feel of his bony shoulders beneath her hands.

Despite his reprieve of torture, Thol had remained hollowed out, haunted. Tanwen had been worried he wouldn't be strong enough for the flight, but she had quickly pushed that fear away.

He had no other choice but to be strong enough.

He will make it, she thought, prayed.

He had to.

They all did.

A deranged laugh snapped Tanwen's attention back to Thol. She watched with concern as his mirth grew until he was bent over, gasping for breath.

"Thol?" Tanwen asked hesitantly, brows drawn in. "Are you all right?"

"He's dead." Aberthol looked up at her. Exhausted relief mingled in his green gaze, tears welling in the corners of his eyes. "Is he really dead?"

Anguish pooled within Tanwen as she gripped his shoulder.

Her brother's months of pain, which he had harbored quietly, tightly, within his soul rose to the forefront of his features. A rippling devastation that robbed Tanwen of air.

In that moment, the depths of her brother's fear of the king became glaringly apparent, as did his burning hatred.

"Yes," Tanwen said softly. "The king is dead."

He can no longer hurt you.

Words she wished to say but could not. Tanwen knew the king's torment would forever be with Thol.

Tears streamed unchecked down her brother's cheeks, his body curling inward within her arms as he struggled to contain his overwhelming emotions.

Tanwen swallowed her own rising agony, as well as her guilt for not delivering the news more sensitively. She hadn't thought about Thol's position when hearing it.

Yet despite the delicate moment, her worry still slid to the palace, to the kidets who continued to fill the skies. They would not be left alone much longer.

"Is that why there were no guards outside the cottage?" asked Gabreel.

Tanwen glanced up at her father, a new twist of uncertainty filling her chest. "Yes and no," she answered. "The . . . prince sent them away."

"The prince?" Gabreel's brows rose, a wash of horror.

"Yes, he's . . . not as he seems. He's our ally." She stumbled over the admission, unable to contain her overwhelming desire to defend Zolya. Tanwen kept her thoughts from dipping too far into despair, the agony of leaving him earlier still raw and bleeding. "But we haven't the time for this," she urged, still holding a wilted Thol. "We can talk about everything once we've landed."

Gabreel remained speechless, gazing down at her. His features were hard, a slip of distrust marring his brow. A look that said, *What have you done?*

Tanwen hated the shame that filled her chest at the thought of disappointing her father. But there was so much he did not know.

"Father, *please*," she begged, forcing this topic to the side as well as her feelings surrounding it. "We. Must. Leave. *Now*."

To emphasize her point, a bolt of lightning streaked across the sky. A storm was rolling in, though the air carried a metallic tang rather than the promising scent of wet soil.

Tanwen glanced to the palace, to the dark clouds forming above the pristine white citadel. It never stormed in Galia.

Magic.

Powerful magic.

Zolya, Tanwen thought with worry, *or a High God.*

Fear was a sharp lashing through her veins.

"We must go!" she demanded, hauling Thol to his feet.

Blessedly, her family didn't put up a fight.

Quickly they finished assembling their gliders before strapping themselves in. They lined up near the cliff's edge, Tanwen's pulse a pounding drum as the wind fought against her.

"Do you have Eli?" asked her father.

And just like that, another near-crippling pain tore through Tanwen. She retreated a step.

Gabreel noticed her distress, for he settled a hand on her shoulder, his eyes questioning, brows furrowed with concern.

Whatever he saw in her gaze gave him his answer. "I'm so sorry, Wen," he said.

Tanwen shook her head, forcing away the rising ache in her throat. *Later,* she thought. *We will have time to mourn everything later.*

"Let's go," she replied, stepping back to their line.

Gabreel held her gaze for another breath before nodding. He handed them each a strange-looking belt with two round glass pieces.

"They are for our eyes," he explained. "Protection that goes around your head like this." He slipped his on, then tightened the strap at the back of his head. He blinked at them through the round glass, looking like an odd bug. "Falling from this height won't allow us to keep our eyes open. The cold and wind are too great. We'll need to wear these to see."

The contraption was terribly uncomfortable but felt sturdy, and Tanwen could see well enough out of them.

"Make sure you jump with your head high." Her father quickly repeated the lesson he had made them both memorize. "Your eyes and chest need to be thrust to the horizon to achieve the correct body position for flight. And keep your legs straight, arms strong and level, and toes pointed. Otherwise, you risk spinning out. Remember, *use* the wind; don't fight it."

Tanwen and her brother and father faced the dark abyss in front of them.

A terror like nothing Tanwen had ever felt gripped her as she gazed into the void. Dark clouds lit by moonlight swirled beneath her feet, nothing but down, down, down.

"Bring me!" shouted a familiar voice, piercing through Tanwen's panic.

Tanwen turned, finding Huw racing toward them up the hill.

Like Tanwen, he had changed out of his atenté garb and into his northern-clan attire. He wore black trousers and a brown tunic. His blond hair was in disarray from his run, his pale cheeks stained red from his exertion.

"Huw?" Tanwen questioned, her shock and confusion swirling. She tore off her eyepiece to see him better. "What—why are you here? How did you know *I'd* be here?"

Huw bent over, hands on his knees, gasping for air. "There's a lot someone can learn," he panted, "when others think they are alone."

Tanwen frowned, not understanding.

"I am like you," he said, forcing himself upright to meet her gaze. "I am Mütra."

Tanwen nearly fell from the cliff, his words barreling through her. Huw was Mütra?

In quick flashes Tanwen recalled all the times he'd suddenly appear or disappear, his uncanny ability to blend in seamlessly.

Was this his Mütra power? To be a chameleon of sorts?

"*Please,*" said Huw, his desperation palpable. "Take me with you."

Behind him, the sky flashed once more before raindrops began to fall.

"*Tanwen,*" warned her father. "We must go."

"Huw," said Tanwen, anguish ripping open her heart. "I'm sorry... I can't. These gliders only support our own weight."

Huw's features crumpled, a devastation, but before he could respond, a blur of blue and green came barreling toward them from the sky.

"*Princess.*" Tanwen yelped as she awkwardly tried to bow in her contraption.

Azla was a storm of despair and panic as she took fumbling steps forward. "Essie," she croaked, nearly falling into Tanwen's arms.

Oh gods, thought Tanwen, holding the princess awkwardly. Her emotions were growing overwhelming, dizzying. Too much was happening! None of which was what *needed* to happen—them leaving!

"She's gone," Princess Azla sobbed into Tanwen's shoulder. "Gone!"

Tanwen tightened her grip, her pain surging. "I'm so sorry," she whispered. "I'm so sorry, Princess."

"Zolya told me where you'd be. That I was meant to find you," explained the princess. "He told me you were in the room when . . ."

"Yes," said Tanwen, voice thick with emotion, with regret. "I was there when it happened. You must know, she didn't have a choice, Princess. The king . . . Lady Esme didn't have a choice."

"Tanwen." Her father's voice reached her through the wind. "What's going on?"

Her family and Huw were looking at her in a swirl of confusion, disbelief, and urgency, waiting.

The clouds rumbled ominously overhead, heralding harsher rain.

If they didn't leave now, flying in such a storm would grow impossible.

Without thought, Tanwen turned back to Azla. "Come with us," she urged. "We are leaving Galia and have somewhere safe to go."

Princess Azla momentarily blinked through her grief, finally taking in her surroundings. She looked to the odd mix of company who watched them and then to where they all stood, dangerously close to the cliff's ledge. "What are you wearing?" she asked, brows drawn together.

"Something that will allow us to fly," explained Tanwen. "But I need to know your answer now. Will you come with us?"

Princess Azla bit her lower lip, indecision swirling as she glanced back to the palace. "Zolya told me to go with you," she admitted, though she still gave no definitive answer.

Tanwen tried to ignore how her heart filled hearing that Zolya had entrusted his sister to her.

"Lady Esme would want you to be free of this place," argued Tanwen. "Especially without her here. She always wanted you to see the world."

Over the princess's shoulder, Tanwen noted a group of kidets angling their way.

Tanwen's heart stopped beating.

"We must go!" yelled her father, seeing them too. "Now!"

"I will come," said the princess.

A wave of relief crashed into Tanwen. "Good," she breathed. "Then you can carry my friend." Tanwen pushed Huw toward Princess Azla.

Each of them looked at one another, eyes wide, startled.

"You are strong enough to carry him, yes?" Tanwen challenged.

Offense flared in Princess Azla's features. Without a reply, she scooped up Huw with deceptive strength, spread her wings, and descended over the ledge.

Huw's cry of terror got swallowed in the clouds.

The guards had seen Gabreel now, out of his cottage. They sped faster forward.

Tanwen and her family toed the cliff's edge.

"Remember," yelled her father over the storm. "Whatever you do, don't faint."

Together, they jumped.

59

Within the opulent chamber, Zolya was frozen.

His eyes were fixed on the lifeless form of the king, who was sprawled, motionless, on the floor.

The sight of his father's pallid skin and bloated veins—tainted black from the poison—sent a chill down his spine, the once all-powerful monarch now defeated.

Zolya waited to feel grief or pain or *something*, but he remained numb, disbelieving.

In shock.

It was clear his father had fought against his death. The room was charred with his magic, a tangy smoke filling the air.

Close by lay the unfortunate victims of his battle, courtiers who were now unlucky to have been chosen for his private gathering.

Their wings were half-singed, flesh bubbled and burned, mouths open in silent screams. It was a gruesome scene.

But untouched among the devastation, the king's crown, pristine white, lay where it had fallen from his head. The diamond-tipped laurel cast a foreboding shadow along the marble floor, where it waited for a new bearer to claim its burden.

Zolya turned from it.

His vision became consumed by Lady Esme. Her once graceful form was now contorted in the agony of her death, her poisoned veins mirroring the king's, parts of her burned away in a grotesque display like the other guests. His father's magic had no doubt been her final blow.

It was then that Zolya finally felt the weight of this moment.

Here lay the chaotic aftermath he was meant to clean up.

A tumultuous whirlwind of emotions surged within Zolya: terror and calm, uncertainty and determination, sorrow and relief—all so raw and opposing they threatened to bring him to his knees.

Zolya's magic churned like the storm he had created outside, a mirroring of his internal chaos. A roar of frustration edged up his throat.

"Sire?" A kidet standing behind Zolya snapped him from his gathering destruction. He could sense the young soldier's nervous energy. "What would you like me to do?"

Zolya forced in a steadying breath, clenching and unclenching his hands at his side. "Inform the families of those lost tonight," he said. "And gather the men of my personal unit to help carry away the bodies."

The kidet snapped into a low bow before departing.

Osko entered just as the young soldier exited.

"All guests have been cleared of the palace," Osko informed.

Zolya noted his friend took extra care not to look at the scene splayed at their feet, his chin tilted stubbornly high. It was no secret Osko had been a great admirer of their king. He would be grieving, Zolya realized.

Guilt worked uncomfortably through Zolya, knowing his own grief had nothing to do with the king. His sorrow surrounded the loss of Tanwen, his sister, and whatever future he might have had for himself if tonight hadn't needed to happen.

He grieved selfishly.

"Good," replied Zolya, forcing his voice to be even.

"And the king's council awaits in the west tower whenever you're prepared," said Osko.

The exhausting weight of his impending responsibilities pressed against Zolya's wings. From tonight onward, his path would be fraught with more challenges and uncertainty than any other time in his life.

The true test of his abilities started now.

There was much Zolya would need to answer to, organize, prepare, and assuage. His people most of all. They were about to get a new king, assuredly not in the way any of them would have preferred.

"Thank you," said Zolya, this time unable to keep the tiredness from his voice.

His friend regarded him, a worried crease to his brow. "There's one more thing," Osko began slowly. "Princess Azla, she still has not been found."

Shame worked its way through Zolya because this was the good news he needed.

If Azla still wasn't accounted for, then she was most likely gone, just like Tanwen and her father and brother.

After he and Tanwen had split ways, the alarm in the palace intensifying, Zolya had flown straight to the princess within the turmoil of guests.

She had been panicked to get into the king's private chambers, to get to Lady Esme, but Zolya had forced her away and behind a nearby column. He then told her how he knew about the poison, that Tanwen had been inside and had seen everything transpire.

Azla appeared to be only half listening, her mind clearly distracted by their swirling surroundings. That's when the guards appeared, positioning themselves in a circle around the prince and princess, facing out, protecting their royalty as they had been trained.

But despite their audience, Azla had pulled Zolya close, her gaze panicked as she erupted in a whispered confession. There *was* a poison, a tear from Maryth, the deadliest of any kind. She was meant to do it, but then Essie got pulled away instead. *But she did it!* she had exclaimed, a burning hope in her gaze. *She must have! Father must be dead.*

Hush, Zolya had commanded, eyeing their guards, but they were all thoroughly preoccupied with the turmoil around them.

Zolya did not fully understand how Azla or Lady Esme could have gotten such a deadly item, but they had no time for further explanation. He needed to get his sister somewhere safe, somewhere *not* in Galia.

With Lady Esme being so near to the king at the time of his poisoning, clearly the only other to have drunk the poison, her connection to the treason would be investigated. A motive could easily be created, suggesting she wanted to save her lover, the princess, from being taken away, thereby implicating the princess as well.

All inarguable truths.

Azla needed to leave.

And the only way to get her to go would be to break her heart.

Zolya had then told the princess about Lady Esme, what Tanwen had shared.

Azla's painful scream had taken years off his life, as did him shoving her away, telling her to lose the guards and where she could find Tanwen. To *go* with Tanwen.

Zolya blinked back to the king's chamber and the massacre at his feet.

"Keep looking for the princess," he commanded. "She's never left Galia, so she could not have gotten far. Look in Fioré," he suggested.

"Yes, sire," said Osko. "And the inventor and his son?"

Zolya kept himself from shifting with his unease. "Is there a new report?" he asked.

"No, sire," said Osko. "There still is no sign of them, in the sea or on the closest edge of Cādra, where their gliders seemed to be angled. But I was curious what you wish our men to now do?"

"Well, it certainly is too soon to stop looking," Zolya began coolly, forcing his tone to be hard instead of filled with his all-consuming dread that Tanwen might not have survived her escape. "Have a unit continue to scour the sea. And have those stationed at Cādra's northern checkpoint set perimeters near the Zomyad and Pelk Forests. They are the closest sanctuaries."

Zolya knew where they were headed, to Drygul, the territory of the Low Gods. But who would presume they'd dare seek solace in such an unknown and perilous land? No matter the level of fugitive.

Zolya had tried to dissuade Tanwen many times from traveling there, but she had been resolute, explaining they would be welcome. And that's where she had left it.

Zolya eyed Osko, his farce of commands coming more naturally than he would have liked, but above all he needed to appear innocent, *against* what had happened tonight. The future of Cādra depended on it.

"Yes, sire," said Osko, though he did not depart.

"Is there more?" questioned Zolya.

"No," said Osko. "Nothing more to currently report."

"Thank bloody gods," Zolya muttered, scrubbing a hand down his face in exhaustion.

Osko surprised Zolya by placing a supportive hand on his shoulder. "I'm so sorry, Zol," he said gently.

His friend appeared to take his crack of emotion as a sign of something else—despair, perhaps, for his dead father, his fugitive sister, that once Orzel learned of tonight's tragedy, the agreement regarding the mine would be—

A painful, wet gasp drew Zolya's and Osko's attention to where the king lay on the floor.

His chest heaved with his sudden desperate intake of air, his eyes flashing open.

"Father?" Zolya was instantly by his side, hands hovering awkwardly over his large form. Never had he touched his father. It was always the king who laid hands on him.

King Réol's gaze locked to Zolya's, clouded, bloodshot, and unseeing. He worked to say something, but only a strained gargle came out. He collapsed back onto the ground, eyes closing.

Panic swirled through Zolya as he forced himself to feel for a pulse. His father was like ice, but there, beneath his taut skin, was the smallest flutter of life.

Zolya was momentarily paralyzed, reeling in disbelief.

His father was alive.

The king still lived.

What did this mean?

"We must get him to his chambers," Zolya instructed in a rush. "And summon meddyg Hyrez!"

Osko soared from the room, leaving Zolya now alone, with his father.

His clearly dying and very weak father.

A terrifying temptation slithered through Zolya, how easy it would be to finish his sister's and Lady Esme's plan.

This man might be Zolya's king, but he had never truly been his father. Never once had he shown Zolya mercy when he was weak, only the brutality of his own strength. Why should Zolya extend grace now when it had been absent throughout his entire life?

Resentment was a poison through Zolya's veins. A dark coaxing whispered from the goddess of death into his ear. *Send King Réol where he belongs, child, to me.*

By some miracle, Zolya stepped away.

While he might have been the son of the king, he refused to begin his reign like his father.

Heartless.

60

On the barren edge of the Cactus Forest, Tanwen didn't know if she was going to retch or scream.

Perhaps she would do both, preferably in that order.

Their flight had been harrowing, an endless descent.

And freezing.

But as Tanwen stood shivering, it wasn't from the chill in her bones but from the adrenaline surging through her veins.

They had done it!

They had flown from Galia and survived.

She felt powerful, unstoppable, and mad—because she wished to do it again.

"That was horrible," groaned Thol, who was slumped in the dirt near her feet.

He had collapsed upon landing and hadn't tried to rise since. His wingsuit weighed heavily on his thin, hunched-over form.

Despite his exhaustion, Tanwen felt immense relief that he had mustered the strength to complete the flight.

"I can't believe these worked," muttered Gabreel as he checked each joint and strap and compartment of his glider. He had neatly unhooked his suit and was inspecting it on the ground. Even with the gravity of their predicament, her father wore a strange, giddy smile. His inventor's delight outweighed his current worry.

"Where are we to go now?" asked Huw, who stood beside the princess.

The pair had remained on the fringes of Tanwen and her family, awkward guests to their planned escape.

"We're to go in there." Tanwen pointed behind them, into the shadows of the Cactus Forest.

Though dawn approached, the night still lingered, casting an eerie glow from the twin moons over the landscape. The towering cacti stretched out like skeletal fingers, their sharp outlines reaching toward the dark sky.

"I can't go in *there*," said Princess Azla, her eyes wide with her panic. "My wings will get shredded."

"We can bind your wings to keep them safe," offered Gabreel.

"Bind my wings?" The princess looked further horrified as she took a step back, her plumage flexing as though bucking the very idea.

"It won't be forever," explained Tanwen placatingly. "Just until we get to Drygul."

"The Low Gods' territory?" exclaimed Huw, his turn to look horrified. "You said you had somewhere *safe* for us."

"Drygul *is* safe," said Tanwen. "Bosyg has—"

Her response was interrupted by the snapping and crunching of soil as it shifted. The group turned to the forest's entrance as it warped and expanded. Cacti flowers burst into bloom in a cascade of colors, accompanied by an overwhelming prickling sensation in the air.

Bosyg emerged from the ground, a manifestation of endless nature and ancient power.

Tanwen fell to her knees, a heavy anticipation settling in her chest.

Out of the corner of her eye, she saw the rest of her group in similar prostrations.

Even the princess joined them in reverence.

"You have defied many odds to be standing on this soil," declared Bosyg, her voice the scratching of bugs over a forest floor. "But I never doubted you'd find your way home."

"Almighty goddess," began Tanwen, head remaining bowed. "I have fulfilled my favor," she declared. "The king is dead."

Nearby, Tanwen sensed the heightened tension pulsing from her father and the princess. Her words had been more than revealing. A pang of unease and guilt swam in Tanwen's gut for not being truthful with them, but she pushed it away.

She had done what was necessary.

"The king is not dead," said Bosyg.

Tanwen snapped her gaze up, heartbeat stumbling into a sprint. "What?"

"King Réol is alive." Bosyg's eyes, like shards of obsidian, bore into Tanwen.

"But . . . he drank the poison," Tanwen reasoned, her breaths growing panicked. "I *watched* him drink the poison."

"Evidently he did not drink enough," stated Bosyg. "His mortal body still holds on to this plane, though where his mind lingers is yet to be determined."

"I don't understand." Tanwen frowned.

"He is trapped in the unconscious," explained Bosyg.

"He's in a coma?" Tanwen whispered, distraught. "What . . . does this mean?"

"That we must wait," said Bosyg. "And see what my cousin Zenca decides."

Zenca, the High Goddess of destiny.

Despite kneeling, Tanwen felt as if she were going to fall over, her mind a race of uncertainty and frustration and—

A howl had her turning to find Princess Azla bent over, racked with grief. *"Essie."* She moaned her lover's name. "She died in *vain*."

"No." Tanwen quickly came to her side, arms wrapping around her shaking shoulders as she sobbed. "Your father may live, but that doesn't mean he won't die soon. He clearly is weak, in a coma. He cannot rule in a coma," she reasoned. "Lady Esme did what she did for *you*, to free you from the king and his commands over your life."

"But my marriage to Orzel," the princess scratched out. "It still stands."

"Your brother will be prince regent," Tanwen explained. "He has the power to annul the contract. He *will* annul it."

"Thol!" Her father's holler brought Tanwen's attention to where her brother was running away. "Thol, *stop*." Gabreel chased behind him.

In a panic, Tanwen was on her feet, racing to catch up to her father and brother. *What is he doing?* she thought in confused dismay, her lungs burning with each quick breath.

"You are supposed to be dead!" Aberthol roared into the night, up into the sky. "You need to be dead!"

He spread his arms, activating his glider.

"No!" shouted Gabreel, stumbling.

Tanwen was quickly at his side, steadying him before they continued to charge forward.

"Thol, no!" she desperately called out.

"You don't have enough power!" bellowed her father.

The meaning of his words crashed into Tanwen. Aberthol's elixir would be near empty; it could not propel him back up, least of all to Galia. It held only enough to—

Tanwen's heart stopped as Aberthol lifted into the air, higher and higher, his silhouette growing minuscule against the rising sun.

Ré's light began to fan out from the horizon, painting the sky in pinks and oranges.

Her brother flew toward it, determined, until his trajectory faltered, the elixir gone.

Tanwen felt a jolt of relief; he'd be forced to glide back down.

But Aberthol's strength slipped, his exhaustion too great to keep his arms steady.

He stumbled before spiraling downward.

A piercing scream sliced through the air: Tanwen's scream.

A gust of wind slammed into her back as Princess Azla soared into the sky toward her brother.

She wouldn't reach him in time.

Aberthol fell.

And met the ground.

61

The weight of her brother's body strained Tanwen's arms.

Yet the physical pain was nothing compared to the devastation coursing through her veins. Blinking back her endless tears, she tightened her grip on the strap that supported her brother, summoning all her strength to hold on.

She had no idea how she managed to keep standing, to keep moving, but her chance to properly mourn would have to wait until they were through the Cactus Forest.

Ré had awoken, forcing them to escape into the sharp covering of cacti. The air had been cool but dry, a sweet aroma that contradicted the brutality of their surroundings.

Spikes protruded at every angle, their route taking them through a thorny burrow of harsh shadows, causing them to suffer more than one scrape and cut.

But none of them complained, not even the princess, whose wings she had agreed to bind tight at her back.

Their only direction from Bosyg had been to go forward.

So Tanwen, her father, Huw, and Azla had silently carried her brother, Aberthol, forward.

Yet despite their quiet procession, Tanwen could still sense her father's and the princess's sorrow and Huw's pensive worry.

All of which only weighed down her own grief, compounded it.

Unwillingly, Tanwen glanced to the wrapped form swaying at her side.

Her brother.

His broken and bloodied form was covered in seafoam silk. The material had been an offering from Azla, torn from her own skirts.

Suddenly, Tanwen could not breathe, her air lost in a rising sob.

Her brother was dead.

Her Aberthol gone.

Together with Eli.

Grief was a cleaver lodged relentlessly in Tanwen's chest.

Each death was on her hands, but most of all Aberthol's.

She had failed to kill the king.

Had failed her brother in slaying his monster.

And it had cost him his life.

Her steps faltered, her arms about to give out, when she noticed the rapidly rising fog.

The group stopped, staring at the thick gray mist.

Beyond, the cacti were no longer visible.

Nothing was visible, in fact.

Only the touch of chill, a pressure of warning that said *Turn back*.

Tanwen met her father's gaze, ignoring how red and puffy his eyes were from crying.

"We go forward," he scratched out. "As Bosyg said."

Tanwen nodded.

Tightening her grip on her brother, she stepped forward.

The transition was abrupt—a squeezing pressure in her mind, ears popping, and a metallic taste rushing across her tongue.

And then, where she and her companions had been traveling through a thorny forest, they were no longer. The clouds lifted, unveiling the most breathtaking landscape Tanwen had ever seen.

The sun bathed the territory of the Low Gods in a radiant glow. The azure sky was certainly not of Cādra, for it sparkled with a brilliance that gave away the ancient magic of this land.

Clouds drifted lazily, their colors shifting between pristine white, soft pink, and warm orange. Even the animals were extraordinary, with birds boasting vibrant plumage and deer grazing in a nearby meadow, their fur adorned with shocking patterns and colors.

A glimmering river wound through the landscape, adding to the surreal beauty. In the distance, a towering forest rose, its leaves a dazzling mix of green and blue, completing the otherworldly scene.

For one relieving moment, Tanwen allowed herself to marvel.

To breathe.

"Tanwen!" The echo of a familiar voice drew her attention to the forest line. "Gabreel?"

Her mother was dwarfed by the large trees, but it was unquestioningly her mother, with her dark hair that matched Tanwen's, her long legs, and her pale skin.

Tanwen's heart gave a leap just as Aisling ran forward, down the small hill toward them.

Tanwen hardly registered their group gently lowering Aberthol's body to the ground or she and her father rushing forward before colliding into Aisling.

They fell to their knees as they embraced, cried, allowed relieved laughter.

Aisling leaned back to kiss her father. A passionate, desperate kiss that made Tanwen turn away, cheeks flushing.

And then Tanwen was tugged back into her mother's arms, her hug backbreaking but healing.

Eventually Aisling drew away, holding Tanwen at arm's length, wide smile lighting up her features. Tanwen took this moment to notice the change in her mother. Her face had regained its fullness with a flush of health to her skin, a spark of her old self returned.

"Where's Thol?" her mother asked, gaze searching the group behind them.

Tanwen's breath of reprieve left in a whoosh, her agony returning to claw open her chest.

She knew the moment her mother saw the wrapped body, for Aisling's features fell, her brows pinching as a silent gasp left her lips.

"*No*," she whispered, eyes slicing back to Tanwen before Gabreel.

When neither of them replied, she pushed to her feet.

"*No no no no no no.*" She stumbled forward.

Gabreel was quickly at her side, to hold up either her or himself—Tanwen couldn't say.

"It happened after we escaped," Tanwen heard her father mutter. "He tried to use the gliders again when there was no elixir left."

Aisling collapsed beside her son's body, hands shaking as they fluttered over his wrappings. "No," she continued to utter in disbelief. "No."

"I'm so sorry." Gabreel knelt at her side, his expression ghostly as tears streamed down his face.

"No!" Aisling threw herself over Aberthol, lifting him into her arms and rocking him as she sobbed. "My baby, my boy." She smoothed her hand over his wrapped head, over and over, as if the gesture might wake him.

Tanwen's despair was a poison slinking through the air, pouring into her lungs, suffocating with each drag of her breaths. Her vision was gone from the spilling of her tears, hot and branding down her cheeks.

She kept her distance, terrified to enter the cloud of devastation that was her father, mother, and brother, fearing she might never find her way out.

After a moment, she sensed company moving to either side of her. Cool, thin fingers laced into her hand, and a strong arm wrapped around her shoulders.

Huw and Azla.

They had come, carried her brother, entered Drygul, and stood by as silent supports.

As more tears fell, Tanwen squeezed Azla's hand while lifting her other to place it atop Huw's on her shoulder.

Thank you, the gesture said.

We are here, their embrace replied.

A movement at the forest line redirected Tanwen's gaze.

From the depths of the woods, forms began to emerge, gradually stepping into the soft embrace of the morning light.

Tanwen frowned, feverishly blinking to clear her vision.

Her heart stilled, mind spiraling in astonished confusion.

Their numbers spilled into the hundreds, a crowd of mismatched forms.

Some boasted odd, curling horns that were of no clan Tanwen had ever seen, while others possessed only half-formed horns or none at all. A few displayed full majestic wings, while others bore one or four. A few hovered as if they could fly despite no plumage; others arrived as a buzzing cloud of birds or bees before reforming into a perfectly normal-looking Süra.

But Tanwen knew none of them were Süra or Volari.

They were Mütra.

A horde of Mütra.

No, thought Tanwen, pulse thundering.

An army.

62

Within the throne room, Zolya hovered at the base of the stairs.

His gaze was fixed upon the vacant seat high above.

Morning light poured in through the large skylight, illuminating the polished marble and casting a severe spotlight on the empty seat of power.

Unease—Zolya's now-constant companion—churned in his gut.

He had yet to allow himself to sit on the throne.

Something he would not attempt with his father still alive, unconscious or not.

The seat held too many tainted memories.

In fact, this entire room did.

Zolya's gaze danced over the opulent adornments.

He remembered all too vividly the countless occasions he had witnessed his father's cruel displays of authority in this room.

A surge of resentment mixed with sorrow worked through Zolya, a whirlpool.

He hated that his father could not have been different, better, fairer, or kinder. If only he had been, perhaps Zolya wouldn't be here now, praying for his death.

Scorched Skies

The kingdom needed to be reawakened, cleansed of the centuries of oppression his father had placed upon it. But none of that could be done with King Réol still alive.

"My child," said a sympathetic yet commanding voice.

Zolya's magic leaped in his veins as he turned, finding Queen Habelle gliding into the throne room.

She was a vision of emerald silk, her dark-brown skin luminous, her braided hair loose around her shoulders, reaching her waist, while her dazzling jeweled crown adorned her head.

Zolya couldn't remember the last time his mother had worn her crown. Nor could he remember the last time she had been back on Galia.

Zolya's disquiet grew, though he flawlessly masked it as he greeted his mother.

"My queen," he said, taking her outstretched hand and bowing over it. "I was not expecting your visit."

Queen Habelle's brows rose. "I could hardly stay away after everything that's transpired. How are you, my darling?"

A cacophony of replies filled his mind, but he settled on honesty. After all, this was his mother. "Tired," he admitted.

Queen Habelle raked her gaze over him. "Yes, you look it."

"Thank you," Zolya muttered.

His mother ignored his sardonic tone. "How is the king?" she asked.

"Still unconscious."

It was subtle, but Zolya caught her flash of delight. "How very tragic this all is," she remarked in mock sorrow.

Zolya fervently surveyed the kidets standing around the room before returning his gaze to his mother. *Careful.* He sent her a silent warning.

She dismissed his concern with a wave of her hand. "You have inherited quite a mess, my son," she unhelpfully observed.

"Yes," he agreed, tone holding an edge. "More than I had even anticipated."

"I hear Orzel has destroyed what had been built of the new mine."

Zolya frowned, disliking the brazen way his mother could discuss such a tragedy. "Yes," he replied stiffly. "It appears he doesn't take kindly to being stood up for his wedding."

A drastic understatement, of course.

As soon as Orzel had learned his bride had fled, the High God had disappeared into his basin of water, hardly remarking on the king's attempted murder.

Within moments, reports had flown in of the rise in the Aspero Sea.

The waters that Orzel had agreed to hold back at the excavation site had surged, landing a quick but devastating blow.

But what had hurt Zolya more than the loss of expense that had so far gone into the build was the loss of lives.

Nearly sixty Süra had perished in Orzel's attack, innocent workers who had been unaware of what was about to ascend upon them.

Which had caused only more problems.

"And what of these fires at the Volari checkpoints on Cādra?" asked his mother. "I hear almost all of them have been attacked."

"Yes." Zolya tightened his hands into fists at his side, a new tension flaring across his shoulders, grief and guilt. "It was retaliation from the Süra families who lost loved ones at the new mine."

It was the Dryfs all over, but this time King Réol wasn't around to slam down his unyielding hammer to stop an impending uprising.

The world was holding its breath, waiting to see how the new prince regent would retaliate.

The problem, of course, was that Zolya didn't *want* to retaliate. He wanted to make things right.

Not a popular opinion for the royal council to swallow—or his people.

It had been a week since the incident and the longest one of Zolya's life.

He couldn't remember the last time he had slept.

The royal advisers were demanding in their wavering faith, clearly wondering if Zolya had what it took to command in the king's absence.

The treasury was even more suffocating, though for good reason.

As for his court, well, they were one complaint away from their own revolt.

Evidently, there were servants growing defiant in the wake of King Réol's incident. Unhappy recruits who were using the opportunity of instability within the royal family to voice their needs and concerns to their employers. A quicker way to disturb the aristocracy, Zolya could not imagine.

There was truly too much for him to juggle at once and keep a clear head.

Zolya hardly even had time to absorb the reality of his losses, in both Azla and Tanwen.

Their whereabouts, along with Gabreel's and Aberthol's, were unknown.

A blessing he knew he should be happy for, despite the pain he was suffering with their absence. His heartache was too great to contemplate, like trying to measure the depths of the oceans or expanse of the sky. It was merely endless.

The only solace he held on to was that they were alive. They *had* to be. His heart would certainly have known otherwise.

"Fear not, my child." Queen Habelle laid a gentle hand on his arm. "I am here to help."

Zolya blinked, a surge of a new emotion filling his lungs, one he wasn't accustomed to—relief.

He had not known he needed those words—and from someone who actually *could* help him—until they were spoken.

"I would be honored for your counsel," he replied.

"You should be, darling," she retorted. "I am much older and wiser than you."

Zolya almost smiled, his mother's energy a fresh intake of air.

"Now," she began, smoothing her skirts. "I must visit with my husband," she announced, forcing her features to be somber.

Despite his father's current state, Zolya didn't much enjoy the thought of his mother anywhere near the king.

"He's not much for company," he admitted.

Queen Habelle's eyes sparkled as she leaned in. "All the more imperative that I see him."

His mother strode from the throne room, leaving Zolya standing as she had found him, alone.

However, this time, he didn't feel as lonely.

63

Nestled along a cliff's side, Tanwen waited impatiently within a dark gazebo.

Nocémi's protective night stretched endlessly from where she stood, gazing out at the Onis Ocean. The rolling waves caught the light of the crescent moons, a glistening dance.

Tanwen leaned against a pillar, crossing her arms as the warm breeze tangled in her hair, sending it spinning around her face.

He should be here by now, she thought, her concern rising as she scanned the empty sky.

Behind her rose the rugged cliff face, where a winding staircase would lead her back up to the perimeter of Drygul. She was no longer technically in the Low Gods' territory.

In the expansive night, a flash caught Tanwen's eye.

She straightened, pulse thrumming.

Zolya soared toward her like a falling star, his powerful alabaster wings illuminated under the light of Maja and Parvi.

The sight of him never ceased to cause Tanwen's body to heat, her heart racing.

He's here. He's here. He's here, her rushing pulse sang.

He landed in a great whoosh, his wings tucking in as he took two long strides to reach where Tanwen had retreated into the shadows of the gazebo.

His presence consumed the space, like a roaring fire in a small hearth. Alluring as well as alarming.

Tanwen swallowed against her buzz of anticipation as Zolya greeted her by pulling her into his arms, his azure eyes shining predatorily.

Tanwen barely released a surprised gasp before he was claiming her mouth, dipping his head as his fingers slid along the base of her neck, holding her in place. It was a possessive grip that said *Mine*, whispered *Finally.*

Tanwen's body untethered as she became nothing but sensation. The rhythm of his mouth lifted and fell against hers. His lips were soft but demanding, his embrace warm despite the chill that clung to his coat. He brought with him the scent of wind and night.

Zolya's rumbling moan of pleasure vibrated down Tanwen's throat, igniting a fire in her belly. She wound her arms around his neck, pressed up on her toes, desperate to reach more of him.

For a slow dip of the stars, they became lost within each other.

And then . . .

"You're late," accused Tanwen, breaking their kiss with a frown.

Zolya's gaze was dark with his desire, but his lips twitched, fighting his grin. "It was hard for me to get away. Mother demanded I dine with her."

"I was beginning to worry," she confessed.

A state Tanwen felt trapped in.

Too much had happened, and too much was still happening, for her to feel calm for long. After losing Eli and her brother, she was terrified of losing anyone else, especially someone else she loved. Especially *him*. She had once believed she had already lost Zolya, and her heart couldn't endure that agony again—not with the stitches holding it together still so fresh and fragile.

Zolya's features flashed with quick remorse. "I would never miss our meetings," he explained, tone serious.

"Which is what had me worrying when you were late."

"I am here now," he reassured, his hand coming up to gently run his knuckles along her cheek.

The trail of heat it left along her skin slightly eased her simmering anxiety.

"Yes," Tanwen agreed. "You are here." She sounded breathier than she would have liked.

It had been two weeks since her and Zolya's last meeting. Two weeks of Tanwen existing half-formed, her heart half beating.

After settling within Drygul, she had enlisted the help of ravens and other fowl to pass notes back and forth with Zolya.

Finally being able to communicate with him felt like taking her first real breath of air since her escape. She could share that she was alive and that they had reached their sanctuary, despite the devastation that had unfolded when they landed.

Zolya's letters were filled with a similar sense of relief and grief.

Too often Tanwen had lain awake in her bed, rereading his words by candlelight, tracing the fine swoops and curls of his penmanship. As if the touch of his quill to paper could awaken the sensation of his fingers tracing her skin. Her yearning to see him, hold him, hear his reassuring, deep rumble of a voice became excruciating. Like she was adrift at sea, surrounded by water—but none she could drink.

Thankfully, Tanwen eventually discovered this hidden spot where they could meet just outside the Low Gods' territory. It was an unwatched corner of Cādra, and beneath the compassion of the twin moons and Nocémi's safe blanket of stars, it became their sanctuary.

Initially, their encounters were consumed with them consuming each other, sating a hunger after an eternity of starvation. Never long were they clothed before shirts were torn open, trousers were discarded, and skin was blessedly meeting skin.

Over time, their meetings evolved into more productive exchanges.

Each shared updates from their respective corners.

And though they never said so, it felt as if they were laying the groundwork for something significant, its shape and purpose still elusive.

However, tonight Zolya seemed of one mind, and that was to taste every part of her.

His soft caresses fell away as he bent once more to capture her mouth with his. Exploratory hands slid down to her backside, pressing her tighter against him, so she could *feel* him and how much he desired her, needed her.

Tanwen groaned, skimming her hands over his broad shoulders and up his neck to dig her nails into his hair. She gave a gentle tug.

Zolya growled his approval as he pushed her against a nearby column.

The hard stone dug into her back, but it was nothing compared to the formidable strength of Zolya pinned to her front. He was a wall of fervor and heat and possession.

With quick, sure movements, he had her top unbuttoned along with her trousers. The night breeze settled over her breasts, pebbling her nipples before the warmth of Zolya's mouth claimed them. His satisfied purr seeped into her skin, hot wax fallen from a candle, as he licked and sucked. His hands were everywhere but *there*, where she ached for him the most.

Tanwen ground against his thigh that he had wedged between her legs, eliciting a whimper of need that she would later blush about.

Currently, she could think only of Zolya and his deft fingers sliding teasingly low, maddeningly slow, before stopping right above the last open button of her pants.

"Tell me, my love," he rumbled as he gazed down at her, blue eyes as dark as the night sky. "Is this how you touch yourself while I'm away?"

Tanwen could only pant, her anticipation overwhelming.

"Do you imagine your fingers are mine as you slip them inside?" As he spoke, he did as he described. Tanwen arched her back, gripping his biceps as a gasp of pleasure feathered over her lips.

"Do you make yourself as wet as I make you?" His deep rumble of a question was flint hitting stone, igniting.

"Zolya," she breathed, pleaded.

A wicked smile stretched over his mouth before he was kissing her again, his fingers working in and out, in and out.

"I need you," she begged against his lips. "*All* of you."

Something flashed, sharp and satisfied, in his eyes before he pushed down her trousers.

And then with strength that always left her breathless, he picked her up, cradling her legs, which were still trapped at her ankles by her clothes and boots, before he slowly eased his length into her.

They collectively moaned their pleasure as he filled her to the hilt before dragging out and then in again.

Over and over and over.

Zolya stood like a demigod, holding her to his hard chest while he kissed and thrust into her with carnal need.

It was too much.

It was not enough.

It was a ravishing that overtook all her senses.

"Oh *gods*," Tanwen groaned as the gazebo fell away along with the stars and the sound of the crashing ocean below.

There was only Zolya's grunts of desire, his intoxicating scent, his powerful hands holding her securely as he claimed her body and soul. His wings shifted with each drive of his hips, their plumage half-spread as if to offer privacy to their hedonistic coupling.

This was not a tender lovemaking but a desperation to brand one another. They continued to move together deep into the night, until their sheen of sweat mingled and became one, until their sounds braided into a singular pulsing of lust, and until their unified climax trembled the stone foundation where they eventually found themselves collapsing.

Tanwen lay splayed on her back.

Zolya's weight on top of her was a heady reassurance as they caught their breath.

A blanket was spread beneath them as Tanwen had grown better "prepared" for their meetings.

A smile edged up her lips as she relished this rare moment of peace.

Time drifted by in a satisfying silence, their heartbeats a matching rhythm where their chests pressed against one another.

Eventually, Zolya pulled himself up to lie beside her, resting his chin in his palm.

His gaze was liquid blue, tranquil, but she caught the shadow of concern within its depths.

"How are your parents?" he asked.

Despite the lazy caress of his other hand along her collarbone, Tanwen's stomach clenched.

Her parents had no idea she and Zolya met like this. *No one* knew, not even Azla or Huw, and it needed to remain that way.

If anyone in Cādra discovered the prince regent was having a secret affair with a deserter recruit, especially one who'd aided Gabreel and his son's escape, it would shatter any hope Zolya had of securing the throne and fixing their world.

And if those in Drygul learned that Tanwen was slipping out of their hidden sanctuary to be with the successor of King Réol—the very man who persecuted Mütra—they likely wouldn't let her return.

Tanwen had already had to dispel certain notions about her and Zolya's previous relationship to her parents. Her father had been relentless in his anger when questioning why the prince of Galia, the very man who had stolen them away, would help them escape. Tanwen had quickly realized that the truth—that the prince loved her, and she him—would never be accepted or tolerated.

She had concentrated instead on a different truth: that Prince Zolya was nothing like the king, nor did he wish to rule as such.

This, of course, drew more questions around *how* Tanwen could have known this, but thankfully Azla had been present and backed her statements: her brother was not their father, and she guaranteed he'd be a better ruler. Despite Azla being the princess, her friendship was far more permissible given her history as the king's illegitimate offspring and the one who'd ultimately tried to kill him.

Huw had merely stood silently in the corner of the room, watching Tanwen as if he knew she was hiding something.

Which made Tanwen extra cautious whenever visiting the gazebo, ensuring no one, not even an invisible friend, followed. Huw's Mütra ability to blend in was becoming a real nuisance.

But Tanwen understood that Zolya's question about her parents had nothing to do with any of that. It was his gentle way of bringing up Aberthol.

Nearly three months had passed since they lost him, yet Tanwen's sorrow remained raw.

"They are still grieving," she admitted, "but getting through it day by day."

During their first reunion, Tanwen had revealed that her mother was alive and hadn't died during childbirth as Zolya had been led to believe. He had surprised her by not being very surprised but rather relieved.

"And you?" questioned Zolya, his hand moving up to cup her cheek. His brows were pinched, his stare patient as he awaited her answer.

Tanwen swallowed past the lump forming in her throat. "The same," she replied. "I still find myself looking for Thol beside Father or putting out a dish for him each meal, as though he'll come striding through our door any moment." She huffed a laugh, understanding the absurdity of her words.

Zolya didn't share in her forced mirth. His expression grew only more severe. "You have never known a world without your twin," he said. "Nor a womb."

For a moment, Tanwen could focus only on breathing, his statement a weighted fist against her lungs. Though she understood he did not say them to be malicious but to remind her that her grief was allowed.

"No," Tanwen said, her reply a mere whisper. "I haven't."

Zolya slid his hand from her face and intertwined their fingers.

He gazed down at her, expression soft, aching, and despite the heaviness of the moment, Tanwen could only marvel at his beauty.

The glow of the night framed his tousled hair and drew a sculpted line along the edge of his bare muscular form. The angular planes of his face were cut with shadows, while one of his magnificent wings he had draped across Tanwen's stomach was a white, silken, soft blanket.

Though she lay naked under the stars, she felt warm and safe tucked in beside Zolya.

"Aberthol's shrine was completed last week," she found herself eventually sharing. "The build progressed faster than expected with everyone's help. It's been nice to have a place my family can go to talk to him and imagine his presence."

"Yes," agreed Zolya gently. "That's important."

"Lybel, the young girl with the four wings who I told you about last time," said Tanwen. "Well, turns out she's an incredible artist and was able to draw a portrait of my brother for the shrine. Based off only our descriptions, the result was remarkably accurate."

Silence momentarily filled their gazebo, a thick tension collecting in the air.

It was something that transpired anytime Tanwen mentioned the other Mütra living in Drygul.

She didn't know if it had been disloyal to share their secret existence, but if Zolya was meant to help her kind, he needed to know that so many lived—as well as lived under the protection of the Low Gods.

Volari couldn't argue that a Mütra's existence was blasphemous if half the divine gave them sanctuary. Right?

This was one of the burdens Tanwen knew Zolya worried over and what kept him quiet now, thoughts clearly churning.

"I'm glad to hear it," he finally said, hiding his thoughtful expression behind a neutral mask. "I like knowing you and your family are feeling settled here." He squeezed her hand. "How's Azla getting on?"

"She has her moments of grief, like we all do," admitted Tanwen, frowning. "But Lady Esme's shrine is near Aberthol's, which has helped."

Zolya nodded, features somber. "And the . . . others, they are still welcoming of her?"

"Very welcoming," assured Tanwen gently, her heart tightening with his worry. "Misfits enjoy meeting other misfits. Some have even taken on the challenge of teaching her to cook. She made her first meal for my family the other day."

Zolya blinked, his astonishment clear. "And you *ate* it?"

Tanwen laughed. "Once we got past the burnt layer, it was pretty good."

"Oh gods," declared Zolya. "You truly are braver than I."

Seeing Zolya's grin was like a cool mist of rain on a blistering day: refreshing.

"She'll get better," said Tanwen. "Everything takes practice."

"Mmm," he agreed as his hand moved to her stomach, tracing soft patterns across her skin. "I can think of a few things I'd like to practice now."

Tanwen flushed, her veins filling with fire. "I'm sure you can," she mused.

Zolya leaned down, his lips warm and inviting as he pressed them to hers. He took long slow drags, a lazy swim in a lake. He cupped her cheek in his hand, controlling the kiss, angling it where he knew she wanted and he needed. Tanwen was a puddle of desire by the time he broke the spell, lifting away.

Zolya's smile gleamed above her, mischievous delight.

"Well," Tanwen breathed. "I don't think you need to worry about getting better at *that*."

His laugh was a soft rumble that feathered across her side, slid like honey down her throat on a satisfied inhale. "Perhaps," he began. "But there's no harm in continued practice."

"I certainly won't argue with that logic." She grinned.

A contented quiet drifted between them as Tanwen ran gentle fingers through Zolya's hair. He leaned into the touch like a pleased cat.

"Zolya," began Tanwen, her thoughts turning back to their earlier conversation.

"Mmm?"

"I know you worry about Azla, but I want to know, I will *always* look out for her. Her role as my charge does not end because we are no longer in Galia. I will make sure she is taken care of."

His eyes held hers, a burning in their blue depths, before he lifted her hand to his lips. "Thank you," he said. "Knowing this is a greater relief than you realize."

Zolya grew pensively silent after that.

His gaze drifted to the view beyond their gazebo, to the stretch of stars and glowing moons. Tanwen noticed the invisible weight pressing down on his shoulders.

"Has something happened today?" she inquired, an unease sliding awake in her veins.

It was another beat before Zolya answered. "Ré still has not visited," he admitted, revealing a worried crease between his brows.

Tanwen sat up slightly, pulling part of their blanket to cover her chest. "Isn't that good?" she asked.

"I'm not sure." He frowned, still looking beyond where they lay. "Most of the other High Gods have come to see the king and offer my mother and me their condolences. Of course, I'm not naive." He glanced back at her. "It's all an act to investigate my intentions for ruling," he added, tone sardonic. "If I will continue as my father had."

"I'm sorry," said Tanwen, knowing her reply was lacking but unsure what else she could say to help.

While she had burdens of her own, they felt inconsequential compared to what Zolya suffered daily as prince regent.

The situation in Galia had worsened after the king's attempted murder. Tensions were rising without a clear ruler on the throne—and not just within Zolya's people but all across Cādra. The fires at the Volari checkpoints had awoken the repressed. News of other Sūra revolts had even made their way to Drygul. Garw's clan leader evidently had claimed more rights to their minerals, weakening any new builds on Galia. Which had only raised more conflicts between Volari and Sūra stationed on the outskirts of every forest.

Tanwen knew Zolya was trying his best to manage everything, but without full control of the crown, it was like trying to plug leaks in a sinking ship with strips of cloth—futile. The only real solution was to rebuild.

Tanwen held tight to her rising guilt, knowing she was partly to blame for Zolya's troubles. While he knew of his sister's involvement in trying to kill the king, Tanwen's was still very much a secret.

Her fear of whether he could forgive her was too great for her to confess. She knew only that she had done what was necessary to save her family, yet it had still cost Thol his life.

"It's only going to get worse." Zolya's gruff declaration returned Tanwen's attention to him, his features tight. "Especially the longer my father remains in the state that he is."

"I still don't understand why you can't change some of the laws as prince regent."

"Because my father's council remains in place. I cannot replace any members as long as the king who appointed them is still alive. If my father had passed the crown to me, the situation would be different. For now, his council remains to ensure I rule according to his intentions, given he could awaken and reclaim the throne at any moment."

"So many rules," she groaned.

Zolya grunted his agreement. "That's only a fraction of them. Politics is riddled with barriers."

"No wonder things have stayed the same for so long."

"Yes," said Zolya, jaw clenching. "Though the world appears ready for change."

"Which is good," Tanwen offered hopefully. "Galia can't ignore the demands of those on Cādra if they are loud enough."

Zolya shook his head, expression growing as hard as granite. "Historically, uprisings never end well for those who instigate them. I do not want to see Süra or Mütra suffer through famines and floods."

"Nor do I," said Tanwen, "but I think the history books have misrepresented who truly provoked those uprisings. I do not recall Süra controlling the trades, creating the Recruitment, or putting a bounty on Mütra's heads. Living in hunger or fear is hardly ever a choice one enters willingly."

Zolya regarded Tanwen, a spark of wonder and admiration in his gaze. "You are a formidable ally," he admitted.

"Yes," she agreed, smile flashing. "You should be very glad I no longer see you as my enemy."

It was meant to be a jest, but Zolya's features sobered, his thoughts clearly growing inward.

"Zolya," she began hesitantly, touching his shoulder. "What is it?"

"I didn't want to bring this up tonight," he said. "In fact, I hate that I must bring it up at all, but . . . we need to be prepared."

Despite the warm breeze, ice slunk across Tanwen's skin. "Prepared for what?"

Sparks of blue clung to her, Zolya's mouth set in a stern line. "With all that has begun to happen in Cādra, I will need to navigate everything carefully," he explained. "My people are watching my every move, the council and court most of all."

"Yes." Tanwen nodded. "I have always known that."

Her words did not alleviate the pinch between his brows.

"Some of my decisions that I'll soon make . . ." He paused for a breath, gaze pained. "You will not agree with, Tanwen," he admitted, voice rough. "I chance to say you may even come to despise me for them."

At his declaration, sharpened fingernails gripped her heart. "Zolya, I could never—"

"But you must know"—he cut her off, seemingly determined to finish his confession—"I'll despise myself ten times over. But for me to work from within the court, I must gain their trust. They must believe I am my father's son and that I have their best interests in mind, as well as our High Gods. Otherwise, everything I do will continue to be questioned, scrutinized, and any change we wish to make in our world, any minds I must turn, will be futile."

"Zol," Tanwen said softly, hating the shadows haunting his expression. "I understand."

"Do you?" he asked, gaze weighing down on her. "Really understand?"

The quiet that stretched between them was so thick and tense Tanwen braced herself for when it snapped back. Still, she was not prepared for the sting when it did.

"For a time," Zolya rumbled, eyes laced to hers, "I must become your enemy."

Despite being in an open-air gazebo, Tanwen felt as though walls were closing in on her. Each of her breaths felt pained, desperate. As if they might be her last.

Zolya's words hung in the air like poison, invading and clogging her lungs.

She wished to contradict him, fight such a notion.

But she didn't, because she realized with a dreaded clarity his declaration went both ways.

I must become your enemy.

For that, too, was what Tanwen would appear to him.

An enemy, working to free Mütra, helping the oppressed Süra.

She hadn't outwardly admitted to such a stance, but she knew in her heart that was to be her future.

While Zolya ruled from Galia, Tanwen would be fighting on Cādra.

An invisible grip tightened around her throat, choking away any response as despair folded in and around her.

Zolya seemed to understand her suffering, share in it, for he answered her silence by drawing her back into his chest. As they lay on the warm blanket, he covered her more securely with his wing, wrapping them both in a tight embrace as if it were a desperate grip on a ledge. To let go would be the death of them.

These meetings were already hard to arrange, and soon they might become impossible.

As she fully realized the future that awaited them, tears brimmed in Tanwen's eyes, her throat burning as she fought down a sob.

She angled her head up and found Zolya's lips.

Their kiss began gentle, reverent, before growing hard and demanding—a public defiance of their forbidden union.

Still, despite the pleasure they gave each other, Tanwen knew it didn't change their fate.

Here lay two souls in love, standing on opposite sides of a war.

ACKNOWLEDGMENTS

Although this section is titled Acknowledgments, brace yourself, because it's also an Author's Note—or musings, if you will—on how this story came to life. But, I promise, there are reasons for my ramblings.

Of all the Greek myths, the story of Icarus has been the one to grip me the most. Perhaps it was a product of reading it when I, too, was a defiant youth, when my ambitions and dreams for my future were loud and intrusive and blinding. But I also know, like so many, the thought of being able to fly just seemed insanely cool. Now, as definitively *not* a youth in age any longer but still one at heart, I continue to find myself fascinated by this parable and how it applies to so many realities of today. I felt compelled to write a story that dived into the complexities of human ambition, the pursuit of dreams, and the consequences when overreaching (even for a king), hoping to capture the essence of this ancient myth while offering up a new world and characters.

I also wanted to explore these themes partly through a woman's lens. While Icarus was a son, so much of what he was warned against doing felt like the proverbial glass ceiling. To me, his actions seemed like a reaction from his years of being ordered to obey, keep quiet, "know his place." A historic script many women have been battered down by for millennia. Because of this, I wanted to rewrite Icarus's tragic failings of hubris into a woman's desperate need to succeed. For herself and for her family. Although this time, despite the tragedies she faced along the way, she ultimately survives her flight.

Which brings me to the gratitude section of these acknowledgments. While writing this story, like Tanwen, I experienced a loss. It was the kind of heartbreak that paralyzes, strips you raw, hollows you out, and leaves you drifting so deep underwater that no light can penetrate to show you which way is up. Thankfully, I'm surrounded by incredible souls, and their combined brightness turned into my blazing sun. With their help and grace, I found my way back to the surface and eventually to the end of this book.

To my husband, Christopher, to whom this book is dedicated: I couldn't have written a single word without your unwavering support, superhero parenting, and patient listening to my plot rambles at all hours. To my son, who is often chaos incarnate, thank you for inspiring me daily with your nonstop imagination. To my parents and sisters, with whom my curiosity for storytelling was first tilled, thank you for being you. I love you all so very much. Also, a special shoutout to my father, Emil Mellow, who so graciously agreed to work his artistic genius in illustrating Cādra's map, which is at the front of this book. You brought my world to life so perfectly.

To Aimee Ashcraft, my agent, sounding board, brainstorm goddess, and occasional therapist, this is our fourth book we've created together, and I am forever and always grateful for your wisdom. Kimberly Brower, the velvet hammer and queen of Brower Literary, I am thankful every day you are in my corner. To my editors Lindsey Faber and Lauren Plude, your faith in my abilities humbles. After every editorial call and handoff, I can feel my craft in writing level up. Thank you for extending your teachings. To the entire crew at Montlake, from the art department to the marketing-and-production team, you make my work look like I know what I'm doing. Truly magical!

To you, my fiercest reader, I quite literally cannot do this without you. Thank you for taking a chance on my story, spending your valuable time in this world, and supporting my passion. I may not know you personally, but I know I'm in love with you.

Last, I want to thank myself. (Narcissistic? Nah.) This writing thing is way harder than the movies make it look. Thank you, E. J., for giving yourself grace when you needed it so you could eventually forge ahead toward The End. This is your eighth book, your eighth dream come true. Keep soaring.

ABOUT THE AUTHOR

Photo © 2020 Jacob Glazer

E. J. Mellow is an award-winning and bestselling author of magical mayhem. Her work has been translated into multiple languages and has appeared on best-of lists such as BuzzFeed and Gizmodo, reaching number one on multiple Amazon charts and receiving medals from eLit Book Awards and Next Generation Indie Book Awards. Readers have said her "lyrical, vibrant, and imaginative" writing sweeps them into "stunning worlds." Mellow is also the cofounder of She Is Booked, a literary-themed fundraising organization that supports women's charities.